"**War is a very un**[...] Garak said. "I don't need [...] even more unpleasant. F[...] it should remain just tha[...]

Sisko turned his head [...] ing straight at each other. Neither of them blinked. Then, on the console, just within Sisko's field of vision, he saw a green light wink at him—and it passed through his mind once again to wonder whether Vreenak had even had the chance to see the lights turn red. He blinked. Then he saw Garak's eyes widen, ever so slightly; bright blue and icy.

"Oh," Garak said, as if something had just become manifestly clear to him. "I see." He eased himself back in his chair, and Sisko watched with a rising wave of distaste. He had spent enough time around Garak recently to recognize a prelude to one of his monologues.

"Cardassians, Captain," Garak said, "have an intimate relationship with guilt. We are, as a rule, very familiar with it, in all of its hues and shades. And yet, despite this shared cultural experience, it can be a very private relationship. For example, we tend—as a rule—to consider it ill-mannered to require that those around us become intimately involved in our own crises of conscience."

"What the hell are you getting at?"

Garak's voice had gone quiet. "It was murder, Captain—twice over. And I didn't do it just so you could lose your nerve and go begging for forgiveness from your superiors. So if your conscience is whispering again—a little late in the day, I might point out—you'd better not forget that you *owe* me."

At that, Sisko could not help but laugh out loud. "I *owe* you?" he said.

They were almost note to nose now, and Garak's eyes had become very cold. "You came to me—just remember that. Not the other way round."

STAR TREK
DEEP SPACE NINE®

HOLLOW MEN

UNA McCORMACK

Based upon STAR TREK® created by
Gene Rodenberry,
and STAR TREK: DEEP SPACE NINE,
created by
Rick Berman and Michael Piller

POCKET BOOKS
New York London Toronto Sydney Hamexis

An *Original* Publication of POCKET BOOKS

 POCKET BOOKS, a division of Simon & Schuster, Inc.
1230 Avenue of the Americas, New York, NY 10020

Copyright © 2005 by Paramount Pictures. All Rights Reserved.

 STAR TREK is a Registered Trademark of
Paramount Pictures.

This book is published by Pocket Books, a division of
Simon & Schuster, Inc., under exclusive license from
Paramount Pictures.

ISBN: 0-7434-9151-3

First Pocket Books printing May 2005

10 9 8 7 6 5 4 3 2 1

POCKET and colophon are registered trademarks of
Simon & Schuster, Inc.

Cover art by Tom Hallman
Cover design by John Vairo, Jr.

Manufactured in the United States of America

For information regarding special discounts for bulk purchases,
please contact Simon & Schuster Special Sales at 1-800-456-6798
or business@simonandschuster.com.

For Matthew—who feeds me.

I invested my life in institutions—he thought without rancour—and all I am left with is myself.

—John Le Carré
Smiley's People

ACKNOWLEDGMENTS

Thank you to Matthew for spending his childhood learning about World War 2 so that I didn't have to.

My love and thanks to all friends and e-friends for encouragement while I was writing. Particular thanks to the Whitecrow crowd—not least for arranging my first book signing. A nod of appreciation to LiveJournal for giving me a whole new way to waste time online.

"In the Pale Moonlight" stunned me when I first saw it and that is thanks in no small part to Peter Allan Fields's story and Michael Taylor's teleplay. It is fantastic to have the chance to take the story a little further.

The works of Chris Boucher, Troy Kennedy Martin, and several other twentieth-century greats have also provided inspiration.

Tom Hallman's outstanding cover art is everything I wished for.

Thank you to Paula Block at Paramount for excellent advice as the story was coming together. And my grateful thanks as ever to Marco Palmieri for all the ideas and guidance and support, and most of all for taking a chance on me.

HOLLOW MEN

PART ONE

DEAD MAN'S HAND

Only connect.
—E. M. Forster

PERHAPS IT STARTS LIKE THIS. A man goes on a journey, to an island in the sky. He brings his son with him; and he also brings his sadness. It takes him time, but, surrounded by strange people, and their even stranger ideas, he learns many things. He grasps that he can put the past aside; he learns to live with it; he begins to hope for the future. And that is not all that he learns from the strangers around him. He finds, as well, that he can do things differently.

Or perhaps it starts later than that. A stranger comes to town, to the island in the sky. He brings suspicions with him, and so it does not take much time for him to grasp that he has been deceived. He leaves in anger, but it is not until later—not until far too late—that he realizes he has not seen everything. He has failed to see the full extent of the deception.

But perhaps it all started much earlier. A man goes on a journey. He has been cast out of his home, and now he is stranded on an island in the sky. He brings regrets with him, and scores as yet unsettled (and some not yet even made). He knows that the past cannot be wholly put aside, and he bides his time, and he watches, and he waits for his opportunity. And when he sees it, he grasps it with both hands.

And where does it start right now? A message is sent out, perhaps, summoning someone to a rendezvous, or giving someone her instructions. A message is received, instructing a path to be diverted, foretelling events to come. Slower than messages, ships set out, and pass; and, as they journey, other communications are sent, weaving between them, weaving them together. In time, it's hard to see how they're connected; like looking at a picture of old friends found in a drawer, it is hard to guess exactly where it is that they would go. But this is how it always starts. Some men go on a journey. Some strangers come to town.

What is it about a tuxedo?

Jadzia smiled as she saw Julian catch a glimpse of himself in the two-way mirror, stop, and smooth away some of the creases in the dark jacket. He started playing with the bow tie. His other hand was holding the gun.

"Is that a real one?" she said.

He looked down at the gun and then up at her. "Of course not."

"I meant, is that a real bow tie?"

"Well, of course it is!" He sounded piqued.

"Aren't the ready-made ones less trouble?"

"They *are*," he said, "but they don't look as good. Garak said that wearing a fake bow tie was like taking someone on a date to the Replimat. You might as well not bother."

"Oh, well," she murmured, turning away to gaze out beyond the mirror, "if *Garak* said so . . ."

Jadzia sighed and lifted up one aching foot, squeezed

into a sparkling and thoroughly unreasonable shoe. On the other side of the glass, the banquet was well under way. Soft strains of some exquisite music floated round the hall, to the clatter of silver and the tinkle of crystal. A lavish, fabulous occasion, attended by lavish and fabulous people—politicians, diplomats, ambassadors, even the odd scion of some royal family tree here and there, *very* odd—and all of them upstaged by their surroundings. The hall was wide enough that there were rows of chandeliers hanging from the gilded ceiling and, beyond the huge table, in front of the long row of windows, a line of golden candlesticks, each almost as tall as a man and crowned in glass lamps. The light glanced and shimmered off every surface, seeming to fill the room with jewels. From where they were hiding, Jadzia couldn't even see the hall's most spectacular feature. Seventeen huge mirrors lined one wall, facing the long windows, and reflecting all the opulence back upon itself, duplicating it. And behind one of them, looking out through a piece of fake glass, stood Julian Bashir, Secret Agent, and his beautiful assistant, Jadzia Dax, waiting to make their entrance.

She switched feet. The other was hurting just as badly. So much for glamour.

"Julian," she whispered, "when are things going to start happening?"

"*Sssh . . .*"

"Are we going to be standing here much longer? My feet are *killing* me!"

Julian looked down at her shoes, and relented. "Not long now," he said. "In about two minutes, the main course will be served. Just after the waiters have finished, but before the doors close, five armed and masked terrorists will burst in and fire at the ceiling—"

Jadzia glanced upward. "I don't hold out much hope for those chandeliers."

"They're only holograms, Jadzia."

"Still, they're very impressive. It seems a shame to ruin them."

"Can I carry on?"

She lowered the fake eyelashes at him, granting him permission.

"As I was saying, the terrorists will come in and take all those very prestigious guests hostage. But a moment or two after *that*, we burst through this false mirror, I shoot the ringleader, and then swing round to take out the other four gunmen before they know what's hit them." He stopped and frowned. "I should probably make a quip about coming through the looking glass, but that still needs a bit of work. . . ."

"Don't worry about it," Jadzia advised. "They'll all be too busy admiring your bow tie."

He gave her a cool look, and then went back to staring through the glass. Jadzia rocked onto her toes. How she was supposed to leap through a false mirror wearing these shoes she wasn't sure. She had a vision of herself falling flat on her face. The evening gown she was wearing was a fabulous emerald green affair, but seemed unsuited for acrobatics, and, despite everything, there was nothing in Emony's memories which might help in a situation like this. . . . *Maybe I'll let Julian do the leaping, and I'll just do some elegant strolling.*

This had seemed such a good idea at the start of the evening. Julian had been so moody recently; preoccupied. She had thought asking him to take her round his spy program might cheer him up a bit. She had even hoped it might take her own mind off the casualty list she had read that morning. She certainly hadn't expected to find herself hiding behind a mirror and teetering on ludicrous heels. She wondered, mischievously, what he would say if she suggested swapping shoes, but when she turned to speak to him, she caught sight of his face, and stopped herself.

Julian was looking down at the gun. He was running his thumb along it. After a moment, he switched the gun over to his other hand, and pressed his free palm against the back of the mirror. It left a print there, the image of his fingers splayed out across the glass. He stared at it, seeming almost to be entranced by it. Jadzia frowned— and then, from the corner of her eye, she caught the door at the far end of the banqueting hall open. It was all about to start happening. . . .

"Computer," Julian said, from beside her, his voice soft, "end program."

Everything went very quiet. Jadzia looked round. It was all gone. The mirrors, the hall, the great and the good; all the glitz and all the glamour. All of it fake. All that remained was the blank wall of the holosuite, graygreen and a bit scuffed from overuse. From too many fantasies, and too much fiction.

"Julian?" She turned to him. The gun had gone too. He was standing with both arms slack by his side, staring at the holosuite wall. "What's the matter?" she said.

With an effort, he roused himself. "I don't know. . . . All of a sudden it seemed a bit . . . well, childish. Not the real thing." He shrugged. "You know, I think I may have outgrown it all." He gave her a smile. "Sorry about your shoes," he said, nodding down at them. "And sorry to break up the evening. Shall we just go and have a drink?"

"If that's what you want," she said. She followed him as he made his way out of the holosuite. She felt that she had missed something crucial, but she was not sure how to ask him what had just happened.

Out in the comfortable bustle of the bar, Worf was waiting for them. "Did you have a good time?" he asked, reaching for his wife's hand.

"Fine," Julian said, before Jadzia could speak.

"What do you want to drink, Julian?" she said instead.

He fumbled with the bow tie and looked around the bar. "You know, I'm actually feeling a bit tired. I think I'll just head off to bed. Thanks for a nice evening, Jadzia."

They said goodnight, and Jadzia watched him cross the bar, and worried. She reached out to lean on Worf's shoulder, supporting herself against him, and began fiddling with the strap at her ankle. Worf watched her struggle impassively.

"I do not like those shoes," he said.

"Don't worry," Jadzia replied, still watching Julian as he disappeared onto the Promenade. "I don't think I'll be wearing them again."

The cargo ship *Ariadne* threaded its way through space, small and purposeful, casting a line between Lissepia and Yridia. On its cramped bridge, its youngest crew member yawned and stretched and checked the time. Still an hour to go before the end of his shift, and Auger was having trouble staying awake. He thought about going to get another coffee, but decided it was too much effort. He eased back into his chair, a slight young man who twitched, with pale eyes that did not always seem to be quite focused on the here and now.

Auger stuck his legs out on top of the console in front of him, crossing his booted feet at the ankle. It was something he had seen Trasser do; he was trying the habit out to see if it fit, but it made his feet get in the way. He stared past them at the screen beyond, at the bright lights, at the specks of stars against the darkness. He picked out patterns in them; tried to see the shapes that Steyn had just taught him. One set of stars made up a club, another was like a diamond—if you ignored the missing point. He wondered what they were called. He could always check, he supposed, but a set of figures and letters wasn't really what he wanted to know. Did people on different planets see them differently, he wondered. Did they give them their own names? Make up their own stories about them? Connect up the dots in their own particular ways—

"Those boots have an impressive shine, Auger. I bet you can see your face in them." The captain's voice, deep for a woman's; only half-awake right now, but still to the point. "But they're out of place on my helm."

Auger jumped in his chair, and hastily rearranged himself, putting his feet back down. He straightened up before the helm, and tried to look busy and competent. Steyn came up to stand beside him.

"I know I run a casual ship," she muttered, "but not quite that casual."

Auger threw an apologetic glance over his shoulder. Steyn was standing with a mug cradled to her chest, and was staring down at the control panels in front of her as if hypnotized. Her eyes were hazy.

"Sorry, Captain," Auger said, brightly. "I got comfortable. . . ."

She waved her hand at him. *Stop talking.* Steyn was no good first thing. She took a swig from the mug. Her eyes seemed to become a little less blurred. Black tea, Auger knew, having delivered enough cups of it to her, even in the short amount of time he had been on board. Black tea, very sweet.

She blinked a couple of times and came into focus. "Status report?" she said. "Are we still alive?"

She said something like this every morning. Auger grinned, and he caught Steyn's own smile before she hid it behind the rim of the mug.

"Looks like it," he said. "All systems running smoothly. Still right on schedule for our arrival on Yridia."

Steyn grunted an acknowledgment. She drank a little more of the tea, and then fell into the chair next to him. She heaved a deep sigh. "Any word from our guest?"

"Not a sound from him all night."

"*Good.*" Her voice held a grim satisfaction.

Auger had not quite got to the bottom of the dislike that lay between the captain and their Lissepian client. He knew—because Steyn had said so, and often—that she took exception to how humorless Mechter was. Auger himself took more exception to how armed he was. It seemed to him to be impolite, never mind how nervous it made him feel whenever Mechter was around. . . . The details of their antagonism were in fact unimportant, since Auger was firmly on the side of the captain. But given how even mention of Mechter seemed to make Steyn grind her teeth, it had to be something serious, Auger guessed. It was either that or Steyn just liked something to complain about. Whichever way, as long as the captain was happy, then Auger was happy.

"I bet you'll be glad to see the back of this cargo, Captain," he said.

Steyn sighed. "Two more days," she said, "and that'll be it. I tell you, Auger, if I'd had the choice, I'd never have got myself stuck with this job. Still, you have to play the hand you're dealt."

Auger nodded, trying to look wise or, at least, trying

to give the impression that he understood what the captain was talking about. He watched anxiously as Steyn brooded into her cup. He tried a safer topic.

"Do you want some more tea, Captain?" he suggested, tentatively, hoping to cheer her up. For a fleeting second, the thought of more tea did seem to perk Steyn up. Then she shook her head.

"No, I'll pass. Thanks though."

Auger went over to the replicator and got himself a coffee. He had never had the stuff before he had come on board the *Ariadne,* and now he was nurturing a fair addiction. He balanced his mug on the edge of the console, pulled out his chair, and started the complex maneuver of sitting down. Hundreds of muscles must be coordinated—relaxed and tensioned *just* so—to fold and lower the body safely to the cradling framework of upholstery, designed by experts to support the lower back during a long and arduous space journey. His mind had wandered by now far from the confines of the *Ariadne* to contemplating what they were going to do when they got to Yridia; this meant that his whole sitting-down maneuver was orchestrated—unintentionally and yet perfectly—to knock his coffee over. He flung out both hands and caught it just before it went flying, and then noticed how hot the mug was and said, under his breath, *"Ouch."* He glanced over at the captain. She had been watching his efforts with a detached and benign fascination, gnawing at the knuckle of her thumb. Auger put down the mug, and began blowing furtively on his hands. He was still busy cursing his clumsiness and thinking how much he hated looking like a fool in front of the captain when Steyn leaned forward in her chair. Her morning fog had completely lifted.

"Auger," she said evenly, "what the hell is that red light?"

The communication had come late in the station-day, the chime of the console echoing brash and loud around the empty office, and just when he had been contemplating sleep. Now Sisko sat running his finger along the edge of the desktop, trying to listen to Bill Ross.

His back ached a little, and he shifted in the seat. Reaching quietly to one side, he touched a button on the console, flipped open a file, and started to read. He kept nodding as Ross talked, made the occasional noise of agreement. He kept one eye on him, the other scanning down the data in the file. *Romulan Activity in the Benzar System—A Strategic Assessment.* Slow going, picking off the system rock by empty rock, but still, ineluctably, advancing.

A dream had been troubling Sisko the past few weeks. He would find himself standing on the bridge of the commandeered Jem'Hadar ship, pushing back the headset, rubbing at his eyes, the crew shifting in and out of his field of vision—and then they were rocked bow to stern. Unfriendly fire—very unfriendly. Smoke began to fill the bridge, he heard someone yell, *"Hold on!,"* and when he flipped the headset back in place, he could see them plunging down, down, toward the planet's surface, and there was nothing he could do to stop it. . . .

It was at this point that Sisko would most usually wake up, sweating and wondering whether Vreenak had seen something like that. Whether he had known that he was going to die. Whether he had had that moment of terrible grace. Maybe, he would tell himself, Vreenak just never knew what hit him. Maybe the ship was gone in an instant. Maybe. Either way, you had to live with the uncertainty. You had to live with it.

He had been contemplating sleep. But not quite risking it.

"This offensive was a mistake," Ross was saying. *"It turns out we thought we knew more about the defenses at Sybaron than in fact we did."*

"Cardassian intelligence is still tricky," Sisko murmured. "Even without the Obsidian Order." He read on. Details of Romulan incursions into Dominion space; attacks on ketracel-white manufacturing facilities; high rates of success.

"And the Seventh Fleet has paid the price." Ross shook his head. *"It's hard, Ben. Thinking of those ships going out there. Expecting . . . well, not what they must have hit up against. And what do we have at the end? Stalemate."*

"It's a bad business," he muttered. "A bad business." The report and the admiral's features blurred together, his eyes heavy. He glanced up from the file. Ross was looking at him quizzically. With an effort of will, he marshaled his attention.

"When do you set out, Ben?"

"First thing in the morning." Sisko sat up straight in his chair. "How are the conference preparations going?"

"Well, everything seems *under control. The Romulan and Klingon delegations are being quartered at opposite ends of the building."*

"Perhaps they should be put in separate cities."

Ross gave him a dry smile. *"I'd like this summit to lay the groundwork for coordinating military strategy. But what I'm hoping for is simply that all the delegates will be in one piece by the end of the week."*

"I'm sure it'll all work out just fine," Sisko said. He

looked back at the file and wondered who would be part of the Romulan delegation.

"I'd be more confident we could come to agreements quickly if military coordination were the only thing the delegations were concerned with. But I have no doubt this summit is going to be as much about the peace as about the war. About what will happen next."

"Inevitable, I guess. Some politicians always seem more concerned with fighting tomorrow's battles."

"Don't be too hard on them, Ben. You know that, sometimes, we all have to be politicians." He paused for a moment, as if weighing something. *"This you won't have heard about yet."* Ross paused again. *"We have some representatives from the Cardassian government-in-exile."*

Sisko looked back in surprise. "Is there one?"

"Apparently so. There are two representatives coming—Rhemet and Tehrak." Ross shrugged. *"I gather they were both prominent in civilian life before leaving Cardassia. Rhemet was part of the government before the Dominion took over."*

"He was lucky to get away." Sisko started thumbing up and down the file on the Benzar system. All the data—all the figures on strike rates and targets met, on Dominion and Cardassian casualties—began to scroll past, far too quickly for him to read. A blur of light and color.

"I don't know the details. And while we're on the subject of Cardassians," Ross gave him a shrewd look, *"I assume your friend Mr. Garak is still planning to come along?"*

That pushed the definition of the word *friend*. "Yes, he's coming," he said. "And I'm sure he's looking forward to enlightening all of us about Cardassian tactics, technology, psychology, art, music . . . Mister Garak," Sisko explained, "likes to talk."

"*Good. Because Starfleet Intelligence are keen for him to talk to them.*"

Sisko stopped the file dead.

"Starfleet Intelligence?" he said.

"*Questions about the information he gave us when he was at Starbase 375.*" Ross shrugged. "*More detail, if he can give it. And his recent report aroused a certain amount of interest. I think that several people are keen to find out what else he can do for us.*"

"I see. . . ."

"*So if he's feeling talkative, or feeling helpful, I'm sure they'll appreciate it.*" Ross smiled at him. "*Anyway, we'll speak again when we meet, Ben. Safe trip home!*" He leaned forward, cut the com, and then he was gone. Quietly, discreetly, the familiar emblem of the Federation displaced Ross's face upon the monitor. Its colors were muted and entirely lacking in their usual reassurance.

Sisko swiveled in his chair, turning to look out at the pale starlight. He sat for a little while, watching the stars wink back at him, and he wondered whether Vreenak had taken comfort from them, or if he had cursed them, just before he died. . . .

"Dammit!" Sisko slammed his palm down against the desktop. He stood up, and began to pace the room, thinking hard. Starfleet Intelligence wanted to know what else could be *done* for them? That was all supposed to be finished, he thought as he paced. All in the past. Garak's deeds done, report filed—now they could just get on with the job of winning the war. No more deals with the devil.

Sisko came to a halt near the exit, rocking on his heels and staring out into ops. Beyond the tinted surface of the doors, he could see one or two people moving about quietly. Late shift. He could almost convince himself that it was peaceful out there—if it wasn't for the war. He stood and watched through the door as the routine business of the night went on, and he was not comforted by it. All in the past?

Sisko raised his hand to his head, pressed his thumb and forefinger against the bridge of his nose, and tried to order his thoughts. Two dead men, a guilty conscience—and nobody paying the price. Nobody paying the price for any of it. Perhaps there was something worse than crimes being discovered. Crimes remaining covered. Crimes willfully ignored.

"Computer," he said unwillingly, cursing once again the day he had decided to dance with the devil, "locate Mr. Garak."

The *Ariadne* rocked, bow to stern, and then everything went unpromisingly still. Steyn started swearing under her breath, remembered Auger fluttering next to her, and swallowed back the rest of her tirade. She drained the last of her tea and set the mug into its holder, hoping the shaking of the ship disguised her own trembling. She punched on the com, opening up a channel to the engine room.

"Trasser," she said calmly, not wanting Auger to hear her sounding anxious, "I could do with an engineering report . . . *now?*"

Silence. Steyn watched the lights on the console flashing madly at her, jerking and dancing at random, nothing like their usual measured ballet.

"Trasser?"

As Steyn waited for her engineer to speak, she heard the door to the bridge open. She closed her eyes very briefly. No surprise that her guest was awake, given how hard the *Ariadne* had just been shaken. But she could really do without Mechter's attentions right now. . . .

Through the comm came the sound of something clattering. Then the *Ariadne*'s engineer began to talk. *"Sorry, Captain . . . things have become pretty hectic down here. . . ."*

Just behind her left shoulder, Steyn heard Mechter start to murmur.

"Thanks for that," she said, a little sourly. "How about something a bit more informative than 'hectic'?"

"Well, I think I know what the problem is . . ."

"Yes?"

"And there's good news and bad news."

Steyn imagined she could feel Mechter's breath upon her neck. Not a happy guest.

"Mr. Mechter and I are eager to hear both, Trasser," she said, pointedly.

There was a pause.

"Oh. Right."

He'd taken the hint. Good.

"The primary engines have failed, Captain—"

"I'm going to take a guess and assume that's the bad news?"

"Yes, I'd say that was the worst of it. I've not quite got to the cause of the failure yet—though, to be honest, these retuned drives can sometimes be a bit off—"

Steyn felt Mechter take hold of the back of her chair.

"How about that good news?" she said sweetly.

"Well, I've got the systems offline now—we won't get any more of that shaking, which is good news for stopping the ship from falling apart . . ." He stopped. Perhaps—Steyn could only hope—he was thinking a little better of conjuring up such images. *"Well, we're stable now but we're not exactly moving at full speed."*

Had Trasser ever moved at full speed? Steyn put the question aside. "And how soon will we be moving again? At full speed or otherwise?"

"All right, that's the other bit of bad news—I'm not going to be able to fix this, Captain. Not quickly, anyway."

"Oh, come on—"

"Don't start, Steyn! Come down here and have a look if you don't believe me. These systems are fried. It's not a question of skill, it's a question of manpower."

Steyn played with the controls of the com, thinking hard. "All right—keep at it down there. And keep me posted." She cut the link, took a deep breath, and then turned in the chair to speak to Mechter.

"Mr. Mechter—" she began.

Moving with speed and ferocity, Mechter spun her right round, slammed the chair to a halt, and grabbed both of its arms, trapping Steyn in her seat. He leaned in close. Steyn stared up at the greens of his eyes and then down at his well-cut cuffs. Lissepians did have the edge when it came to polished villainy, she thought, with a certain fleeting admiration.

"Steyn," Mechter hissed, "you lowdown, cheap, third-rate excuse of a pirate, I am going to gut you from neck to tail like a copperfish."

No, Steyn thought, he really wasn't happy.

2

THE DOOR TO THE TAILOR'S SHOP opened on approach. It was dark inside. Sisko stood for a moment or two on the threshold, letting his vision adjust, and then he went in.

"Garak?" He kept his voice low.

The gloom echoed no answer. He took a step forward. Ahead of him, the far end of the shop was in darkness, although he thought he caught a faint flicker of light. The door slid shut—a quiet, automatic, familiar sound. Sisko went further in, peering around for the proprietor. As he walked on, he passed a row of tailor's dummies, standing huddled together, like mourners at a funeral, or conspirators in a plot. Their figures cast long shadows, slanting across the floor of the shop, more like feelings than visions.

"Garak, are you in there?"

Still no answer. Sisko stopped and reached out to touch one of the mannequins. Garak had to be lurking in here somewhere; he would never leave the shop unattended and unlocked. Sisko punched the dummy lightly on the chest, and it made a dull *thud*. "Computer," he said, his patience finally running out, "give me a bit more *light!*"

He blinked as the room became suddenly bright, until his eyes adjusted once more. Garak could be seen now, sitting behind the console at his desk, and looking up at the lights with an expression of distinct exasperation.

"What the hell are you doing back there, Garak? Didn't you hear me call?"

"I *was* concentrating," Garak replied pointedly and, Sisko did not fail to notice, only answering the second of his questions. He let it pass.

"In the dark?" he said, suspicion mounting.

Garak closed his eyes for a brief moment. "Dark, by *human* standards, Captain."

"Ah yes," Sisko muttered. "Sorry." He went a little closer and nodded towards the console. "Still—you're working late," he said.

Garak shifted toward to the viewscreen and, with a quick flick of the wrist, turned it off. Sisko frowned.

"Designs," Garak said smoothly, "for Lieutenant Nedani's elder daughter's *ih'tanu* ceremony. She is very anxious," he added, keeping his eye fixed on Sisko, "that the dress be kept a surprise for her big day."

"Is that right?"

"That's right." Garak shifted back slightly in his chair. He seemed, Sisko thought, to want to keep a little distance between them. Not surprising, perhaps, given just how hard Sisko had hit him last time he had come into the shop. Hard enough to knock him to the ground.

"Was there something in particular you wanted, Captain?" Garak said. "Or are you just late-night shopping?"

"In fact, there *was* something in particular." Sisko glanced uneasily about the shop, and then gestured around him. "Can we talk . . .?" Safely, he meant.

Garak took the hint. "Captain," he said, "If you can't trust your tailor to be discreet, then really—who can you trust? Ask Nedani Iriya." He slithered out a smile. Sisko's palms began to itch. "Talk away," Garak finished. He turned his attention to a pile of samples spread out over the table in front of him, and started folding them. Sisko watched this ritual for a moment or two, and then began to ease himself cautiously into the conversation.

"The *Rubicon* is all ready to leave at oh eight hundred tomorrow morning," he said. "Runabout pad A."

"Of course," Garak murmured, casually. "Our trip to Earth." Sisko watched a muscle in his cheek twitch. "So you *are* shopping?"

"This is business, Garak, not pleasure."

"What a shame." Garak looked back down at his work, and began smoothing out a piece of bright blue silk in front of him. "Captain," he said, folding the silk with exaggerated care, "as you know, I have been eagerly anticipating this conference ever since the invitation to attend was extended. And I'm grateful you've taken the time to let me know our travel arrangements. But it does seem the kind of information you could have passed along rather than brought in person. So"—he looked up again at Sisko; his eyes had gone wide and, for a second, they were very intent—"why are you here?"

Sisko managed not to recoil. "I was just speaking to Admiral Ross," he said.

"How nice for you."

"And he had some news which I thought you might find interesting." Sisko made his tone almost conversational. "It turns out you won't be the only Cardassian at the conference."

The silk went on top of the pile. Garak picked up another bit of material; red, with a darker, crimson pattern upon it. He didn't fold it straightaway, and instead began rubbing it between his fingers. "Is that right?" His voice was very bland.

"That's right," Sisko replied. "Your government-in-exile will also be attending."

The motion of Garak's fingers stopped abruptly. "There is no Cardassian government-in-exile," he said.

"It seems there is now—"

"That idea died with Tekeny Ghemor." He had started running his fingers along the cloth again, tracing the lines of the pattern.

"And now it has a new lease of life," Sisko said. "Ross mentioned some names—Rhemet, Tehrak . . . Do they mean anything to you?"

"Never heard of them," Garak said flatly. He folded the patterned cloth, set it in its place, and then picked up a long piece of creamy linen. "Take hold of that end, please," he murmured. Sisko did so dutifully. They pulled the cloth out taut, brought it together corner to corner; then Garak took it back, folded it once more, and put it down on the pile. Sisko watched his face and tried to anticipate him.

"In the light of this news," Garak said at last, "I think that my attendance at this conference would be a bad idea." He bent back over his desk, his focus returning entirely to his work.

"*What?*" Sisko had not seen that coming.

"The Federation is of course free to recognize whoever they want as the legitimate government of Cardassia," Garak said. "But they can do it without my endorsement."

"You haven't even *heard* of these people!"

"Which is reason enough not to trust them with Cardassia's interests. Besides"—Garak's eyes sharpened with malevolence—"with such an *exceptional* resource now at its disposal, what could the Federation possibly want with *me?*"

"Starfleet Intelligence wants to talk to you."

Garak froze, leaning on the desk in front of him. He did not look up at Sisko. "They've already had my report," he eventually said.

Sisko watched Garak's hands, pressed out flat. "Not that," he murmured. It was the first time they had referred to the events of the previous weeks; the first time since . . .

Since Sisko had come in here so angry that he had punched Garak to the ground. Interesting to learn, Sisko thought, just how close to the surface it still was for Garak too. Who would have thought that Garak was not entirely reconciled to what had happened? He watched on with almost clinical detachment as Garak's fists clenched briefly, and then were made to relax. Sisko doubted it had anything to do with guilt on Garak's part. More like fear of detection, he guessed.

"Your talents," Sisko said, "have not gone unnoticed."

"How very gratifying to know that." His voice was brittle.

"And various people believe it's possible they could be put to good use again—"

Garak's head snapped up. "By Starfleet Intelligence?"

Sisko shrugged. Very slowly, Garak began folding the next piece of cloth on the pile. Watching, Sisko thought that perhaps the tailor's hold on it was shaky. Just a little. A tiny smile was playing at the corner of the Cardassian's mouth. He had been wrong, he realized, to think that Garak was trying to slide out of the trip to Earth. He had just been waiting for something else to draw him there.

Garak's voice was steady; he even managed to make it sound a little bored. "You'll forgive me if I say that isn't the most appealing offer I've ever received."

They stared straight at each other.

Liar.

"And so I must regretfully continue to decline your very kind invitation."

It was tempting, Sisko thought, so very tempting to knock him to the ground again. Just as Garak reached for another piece of cloth, Sisko slammed his hand down upon the pile. "What the *hell* are you playing at?" he said. "You know full well this is the best way you can help Cardassia against the Dominion—"

"You're assuming I'm not doing that already—"

"All your resources were used up, you told me." Sisko jabbed a finger at him. "I'd think you'd welcome the opportunity to make some new friends!"

Sisko caught the hissed intake of breath, quickly cut off, and felt a vicious satisfaction that he'd hit the mark. "Besides," he said, turning the screw, "you're hardly in a position to refuse, are you?"

"And *what* do you mean by that?"

"You know exactly what I mean."

Garak's eyes narrowed and Sisko knew that he had understood. He had blackmailed Garak once before to get him to leave DS9. He was prepared to do it again.

And then, all of a sudden, Garak began to smile. "I will say one thing for you, Captain," he said. "I always know exactly where I stand with you." He reached for another piece of cloth, tugging at it gently until Sisko lifted his hand up from the pile. Sisko looked at him in confusion. Did Garak really want to be threatened? Both of them knew he was going to come to Earth. What the hell did he want? Garak was still watching him closely, his head tilted in—what? Challenge? Expectation?

And then Sisko suddenly knew what was going on. Garak wanted to save face. *Well,* Sisko thought dryly, *I did knock him to the ground.* . . . "I would put it to you," he said, "that Starfleet wishes to benefit from your *exceptional* expertise."

Garak beamed at him. "And that, Captain, would be most prettily put." He picked up the pile of samples, shoved them unceremoniously out of sight under his desk, and set his hands down flat on the table. "Oh eight hundred hours?" He sounded eager now, almost excited. "Is that correct?"

"At runabout pad A," Sisko confirmed.

"I'll be ready."

"I'm glad to hear that."

They exchanged smiles that went nowhere near their eyes, and Sisko turned to go. As he walked back through the shop, the lights went down again. He went out, and the door glided shut behind him. He stood for a moment just beyond it, staring down the Promenade. He felt exhausted from the interview. And they hadn't even boarded the runabout yet.

Sisko walked on slowly along the deserted Promenade, looking at the shopfronts that were darkened and closed for the night. Quark's was still open, the late shift there going strong. The door slid aside, and he saw the bright lights spill out, heard clearly the shout of a punter scoring at the dabo wheel. Bashir walked out onto the Promenade. He was out of uniform, wearing a suit, and had what looked like a bow tie thrown over his shoulder. Probably been in the holosuite. Sisko thought of calling out to him, but with his shoulders slumped, Bashir looked pretty tired. Sisko held back and watched him walk away.

His combadge chimed, too loud, and he reached up quickly to cut it quiet.

"Sisko here," he murmured.

"Captain." Odo's voice. *"I would be grateful if you could come to ops. We have a small problem."*

"On my way."

A small problem? Perhaps it would take his mind off the larger ones.

Garak switched the viewscreen back on. Sisko was standing just beyond the closed door of the shop, his fingers pressed up against his eyes. After a moment or two, the captain straightened himself up, and walked on down the Promenade. Garak switched the viewscreen off. He rummaged around under the desk, pushing aside the accumulated pieces of material and equipment, digging around until he found a glass. He considered the bottle of *kanar*—a decent vintage, left behind by the Cardassians that had recently visited the station—and then chose the whiskey Bashir had given him once as part of his general cultural education.

He had always intended to go with Sisko, of course. As the captain had said, it was surely the best way to help Cardassia; in fact, it was the only real way available to him at the moment. But Garak had seen no reason why his assistance should be taken for granted, whether by all the machinery of Starfleet, or simply by the cog that was Captain Benjamin Sisko. He pulled the cork out of the bottle, and sniffed the contents. The scent was sharp and sour, and seemed to coat the back of his throat.

He would have to watch Sisko, he thought, with a sigh, as he poured out a generous measure into his glass. It was not hard to see that the captain's conscience was still troubling him, and a return to Earth might bring recent events into sharper relief. Garak had no desire to find himself playing a part in that particular moral melodrama. He had more pressing matters on his mind; matters concerning Cardassia.

So now there was a government-in-exile? Garak swirled the golden liquid around and tried to put faces to the names that Sisko had given him. Rhemet he remembered well enough; a state conservator who had made his name in literary trials, clamoring in a voice just like everyone else's, only that bit more strident. He had briefly been a member of Cardassia's ill-fated civilian government, and one of the few to get away when the Dominion had taken over. Tehrak was a little more elusive; something at the Science Ministry, Garak seemed to recall. Not military; certainly not part of the Order. Just a relatively ordinary functionary; another cog in a now-broken bureaucratic machine. Garak watched the liquid slide down the inside of the glass. He had to wonder if these men really were the best that the Cardassian émigré community could manage. Tekeny Ghemor had always made his dislike of Garak clear—which had not exactly inclined Garak toward him—but at least he had had intelligence. Despite their differences, Garak would have felt a little easier at the prospect of a government-in-exile with Ghemor at its head.

Not for the first time, Garak was struck with a sense of how few good people there seemed to be left these days. The old Order was gone, the military had surrendered to the Dominion, and Garak had never been wholly persuaded of the purpose of civilians in the state machine. A new anxiety had been presenting itself to him, ever since he had murdered Vreenak, ever since he had begun to believe again that this war could be won: What would Cardassia be like, afterward? Whose hands would hold it, care for it, punish it? The forthcoming conference had brought these questions to the fore: Against the assembled ranks of all the other powers in the quadrant, Cardassia's hand, it seemed, consisted of nothing more than some second-rate civilians and the very last remnant of the Obsidian Order.

Garak looked around for a distraction, searching the shadows of the shop. *Earth,* he thought, absently. It had promise—and hazards, too, it had to be admitted. He contemplated both. His instincts told him that this conference would be as much about the peace as about the war. And he really needed to keep an eye on Sisko. He leaned back in his chair, tipped his glass at one of the mannequins standing by, and drank, savoring the taste. He glanced down at the sewing that he had put aside when Sisko had come in. Back to work, he thought.

Their guest was certainly awake now. Awake and angry. Auger pressed back against his seat and prayed he was inconspicuous. He was relatively hopeful on this score. Mechter was too busy yelling at Steyn to pay much attention to Auger, but if anyone could handle Mechter it was the captain. Still, her eyes kept drifting down to the weapon at Mechter's side. It seemed to Auger to have a glossy, well-kept look; in even better condition than Mechter's suit, and that was pretty sharp.

"Captain Steyn," Mechter said. "When, back in the gray mists of time, you first approached my employers, I believe you were at pains to point out your professionalism, your good reputation, and your foolproof security—"

"Mr. Mechter," Steyn said quickly, before he could get

further under way, "Let's skip listing my shortcomings and focus for a minute on solutions. From where I'm sitting," she shifted a little in the prison of the chair, "I think we have two reasonable options. Either we can carry on to Yridia on limited power, or we can divert the ship and stop off for repairs."

Auger's guess was that Steyn was gambling on her bluntness sidetracking Mechter and stopping him from shouting at her any longer. The captain was not, from all Auger had seen, on the whole very fortunate when it came to taking risks, but she certainly knew how to talk her way out of a tight spot. Literally, in this case.

Mechter blinked back at her. "What do you advise?" he said at last.

"Well," Steyn drew in a breath, "we could probably get there a day or two sooner if we don't stop off. But diverting will make it a safer ride. Trasser's good at his job, but I know from experience that I wouldn't want to fly under one of his patch-ups for longer than strictly necessary." She looked up at Mechter slyly. "Choice is yours, Mr. Mechter. We can carry on limping toward Yridia if you like. But which do you think your employers will prefer?"

Mechter released his grip on the arms of the chair and stood up straight. Steyn straightened up, pulling her jacket straight. Mechter was looking a bit harried, Auger thought, and he wondered—not for the first time—what these mysterious employers must be like if they had Mechter running scared.

"All right," Mechter said at last, "where can we go?"

"Auger," Steyn said, and when he turned to look at her, she winked at him. Auger risked a smile back. "Open a channel to Deep Space 9," she said. "We should let them know we're on our way."

• • •

A quiet buzz had spread through ops—restrained, but expectant. Striding out of the turbolift, Sisko registered the change in atmosphere straight away, and welcomed the distraction.

"There was a small problem, you said, Constable?"

Odo looked up at him, and inclined his head in greeting. "Captain. We've just received a distress call from a freighter—a failure in their primary warp engines."

"And they want to dock at DS9 for repairs?" Sisko frowned slightly. This was routine—not something Odo would usually trouble him with, not even with the heightened security that came during war. "What's the catch, Odo?"

"Their cargo. One hundred vials filled with liquid latinum."

Sisko whistled softly. "Now, that *is* a catch."

"In every sense of the word," Odo agreed. "Given that, I believe it's reasonable to conjecture that this might not simply be engine failure, but could well be sabotage. And I am certainly *not* ruling out the option that the ship has been intentionally diverted to the station."

Sisko nodded his agreement. "Draw whatever security you need onto this, Odo. We don't need any trouble right now." *Any more trouble.* "Have you let the chief know he has a little extra work coming his way?"

"Naturally. And I'm sure you can imagine the delight with which the news was met. But he's assured me that he can cope with the repairs." Odo paused. Which meant there was something else he wanted to say. "You leave very early in the morning, Captain, am I correct?"

As if the constable wouldn't have the precise time committed to memory. "That's right," Sisko said. "Oh eight hundred hours." He waited patiently for the next question.

"Captain," Odo said, "if I may say so, you have been unusually preoccupied in recent weeks. Is there something about your forthcoming trip of which I should be aware?"

"It's an important conference, Odo," Sisko said, wondering if anything could happen on the station without the constable getting wind of it. "Klingons, Romulans, Federation—hardly what you'd call natural allies. Plenty of room for misunderstandings. Particularly with the Romulans, at this early stage."

From the extent of Odo's impassivity at this response, Sisko guessed he was not satisfied with it.

"Captain . . . I would say that your preoccupation predated the announcement of this conference. I appreciate that Starfleet has an increased need for secrecy in wartime, but the security of this station is my primary concern—"

"I know, Odo. I can assure you that in no way is the station at risk."

It was a half-answer, and Sisko could see it did not even half-satisfy.

"I see," Odo said. "A matter of Federation security, I imagine?"

It had almost become shorthand between them: Federation security, Constable. Don't ask me any more, Constable. You really don't want to hear any more, Constable.

"There really is nothing for you to worry about, Odo," he said.

"Well, I hope you in turn will rest assured that the station is in safe hands while you're away, Captain."

"Of course I will," Sisko murmured. "Keep me posted

about this transport ship until my departure. I have to go and speak to the major." He stopped on his way up to his office. "I suppose you're glad to see the back of my fellow traveler," he said. "One less thing for you to worry about."

Odo looked up at him. "Your fellow traveler, Captain?"

"Garak's coming with me."

There was a slight pause. He hadn't heard, Sisko realized. Something that had got past him. But there was no double take. Not even a flicker. You really did have to give Odo credit.

"Garak?" Odo said, eventually, and rather blankly.

"That's right."

"Captain . . ." And now just the merest suggestion of doubt was allowed across those controlled features. Sisko waited for him to come right out and say it. He knew that Odo had been waiting for the opportunity.

"It . . . has not escaped my attention," Odo said, "that you've been spending a great deal of time in Garak's company recently."

"Perhaps I like his sense of humor."

"You'll forgive me if I say I find that explanation rather unlikely," Odo answered bluntly. "May I lay out my evidence?"

Sisko glanced meaningfully around ops. Odo lowered his voice.

"Time closeted away with Garak. A whispered conversation with Quark which results in charges being dropped against a man who stabbed him. A very angry Dr. Bashir. Let me ask in the plainest terms: Is there something happening on this station about which I should be informed?"

"No, Odo," Sisko said, in perfect honesty, shaking his head. "There isn't."

"Which, of course, is not the same as saying that nothing is happening."

"No," Sisko agreed, "it isn't."

"I see." Odo's dissatisfaction was plain. "Let me guess—a matter of Federation security?"

Sisko shrugged. Odo turned away, and Sisko was sure he heard a growl.

Sisko retreated upstairs, back into his office. He'd been contemplating sleep, he recalled. Perhaps it could wait a little longer.

A night falls here, a day breaks there. A moon sets and a sun rises. Stars wink in and out. People are talking, sending out messages, laying down line upon line in the pattern of infinity.

3

SEATED IN THE REPLIMAT, Odo was beginning to feel like a man at sea. The wave of chaos that was threatened by the arrival of the *Ariadne* was drawing ever closer. And, right now, he was trying to navigate the shoals of what was turning into an unexpectedly rocky breakfast with Lieutenant Commander Dax. Dax was on a rescue mission, and Odo was beginning to fear that he was about to find himself turning into her backup.

"He's been *moody,* Odo," she said, emphasizing her words with a wave of her fork. "And has been for a couple of weeks now. It's just not like Julian at all! I even went to play that stupid secret-agent program with him last night—I thought it might cheer him up a bit." She shook her head. "He turned it off halfway through!"

Odo slid the level of coffee in his cup down by exactly 1.5 centimeters. It came as no surprise to him to learn that Bashir's game had lost some of its appeal. He looked across the table and, with a guilty start, realized that his attention had wandered. Dax was looking at him as if expecting an answer.

"Perhaps," he said, twitching a little more coffee into himself, "the doctor simply needs some time to himself at the moment."

"It's ever since he went to that conference," she said, attacking the second of her fluff pastries with a merciless stab of the fork. A few flakes fell away onto the plate. "Did he say anything to you about it? Anything about how it went?"

"He's said nothing about it to me," Odo replied honestly.

"Hmm." Jadzia frowned. "Maybe someone didn't like his paper. Those academics can be very cruel sometimes." She sat for a moment staring thoughtfully at her breakfast. "Usually I'd just have a word with the chief, but he's going to be busy over the next few days with the *Ariadne*. . . ." Her attention fell on Odo and her eyes glittered slightly; she was looking at him like someone suddenly handed the key to a treasure chest. "Maybe *you* could do something to help. . . ."

An anxious millimeter retreated from the coffee and the handle of the cup thinned.

"I'm also going to be extremely busy over the next few days with the *Ariadne*," Odo said quickly, striking out before he was pulled under. "The security arrangements over its cargo will be taking up a great deal of my time—"

"Odo, I'm not asking you to lay on all-night parties and dancing girls! Just check in on him now and again, make sure he's not sitting by himself with the lights dimmed. I don't know—ask him to teach you darts or something!"

Odo grunted. "The competition between the chief and the doctor has always seemed to me to be a great waste of time, not to mention their talents—"

"I think," Dax said absently, "that it's probably more about the playing than the winning."

"I'm not entirely sure that either of the competitors would agree with you," Odo replied. But Dax was no longer listening. A little coffee slumped from the cup as Odo saw the gleam appear in her eye again.

"I know!" she said. "You could get him involved in some sort of mystery. Get him to help you on one of your cases—"

Odo stared at her. Just the thought of someone else interfering in one of his investigations was alarming. "I don't think that would be a very good idea—"

"But it's *exactly* the sort of thing that he'd enjoy. Something for him to puzzle about." She leaned a little toward him, her eyes shining now not as she plotted, but with enthusiasm for her new idea.

Odo had often thought that Jadzia Dax would make an excellent interrogator. The combination of her host's youthful charms and her symbiont's old, low cunning made her almost impossible to refuse. Nevertheless it was time, Odo thought, to put a stop to this conversation—before he found himself committed entirely to something he would regret. Briskly, he put his hand over the top of the mug, reabsorbing it and the coffee discreetly. Then he stood up. "*If* something comes up," he said firmly, "*then* I might consider it."

Jadzia gave him an enchanting smile. "I knew you'd help," she said.

"I'll take that as a compliment, Commander," he said. "Now, you must excuse me—I have an appointment to speak with the captain of the *Ariadne.*" He nodded his farewell and turned to go. The safe haven of his office was very close now.

"Besides," Dax called after him, "it might take *your*

mind off things too." He turned to look at her, and she smiled sweetly back at him. "I'll mention to Kira that you'll be speaking to her soon about the *Ariadne*," she said.

Odo glared back at her. He should have guessed that Bashir was only one of Dax's projects.

Breakfast at the bar was slow this morning, but Quark was philosophical about it. Even without profit, there was still opportunity, and watching the traffic on the Promenade had always been a good way to find it.

For example: Was there opportunity, Quark had to wonder as he dried a little crystal glass, in being the only one up early enough to have witnessed the uncommon sight of Garak walking slowly toward the turbolift, deep in thought, a bag slung over his shoulder? Probably not, although Quark did have a superstitious recollection that the last time Garak had left the station—the Starfleet withdrawal notwithstanding—had coincided with Cardassia joining the Dominion. . . . Hardly the tailor's doing, Quark would admit, but perhaps it was worth bearing in mind that when Garak was not safely tucked away in the shop, things had a tendency to happen. . . . Quark looked down at the glass in his hand. There was a slight smear still on it. He rubbed more vigorously.

So was there opportunity in seeing Captain Sisko striding toward the same lift five minutes later, in earnest and energetic conversation with Major Kira? Quark examined the glass in the light and, now satisfied, he put it away and picked up another. It *was* worth finding out that the captain was going off-station; it was certainly worth overhearing a mention of increased security as the captain and the major marched past the entrance to the bar; and it was *definitely* worth seeing the particularly stern set of the major's jaw as she glared inside the bar. From that alone, Quark was able to determine that it might be advantageous to tread carefully with her over the next few days. He polished the glass with slow, thoughtful care. No, there was no profit in Garak and Sisko being away—in fact, Quark might have paid a slip or two of latinum to be able to listen in to the conversation on the runabout—but was there opportunity? Quark regretfully decided not. Only an idiot would try his luck with the major when she was looking that humorless, and only the suicidal would take advantage of Garak's back being briefly turned.

Quark put away the second glass, started work on another, and considered the view beyond the doors of the bar. The traffic on the Promenade had gotten busier as the morning went on—busier than usual, in Quark's expert opinion. This was what made him sure that what he was hearing was the first whisper of impending profit. O'Brien had been running around like a Scalosian. There was a more than usually heavy security presence on the Promenade too; Quark would hardly miss a thing like that. And now there went Odo, hurrying past toward his office, looking even more cantankerous than, in Quark's long experience, he should at oh-eight-hundred-and-a-bit. . . . Must have just finished one of his beyond-frugal breakfast meetings, Quark guessed. He felt sorry that Odo failed to realize that such meetings could be both a social occasion and an information-gathering exercise— and he wondered who the constable's sorry companion might be, given Garak's absence. The only opportunities that came with Odo were lost opportunities, and he appeared more on the deficit side of the ledger than as a source of income, but he *could*, Quark thought with a long-held sense of injury, at least *think* about bringing his breakfast partners here rather than taking them to the Replimat. . . .

Quark put the old hurt aside for nurturing later, rubbed hard for a little while at a fourth glass, and listened, as he worked, to what the traffic on the Promenade was trying to tell him. Yes, he thought, there was a definite change in tempo. People were anticipating something; so what could it possibly be? Nothing too serious, or with consequences for the war, or the captain would not have contemplated leaving the station, and from the way the captain and the major had been talking, Sisko had definitely known what was going on before he left. So whatever it was that was about to happen was not critical, but it was enough to make O'Brien look harassed, and make Odo look tetchier. . . . A situation that demanded engineers? The arrival of a ship, perhaps? A damaged ship? But why all the security passing down the Promenade? Why did Odo look even more dismal than usual?

Quark put the last piece of crystal away, threw the cloth over his shoulder, and turned back to his sole customer. His own brother. *Speaking of idiots* . . . Quark watched with disapproval as Rom shoveled fork after fork of food into his mouth. He was halfway through a plate of that revolting pink and yellow *hew-mon* breakfast he had seen O'Brien eating. The slick sound of the cutlery slipping against the grease made Quark feel queasy, but it wasn't slowing Rom down for a second.

Quark reached for Rom's cup and filled it. Rom took it from his hand and drank with enthusiasm. *Coffee,* Quark thought with distaste. Noxious, bitter, addictive stuff; the very reverse of root beer and yet somehow still so intrinsically *hew-mon.* . . .

"The chief looks busy this morning," Quark said.

Rom put down his cup and stared, slack-jawed and trusting, back at his brother for a moment or two and then, increasingly, looked upon him with the soft sad eyes of a Bajoran silk deer that knows it's being herded into the hunter's trap. "Oh no, brother . . ." Rom said, sorrowfully. "I can't tell you anything about that."

Quark leaned in hungrily. "So there is *something?*" he said.

"Oh no . . ." Rom said again, shaking his head this time. "Not a word, the chief said. Not. A. Word."

Quark turned away. He flicked the cloth across the bar. "Fine," he said. "Fine." He sighed deeply. "I know you've made your choice, Rom." He tried to keep the grief from his voice not at all, but drew the line at dabbing the cloth against an eye. Not even Rom was that stupid. "I just can't help it if it *hurts* . . . when I *try* to take care of you. . . . Have you had enough to eat?"

Rom slid uneasily from his chair. "Yes, brother," he said, making it sound like an apology. "Thank you. But I must be going now. A lot to do before the *Ariadne* arrives."

As he watched Rom scurry from the bar, Quark gave his widest grin. He picked up Rom's abandoned plate and cup. *Ariadne*. That was all he needed. Quark turned to his interface console and began to investigate the ships that were scheduled to pass through the sector.

The runabout's systems hummed quietly, and the lights on the console seemed to be synchronizing with them. Sisko watched his fingers drum in time for a beat or two; then he stopped them and sighed.

"Is something the matter, Captain?"

Sisko turned his head to see Garak standing in the doorway, holding a mug. Since they had boarded the *Ru-*

bicon, Garak had hidden himself away at the back. Now he had surfaced again. "I thought you were asleep," Sisko said. It came out rather more accusatory than he had intended, so he softened his tone, just a little. "Is something the matter with *you?*"

Garak shrugged. "Maybe I had a bad dream," he said, flippantly. Sisko watched him as he came a little closer. Garak did not look as if he had slept well. Sisko wondered whether he dreamed of Vreenak too. "But you haven't answered my question, Captain—is there something the matter?"

Sisko considered his options. In theory, it was a classified report that he had been reading. He suspected, however, that once they got to Earth, Garak would be issued with a high enough security rating to read it; he would have to be, if Starfleet Intelligence were serious about using him. Plus the chances were pretty damn high that Garak would just wait until Sisko was finally sleeping to rummage around and find out for himself. And it was hardly as if there were no secrets between them already. Garak, he noticed, was watching him, a smile playing across his face, almost as if he could follow the lines his thoughts were taking. Sisko looked back down at his hand. A muscle in it was twitching slightly. He really had to get some sleep.

He passed over the padd. Garak put down the mug and began to read. "Continued Romulan advances in the Benzar system," he said, after a moment or two. He chewed thoughtfully at his bottom lip. "And from your face I thought it had to be *bad* news. . . ." He glanced up, his eyes glittering, and looked straight at Sisko. "You really can say this for the Romulans, Captain—when it comes to fighting a war, they do make *exemplary* allies."

Sisko stared at him for a moment, and thought about

just how much better or worse he would feel if his fist got another chance to connect with Garak's jaw. Then he shook his head, and laughed, and looked away. *You really are a bastard, Garak.*

"All in all, this is something of a success," Garak said, and then he laughed himself. Another bitter sound, Sisko thought. "Particularly," Garak continued, "as Cardassian losses are comparatively few. I would find it more than a little galling if our Romulan allies killed *too* many Cardassians."

Sisko looked over at him again. Garak was smiling.

"All these ironies, Captain," he said, putting down the padd, and smiling at him. "Whatever shall we do about them?" He handed the padd back to Sisko, and reached for his mug again.

Sisko began thumbing at the padd halfheartedly. It *was* good news from the Benzar system, and it was long past time for some good news. He thought tiredly of the failed offensive at Sybaron.

"I believe," Garak said, interrupting Sisko's strategizing, "that I may at last have come to an understanding with Earl Grey."

Suppressing a sigh, Sisko turned to look at Garak again. He was staring down into his mug.

"An understanding?"

"The problem, I have decided," Garak continued, "is that it tastes of flowers."

"Flowers?"

"Flowers. And the *smell*—"

"This coming from a man who drinks fish juice."

Garak ignored him. "And I do find myself wondering precisely what it says about a culture that it drinks flowers—"

"Again, I'm thinking of the fish." Sisko threw aside

the padd he had already been struggling to read. "And it's not flowers. The oil in Earl Grey tea comes from the rind of a citrus fruit."

"A fruit?"

"A fruit."

"Like prunes?"

With an effort, Sisko covered his smile. "Yes."

Garak waved his hand, as if encouraging Sisko to say more. "And what insights do you think I should gain about Earth and its culture from this information, Captain?"

Sisko shrugged, and tapped his own mug, resting by the abandoned padd. "I don't know. I prefer *raktajino*."

A silence fell between them, disturbed only by the quiet but persistent hum of the runabout's engine, the soft and repetitious pulse of the systems on the console at the fore. On the padd, the marker in the text flashed, urging Sisko to turn back to the work still as yet undone. He picked it up again, and stared down, but did not begin to read. There was a slight clatter as Garak put down his mug. Sisko watched from the corner of his eye. Garak had begun to run a gray finger along the console. Sisko waited.

"It has not escaped my attention," Garak said at last, "that we have not spoken again in depth about our recent . . . collaboration. Not, at least, since you visited me in the shop and expressed such great displeasure about the turn of events."

That was certainly one way of putting it. . . .

"I meant what I said the other day," Garak continued, seemingly engrossed by the slow back-and-forth motion of his finger, "that I have nothing more to add to my report. And I sincerely hope that you have nothing more to add either." He turned his head, quite suddenly, to look at

Sisko, who managed to resist the urge to look back. "War is a very unpleasant business, Captain—I don't need to tell you that. And covert war is even more unpleasant. For which reason—among others—it should remain just that. Covert."

Sisko turned his head now, slowly, until they were looking straight at each other. Neither of them blinked. Then, on the console, just within Sisko's field of vision, he saw a green light wink at him—and it passed through his mind once again to wonder whether Vreenak had even had the chance to see the lights turn red. He blinked. Then he saw Garak's eyes widen, ever so slightly; bright blue and icy.

"Oh," Garak said, as if something had just become manifestly clear to him. "I see." He eased himself back in his chair, and Sisko watched with a rising wave of distaste. He had spent enough time around Garak recently to recognize a prelude to one of his monologues.

"Cardassians, Captain," Garak began, "have an intimate relationship with guilt. We are, as a rule, very familiar with it, in all of its hues and shades. And yet, despite this shared cultural experience, it can be a very private relationship. For example, we tend—as a rule—to consider it ill-mannered to require that those around us become intimately involved in our own crises of conscience."

"What the hell are you getting at?"

"What I'm trying to say," Garak said, leaning toward him, "is that I sincerely hope that troublesome conscience of yours isn't going to make you do something stupid—"

"*Stupid . . . ?*" Sisko rolled the word around his mouth, as if unsure of the taste.

"All right then, if you prefer—don't do anything that *I*

will regret. You do fully grasp the gravity of the situation in which we could find ourselves—?"

"We're already in a pretty serious situation—"

"Let me impress upon you that nobody knows the full extent of it—"

"Starfleet Intelligence already knows about the bio-mimetic gel. They already know about Tolar, they know about the forgery—" Sisko counted off the points violently, one to each finger.

"Oh, *please!*" Garak pushed back in his chair and looked at Sisko scornfully. "Don't delude yourself! You think because they let us off some petty crimes they'll pass over the larger ones?"

Sisko bit down on his anger, bit down hard.

Garak leaned in again. His voice had gone quiet. "It was murder, Captain—twice over. And I didn't do it just so you could lose your nerve and go begging for forgiveness from your superiors. So if your conscience is whispering again—a little late in the day, I might point out—you'd better not forget that you *owe* me."

At that, Sisko could not help but laugh out loud. "I *owe* you?" he said.

They were almost nose-to-nose now, and Garak's eyes had become very cold. "You came to me—just remember that. Not the other way round." He had raised his hand from the console, and now he lifted a finger, as if in warning, and jabbed it at Sisko. "*You* asked for *my* help—"

"Well, you know what they say, Garak," Sisko replied, staring back at him. "No good deed goes unpunished."

A long moment passed. Garak didn't move a muscle. And then he withdrew. Sisko nodded across at the mug. "Finish your tea, Garak," he said softly. "Before it gets cold."

Garak picked up the mug, and looked down into it. "Do you know, Captain," he said, after a moment or two, "I sincerely doubt I'm ever going to acquire the taste." He glanced up. "Nothing I'll regret," he said again—and then something passed very quickly across his face. Something new. His eyes lit up with amusement. Sisko felt his skin begin to crawl.

"Perhaps," Garak said, his voice smoother than silk, "I shall have more success with other human delicacies. I'm very much looking forward to sampling the offerings at your father's restaurant. In fact, I'm just looking forward simply to meeting your father."

My father . . .

He had so much to do lately, and it had always seemed to be the last thing on the list, or it was night back in New Orleans . . . Then, yesterday, the call from Ross had come in so late. . . . He'd had to see Odo about the transport ship, speak to Kira, speak to Jake. . . . So much to do he had forgotten to let his father know he was coming home. Sisko rubbed at the back of his neck—and then another thought crossed his mind.

My father . . . meeting Garak?

Just beside him, Garak was waiting—and smiling, benignly.

"Could you excuse me for a little while, Garak?" he said.

"By all means."

They stared at each other.

"I mean," Sisko said, pointedly, "that I'd like some privacy."

"Oh, I see . . . of course." He stood up, and Sisko watched him amble toward the back of the runabout, and then look back. "You seem a little distracted again, Captain? Are you sure that everything is quite all right?"

Go to hell, Garak.

"It will be," Sisko muttered, turning away and taking his frustration out on the console in front of him. "I just need to speak to somebody on Earth."

Having escaped from Dax, Odo arrived back in his office with exactly half a minute to spare, walked the four paces across the room to his desk, pulled out his chair, and sat down. He shifted slightly to one side two padds that seemed to him to be out of alignment, and then folded his hands before him and waited.

And waited.

Forty-three seconds later, "Incoming transmission from the freighter *Ariadne*," the computer told him.

"Receive transmission," Odo replied, promptly, and with a mild degree of annoyance. Steyn appeared on the viewscreen, half-awake, brushing her hair flat.

"Captain," Odo said, "is there anything the matter?"

Steyn looked at him in confusion. "No. Why?" She leaned forward, tense. "Has something come up at your end?"

"You were a little late in placing this call."

"Was I?" She looked puzzled, and then shrugged. "Well, sorry about that. No, everything's fine—all on schedule."

All on schedule? Odo checked the time, surreptitiously. Forty-three seconds late, twenty seconds spent disentangling the ensuing misunderstanding—more than a whole minute wasted now because Steyn had not taken the trouble to put through her call when she had said she would. Even after all these years living among them, Odo was certain that he would never understand the flexibility with which humanoids treated time.

"Never mind," he replied, resigned to it. "All on

schedule, as you said." He reached for the nearer of the two padds he had set ready near his hand. "I've read through the security arrangements surrounding the latinum shipment that you have on board the *Ariadne,* particularly concerning these biometric procedures you have in place—"

At the mention of them, Steyn came to life. "It's a great technology, Mr. Odo," she gushed. "Foolproof."

"Unfortunately, Captain, it has been my experience that successful crimes are very rarely committed by fools. Consequently, there are a number of details which I would like us to go through before your arrival at the station." He thumbed at the padd. "If you look at the material which I sent to you in advance—shall we begin with point one-dot-A . . .?"

His attention now firmly on the information before him, Odo neither saw nor heard Steyn give a very deep sigh.

The image on the viewscreen resolved itself into the familiar sight of the kitchen back home. Sisko saw the pots and the pans hanging all about, heard the noise and clatter in the background of someone busy at work, could almost convince himself he could feel the warmth and catch a breath of the heavy, spicy air. The old man leaning before the console sat up and looked straight at him.

"Hey Dad," Sisko said, guiltily.

His father, in return, bestowed upon him something between a frown and a smile. *"Well,"* Joseph said, *"I was* wondering *when I would hear from you. So tell me, were you planning to come all this way and not mention it at all?"*

Sisko looked at him in frank astonishment. "And just

how did you hear I was coming back—?" So much for security in wartime.

"That grandson of mine," Joseph said, *"now, he's a nice young man. Takes a little time out of his day now and again to speak to his old grandfather. I have to wonder where he could have learned good manners like that. Although they do say that kind of thing can skip a generation . . ."*

So *that* was how he'd found out. Jake Sisko, double agent. Looked like there was another father-son conversation to be had when he got back to the station. . . .

"Dad . . ." Sisko said, shaking his head, but now that he had started, Joseph was unstoppable.

"Other people, though, they're just so important. Too busy. Just can't find the time—"

"All right, all right—I surrender!" Sisko laughed, admitting defeat in the face of this intergenerational pincer movement. "I'm sorry—I should have spoken to you much sooner than from the runabout!"

The frown disappeared entirely from Joseph's face. He smiled at his son. *"So you're on your way home then."*

"I am."

"Well, it's about time! It's . . . what, two years since you were last here?"

"You know how it is, Dad, especially now. . . ." *The war.* That all-encompassing excuse. He left it unsaid.

"I know." Joseph nodded slowly. *"And I know you're going to be busy while you're here, Ben—they've been talking about this conference for a few weeks now on the news, and I guess it's got to be pretty serious to bring you all this way back, with things as they are right now."* His voice took on an almost plaintive edge. *"Will I get the chance to see you at all?"*

Sisko did not answer.

"Ben?"

Sisko jumped. "What was that, Dad?"

"Will I get the chance to see you while you're here?" Joseph said again. The frown was coming back again.

"Of course you will."

Joseph gave him a long, hard look. And then a smile lit up his face. *"Your sister, now, she's not bad at keeping in touch. Too good, sometimes."* Back to the usual. No awkward questions. *Thank you, Dad.*

"Portland *is* a little closer than DS9—"

"Doesn't seem to stop Jake."

"That's a fair point!" Sisko had to admit it.

"She'll be here herself from tomorrow."

"Judith will be there? I thought she was touring right now."

"She got back the day before yesterday. Said she wanted a bit of time at home, and then she'd be coming over." Joseph gave a dry smile. *"I seem to see a lot of that girl these days."*

For the first time since their conversation had started, Sisko took a proper look at his father. It was difficult to be certain—these screens were never as good as being face-to-face—but could it be that he was looking a little older? Were there a few more lines there? It was strange, Sisko thought, how you took so much for granted, relied on it, and then when you came and looked at it again, it was different. Not how you remembered it. Not how it should be. Frailer.

"How are you, Dad?" Sisko asked, softly.

"Well, it's nice of you to ask, Ben. I'm doing just fine."

"Not doing too much?"

Joseph's mouth set in a thin line. *"I'm doing just as much as I want—no more, no less."*

Sisko snorted. Stubborn old man. Some things never changed.

"You know, son—you don't seem quite yourself to me. Something on your mind?" Joseph was watching him closely, and with kindness.

Sisko looked away, around the runabout. "I'm just a little tired, Dad. There was a lot to get done before I left." He risked another look at his father, smiled the strained smile.

"You sure there's nothing else?" Joseph frowned once more. *"Not like last time?"*

Last time Sisko had been on Earth there had almost been a military coup. He sure as hell hoped that wasn't going to be the case this time.

Sisko shook his head. "I can't really say very much about the details, Dad," hearing himself giving the same old excuse he used with Odo: *the war, you see—the war.* "But there's nothing you need to worry about." He was about to say *I promise,* but stopped himself in time.

"Well, that's good. You get yourself here just as soon as you can, Ben. Your sister and I will be glad to see you. Be a bit like old times."

"Can't wait, Dad. See you soon."

His father smiled at him again, and then he was gone, and the UFP symbol filled the place where he had just been. Sisko sat and stared at it for a little while. Dinner with the family—good food, old jokes, the best company . . . It was something to look forward to. He thought of the new lines on his father's face and worried about it all. Maybe he should have brought Jake along after all. These were uncertain times, and everything seemed to be shifting, changing, on the move. You could never know for sure who would be next to go.

He put his elbows on the console, propping up his

head in his hands. He heard a sound coming from the
back of the runabout and gave a short laugh. As if he
would ever allow Jake on the same runabout as Garak.

Somewhere, Sisko thought, *you just have to draw a
line.*

At Starbase 375, Sisko and Garak transferred from the
Rubicon to a personnel carrier taking people back to
Earth from all along the front line. During this last leg of
the trip, Garak began to feel an increasing sense of dislo-
cation. The others on the carrier were surprised, to say
the least, to see a Cardassian journeying with them, and
they kept a wary distance. It reminded Garak a little of
how it had been on Deep Space 9 just after the Federation
had taken over. Although there was none of the overt hostility he had encountered in those early days, many of his
fellow travelers were clearly uncomfortable around him.
Hardly surprising, he supposed, given where most of
them had lately been. As he contemplated this change in
his circumstances, it struck him how much, as the years
had gone by on the station, he had come to take for
granted seeing familiar faces, being a familiar face.
Exile, of course, was as much about mind as about place.

In all of this, Sisko proved to have very limited use as
a distraction. If the captain had been distant before, he
was now verging on the inaccessible. Sisko spent most of
his time either plowing through reports or watching the
starscape. It was, Garak had to allow, an improvement on
the open hostility that had broken out in the confined
space of the runabout, but Sisko's heavy silence made
Garak uneasy too. He had to wonder what it was prefig-
uring, what kind of eruption was coming, and how fero-
cious it was likely to be. As a result, he watched the
captain closely; if only, he told himself, so that he might

see the explosion before it happened, and thus be ready to get out of its way.

When Garak had been invited to attend this conference, he had taken a little innocent pleasure in failing to mention his forthcoming absence to most of the people he had dealings with on the station. He had, however, chosen to tell Bashir that he was going to be visiting the doctor's home planet. And before Garak had set out, Bashir had given him a padd which, the doctor told him, contained everything that any visitor to Earth should have read before going there. As the carrier inched closer to its destination, Garak fell back on this gift. A lot of it turned out to be Shakespeare. Bashir, Garak thought, as he thumbed through the texts, had a persistent streak; hope really did spring eternal in him. Still, he was grateful for it, since it filled the time. As did watching Sisko, shifting his attention between news of the war and the void of space, as if he were trying to force them to fit.

Kira grabbed some lunch from the replicator in ops, and went straight back to her station. She took bites automatically, all of her attention directed toward her work. The *Ariadne*'s imminent arrival was throwing many of the station's routines into disarray; someone had to bring a little order back, and Kira was going to be the one to do it.

"I'm receiving a communication from a shuttle requesting docking clearance," Dax said from her station.

Kira did not look up. "Is it on the roster?"

"Yes, although it's gotten here a little early."

"Where's it come in from?"

"Hamexi space." Jadzia sounded interested by that. "We don't often hear from that part of the quadrant," she added.

"Well, if we're expecting it, you'd better give it permission," Kira said. "Let the pilot know that the station's on a heightened security alert. He can expect restrictions on moving around here."

She pressed on with her work, but it was not long before she was interrupted again, this time by Odo's voice, coming through the com.

"Major," he said, *"Lieutenant Commander Worf and I have drawn up a preliminary outline of the sections of the Promenade that will need to be closed while the* Ariadne *is here. It needs your approval before I can confirm it with Captain Steyn."*

"Send it over, Odo." Kira scanned through her backlog of files and gave a smile. "It just so happens that I felt like doing some reading."

"Also the procedure I have devised for bringing the shipment on to the station."

"I'll be glad to have a look at that too."

The data began streaming onto her console, and Kira started skimming through it.

"Shuttle's docking," Dax said and then added, in a thoughtful voice, "You know, I'm sure that Odo would normally make the effort to come down here with that kind of thing."

Kira had become engrossed in the files and was only half-listening. "Yeah?"

"And given," Dax continued calmly, "that he's no longer avoiding *you*—"

Kira did look up from her station then, for just long enough to give Jadzia a very dry look.

Jadzia smiled back blandly. "Given *that*," she said, "I'm starting to get the strangest feeling that he's avoiding *me*."

Kira reached out for her lunch and took another mechanical bite. "Well," she said, "I wonder what you could *possibly* have been doing to annoy him?"

Earth hung ahead, blue-white and unspeakably fragile. Sisko stood at an observation point and squinted at the vision, staring through the swirling clouds, trying to pick out patterns. He found the bulge of the coast of South America, upside down and a bit to one side, and he leaned his head a little so that the shape became more familiar. Then he closed one eye, raised his thumb and, twisting it up, blotted out the whole planet. He did this several times, and then he became aware that someone had come to stand beside him. He turned to look.

It was Garak, watching him with frank curiosity. "Whatever are you doing, Captain?" he said.

"It's something I read about the first human astronauts," Sisko replied. He blocked out the Earth again, then dropped his thumb so that it came back into sight. "They did this on the first trips to space—I've never forgotten how they described what it felt like when the planet was so small that you could just hide it away." He went through the motions again, and Earth slid in and out of sight. It was something he had done many times before, and it was always an odd feeling. Alienating.

"And why, I wonder, would they want to do that?"

Sisko sighed, and put his hand back down at his side. "It's a story about perspective, Garak, about something that once loomed very large suddenly seeming very small—"

"I believe I understand the metaphor, Captain," Garak said dryly. "I just don't see the point of it."

"Didn't your early space explorers tell the same story?" Sisko said. "About what it was like to see Cardassia from space for the first time? About how they could hide it away?"

"I shouldn't imagine they even thought of doing it," Garak replied. "Not an imaginative bunch, on the whole, the Cardassian military. It wasn't encouraged. And, anyway, it would hardly be worth doing, would it? Nothing can put Cardassia out of mind. Not space, not time . . ." He halted. Sisko glanced over at him, staring out at the alien planet that was fast approaching. "Not distance," he finished, regretfully. Then he lifted his hand, shut one eye, and tried blotting out Earth for himself.

"It's because you only have one moon," Garak declared, after a moment or two.

Sisko frowned. "What?"

"Earth only has one moon—am I correct?"

"Yes, that's right. . . . What's that got to do with it?"

"Then people will have done this for centuries." Garak waved his thumb up and down. "Only they'll have been standing on Earth, and blocking out the moon. It would be natural to try it in reverse, once people got into space. Now, Cardassia Prime has three moons. So which one would you choose to hide away? One of them is called the Blind Moon," Garak went on. "It's never alone in the sky—there's always another moon up there with it. As if it has to have a companion. There's a children's story, about how even the Blind Moon can see." Garak's voice trailed away and then he began to laugh. "Isn't it strange, what comes back to mind?" he said. "I haven't thought about that story in years."

"There's a children's story on Earth too," Sisko mused, "about a man in the moon, looking down." He carried out the little ritual again. "Maybe you're right," he said. "Maybe it's not about hiding something after all.

Maybe it's more about hiding *away* from something."

"And on Cardassia," Garak said, with a smile, "it's always best to assume that there's someone watching."

Sisko did not answer. He tried one more time, but they had come too close now for him to hide it away entirely. He abandoned the attempt. "Is this the first time you've ever seen Earth, Garak?"

Garak roused himself from his thoughts. "Yes," he said. "But for some reason it feels very familiar."

Sisko could not help but smile. He looked back at the planet and felt a little warmth. "Perhaps you've spent too much time around humans," he suggested.

"Captain," Garak sighed, "I don't doubt that for a second."

Once, in an anonymous room, anonymous men met to debate the fate of nations, met to wage a private little war. One of these men is angry, and believes himself betrayed. The other is placatory, still seeking to persuade.

The first confronts the other with his case. He launches the facts across the room like artillery fire. He intends to take no prisoners.

"What the hell have you been doing? What are you playing at? What have you done*?"*

The other tries to deflect the accusations being thrown at him. "Take it easy, take it easy!" All the motions of appeasement. "We can talk about this, surely?"

"Talk about it? What is there to say? What can *there be to say? Have you no comprehension—"*

"Maybe there's been a misunderstanding. A miscommunication somewhere along the line. I know," he's speaking more slowly now, smoothing at the edges between them, "that you and I can come to an understanding—"

"An understanding? How can there be an understanding? This is beyond belief!"

"Let's talk about it—"

"This is not what I signed up for. This is not what we are for!"

From the other, there is the first sign of resistance to the onslaught. "You see, I would have said that this is exactly what we are for—"

"Not this. Not this far. This is well beyond containment. Dammit, this is well beyond going on the offensive!" He plunges on with his attack, reckless, uncaring of the consequences. "This is abhorrent—"

"Think about what you're saying now. Those are strong words you're using—"

"And you'd better believe I mean every single one of them—"

"It's still the same end. Still the very same end that you signed up for. Just the methods have changed—"

"No, no! That's exactly my point—are you deliberately misunderstanding me?"

"I'm about as sure as I can be," says the other, "that I understand you perfectly."

The first at last perceives the threat that the other now poses. Silence falls. A respite. When he speaks again he has now become anxious to consolidate the truce. "I . . . can understand how it might seem to make sense to you; but I cannot in good conscience countenance it—"

"Don't let it trouble you." Back to persuasion. Soothing again. Better the first is coaxed than threatened. "Leave this to me. Let me handle it."

"But that's exactly what troubles me." The fury has left his voice. He is now only stating the facts as they appear to him. "What happens when you are left to handle *things. You've already turned a tool into a weapon. More than a weapon—"*

"Don't make it your problem. Let it lie with me. You have your own work to attend to—"

"My own work?" He is laughing now, gently, making a mockery of all that he has done; grasping fully the limits to his actions. "On your behalf."

"No," says the other. "Our work." He is speaking softly to him, almost as if to embrace him. "You know you're one of us."

A kind of peace has broken out; a kind of resolution. The first man leaves and the door is closed; not slammed—not anything so definite. The other turns to the third man. He is sitting in a chair positioned in the corner; sitting where one might be best placed to observe, to analyze, and, later, to recall.

"Have to wonder if we'll see him again. Have to wonder if that particular alliance might just be coming to an end—"

"No," corrects the third man. "It has already come to its end."

This is how it stands. The lines have crossed each other; they are heading to their end points. All that's needed now is for a ship and its crew to make their entrance. All that's needed now is for two men to reach their destination.

PART TWO

THE BRIDGE

It is well that war is so terrible;
else we would grow too fond of it.
—Robert E. Lee

We are having one hell of a war!
—George S. Patton

WITH A GRUNT OF SATISFACTION, Odo switched off the padd, and set it neatly in place upon the pile. Between them, he and Steyn had at last finalized the procedure for bringing the latinum shipment onto the station, securing it, and returning it to the *Ariadne* after the repairs on the ship were complete. The original plan—Steyn's idea—had been that, since the *Ariadne* was going nowhere, the shipment should remain on board throughout. But this had proven unsatisfactory; now that her engineer had given a fuller picture of the extent of the damage, it was clear that too many people would need ongoing access to the ship throughout the process of repairs. Bringing the latinum onto the station had its own problems—making sure that the route to the assay office and back was secure for one thing—but it was to Odo's mind (and Steyn's, in time, once Odo had finished his explanations) without doubt the better choice. Or, to put it in the plainest possible terms, Odo would be much happier if the latinum was close by, and if his people were working on the territory that they knew best. Steyn's assurance that her security systems were state-of-the-art was no guarantee for Odo. Faults in the system were exploited by people, not technologies—and, in Odo's experience, if the rewards were great enough, then people were endlessly creative when it came to finding faults. He often thanked providence that the chief had not chosen a life of crime.

He got up from his chair, and briefly surveyed his office. All was in order. It was time to carry out his morning ritual, and make his inspection of the Promenade.

He stood for a little while, as was his habit, in the doorway of his office, his arms folded, and watched the ebb and flow of the people as they passed him by. One of the shopkeepers, on her way to opening up, saw him and gave her customary salute. Odo gave a small nod in reply. From here, everything seemed just as it should be.

He progressed out onto the Promenade itself, the door sliding shut efficiently in his wake. He contemplated visiting the infirmary but, try as he might, he could not think of an excuse other than *Dax has asked me to keep an eye on you.* He passed by. As he went on, he glanced around at the shops and the morning trade; the usual people selling their wares; and their customers, residents and visitors alike. He ticked off the familiar faces as he checked automatically for any changes in routine or appearance, and kept a mental tally of the new faces. He nodded approvingly as he passed two of his security staff, making a scheduled sweep, right on time. He saw one of the Klingon liaison officers striding purposefully *(did a Klingon ever stride any other way?)* a little distance ahead. Just to be on the safe side, he resolved to check up on the officer's schedule later. It paid to treat even allies with caution. Odo walked on, briskly. When he got as far as the tailor's shop, however, he stopped and stood looking at the door. It was tempting, so very tempting. . . .

The permanent battle of wits between Odo and Quark was the stuff of legend around the station—conducted openly and to the never-failing absorption of the other residents, who seemed to be most appreciative of this ongoing cabaret. The similar state of hostilities that existed between Odo and Garak, however, went on in complete secrecy. Odo would increase the levels of his surveillance of the shop; Garak would have the devices disabled within the week. Garak would in passing seem to suggest that he had more information about a topic than his very narrow security rating should allow; Odo would promptly introduce new cryptographic protocols around his databases. It was years now since Odo had first put Garak under observation and Garak had first slithered out, but the combatants themselves had not mentioned the situation to each other even once. Odo had a vague impression that Garak would have found the subject vulgar.

He looked over his shoulder. This part of the Promenade was quiet. The shop door was closed, and Odo knew for a fact that its owner would not return unexpectedly. It was more than tempting. It was tantalizing.

What would I find in there? Odo wondered, tapping a finger thoughtfully against his sleeve, and staring at the blank slate of the door. *Would I learn what he and the captain have been up to recently?*

He snorted. It was a pleasant fantasy to think rummaging around the shop might lead to some discovery—a pleasant fantasy but, it had to be admitted, a most unlikely one. As if Garak would leave anything incriminating in plain or easy view. It would only be a waste of time, and Odo had quite enough to worry about without adding another task to his list. Better to treat Garak's absence as one trouble fewer, rather than take more on. And anyway, he reflected, almost as an afterthought, it *could* be construed as breaking and entering. Technically.

A little regretfully, Odo moved on. He took the steps to the upper level, and walked along, looking out past the bright flags draped above the Promenade. He came to a halt at the spot where, in years past and on countless occasions, he would find the younger Sisko and his partner-in-crime lurking. The spot was quiet these days, unless Odo himself was there. He could quite understand why the two had liked it so much. It gave an excellent view.

He had been standing there no more than a minute or two, watching the morning traffic, when the sound of a familiar voice drifted through the muddle of the crowd. It was a voice to which he was attuned.

"No, absolutely *no* way—"

Her companion said something that Odo, high up on his perch, and despite leaning forward a little, was not quite able to hear.

"I don't *care* what Worf has to say about it, Jadzia— it's not going to happen and that's final!"

Odo watched as Dax's shoulders rocked with laughter. Even so, she was still trying to change the other's mind— but Nerys was having none of it.

"Yes, well, *if* he can prove that, *then* I'll think about it." Kira waved her finger, with finality. *"Think* about it, mind you. Look, Jadzia—I've got to go. You get any more trouble from Worf, you send him my way, okay?" She gave Dax her wide and generous smile, and they parted.

Odo hurried toward the steps and made his way down onto the Promenade. As was in his nature, he timed his interception perfectly. "Major," he greeted her.

"Constable!" She favored him with the same smile she had just granted to Dax . . . was it his imagination or was it a little less wide than the one she had given the commander? Was it the same? "Have you heard yet from the *Ariadne?*" she said.

"Indeed I have, Major." He fell in step alongside her. "I've just spent the past hour in discussion with the captain and she has at last been persuaded that her cargo will be safer on the station throughout the time it will take to make repairs to the ship."

Kira gave a brisk nod. "Good," she said. "Trying to keep track of who was going in and out of the ship would have been a real strain on resources. Thank you, Odo." She looked around her. "Hopefully we won't hear too many complaints from the Merchants' Association when we tell them we'll be sealing off this section of the Promenade. I imagine there'll be some talk of lost earnings and so on. . . ." She frowned. "I guess I'd better get on to that next."

"It is unlikely to affect them for much more than a day," Odo pointed out. "And we are fortunate in that at least one proprietor in that section will not be affected at all." Odo looked meaningfully back at Garak's shop.

"Yes . . ." said Kira. "I have to wonder if the captain is getting along all right. . . ."

"Assuming Garak doesn't talk *all* the way to Earth," Odo said, "I have high hopes for the survival of both of them." That earned him another smile, but then there was a beat of silence where once some more informal conversation might have taken place.

"So," Kira said, "when are you briefing your team?"

"In an hour," Odo answered.

"Good," she said again. They were coming up to Quark's now. Odo customarily went in around this time, on his inspection of the Promenade. Kira knew his habits. She had already slowed their pace a little, and when they reached the entrance of the bar, they both came to a halt.

"Well," Odo said, "I should go and check on how Quark's morning is progressing."

"Thanks for keeping me up to date on the *Ariadne,* Odo." Her smile was full and open. He nodded his good-bye and watched her go on down the Promenade. Their accommodation in their working relationship was a great relief to him, but still mixed with regret. No one watching them would be able to tell, but Odo felt the space where their close friendship had been very keenly. It was, he thought, as if they were not quite in alignment with each other. Carefully, he put that thought to one side, and considered instead the security briefing he would lead later in the morning.

Just as he was about to turn to go into Quark's, Odo could not help registering a figure walking toward him along the Promenade. He checked his mental tally of visitors. *I think that's someone new,* he thought, and stepped out a little more to get a better look at the man strolling toward him.

He was carrying a large, formless bag, slung across his larger, bulky body. He capped it all with an elaborate black hat, pulled down over his head at a rakish angle. Beneath the brim of the hat, Odo caught a quick glimpse of something—something that might have been smiling, as if at some private joke. Something disquieting, formless; a face without a face, shifting and swelling behind an invisible skin, the station lights kaleidoscoped within something—something that still might have been smiling. He shuddered involuntarily, then controlled himself.

That's a hat I know, I'm sure. . . .

It took Odo a moment or two to sift through names, and events—and court hearings—but eventually he placed him. *Mexk Brixhta,* he thought, watching the bulbous figure curve along with the line of the Promenade. *What, I wonder, could have brought you here just now?* Breaking the habits he had built across his whole career, Odo turned away from Quark's, and began to follow Brixhta back along the Promenade. His day, he knew, had just become a great deal more complicated.

The shimmer of the transporter beam settled at last, and Sisko was able to take a proper look at his surroundings. His eyes began to water a little, and he blinked in the white glare of the morning sunshine. The light silvered the water on the bay over to the west, hit the glass and chrome of the building ahead and the white stones of the paving of the plaza in front of it, and cast long, deep shadows on the trees and the green grass of the parkland opening out behind them. Sharp, bright colors; the taste and the scent of fresh air—it was too easy to forget it all, he thought, living on the station. Too easy to lose sight of Earth.

He took a quick glance over at his companion. Garak was shielding his eyes against the light, and he was staring all around. He seemed ill at ease. Then he caught Sisko watching him, and produced a dry, closed smile. "So this is Earth," he said. "How dazzling."

Sisko pointed in front of them. "That building over there is Starfleet Headquarters," he said. "I guess we should go straight on in. . . ." He looked around uncertainly. "I *was* expecting Admiral Ross to be here to meet us."

Garak was staring up at the front of the HQ building. "That's the Cardassian flag up there," he said, in surprise. "Why, I wonder, would that be flying here? Have we managed to arrive in the middle of a coup d'état? Someone might have taken the time to inform me."

He *was* edgy. "It's customary to fly the flags of visiting delegates," Sisko explained. "It's meant to welcome them to Earth, and it's also meant as a mark of respect. I guess that flag up there might even be for you. And for your government-in-exile too, of course."

Beneath the shade of his hand, Garak's eyes glittered coldly back. "It is not my government, Captain," he replied. "But that is a revealing custom, to say the very least. On Cardassia, we would certainly try to impress you with a display of pageantry. But you would never see another empire's flag flying over any of *our* cities." His smile twisted. "Well, not until very recently."

Sisko didn't answer. He gestured vaguely at some of the other buildings dotted around the plaza. More chrome and glass. All very glossy. "Starfleet Academy, campus housing, consulates, that kind of thing," he said. He jerked his thumb over his shoulder. "The rest of the city is over that way."

"And I'd like to see more of it," Garak murmured, gazing around. His eyes were still under protection, hidden away, but he seemed to be surveying everything, Sisko thought—the vivid sky, the white light, the lines and contours of the buildings, out to the city beyond. . . . Watching him take the measure of it all, so methodically, so efficiently—so Cardassian—Sisko felt a sudden surge of protectiveness. It felt as if something precious was being intruded upon, invaded—violated, even.

Serpent in Paradise . . .

"A lot to do first, wouldn't you say, Garak?" His voice came out perhaps a little angrier than he had intended. "A lot to talk about."

Garak snapped his attention back to him. "That really depends on whether or not you're feeling talkative, Captain." Ice cold. Alien. Here, on Earth. Right at the center of it all. "I am very clear on exactly what information I wish to share."

Sisko stared up at the building ahead and the flags flying and, with an effort, considered it more carefully. "You know," he said, after a moment or two, "I think they may have tinted all that glass since I was last here."

"Costly," Garak remarked.

"Moneyless," Sisko reminded him.

"Oh yes," Garak murmured. "Of course." Sisko risked another sideways glance at him. Garak seemed to have adjusted now to the daylight; he had dropped his hand, but he was still staring all around. And he still, Sisko thought, had a faint edge of unease.

Garak pointed ahead. "I wonder, Captain," he said, "whether these two officers approaching are coming to meet us?"

Sisko looked up. Two figures were coming down the steps of the HQ building. Considering the identity of his companion, they would, he reckoned, most likely be Starfleet Intelligence. It certainly looked as if they were coming over to them. He was aware that Garak shifted slightly, straightening up and folding his arms across his chest. They both stood and waited in silence as the welcoming committee crossed the grass.

When they got closer, Sisko thought that the two officers, a man and a woman, looked very youthful. *The spies are getting younger every day.* Sisko glanced at Garak and saw that he too had relaxed a little. That gave him a moment's pause, since he had to wonder at the risks of putting Garak into the care of what seemed to be two relatively inexperienced officers. Or maybe Garak wasn't considered as much of a security risk these days? Not as much as he would have been in the past? He had, after all, proven himself useful—even reliable—since the start of the war. Still, in Sisko's own extensive experience, it paid to keep an eye on Garak. If only to make sure he wasn't killing people when you weren't looking.

The woman was the first to speak. She seemed to be slightly the younger of the pair; mid-twenties, tall, with long blond hair tied back in an efficient ponytail. She had a quick, brisk manner that was straight from the textbook. Starfleet, Sisko thought, produced bright young officers like this by the dozen. And was losing them on the front lines pretty quickly these days.

"My name is Lieutenant Chaplin," she said, "and this is Lieutenant Marlow." She gestured to her colleague, standing behind. At first glance he seemed nondescript, almost colorless; on closer inspection Sisko could see his watchfulness, and the patience of a much older man. Marlow nodded a greeting to them both, but did not speak.

"Mister Garak," Chaplin went on, "welcome to Earth. Lieutenant Marlow and I have been assigned to look after you while you're here."

"It is very good to meet you, Lieutenant. Both of you."

Sisko shot him a curious look. No elegant putdowns? Perhaps these two young officers hadn't been such a bad choice after all.

"Captain Sisko," Chaplin said, turning to address him directly, and now only just managing to cover what Sisko realized must be excitement, "it really is an honor to meet you, sir."

"Thank you, Lieutenant," he said, giving her a broad smile. "I'm glad to have the chance to meet you both." He nodded at Marlow. "Although I *was* expecting to see Admiral Ross—"

"The admiral has asked me to pass his regards on to you," Chaplin said, "and also his apologies for not being here in person to meet you. I understand that something has come up that demanded his attention—"

Sisko frowned. "Nothing serious, I hope."

"I'm afraid I really can't say, Captain." Chaplin gestured at the HQ building, and began to lead them toward it. As they walked, Sisko watched from the corner of his eye as Garak unobtrusively put Chaplin between them, letting him walk on the outside. *First point to Garak,* he thought.

"Did the admiral say when he was likely to be free?" he asked Chaplin.

She shook her head. "I'm afraid not. He asked me to direct you to your quarters, and said that he'd meet you there as soon as he was able." She offered him a padd. "He also asked me to prepare and pass on these files."

Sisko took the padd, and started scrolling through, skim-reading. Chaplin began to give him a quick overview. As she talked, Sisko took another look at Garak, who was taking in their surroundings as they walked. Sisko glanced over his shoulder. Marlow was walking behind, hands clasped behind his back, head down a little. He was aware, Sisko realized, of every move that Garak was making; was watching to see what Garak was watching. Sisko smiled to himself. Second point to the lieutenants. With even just a little closer contact there was no doubting their competence. Maybe it was the war, Sisko thought, regretfully, making them older before their time.

He read through some more of the information on the padd. It was pretty much as Chaplin had described. Details of all the conference sessions. Full files on all of the attendees, from across all the delegations. *Very* full files, some of them. And, he thought gratefully, what looked to be some excellent summaries.

"Thank you for this, Lieutenant," he said, smiling up at her, "this is going to be extremely helpful."

She smiled back brightly, and pointed her finger to one line. Details of the quarters assigned to him. Ross would meet him there.

"Chaplin's very thorough," Marlow remarked, from behind, speaking for the first time. Sisko turned to look at him. He was mild and softly-spoken; almost compliant.

Garak answered him without turning to look. "I don't doubt that for a moment, Lieutenant Marlow." For the life of him, Sisko could not judge which one of them had taken *that* point.

"I've prepared some background information for you too, Mr. Garak," Chaplin said, handing him a padd. "Summarizing some of the areas I'd like us to cover in conversation while you're here."

"Conversation?" Garak murmured, as he took the padd. "So that's what we have in mind." He began reading. "All of this looks really very routine," he said. "Very much on the lines of what I had to say when I was at Starbase 375."

"I don't think any of the officers you spoke to there were specialists," Marlow said, from the rear. "I have a number of more technically-oriented questions I'd like to ask you."

"And I'll endeavor to provide whatever you need."

"Thank you," Marlow said, politely.

"And what I have not included in that file," Chaplin said, "is that there are one or two matters arising from your most recent report that we would like to examine in a little more detail."

Garak smiled at her. "If you are both of the opinion that something needs a little clarification," he said, "then

I would of course be delighted to help in any way that I can."

Sisko watched as Chaplin and Marlow exchanged a look. He caught the glimmer of a smile in Marlow's eyes. It was, he realized, no more than the natural response to spending a little time in Garak's company. He looked back down at the routines scrolling past on the padd.

They had reached the steps leading up to the HQ building. Sisko glanced at the flags flying above as they passed beneath them. The steps were wide and made a good meeting place coming in and out of the building. Several clumps of people were gathered there, talking, waiting for friends or colleagues, or finishing bits of business before going on to the next meeting or assignment. As they went up toward the entrance, heads turned, and Sisko thought he could catch a little of the questions rising in their wake, thought he caught the whispered word, *"Cardassian?"* Sisko chewed at the inside of his lower lip. Their arrival was not turning out to be quite as low-profile as he would have liked.

The entrance doors slid back to admit them, and they went inside, into a wide, high atrium. They stopped at the security barrier and, while Sisko was cleared straight away, Chaplin began the more laborious process of getting Garak into the building, and letting him move around it—or some of it, at least. Not too much, Sisko speculated.

He looked out across the atrium. The sunlight was pouring through the glass front, filling the hall—although perhaps, here inside, the light was muted just a little. It was certainly not as warm as it was outside, the temperature regulators keeping everything cool. As he waited for the requirements of the bureaucracy to be fulfilled, Sisko looked out beyond the security gate, at the people hurrying to and fro across the wide hall, at the big green-leafed plants and bits of artwork dotted here and there, at the clear-fronted turbolifts gliding up and down. All so sleek, all running so smoothly.

"That's it," said Chaplin. "You're in."

They went past the barriers, farther into the bright hall. "Mister Garak," Chaplin said, still efficient, still brisk, and obviously wanting to waste no time, "if you're willing, I think we ought to begin straight away."

"Well, I'm quite certain," Garak replied, "that I have no other immediately pressing engagements."

"Then we should get started." She turned to Sisko, and nodded goodbye. "It was an honor to meet you, sir. I'm sure we'll see each other again over the next few days."

"No doubt," Sisko said, and lifted the padd. "Thank you for this."

"My pleasure." Chaplin turned to go, motioning to Garak which way they were heading. Marlow gave Sisko a quiet smile.

"Very good to meet you, sir," he said and then, smoothly, he put himself in position so that Garak was between him and Chaplin. Yet another point to the lieutenants, Sisko thought with a smile. As the three of them headed off together across the hall toward the turbolifts, Garak glanced back over his shoulder at Sisko, and gave him one last, very careful stare. His meaning wasn't exactly unclear.

Don't do anything I'll regret.

It seemed to Odo that Brixhta was stopping at every possible point around the Promenade. It made it somewhat difficult to follow him in a wholly inconspicuous manner. The florist had been bewildered at Odo's apparent and sudden interest in Bajoran *esani*. And at least two people had called out to remark how unusual it was to see him make another round so early in the day.

Brixhta passed under the balcony and, in the relative shelter of one of the stairspirals, Odo contacted ops. "Odo to Lieutenant Commander Dax," he murmured.

Dax's voice came out clear. *"Odo?"* she said. *"Are you whispering—?"*

Odo looked hurriedly at Brixhta, making slow progress ahead of him. "Could you check for me, please, Commander," he said, "whether a ship has recently arrived from Hamexi space?"

"It came in to docking port three earlier."

"Any cargo?" Odo said quickly. "What's on the manifest?"

"Wait just a moment. . . ."

Odo tapped his fingers impatiently against his sleeve. Brixhta was disappearing around the bend of the station.

"Several crates unloaded into the cargo bay. Described as 'historical artifacts.' Something going on I need to tell the major about, Odo?"

"No," Odo said firmly, "I'm well able to handle this. Thank you, Commander."

He hurried on along the Promenade, just in time to see Brixhta go into the bar. Everything, Odo thought, eventually led to Quark's.

Quark took one look at his new customer and decided not to bother trying to work out how to shake hands. "You're a new . . . face around here," he said. "Welcome to DS9."

"Thank you."

Quark wiped the glass he was holding nonchalantly, put it down, and then made his standard opening gambit. "You here on business?"

He edged in a little as he spoke; he liked to be up

close when he asked this question, to see how people's faces changed when he asked it. Some would look hungry, others desperate, others just smug. In this case, however, Quark wasn't entirely sure what he was meant to be watching.

"As a matter of fact—I am," the man replied. He reached inside his jacket and flicked out a small piece of plastic; it was a gaudy shade of pink and the writing on it was gold, ornately curled, and embossed. Quark took it, taking a little care not to touch the hand that was offering it, and as much care not to be too obvious about it. No need to give offense.

"My name's Brixhta," the alien said. "I deal in antiques."

Quark set all cross-cultural concerns aside. *This* was familiar territory—the real universal translator. "Buying," he said, "or selling?" He examined the card. *Brixhta,* it said. *Antiques.* Strange custom, Quark thought, turning the card over. It was blank on the back. Pretty, though. And an interesting idea. Maybe he could get a few made—it might catch on. *Bashir. Doctor.* Or *Odo. Persecution.*

"That depends on where I am," Brixhta replied. "But here—selling."

"Antiques?" Quark said, thinking hard, and leaning on the bar.

A finger stretched out and tapped the word on the card. "Antiques," Brixhta confirmed.

Quark put the piece of plastic down carefully in front of him. "Well, that covers a lot of possibilities, Mr. Brixhta—"

"If you'd like to hear more," Brixhta said, "I have plenty of time. And I do so enjoy talking about my work."

"Why don't you take a seat there?" Quark said, gesturing at one of the stools. Not too close to Morn, of course—he didn't want them to be interrupted. "And what are you having to drink?"

"Tonic water. Bolian. And I prefer to stand," Brixhta said. "It reminds me of my corporeality."

"*Okay . . .*" Quark pulled himself up from his elbows and drew back just a little. Some things always got lost in translation. "Well, why don't you just . . . take a stand there, then, and I'll get you your drink."

Quark turned away, thinking a little brandy might help him in the negotiations he was about to open. Above the clink of the glasses he retrieved and the splash of the drinks he poured, he was tuned in to the ambient noise—the satisfying chink of latinum at the dabo table, the constant drone from Morn's end of the bar . . . and then he heard another all-too-familiar sound, one he had made quite sure he never missed. It was very quiet, but unique—a very particular *ooze. . . .*

"Ah, Odo . . ." Brixhta said, elongating the word. His voice had acquired a slight edge, Quark thought, as he turned back to the bar. It sounded like a piece of velvet—wrapped around a switchblade. "I was wondering how long it would be before you came to say hello."

Quark put down the glasses. Brixhta was looking Odo up and down, and his eyes were glittering beneath the brim of his hat. "You know, Odo," Brixhta said, "you haven't changed a bit."

Odo folded his arms. "I sincerely hope, Mr. Brixhta," he rasped, "that the same cannot be said for you." Quark whistled under his breath. That was the tone of voice Odo usually reserved for more colorful residents of the station—Garak, Prylar Rhit, himself. . . .

"For one thing," Brixhta said, ignoring Odo's reply, "you're still as shy as ever." He sounded almost playful now, Quark thought. In much the same way that a razor-cat was playful—just before it tore open the throat of its prey. "Almost a whole morning you've spent following me round the station," Brixhta said, "and only now you've come to talk to me."

"You may rest safe in the knowledge that I was taking a keen interest in your progress. Very keen." Odo glared at him. "And I shall continue to take a keen interest in you for as long as you remain here on DS9."

Brixhta drew his glass in toward him. "That you should show such concern, after so much time has passed. I'm honored, Odo. Honored."

"It's only natural for the station's chief of security, wouldn't you say?" Odo thinned his lips. "When, exactly, *did* you get out of prison, Brixhta?"

Quark, mouth full of brandy, started to choke. Both Brixhta and Odo stared across the bar at him. "Sorry," Quark muttered. "Didn't mean to interrupt."

"Six months ago," Brixhta admitted. "But you too, Odo, may rest safe in the knowledge that my . . . ah . . . *felonious* days are over."

Odo snorted. "I find that highly unlikely—"

"What you see before you is a new man, Odo."

"And how, precisely, did this improbable transformation take place?"

"Ah!" Brixhta sounded rapturous. He spread back into the bar stool. "Therein lies a tale, and one which I could spend a whole day telling. But the heart of it, Odo, is that I discovered History."

"History?"

"History. And with that discovery, I found worlds of immeasurable beauty; worlds upon worlds . . ." He took a little of his tonic water; it seemed to steady him a bit, Quark noticed. "History, Odo," Brixhta said, "has looked upon me kindly, and she has shown me her treasures." He sounded close to tears.

Odo looked distinctly unmoved by this. "What's the scam, Brixhta?" he said.

Brixhta tipped the brim of his hat upward. "I deal in antiques," he said, and then pulled the brim back down again.

"Antiques?" Odo said, in disbelief.

"Antiques," Quark put in, pointing at the piece of pink plastic on the bar. Odo reached out cautiously and picked it up, looking at it as if it were a piece of evidence.

He growled suspiciously. "Why, if you are selling antiques, have you spent the whole morning visiting almost every establishment on the Promenade? Is the proprietor of the *jumja* kiosk a keen collector? Has Kaga at the Klingon restaurant also had a life-changing encounter with the past?"

"It's called *advertising,* Odo—" Quark said, sighing at having to point out something this obvious. After all this time.

Odo gave him a sharp look. "You keep out of this, Quark."

If it was possible, Odo sounded just a tiny bit more bad-tempered than usual. Quark decided to make a strategic withdrawal back to his brandy. For the moment.

"Mr. Quark is, to some extent, quite correct," Brixhta said, "but, in addition, I have been looking for somewhere to hold an auction of my goods. Somewhere with a fair amount of space, plenty of chairs, perhaps affording the opportunity to offer my customers something to eat, or something to drink. . . ." He looked around him, and then gleamed at Quark from beneath his hat. Quark smiled back broadly. It seemed that they were definitely going into business.

"Have some more tonic water," Quark said generously, reaching over to top up the drink. Brixhta raised the glass and tipped it at him, before sucking out a little more of the liquid.

"If I could interrupt this mutual appreciation session for just one moment," Odo said dryly, "may I ask when you intend to hold this auction?"

Brixhta looked at Quark. Quark looked back. Brixhta shrugged, and then Quark offered, "Tomorrow morning? Eleven hundred hours?" Brixhta nodded.

"I see. . . ." Odo looked at Quark thoughtfully, and then turned back to Brixhta. "Hours yet," he said. "In the meantime, perhaps you won't mind accompanying me down to the cargo bay, opening up all those packing cases you have brought on board, and showing me exactly what's inside, will you?"

Brixhta drained his glass and slid out of the chair. "Odo," he said, "I thought you would never ask." He addressed Quark. "I shall return," he declared. "And bring you my wares."

Just before Odo turned to go, Quark pointed at the pink plastic card the constable was still holding.

"Can I have that back?" Quark said.

Odo looked down at it. "No," he said. "I'll be needing it for the trial."

Sisko put down the padd and checked the time. Still no sign of Ross. He went over to the replicator and got himself a cup of *raktajino,* and drank it slowly, standing by the window looking out across the plaza and toward the Bolian consulate. There was a light mist coming from the sea. He caught himself thinking of the view of the stars that he had from his office, back on the station; white points of light against sheer black. He sighed, then finished up the coffee and looked again to see what time it was. He put down the cup and started unpacking his bag. There were a couple of padds on top; he scanned through one of the reports, reminding himself of the details of the news of Dominion activity in the Calandra Sector. It would almost certainly come up in conversation with Ross later. If they got the chance. If Sisko decided he had nothing else to say first.

Reports. Reports. More reports. He put the padd down, a little impatiently, and pulled out his dress uniform. It had got a little crumpled in the bag. He hung it behind the door and smoothed out some of the creases, then took a step back and considered it. After a moment or two, he turned away and went over to the comm unit to check he had not somehow missed a message from Ross.

There was nothing. He played for a moment with some of the controls, and then came to a decision. It was probably best, he thought, now that he was on Earth, not to leave it too long to speak to Dad. . . . It was not his father's image, however, that appeared on the screen.

"Judith!" he said, giving her a wide smile.

"Ben? Ben!" His sister grinned back. *"We weren't expecting to hear from you for a day or two yet! I thought things were going to be busy at your end?"*

"They will be," he said. "Very soon. I seem to have a little time on my hands right now."

"Well, I'm glad you took the chance to call," Judith said. *"Dad tells me you're hoping to get over here."*

"That's right."

"Any idea when?"

"I'll . . . probably have a better idea later today," Sisko said, hearing himself go cagey. Closed. He could see from the slight shift in her expression that Judith too had heard the note of caution.

"Well, I won't press you to tell me any more," she said. *"You know we'll be glad to see you whenever you can get here."*

"Thanks, Jude." He smiled at her. "I wasn't sure whether you'd be there yet."

"I came over a bit earlier than I'd planned."

Brother and sister exchanged knowing, worried looks.

"How is he?"

She sighed. *"Well, you know what he's like, Ben—he won't slow down, he won't tell me if he's feeling under the weather. . . . He won't admit it,"* she said, *"but I think that trip of his to DS9 took a lot more out of him than he's willing to say."*

"To be honest, I was amazed he agreed to come."

"I think he got a bad fright when the station was taken. Particularly when we heard that Jake got left behind. . . ." Judith narrowed her eyes slightly.

"Now, don't *you* start blaming me for that," Sisko said quickly. "Jake fixed that all for himself."

"Okay, okay . . . well, whoever's *fault it was, it made Dad jumpy. He didn't say anything, but I think he started worrying whether either of you would ever come back to Earth again."*

"Judith, that's crazy—!"

"No, Ben—that's the thinking of an old man who's getting more than a bit frail, and who worries about his son and his grandson." She gave him a wry smile. *"I think he's just about forgiven you for forgetting to let him know you were coming. At least,"* her smile became wicked, *"all he can talk about is when you'll get here. I'm sick of it, the customers are sick of it—"*

"Well, I'm sorry to be the cause of so much suffering. . . ."

"We'll forgive you. Anyway"—she pulled a face—*"I'm used to hearing how proud he is of you."*

In the middle of their banter, something they'd done for years, Sisko almost flinched at her words. *Proud . . .*

Judith was still talking of past times and childhood follies. *"Oh yes, I knew there was something I wanted to tell you—an old friend of yours is making a name for himself on Earth right now."*

"Oh yeah?"

"Tomas Roeder—you remember, from the Livingston? *You brought him to the restaurant once."*

"Of course I remember him." Sisko felt a slow smile pass across his face. "But wasn't he more your friend than mine?" It actually flustered her, he saw, and he grinned broadly at her discomfort.

"Oh Ben," she said, embarrassed, and shaking her head at him, *"that was years ago. I only saw him once. He came to New York when I was studying there. He took me to the ballet,"* she said, wistfully. "Coppélia. *All the other girls in my composition class were sick with envy. He was* very *handsome—"*

"Strange what comes back to us," Sisko mused. "The thing I recall most about Roeder was that he fought like a machine. Came in very useful in the occasional barroom brawl."

"Well," she said, mock-stern, *"you judge him by your standards, and I'll judge him by mine. It was very sweet of him to take me out. That kind of thing matters when you're young."*

"What's all this about him making a name for himself?"

"It's the strangest thing, Ben—you know he resigned his commission?"

Sisko looked at her in surprise. "Last I heard he was with Internal Affairs—"

"Not anymore. Now he's one of the leading lights in the antiwar crowd."

"You're kidding me?" Back on the station, they had heard only a little about this movement—if you could even give it a title that grand. A handful of people who wanted the quadrant to be a more peaceful place, and thought the Federation should start at home. From where they were sitting on the front line, it all seemed very worthy, but hopelessly naïve.

Judith shook her head. *"And he's very influential, too. It was all pretty low-key before. But now Roeder's involved . . ."* She shrugged. *"Dad and I—I guess we have a different perspective on things, because of you."* She gave him a thoughtful look. *"But a lot of people, they don't have relatives in Starfleet, never mind someone holding the line. Roeder asks why we're fighting this war and they listen to him."*

"Why we're fighting this war? The Dominion—"

"You don't need to convert me, Ben," she said, cutting him off.

"I'm sorry, Jude. I just can't believe that people listen—"

"But it's persuasive, coming from someone who used to be Starfleet. People assume he knows what he's talking about. And there's something else about him, Ben, when he talks. When he talks about peace. It's like he's on a mission, or something."

"Yeah," Sisko murmured, "he was always very intense. It worked well with women."

She stuck her tongue out at him. *"Anyway, I thought you'd be interested. He's been in the news a lot, doing interviews, that kind of thing. See if you can call up some files."*

"I might just do that," he said. He checked the time

again. The first session was due to start soon. And still no sign of Bill Ross. "Look Jude," he said, "I've got to get ready for a meeting. . . ."

She nodded. *"I understand. It's good to have you home, Ben. I'll see you again soon."*

She cut the com. The room became quiet, just the hum of the machines. Sisko got himself another *raktajino,* and sat down again with the padd.

Tomas Roeder . . .

Sisko tapped the padd against the desk, remembering mess-room bull sessions with other bright young officers, arguing about how far you could and should go; and he remembered Roeder, one of the brightest of the bunch, smiling down silently into his drink, and then going off and doing his duty with cold efficiency.

Sisko turned to the padd, and began briefing himself on the first session. Troop dispositions along the border. Who was going to put how many of their own people on the front line. That was going to be a tough debate. After a moment or two he stopped reading, and looked up at his dress uniform, hanging up on the back of the door. Something else to be proud of.

"Computer," he said, "how many files do you have on Tomas Roeder?"

"There are two hundred and thirty-nine files containing the name Tomas Roeder."

Sisko whistled. Roeder *had* been busy. "Cross-reference that with interviews," he instructed. "And with Starfleet. And just give me the files from the past three months." There was a short pause, and then the answer came.

"There are fourteen files within those parameters."

"Show me the first of them."

He turned to the viewscreen just as the image came

up. It was footage from a late night political discussion program broadcast by the Federation News Service. Roeder was engaged in what looked like a very heated debate with Admiral Alynna Nechayev.

"I'd be ready to give that statement credit, Admiral, were it not for the fact that, as you and I both know, the Federation was putting out peace feelers shortly before the invasion of Betazed—"

"And I think we'd both agree that the situation has changed markedly since then—!"

"All that has changed is that we now have a new ally—"

"And you don't see that as making a difference to our capacity to wage this war?"

"I certainly do, Admiral, and that's exactly what alarms me. Because no one from either Starfleet or the Federation Council has been willing to answer some very straightforward questions. If we were prepared to negotiate a peace settlement from a position of weakness, why are we not prepared to do it from a position of strength? And, if we are indeed stronger now, are we not more likely to be able to negotiate a more satisfactory peace? What does this mean? That Starfleet wants this war to continue—?"

Sisko sucked in a breath. He scanned through the rest of the files. A couple more debates. Very angry, some of them, particularly if Roeder was up against anyone from Starfleet. There was a lot of footage of Roeder giving speeches at various venues, some a little more charged than others. Sisko watched them and drank his coffee. Judith had been right. Roeder spoke like he had a mission.

Sisko skipped back to one of the debates. This time

Roeder was arguing with a Federation councillor, Huang Chaoying of Alpha Centauri.

"What I want, Councillor, is some clarity when it comes to the Federation's goals in this war. I want to know just how far we are intending to go. Are we attempting to contain the Dominion within their new borders? Are we attempting to push them back into the Gamma Quadrant? Do we intend to go as far as waging war in Dominion space itself? By the way, I should say, at this point, that the legitimacy even of the first of those goals is questionable—the Cardassian Union is not conquered territory and its treaty with the Dominion was not signed under coercion—"

"Mister Roeder, that is quite simply false! There was a coup on Cardassia! And, consequently, not everyone recognizes the legitimacy of the government that took the Cardassian Union into the Dominion—!"

"And not everyone recognizes the legitimacy of waging a war upon the Cardassian people as a result of the actions of their leaders!"

The chime on the door sounded.

"Come in," Sisko said, reaching to switch off the screen. Roeder's face disappeared into blankness.

It was Ross. "Sorry I wasn't here to meet you," he said, as they shook hands. "It hasn't been a good morning so far. . . ."

Sisko took in Ross's drawn face. He looked like he hadn't had a full night's sleep. "What's happened?"

"It's bad news," Ross said, and offered Sisko a padd. "About the Seventh Fleet."

"At Sybaron?" Sisko scanned through the report. After a moment he looked back up in horror. *"Dammit,* Bill! What the hell's happening?"

"Who the hell knows? Dominion counteroffensive started late last night. As if we hadn't lost enough already in the offensive . . ." Ross shook his head. "That was certainly some very bad intelligence."

Sisko thought about all those ships, and all those people, and whether or not they had had their moment of stillness. "When will we hear more?" he asked, abruptly.

"Soon. Throughout the morning."

"Admiral, do we even know whether they're *holding?*"

"Not yet," Ross said, from between gritted teeth.

Sisko looked back down at the report. A sense of dread trickled through him as he thought of the casualty lists that would soon begin to appear. He heard Ross, muttering under his breath. "Hell, the first session is about to get under way. We'd better go down."

Sisko looked up at him, and opened his mouth, to speak.

"Ben?" Ross gave him a questioning look.

He glanced back down at the report.

"Ben? Something on your mind?"

"No," Sisko said, trying to draw himself back fully to matters closer to home. "I was just thinking about all those ships."

"It's hit me pretty damn hard," Ross admitted, as they made their way over to the door. He stopped just before going out, glanced over at Sisko. "Not a word about it, I think, until we have a lot more information."

"The last thing I want to do," Sisko said, "is debate troop dispositions when the people across the table know I'm in the middle of losing a fleet." They went out. "You think it could be that bad?"

"No idea," Ross said frankly. "Still, there's no need to show our entire hand. Not until we have to, at any rate."

He frowned. "Not much of a welcome home, Ben," he said. "I'm sorry about that."

They walked on, each becoming lost in thought, along corridors toward the conference room. When the content of his thoughts became too much, Sisko said, "I watched some of Tomas Roeder's speeches while I waited for you."

He saw Ross frown at the name. "Oh yes? It caused a real stir when he resigned. You know him, don't you?"

"Knew him. Back on the *Livingston*," Sisko said. "Years since we've spoken. No idea what he's like now." Then the door to the conference room opened, and Sisko found himself confronted with a piercing assembly of Romulans.

2

ODO STARED AROUND THE CARGO BAY and then turned to Brixhta. "Just how many packing cases have you brought with you?"

Brixhta began counting them off on his fingers. Even for a shapeshifter, it was a slightly disconcerting exercise to watch. Odo suppressed a shudder, and looked back across the cargo bay.

"Only twelve," Brixhta said at last.

"And just how big a market do you think there is for your goods on DS9?"

"Some of the pieces are *extremely* collectable. And *very* beautiful—"

"Perhaps I should take a closer look?" Odo suggested. He pointed to a large crate standing nearby. "Shall we start with this one?"

Brixhta did not move. "These are old pieces, Odo," he said. "And I am storing them very carefully. I am loath to expose them to unsuitable atmospheric conditions on nothing more than a whim—"

"I never have whims. Open the crate."

Brixhta murmured something to himself, and then shifted toward the case. There was a control panel on the lid, and he began to fiddle with some of the buttons.

Odo folded his arms. "What are you doing, Brixhta?"

"This will help mitigate the possibility of damage. . . ."

The lid popped open, suddenly, and with a high-pitched whine. Brixhta leaned over and began lifting out bunches of packing material. Odo took a step forward and peered inside. The box seemed to contain . . . another box. It was a dark green, and Odo thought he caught a flash of silver. He reached out himself and began to push some of the packaging aside to get a better look. He was rewarded with a sharp rap on the knuckles.

"*If* you wouldn't mind, Constable," Brixhta said sternly. "This is an extremely rare piece. Whitaker and Lambert manufactured only a very small number of them. And I am aware of only one other that survived the conflagration." He began to wrestle the piece into an upright position. "Although it's possible," he grunted, "that a collector has another one hidden away some-where. . . ."

Odo drew back and watched as Brixhta worked. His curiosity was beginning to get the better of him. "What exactly is it, Brixhta?"

"Patience, Odo, patience . . ." Brixhta said breathlessly, maneuvering the box round. "There!" He ran a loving touch along it. "Beautiful thing, isn't it?"

"Beautiful" was not the word Odo himself would have chosen. Bulky, perhaps. It was a large machine—quite a bit bigger than an ordinary, domestic replicator—made of dark green metal, and with chrome buffers curving round each corner and edge. On the front was a silver control panel with various knobs and dials and, beneath it, a plate of some kind of clear plastic.

"And the real miracle, " Brixhta's voice had dropped to a reverential level, "is that it *works*."

"What does it *do?*"

"Watch."

Brixhta started fiddling with one of the dials. The machine groaned and clanked. Odo took a step forward. "This had better be safe—"

"*Perfectly* safe . . ." Brixhta began tweaking some of the knobs. The device lurched forward slightly.

"*Brixhta* . . ." Odo warned. Whatever it was the machine was doing, it had started to pick up speed. It shook up and down, whined, heaved—and then ground to a complete and decisive halt. Brixhta reached out for the panel, and raised it, and lifted out what looked to Odo to be a dish filled with mud.

"Early replicator technology," Brixhta said. "Try a bit, it's perfectly edible."

"I don't eat," Odo said, staring at the contents of the bowl. It bubbled up at him. "Thankfully."

"I have to say that I've acquired something of a taste for it," Brixhta said. He dabbed a finger into the brown mess, and then wiped it along the side of the dish. "But I'll resist the temptation for now." He put the bowl down on the edge of the crate, and beckoned to Odo to follow him. "Now, *this*," he said, hastening toward the next giant crate in the line, "holds some truly wondrous treasures. . . ."

He's enjoying this, Odo thought, going after him reluctantly. *Which means he* has *to be up to something. . . .*

"Not on as grand a scale, I'll freely admit, but still some very lovely pieces . . . *very* lovely. . . ." He hit the panel, and the lid of the crate bounced open. He delved inside, throwing packaging carelessly about him, and then lifted out a smaller box, balancing it on the edge of the crate.

"This was apparently used by some early Earth cultures to select the leaders of their clans," he said. "I have to confess that I have not been entirely able to understand the philosophy behind it. There seems to be a high degree of chance involved." He hefted it back into the crate. "None of the cards it used exist anymore, of course," he said, rather sadly. "They would be *very* collectible." He started rummaging around in the crate again. "I have seen a number of fakes, however."

"What, I wonder, are you going to show me next?" Odo said, dryly. "Toys for children?"

"I do in fact have several things on those lines. . . ." Brixhta shifted toward another crate and began delving around inside it. He pulled out a polished gold metal case, popped open the lid, and lifted out the contents, standing it reverently on the edge of the crate. Odo peered at it curiously. Three Ferengi figures, standing in a line. One was holding a tiny round token, and there was a little key in the back of another of them. Brixhta wound it up, setting the whole device in motion. The figure holding the token dropped it in a box in front of him, it came out of the bottom and rolled along, and the second figure picked it up. He turned and passed it along to the third figure, who twisted round in the middle until he was back-to-front, and dropped the token. It rolled along the back of the other Ferengi, and then the first one collected it, dropped it in the box, and the whole thing started again.

"A first lesson in the Great Material Continuum," Brixhta said, as the token moved round and round. "How all the individual pieces of the universe are part of a larger scheme. Tributaries of a great river that we must learn to navigate." He enveloped one of the figures in a caress. "Ferengi are a most unexpectedly profound species, when one comes to think about it."

"Should this explain your sudden and very fast friendship with Quark?"

Brixhta did not answer. "The design is perhaps rather garish, even for my taste." He wrapped the figures up, and put them away. "Perhaps this would be more to your liking," he said. From the same crate, he took out a little wooden box and offered it to Odo. Odo took it, and turned it over in his hands, examining it closely. There were old-style Bajoran letters painted on the lid; Odo's ancient Bajoran was not exactly fluent, but he thought he could recognize a familiar word here and there, and it seemed to him as if the words made up some kind of rhyme. Nerys would almost certainly know, he imagined, or the captain.

Odo balanced the box on the edge of the crate. The lid was kept shut by a little metal hook that slipped into a tiny, rounded piece of metal. Very carefully, half-expecting something to jump out on him, Odo unfastened the hook and lifted the lid. Nothing happened. He looked inside. Nestling within, securely wrapped in velvet packing material, was a small, colorfully painted figure. Odo touched it, gently. Like the box, it too was made of wood, and it was oddly shaped: smoothed all around so that it curved in and out in the shape of a body, but did not have arms and legs.

"Take it out," Brixhta said softly. "I'm sure you'll find it interesting."

Odo lifted out the figure and looked more closely. It was painted bright yellow, and a little Bajoran face—earring and all—peeked out from under a yellow hat. "It looks like the kai," he said.

"Hold it in both hands," Brixhta instructed him, "top and bottom—and then twist."

Odo did as he was told. To his horror, the doll came

apart: its top half, the head, came away from the round body. He turned anxiously to Brixhta. "Have I broken it?"

"No, no, not at all! Have a look inside!"

Odo lifted off the head—and there, inside, was another little figure.

"Go on, Odo—take it out!"

Putting down the kai's head, Odo lifted out the new doll. This one was very cleverly painted: still the same rounded shape, but the headpiece somehow was unmistakably a vedek's. Odo gave a bark of laughter. He twisted the vedek apart; sure enough, there was a prylar inside. When he twisted that open, there was a little acolyte; and, when he twisted *that* open, there was one last tiny doll. This figurine was no bigger than a thumbnail, but still beautifully painted. Odo could see a tiny spot of yellow paint for the earring. Unable to resist seeing how they looked, he put the halves of the individual pieces together, and set all five of the hollow figures in a row.

"One could say it is just a child's toy," Brixhta said, "and yet she would learn her religion from it. A lesson in infinity too, perhaps. Or that appearances are deceptive." He snaked a finger out to touch the very smallest of the dolls. "So *magnificently* carved and crafted," he said. "But I suppose it's no real surprise that even the toys on Bajor are works of art."

Odo started hiding the dolls back inside each other, carefully twisting the figures so that the designs on the top aligned perfectly with the bottom. *I wonder what Nerys would think of this,* he thought.

Brixhta's voice sounded silkily in his ear. "If you're interested in making a purchase, Odo, I'm sure that we can come to some arrangement—"

Odo put the kai's head back in place. *"No,* thank you,"

he said, firmly. *It's a toy,* he told himself, irritated that Brixhta had almost coaxed him into buying. *Nerys would probably be insulted.* Odo set the doll firmly back into its box. He cast a baleful eye over the remaining crates. "I imagine the rest of your stock is like that?" He gestured back to the food machine.

"Well, that is a *particularly* fine piece, Odo—"

"What I mean is, do people actually give you money for this junk?"

Air was sucked in. Brixhta shrunk back. Beneath the brim of his hat, something seemed to sharpen.

"Junk?"

"They're not exactly what I think of when I hear the word *antiques.* Bits of old machinery, toys—" Odo tapped the top of the box containing the Bajoran figurines.

"Windows onto the past, Odo. Fragments from which we can piece together how people used to live—"

"All right, Brixhta," Odo cut in impatiently, "I get the picture." He looked down the line of crates. They were each as big as the first two. He sighed.

"It's all much the same," Brixhta said smoothly. "Are you sure you want to look inside the rest?"

Odo glared at him. *"Very* sure," he said. "And make no mistake," he added, as they went on together to the third case, "I'll be watching you all the time you're here, Brixhta—you and your toys."

Brixhta seemed quite unruffled by this. "I have to hope you do, Odo," he said. "You never know—something else might just catch your eye."

Perception, Sisko reflected, was a damned strange thing. Not everyone in this room was Romulan. And not all the Romulans were looking at him.

The conference room was already busy, and was rapidly filling. At the center of the room was a large circular table, with places around it for twelve people: three from each delegation, grouped together, with space between each grouping. Fanning out from behind these sets of three places was seating for aides and support staff, with narrow aisles between the rows where the various delegations were to sit.

Sisko looked around the room. He saw Fleet Admiral Shanthi, who was heading the Starfleet delegation and chairing these sessions, in quiet but intense conference with some of her aides; Sisko thought he could make a good guess as to what the subject matter was. She saw him and nodded an efficient greeting. Standing with her was Vice-Admiral Batanides, in charge of security for this whole occasion. She came over to speak to him, and they greeted each other warmly.

"I didn't know you were taking part in any of the discussions, Marta," Sisko said.

"Just sitting in on a few sessions," she replied. "But I'm staying near the back," she added, lowering her voice. "Waiting for news."

Of the fleet. Sisko nodded. Batanides went on her way, and Sisko went back to looking around the room. Over on the left-hand side, staying on the perimeter, he saw three Cardassians—civilians—standing bunched together. That must be the government-in-exile. They looked uncomfortable, and more than a little suspicious. Was that a cultural trait, Sisko wondered, with a grim flippancy, or did they have good reason?

His eye fell on the Klingons; he recognized one or two of them as numbering among Gowron's seniormost generals. He watched as Ross worked across the room, smiling at those functionaries he passed by, touching their

arms or nodding his head as their culture demanded. He
greeted the members of the Klingon delegation formally,
but talked to them cheerfully and with easy bonhomie.
Sisko joined them, made some conversation of his own,
and admired Bill's nerve. No one would think for a moment that he was waiting to hear whether or not one of
the fleets was still intact. Quite a few people around here,
Sisko thought, keeping quite a few secrets. He glanced
across at the Romulan contingent, stiff and silent and
watchful. Now that he was prepared for them, he could
see that there were ten of them in total. Far fewer than
there were Starfleet personnel in the room. He thought of
making an approach, but his usually steady nerve failed
him.

Instead he went to find his own seat. At the front,
next to Ross, on his right-hand side. He sat down and
took out the padd that Chaplin had prepared for him,
and began reading again her summary of the morning's
agenda. Then he skipped on, to the list of the Romulan
delegation, and tried to put names to faces. They were
headed by a senator named Cretak. As Sisko studied the
information in the file, he heard someone take a seat just
behind him, and to one side.

He glanced over his shoulder. It was Garak. He was
leaning on the back of the chair next to Sisko. He nodded
toward the Romulans, still standing apart at the far end of
the room. "So, Captain," he said, his voice low and
amused, "which of them do you think is Tal Shiar?"

"What makes you think they aren't *all* Tal Shiar?"

Garak laughed very quietly. "That's a very good
point," he said. "After all, this conference is of such significance that the whole of the Obsidian Order is in attendance."

Sisko gave a slight smile, and then he looked over at

the three Cardassians. They had already taken their seats. "Have you spoken to your government-in-exile yet?"

Garak drummed impatient fingers against the back of the chair. "They are not my government, Captain—and, no, I haven't. Nor do I intend to, if I can possibly help it."

"You're absolutely sure they're not worth cultivating?"

"Oh, I'm quite sure they'll soon show themselves for what they are."

"Which is?"

"Charlatans. And not particularly accomplished ones."

Sisko grunted. Shanthi had gone over to speak to Cretak, and one of the Romulans had taken the opportunity to detach herself from the group, and begin walking around the table, on the inside. As Sisko watched her progress, he became sure that she was less interested in the name settings, and more interested in him.

"That one seems to be paying us a great deal of attention," Garak remarked.

"And I thought I was just being paranoid," Sisko murmured. "Do you know her?"

Garak considered her. "I don't *think* we've met," he said, thoughtfully. "Although I did have a lot on my mind while I was on Romulus." He gave Sisko a sly look. "Successful gardening does require a great deal of concentration."

"I bet it does." Sisko eyed him back. "So, how was your meeting with the bright young lieutenants?"

"Very correct," Garak said, still watching the Romulan as she came closer, "and a complete waste of time."

"I find that hard to believe," Sisko said. From first impressions, Chaplin had been too efficient, and Marlow too smart.

"We spoke only in very general terms." Garak sighed.

"I sincerely hope I haven't wasted my time coming all this way to Earth, Captain."

"I'm sure they know what they're doing. They struck me as very competent."

"I can only hope so," Garak said. "They want to talk at greater length this afternoon, but I insisted on attending this first session—" He stopped, suddenly. Sisko looked up. The Romulan that had been watching them had taken her place, in the seat a little further along from Sisko. She acknowledged Sisko with a slight nod of the head, and a half-smile. Garak she ignored completely.

"Maybe you do know her," Sisko murmured.

"I dread to think," Garak muttered, and stood up to go to his seat near the back of the room. Shanthi had taken the chair, and was calling the conference to order.

Tomas Roeder, poised and melancholy, put the cap back on his fountain pen, and set it down upon his desk along-side the pages that lay before him. As he waited for the ink to dry, he smoothed the remaining blank sheets of paper.

Roeder had always preferred to write by hand. He liked to feel the weight and the metal of a stylus; he liked to watch dark ink stain plain paper. It suited the way his mind worked: nonlinear, wide-ranging. Serving on star-ships had made this idiosyncracy impossible—swiftness in communication had been essential—and he had used the machinery available as any other officer would, leav-ing all the trails that Starfleet's bureaucracy demanded of him. These days it was different. These days, Roeder worked by hand, taking pains, crafting the message in the medium.

He glanced over at the uppermost page. The ink was now dry. He reached out and set it at the back of the pile.

It was the last one. Then he called through the open door. "Michel," he said, "could I see you?"

"Of course, Tomas." His secretary's voice, from the other room. "Just a moment, please."

Roeder waited patiently and, a minute or two later, Michel came in. He came to a halt standing before the desk, putting a piece of paper down tidily. "Next month's schedule," he explained, and then he glanced pointedly at the pile on the desk. "All done?"

Roeder smiled up at him. "I think so." He picked up the pages and offered them. Michel took them from him and sighed when he saw they were covered in line after line of script.

"Tomas, I do wish you would overcome this irrational dislike of machines—"

"It's not irrational."

"This *paranoia,* then—"

"Again, something of an overstatement, don't you think, Michel?" His tone was sharper this time. They both fell silent. Michel flicked fretfully at the pages.

"Well, whatever it is," Roeder said quietly, firmly, but trying to make peace, "I might just grant you that it's something of an affectation."

It had the necessary effect. Michel smiled back at him, and then tapped the top page. "Are you satisfied with it, at least?"

Roeder permitted himself a sigh. "Oh, I suppose so." He stretched up his arms, bringing them behind his head, clasping his hands together. "It's the usual over simplification and flattery of the audience, of course."

"Whom I'm sure will greatly appreciate your efforts on their behalf."

"Well, I certainly hope so."

Michel waved the pages. "I'll get copies prepared and

sent out to the press. And have you decided yet when you want to leave for Vulcan?"

"Yes . . ." Roeder said. "The day after that embassy reception—"

"You've changed your mind about that?"

"Know thine enemy . . ." Roeder murmured. "And the Councillor does serve up good wine."

Michel laughed. "I'll arrange the shuttle for the morning after, then," he said. "And reply to the invitation."

"Thank you, Michel." Roeder unfolded from his seat and stretched again.

"Anything else you need at all, Tomas?"

"I don't think so."

Michel nodded, and turned to go. Roeder watched him covertly and, when he reached the doorway, Roeder spoke again.

"Oh," he said, perhaps too casually, "there is one other thing."

The younger man stopped and looked back. "Yes?"

"Could you put all incoming communications through to me directly? No need to screen them. Just for the next hour or so."

Michel looked at him oddly. "Are you sure, Tomas?" He pointed at the desk. "You would have to handle the com yourself—"

"Just for the next hour," Roeder said, in a distant tone of voice, "I'd like to find out what it feels like to be neither irrational nor paranoid."

Michel stared down at the desk. "Then of course," he said, collecting himself. "Whatever you wish, Tomas."

"Thank you."

"Let me know if you think I've missed anything in your diary," Michel said, then went out, and the door closed after him.

Roeder watched him go. He picked up the schedule, but did not read it. It had no interest for him. Slowly, he balled it up, then he took aim, and threw it toward the recycler. It went in, first time. If he enjoyed this minor victory, he did not show it.

He came out from behind his desk, and began to pace, restlessly, looking around the room. His taste ran to dark colors, reds and browns. In the evenings it was elegant, and the prints on the walls would glimmer dimly. Now, in the afternoon sunlight, the room seemed muted. He went over to the shelves, traced his fingers on the lines of books, but could not choose. He stood and stared out across the room, and decided that the chair was not aligned with the couch. He went over and moved it a little to the left—and then decided he had been wrong, and moved it back. He crossed to the window and looked out, at the wide view out across the city and the bay. He stared along the streets that ran down to the harbor.

"Computer," he said, "some music."

The opening chords shocked the room. "Skip forward," he said, sharply, and the piano softened almost to a breath. The adagio began, opening with serenity, opening out with patience. It began to fill the empty room.

It was not, in fact, a bad speech. It was well constructed, and well argued. Some of it was even quite stirring. Roeder laughed to himself at this little piece of self-delusion. He had no doubts that he would be doing anything other than preaching to those who were already converted. Nobody in the audience tonight would be persuaded to follow a path other than the one they were already following. Nobody would need the example of Tomas Roeder, formerly of Starfleet, to set them straight. They had all seen through the fictions of this war to the truth long before Roeder had himself.

He closed his eyes, and withdrew deep into himself. The music was unfolding to fill the space, plangent and pure. When the long trill at last began, he found himself thinking that his only comfort was that once he had seen the truth, he had done what was right. And with that decision made, he knew he could continue to do what was right.

A quiet alarm sounded on the console. Roeder jerked forward and opened his eyes. "Computer," he said, "stop the music."

The piano cut out, before the end, before the theme resolved itself. Roeder moved quickly over to his desk, punched at the controls, and read.

It was the message he had been waiting for. He scanned through it quickly, took in the news, and sent out the files that had been requested. Then he leaned over the console and—using all the skills of his last career, using all that he had taught himself while he was serving—he removed all trace of the message and the route it had taken. When he was done, he straightened up and drew in a deep breath. It was strange, he thought; it had all passed beyond his reach now, and yet he could feel a little welcome calm descend upon him.

"Good," he said softly. "Good."

"Come on, hurry up!" Steyn hustled them all toward the table. "Auger, you sit there, opposite me," she pointed him to his place, "I'm south, you're north. Trasser, put yourself here on my left . . . and, Mr. Mechter—this seat here, please, opposite Trasser, he's your partner . . ."

"There isn't a north," Auger murmured. "We're in space."

"Steyn." Mechter stood motionless behind the chair. "What is the purpose of this?"

Steyn sat down heavily. She sighed, and looked around the tiny space, at the emergency lighting, at the little red flashes on the console informing her—persistently and wholly unnecessarily—of the unfortunate state of her ship. "Mr. Mechter," she said wearily, "we have hours before we get to Deep Space 9. We can stare at the walls, we can stare at each other . . . or we can do something productive."

Mechter did not move.

"It needs four to play," she reminded him.

Mechter remained unconvinced.

"You might make some money," she said.

Mechter's eyes flicked closed for just a second. "The rules," he declared, as he took his seat, "as you described them to me, were very complicated."

"You'll pick it up quickly enough," Steyn said, rubbing her hands together. She nodded across the table. "Auger did."

When they were all seated to Steyn's satisfaction, she picked up the deck and tore open the packet. She caressed the contents tenderly.

"Right," she said, looking at each member of the group in turn, and with the air of one officiating at an important ceremony. "You may, or may not"—she contemplated Mechter—"have heard chess described as the game of kings. But what *we* are going to play is the game of convivial couples who can't stand each other. It is called, most appropriately, given our situation"—she gestured around the dim little space in which they had come together—"bridge."

She began to shuffle, expertly. Auger followed the cascade of cards with fascination, and Steyn smiled over at him. "Pretty, isn't it?" she said. She flicked through the deck one last time, and then she began to deal.

Mechter reached over and began to peel the pack away from her clutches.

"I think I'll do that," he told her.

"It would be a lot easier if you let me do it . . ." Steyn replied, tugging at the cards, and then, feeling the weight of his resistance, said, ". . . but probably even easier if I let *you* do it." She relinquished her hold.

Mechter dealt with method rather than speed, and he opened the bidding with a single spade. Trasser inched it up to two hearts. Auger passed. Mechter pushed up to five hearts, Trasser took up his offer and raised the bid to six. Auger passed again, and Mechter did this time as well.

Steyn smirked at him. "I'll double that," she said. He looked back at her impassively as the bid came right round to him.

"And I'll redouble," he informed her.

The bidding reached Auger again. He sat for a short while contemplating the nature of things and then made his offer. "Six spades."

"Ha!" Steyn was triumphant. But, just beside her, waiting to meet the challenge, Mechter was unfolding a slow and thoroughly unpleasant smile.

"I'll double," he told her.

"*Mother of all that is merciful* . . ." Steyn muttered, and passed. So did Trasser, so did Auger. The bidding closed.

"You were absolutely right, Steyn," Mechter said, beginning to lay his cards out on the table. "I picked it up."

"No, no, no!" Steyn slapped her hand down quickly, hiding Mechter's cards from view. "That was just the auction! There's the *game* to play yet!"

The morning wore on. Sisko was aware that Batanides had left the conference room a couple of times throughout, but she had brought no news back with her—or nothing that had been passed up to them at the front. Whatever was happening at Sybaron, it was not enough to interrupt the meeting. Whether that meant success, or disaster beyond anything they could mitigate, Sisko did not want to take a guess. The business of the morning was technical: Who was willing to deploy what, and where. Who was willing to give, and who was willing to take. The Klingons were blunt in both their offers and their refusals. The tiny Cardassian contingent was guarded and saying very little; they had none of the characteristic swagger Sisko had come to expect in his dealings with Cardassians. The Romulan delegation seemed to delight in the intricacies of the discussion; in the debate itself as much as the outcome. Shanthi too seemed to enjoy more than a little of the cut and thrust. It did have a certain allure, Sisko thought. An academic exercise, without loss or consequence. But it was a false glamour, far removed from the actuality. Too far removed. *Do we grow too fond of war?* he wondered.

He found, throughout the morning, that he was listening less to the proceedings, and thinking more about the delegate between him and Cretak, the one who had seemed to be watching him earlier. He knew her name now, Subcommander Veral. He flipped fretfully through the files that Chaplin had prepared for him. *Veral . . . Veral . . .* Surely the capable Chaplin couldn't have missed her?

When he followed Chaplin's index methodically, he soon found the right file. He read through the details of a more than competent military career, considered the observations on the more-than-likely intelligence career . . . He glanced over at Veral. She was sitting with her elbows resting on the table; her hands were steepled in front of her; her chin was balanced on the very tips of her forefingers. She was a study in symmetry. As he watched, she seemed to become aware of him. She turned, smiled ever so slightly, and then went back to listening closely to the proceedings.

Sisko tried to emulate her. Rhemet had finally begun to talk, saying something about whether an offensive could be launched against the Glintara Sector. *Glintara.* The name sounded vaguely familiar, but Sisko could not place it immediately. He looked at Veral again; she seemed now to be completely absorbed in listening to Rhemet. And then she frowned. Someone else was speaking, from near the back of the room. Sisko snapped back to attention. It was Garak.

What the hell does he want?

"I really am very sorry to interrupt," Garak said, "but I wonder if I might address one of the points just raised by the conservator?"

From Shanthi's expression, she did not look inclined to let him, but she glanced first over at Sisko for his opinion. Sisko shrugged. *Might as well hear what he has to say.* Wasn't that what he'd brought him all this way for, after all?

"Very well," Shanthi said, apparently unable to think of a reason not to allow him to speak. "What is it that you have to say, Mr. Garak?"

Garak rewarded her with his most dazzling smile. Which was when Sisko began to get the first vague sense of unease.

"I'm sure it will prove to be only a very small matter," Garak said, "But my recollection of the Glintara Sector is that it has been a covert base of operations for the Fourth Order for the best part of two decades." He smiled helpfully at Shanthi. "I doubt very much this activity has been scaled back; in fact, I rather imagine the Dominion may have reinforced the area. Conservator," Garak turned away from Shanthi and looked at Rhemet, "surely you must have been aware of the sector's status during the brief period that you were in government?" Rhemet did not reply, and Garak strolled in for the kill. "Unless, of course, Gul Trepar of the Fourth Order did not see fit to pass the information on to you."

It was painfully apparent from Rhemet's face that Gul Trepar of the Fourth Order had not. Over to Sisko's right, he could see that the Romulan delegation had been watching this one-sided exchange with increasing and barely concealed delight. Sisko remembered what Ross had said to him before he had set out for Earth: *It's as much about the peace as about the war.* He glanced at Cretak. She herself was maintaining an exquisite distance, staring decorously at a point on the wall somewhere beyond Rhemet. She was making no attempt to rein in her staff however; and Veral took her silence as indirect permission to score a few points.

"Although I must derive a certain amount of pleasure," Veral said, "in watching the Cardassian delegation fall apart before my very eyes, I do think that discussion of the internal arrangements of the Union strays somewhat from the specific purpose of this meeting."

"Oh, I would have to agree," Garak said cheerfully, from his seat. "It's none of your business in the slightest. Nevertheless, I do think that my point stands. Send your ships in that way, by all means. I can't exactly stop you. But I feel I'm being remiss in not pointing out that you'll almost certainly be sending them against one of the more highly fortified sections of the Cardassian border."

Rhemet had collected himself. He ignored Garak and addressed Shanthi directly. "This man has been away from Cardassia for many years," he said pointedly. "It is more than possible that his information is out-of-date."

"Perhaps what we should draw from that," Shanthi said, cutting in before anyone else could speak, "is that we need better intelligence about this particular sector."

It was a remark aimed substantially at face-saving on Rhemet's behalf, but no one was going to point that out, not even from the Romulan delegation. It still did very little to restore orderliness to proceedings. The various delegations were now talking rapidly among themselves. Sisko shook his head. He should have seen this coming. What had Garak said to him earlier? *They'll soon show themselves for what they are.* One of Garak's coded warnings, and Sisko had been too distracted to register it. And he had not even been thinking about the Seventh Fleet. He'd been thinking about Romulans, about Veral. No, Sisko thought, no more deception. He had been thinking about one other, very particular Romulan.

From the chair, Shanthi managed to restore a little order. "This is as good a point to stop as any," she said. "Let's take a break. We'll reconvene at fourteen hundred hours." She stood up to go and speak to Rhemet, and shot Sisko a slightly irritated look on her way past. Sisko tapped a fingertip against his brow.

"Bill." He leaned toward Ross, and kept his voice very low. "We have to talk."

Ross looked at him, frowned, and then glanced quickly toward the door of the conference room. Batanides was on her way over.

"Now?" Ross said.

"Now, Bill."

They sat together uneasily, watching the room empty around them. When Batanides came up, she had no more news than that the fleet was still holding, but the losses were going to be high. Then Sisko saw her take in the expression on his face. "This looks pretty serious," she said. "Do you want me leave you?"

"No," Sisko said. "I think you should hear this too." He leaned back in his chair as she got settled into one of the seats just behind him. He folded his hands on top of each other. It was not comfortable, so he unfolded them, set one on each knee. He looked down, and saw that they were spread out and taut.

"All right, Ben," Ross said. "What's the matter?"

Sisko studied the lines of the tendons for a moment longer, and then he looked up. The room was empty now; it was strange, he thought—it had been so charged only a few minutes before. Now it felt deserted. The door was firmly closed. Only the three of them left in there. Sisko listened to the quiet for a moment, then looked directly at Ross, and began to speak.

"You both read my report on Senator Vreenak's visit to DS9," he said. They each nodded.

"I should tell you now," Sisko said, "that I omitted a number of significant details from that report."

Ross and Batanides glanced at each other. "Go on," Batanides prompted. Ross was frowning.

"Concerning the senator's death," Sisko said.

"Vreenak was assassinated by the Dominion," Batanides said. She was frowning now. "They put a bomb on his ship while he was at Soukara. Lucky for us."

"Vreenak *was* assassinated," Sisko said. "But not by the Dominion." He jerked his head toward the closed door of the conference room. "Garak planted the bomb on Vreenak's ship while he was on DS9."

There was a silence. Batanides spoke first. "You knew about this?" she said. Her voice sounded very neutral.

"I knew about it . . . later. When the ship blew up," he

said. "That's when I knew what had happened. And Garak confirmed it."

"He *told* you that?" Batanides's tone had sharpened; she sounded as if she were more than a little disbelieving of Garak's testimony.

"I did hit him quite hard," Sisko murmured, flexing one hand and remembering.

"I bet you did," Batanides muttered. "Look, Ben, back up a minute—I need you to take me through this from the beginning. The idea of bringing Vreenak to the station; the idea behind the . . ." She hesitated, seeming to consider how to phrase it.

"*Fraud,*" Sisko said, "is the word you're looking for."

She gave him a very narrow look. "The idea, as I remember," she continued, "was to send Vreenak home with evidence that had been prepared of a planned Dominion invasion of Romulus—"

"Yes, that's right—we brought Vreenak to DS9 to give him the evidence we had prepared of that. And when that plan fell through—Garak murdered him. Garak killed the forger too—no loose ends, you see. His name was Tolar. Graython Tolar." Sisko trailed off. He licked at dry lips. "When the Tal Shiar investigated Vreenak's death, the imperfections in the faked files looked like they were caused by the explosion on the ship." He lifted one hand. "Details of invasion," he said. He lifted the other hand to weigh against it. "Dead senator. You do the math." He stopped, drew his hands together, then added, "And then I left all of this out of my report." On balance, Sisko thought, that was probably the least of the crimes he was exposing, but he felt it was important at this point to be complete.

The silence fell again. That really was everything, Sisko thought. He felt light, as if he had been emptied out. It was relief, he realized. Whatever happened next, he really believed he could live with it. Because he had done the right thing.

Batanides sighed. Sisko saw that she was running her fingers around the insignia on her collar. She glanced over at Ross, waiting for him to respond before she said any more. Ross sat back in his chair, and looked Sisko straight in the eye.

"Well," he said. "That's quite a story."

Sisko met his gaze firmly. He and Ross had worked together so closely, and he had lied to him. "I'm sorry." he said. "It was wrong. I should have had the situation under control, and I failed to admit the . . . consequences of my judgment. I'm ready to accept it; whatever you decide you have to do—"

"I don't intend to do anything," Ross said. His voice had gone very soft.

Sisko stared back at him. "What?"

Ross sighed. "It's happened; it's done. We'll leave it at that."

Sisko began to fill up now, with anger. "That's all? No committee of inquiry? Nothing at all?"

"Ben." A single word from Ross, stopping Sisko in his tracks. He watched as Ross leaned forward, resting his elbows on the table, putting his hands up to his face, and sitting hidden behind them. Sisko recalled how tired Ross had looked when they'd met earlier. And it had been a long morning since.

After a moment or two, Ross looked up. "What do you expect me to do?" he said. He jerked his thumb toward the door. "Go out right now and tell Cretak what you've just told me? Where do you think that would leave us? Where would it leave the alliance?" Ross carried on, without mercy. "Right now, I'm waiting to hear whether or not we even have a Seventh Fleet. But for the first time, we have everyone sitting in the same room—Klingons, Romulans, Starfleet; dammit, even some Cardassians!—and for the first time we have a real chance to win this war. Not to lose, or make a peace that will mean we lose in the long run. *Win.*"

Sisko had to look away. "It was murder," he said. He shook his head. "Twice over."

"I know. But I can't regret it." Ross looked Sisko straight in the eye. "I'm not going to give you some crap about the greater good," he said softly. "But think about this—a month ago we were losing this war. Now we have a chance to win it, and it's all because the Romulans are our allies. It's all because of what you did."

"In all fairness," Sisko said bitterly, "that particular medal really should be Garak's."

Beside him, Batanides drew in a sharp breath.

Sisko shut his eyes for a moment. "I'm sorry."

Ross nodded."Was there anything else, Ben?" He sounded weary.

"No," Sisko said. "No, I think *that* was all I had to tell you right now."

"All right." Ross stood up. Sisko and Batanides followed suit. "The matter's closed, then."

"So it seems," Sisko murmured. He watched as Ross and Batanides exchanged troubled glances. Closed. So that was it. Atonement? Acceptance? It didn't feel like much. It didn't feel like anything at all.

Ross cleared his throat, clearly wanting to move the subject on. "Garak certainly made his mark this morning."

Sisko looked past him. "I think that was pretty much inevitable," he murmured, hoping that the words he was saying were somehow coherent.

"And I think," Ross replied, "that I'd prefer things to run a little more smoothly from here on. Our credit's going to be stretched enough as it is once we have to release the information about Sybaron. Plus Rhemet may just turn out to have some useful input, but he's not likely to give it if he thinks Garak is scoring points." He gave Sisko a sharp look. "What's your reading, Ben? Is Garak likely to do something like that again? Can we make sure he won't?"

It was, in Sisko's considered opinion, probably a little late in the day to be thinking about whether or not they could control Garak. "Who knows," he replied. "I certainly don't know how to keep him in line. I doubt the whole of Starfleet could." As he spoke, he marveled to hear himself, talking as if everything were normal. As if the whole universe hadn't just taken a sideways swerve.

"Well, have a word with him, will you?" The door to the conference room opened, and Ross looked across. One of his aides was standing there, trying to catch his attention. "I have to go. Marta," he said, as he got up to leave, "come and find me when you're done here."

Batanides nodded, waited until he had gone, and then turned to Sisko. "Are you all right?" she said.

"Fine," he answered. "Just fine."

She watched him for a moment or two. "Look," she said. "Do you want to go somewhere and talk a little more? It's lunchtime. Let's get something to eat."

Life goes on, Sisko thought, abstractedly. *We all go on eating, and sleeping, and holding meetings, while wars are fought, and men are murdered.*

"No," he said. His voice seemed to be coming from a distance. "No, I think I'll sort out this problem with Garak right away." He recalled himself and turned back to her. "Thank you," he said.

Just outside the door, he found the man he was looking for. Waiting for him. "Captain, I wonder if I might have a moment of your time—" Garak said, anxiously, just as Sisko growled, "I want a word with you."

"We must speak quickly. I suspect I have very little time remaining. Have you familiarized yourself with the immediate area?"

"I have familiarized myself with the immediate area."

"You have located the exit?"

"I have located the exit."

"You do realize there is no need for you to repeat everything that I say?"

"Indeed I do. But I find it brings it all to life."

Sisko and Garak went out of the HQ building into the blaze of the midday sun. They had barely stepped outside when Garak's eyes began watering. He stopped on the steps and pressed the heels of his hands into his face. "I do hope this stops soon," he muttered. "All this natural light seems to be getting to me."

"You'll adjust," Sisko said, not wholly unkindly.

"And quickly, I hope. I don't want to give the impression I'm weeping with gratitude just to be here on Earth." He wiped his eyes.

Sisko feigned disappointment. "I'm sorry to hear you're not."

"Trust me, Captain—it takes more than San Francisco to move me to tears."

They walked across the plaza. Sisko glanced back over his shoulder at the building. It seemed to be catching the bright noon light, warm and golden, within its broad curve. Sisko led Garak along the well-ordered paths of the park. Neither of them spoke. Garak was

rubbing at his left eye, ill at ease. Sisko himself was still
trying to work out what the hell had just happened with
Ross and Batanides and why right now he wasn't being
locked up with someone busy throwing the key into the
ocean.

They came to a halt by some railings. From where
they were standing they could look out across the bay,
but Garak put his back to it, and pressed his fingers
against his eyes again. Sisko waited until he was done before he spoke.

"Lay off Rhemet," he said. His voice came out ser-
rated.

Garak's head snapped round. *"Rhemet,"* he spat, not
bothering to hide his contempt. "He and his friends are
amateurs. It's like watching children playing with plasma
grenades."

Sisko watched as Garak's hands curled around the
railings. "I don't care," he said. "Cut them some slack."

Garak's hands tightened their grip. "Cut them some
slack?" He had kept his voice low, but still injected it
with venom.

"We've got *enough* problems right now without *you*
deciding to undermine your own government!" Before
Garak could challenge him on that point, he went on:
"There's been a Dominion counteroffensive at Sybaron.
Right now we're losing; losing ships, losing people . . . if
we manage to hold the line there, we're going to be damn
lucky."

He saw Garak take this information in; watched him
turn it over and process it. Counting the cost to Cardassia,
no doubt. Sisko thought of all those ships again. "Our position at the conference is going to be weakened enough
as it is, and your stunt this morning won't have helped,"
he said, and was satisfied that he had struck when Garak

glared at him. "We don't need to be dealing with distractions. *Dammit*, Garak! I don't have time for this right now!"

"And *I*, Captain," Garak said, angrily, "don't have time to be playing children's games. *Cardassia* doesn't have that kind of time—"

"I'm sure Rhemet appreciates that—"

"*If* he were a true patriot," Garak shot back bitterly, "then he *would*."

Sisko did not reply. He should have delayed this conversation with Garak, he thought now. There was something unnerving about just how quickly their exchanges could collapse into savagery; something disturbing about the violence that simmered behind even their most polite conversations. Once again he loathed the reaction Garak invariably provoked in him; once again he regretted ever approaching him. They stood in silence. The sky above was blue and unruffled.

"I notice that in the midst of all these troubles you took the time to chat with some of your superiors," Garak said, eventually. And smoothly. Too smoothly. That was something else about him that was particularly irritating. "I have to wonder—how did that go?"

"Fine."

"Was there anything discussed that you would like to tell me about?"

"No."

Garak studied him, closely and coldly. He had released his hold on the railings, and now was rubbing the palm of one hand with the thumb of the other. Sisko had the distinct impression that there was nothing Garak would welcome more right now than the opportunity to interrogate him; nonetheless, he did not feel intimidated. Hell, he'd confessed once today already, and to no effect, ill or otherwise. He folded his arms and looked right back.

After a moment or two, Garak sighed, and subsided. "Given that I am still at liberty to move about," he murmured, "I shall have to assume that you're telling me the truth." But he was obviously unhappy. He really had been worried, Sisko realized; and still was. Which had to be the biggest joke of all. Because even though Sisko had told everything, it turned out that neither of them had had any need to worry. Because nothing was going to happen. Two dead men, and nobody was going to do anything about it. Not a damn thing.

"Nonetheless," Garak was saying, his tone considerably more civil, "you do seem distracted. And on such a beautiful day. It seems a shame."

"I'd like more news about what's happening to the Seventh Fleet."

"There really is nothing you can do about that right now," Garak pointed out. "You shouldn't worry about something you can't control."

That was good advice, Sisko thought. Perhaps he should listen to it.

Garak was examining the backs of his hands. "We *are* on the same side, Captain," he said. "Don't forget that." He hesitated for a moment; moved so that he was now subjecting his palms to scrutiny. "I do have some grasp of what's troubling you," he added.

Did he just mean the details, Sisko wondered, or was he talking about something that went beyond that? Sisko could not be sure. Still, he thought, it sounded very much like the offer of a truce—and he figured there were enough battles for him to fight as it was. Sisko leaned back against the railings and looked around the parkland; let himself feel the heat and the sunlight. Some of the strain of the morning ebbed away. "You know, it feels odd being home," he confessed. "I don't get back as often as I'd like."

"That is also a sentiment with which I can sympathize," Garak said.

Sisko turned to look at him. Garak was staring out across the park at some vague point in the distance.

"Just how long is it," Sisko asked, "since you were last on Cardassia?"

Garak gave him a cool, amused look. "You mean, not including the time you blackmailed me?"

Sisko flinched, but figured he had probably asked for that. *"Not* including that."

"Then, it must be six . . . no, it's more like seven years, now. How time flies."

"That's a long time away from home," Sisko said softly.

"Oh, one can adapt to anything, Captain," Garak said, with false levity. "For example," he glanced around, and a smile began to play across his lips; a more genuine smile, Sisko thought, "having the freedom to move about wherever one wishes, or being debriefed rather than interrogated. These are things I imagine anyone could adapt to, given enough time."

Just so long as it stayed that way. Last time Sisko had been home there had been troops standing on the street corner by his father's restaurant. Last time, Sisko had ended up sitting and waiting in a holding cell with Admiral Leyton on the loose and no one willing or able to stop him. . . . How fragile it had all turned out to be, when it came down to it. How strong was it now, under the stresses of war?

A couple of members of the Romulan delegation walked past, deep in conversation, a not-so-discreet security detail following a few yards behind. Sisko watched them as they went past. He supposed he should take heart at seeing them walking around, here, at the center of things. They were all allies together, now, after all. They had fixed that—he and Garak. Something for them to be proud of.

Garak had already moved on ahead. "Now this is something that puzzles me," he was saying. *"What* are all these?" He had come to a halt before a wall, covered in posters—vivid colors, sharp slogans, layer upon layer of them, many ripped and weather-beaten. The rest of the park area was orderly, even the bright beds of flowers were laid out with considered geometry, and yet they didn't seem out of place. They seemed just another part of the whole.

"They're just posters," Sisko said.

"What for?" Garak inspected them more closely.

Sisko came to see. "The usual . . . bands, theater . . ." A part of the academy campus lay close by and this particular path was a much-used shortcut down to the harbor. "Cadet stuff, mostly." He glanced at the display. "Oh, here's one I bet will interest you. . . ." He gestured at one of a series of bloodred posters with bold print that had been plastered at uneven intervals along the whole of the wall. Each had a big black and white logo, a stylized dove with a single, urgent word beneath it: *Peace!*

"What is it?" Garak said, leaning in to read.

"It's advertising an antiwar demonstration." Sisko scanned down the list of names, and pointed one out. "I'd certainly be interested to hear what he has to say."

"Tomas Roeder," Garak read out, and looked up from the poster with interest. "Why him in particular, Captain?"

"I used to know him on the *Livingston*—he was chief

of security. He resigned his commission just before the offensive to take back DS9. He's thrown himself in with the peace campaigners since then."

"Yet another disillusioned idealist," Garak murmured. "Starfleet does seem to specialize in producing them. And where, do you think, will this event be taking place?"

"It's in the square," Sisko said. "Later this evening."

Garak stared at Sisko in amazement. He jerked his thumb over in the direction that they had come. "In the square back there?"

"Yes."

"Tonight?"

"Yes. . . ."

"In front of Starfleet Headquarters?"

"Yes!" Despite himself, Sisko started to laugh. "What's the problem, Garak?"

Garak shook his head and stared back at the poster. "You're insane. You're all absolutely insane."

"What do you mean by that?"

"A demonstration *against* the war, while the Federation is fighting for our very existence?"

"And what's wrong with that?"

Garak looked at him in exasperation. "Do you people understand *nothing* about the value of censorship?"

"Thankfully, no!"

Garak started to examine the poster more closely. "What do you think these numbers are?" He pointed at some print running down in columns, dates and numbers. The numbers got larger as time went on.

Sisko sighed. "They're casualty figures. Servicemen and women lost since the Dominion War began."

"You *publish* that information? *Openly?*" Garak was aghast. "For *anyone* to read it?"

"Of course we do."

"Well, no wonder you have civil unrest—"

"I wouldn't exactly call it *unrest,* Garak—"

"People coming out and demonstrating in the streets against the government?" Garak looked at him in horror. "What *else* can you call it?"

"I'd call it democracy."

Garak pursed his lips. "Well, it simply isn't *right.*"

"So, I guess you wouldn't see an antiwar demo in Cardassia City then?"

"We have laws against that kind of thing," Garak said, seeming affronted even by the idea. *"Thankfully."*

Sisko folded his arms and smiled. "And I bet the Dominion hasn't seen fit to repeal them," he said. "Something you would find hadn't changed, if you went back."

Garak looked at him narrowly for a moment, and then his eyes lit up in amusement. "I rather doubt you would see this kind of thing cluttering up the Promenade either," he said, and gestured at the posters. "I suspect that the constable would find them terribly untidy."

Sisko managed a wry smile. "You know, I think you might just be right there."

Garak turned back to the poster, and stared at it intently. He ran a finger along the edge of it, began picking at the paper with his nail, trying to straighten the edge, trying to make it align with the others on the wall. "Do you know," he said, thoughtfully, "even after so long away, I can still picture Cardassia City very clearly. I can remember all the streets and the squares as well as if I were standing there. But these days, I picture them a little differently. In my mind's eye, I can see Jem'Hadar, in all the places that I knew." He turned to survey the park, the way they had just come. "All the places that I *know,*" he corrected himself, emphatically.

Sisko looked around too, at the well-kept lawns, the lines and circles of the flower beds, the rows of trees. And, behind them, the glass building of Starfleet HQ, and the square in front, where later that day Federation citizens would gather together in order to tell their leaders what they thought they were doing wrong.

"Look at all of this, Captain," Garak said. "You've fought the Jem'Hadar. You've seen them up close. Imagine them here."

Sisko shuddered, and shook his head. "It doesn't bear thinking about," he murmured.

"They got to *Betazed*, Captain." Garak's voice had gone very low too. "And I know that only time can really tell, but what we did . . . well, I'm sure, as sure as I can be, that it was the *right* thing to do."

"It would be good to believe that, Garak."

"War requires sacrifice, Captain. Of principle." Garak gave a short laugh. "That goes without saying, surely? And there are other sacrifices too. Sacrifice of self, for one. Or sacrifice of the innocent . . ." He stopped.

Sisko glanced back at him, staring down again at the casualty figures on the poster in front of them. He thought of Jennifer and the terrible moment they had shared. He thought of Ziyal's funeral, and how it had taken a murder for Garak and Kira to have something in common. *You don't need to tell me any of this,* he thought.

"Sometimes it turns out to be a waste," Garak murmured, "and sometimes not." He cut himself off abruptly. "You're a soldier. I am . . . preaching to the converted." He gestured around, almost dramatically, and gave Sisko a genial smile. "You have a very beautiful home, Captain. You're right to want to fight to preserve it. To the best of your ability."

Cold comfort. Ice cold.

"Maybe," Sisko said, finding no conviction to put into his voice. It was easier, he imagined, to believe that. But what about those occasions when the best of your ability took you way over the line? He gestured at the poster. "You know, Garak—I think we should attend this later. So you can see Federation democracy in action."

Garak began to laugh. "You think I might learn something?"

"You never know. You might be surprised."

Garak examined the poster again. "Thank you," he said, "that would be most interesting." Then, without looking back at Sisko, he added, "I shall endeavor from hereon to treat Rhemet with all the respect he does not deserve."

"That's all I ask," Sisko replied. They walked back through the noonday heat to the HQ building. Inside, Chaplin was waiting to collect Garak for another debriefing session. She told Sisko that Ross had been looking for him; when he found him, he had news that the Seventh Fleet had held at Sybaron, but with significant losses. They took that to the rest of the conference. A reprieve, but a costly one.

3

MID-EVENING, Odo came out of his office to meet Kira, who was heading along the Promenade. They walked together a while, discussing the day's business. Kira related a few tales of shopkeepers who had not been pleased to learn that parts of the Promenade would be out-of-bounds once the *Ariadne* arrived, and told with relish how she had handled them. He listened happily. He had always enjoyed her triumphs, as if they had been his own.

"I knew there was something I meant to ask," she said, as they drew nearer to Quark's, "you have run background checks on the crew of the *Ariadne*, haven't you?"

"Of course," Odo replied. "The captain of the ship is an interesting case; a Federation citizen who seems to prefer a less ordered life outside in the wider universe."

"Or found herself unable to come back," Kira suggested.

"Maybe," Odo said. "But the crew of the *Ariadne* is not really my concern at the moment," he confessed. "I'm more interested in someone else who has recently arrived on the station; particularly in the light of the business arrangement he appears to have struck with Quark."

"Anything I need to be worried about?"

"I believe I have the situation well under control, Major. I'm on my way to Quark's now to make sure no mischief is being planned this evening. Beyond the usual, that is."

Kira laughed, and they walked on companionably. "You know," she said, after a moment or two, "Jadzia has got this strange idea that you've been avoiding her."

"And she would be entirely correct in her assumption," Odo confirmed. They exchanged smiles. "She is very keen for me to involve the doctor in one of my current cases. I myself am less enamored with the idea." They had reached the entrance to Quark's, and came to a halt.

"Well, I think it's a *good* idea, Odo!" Kira said. Her eyes were sparkling at him, something like they used to. "You know, we hear a lot from Julian about just how smart he is—I think he should prove it!"

"Perhaps it *would* be interesting to see whether he has the makings of an investigator," Odo conceded.

"I can't imagine anyone doing the job as well as you," Kira answered, quickly. There was a slight pause, and then she looked past him. "Well," she said, "I should let you get on. Good luck with Quark!"

"Thank you, Major."

He watched her head off down the Promenade, and then went into the bar. It had been something like their old warmth, he thought. Something very like.

The evening was hazy; a thin mist was hovering over the bay and the plaza. The sky was gray, and reflected gray in the glass of the building. In front of it, a stage had been erected, with large screens so that those at the back of the crowd could still see the speakers. Crash barriers had been put in front of HQ building itself, and around most of the plaza, to keep those gathered contained within a set space.

Sisko had taken Garak to an inconspicuous spot toward the back of the square near a little artificial lake. Chaplin had followed them, keeping her at a distance. From where they were standing, they could look out across the whole of the arena. It was beginning to fill up. The people arriving were a mixture: many of them were young—students, Sisko guessed—but most were just ordinary folk. Some had even brought their kids. There was a buzz of expectation, but the people were gathering themselves together in an orderly way. Some recognized friends and called out to them. Others started up eager conversations with strangers, all here together on a common purpose. Sisko thought about the crash barriers and wondered idly if the organizers were really expecting any trouble. He dismissed the idea. Not at a peace rally. Not in front of Starfleet HQ.

He was aware that quite a few people were looking at them. Never mind the Cardassian standing next to him; Sisko was beginning to feel a little conspicuous himself in his uniform. He folded his arms and turned to look at Garak.

Garak was certainly oblivious to the looks being thrown at them, and apparently unaware of the crowd. His whole attention was on the lake. "So much water," he said, staring out across it, transfixed. "I can see why they chose to put the buildings here."

"It's artificial," Sisko said.

"What?"

"The lake. It's man-made."

Garak blinked at him. "Of course." He smiled wryly,

as if coming to some kind of understanding. "You don't see that much on Cardassia. Or you didn't, when I was last there. Who knows what's going on these days." A couple of swans glided past, imperiously. Garak watched their course with undisguised fascination. "You don't see that either."

"They're swans," Sisko said, and then gave a short laugh. "If I'd known we were going to come this way, I'd have saved some of my breakfast. We could have fed them."

Garak looked at him in horror. "Why?" he said. "Are they *starving?*"

"No . . ." Sisko struggled to think how he could explain. A brief memory came back, of Jake as a very little boy, standing next to Jennifer, both of them laughing as they tried to throw their bits of bread as far as they could, both of them laughing at the ducks as they rushed and dived to be the first to the prize, then rushed and dived again and again. "It's fun, I guess."

"Well, I'll take your word for it." Garak propped himself against the railings and sighed, drawing in a deep breath of the clear air. Sisko watched him, covertly. Garak looked around until he could see where Chaplin was, and then stared out across the water again. "I must say, I continued to be disappointed in Chaplin and Marlow this afternoon."

"Why's that?"

"All we did was talk," Garak said. It was clearly a source of frustration. Sisko thought he had a better idea now why Rhemet had provided such an irresistible target.

"I think I learned more about them than they did about me," Garak was saying, "and how very exceptional their careers have been. Oh yes," he cast Sisko a dry look, "somehow I found myself fully apprised of all that." He nodded in the direction of the lieutenant. "Did you know that Chaplin there is one of the youngest people ever to serve as an adjutant to an admiral? A field promotion of course; if the previous holder of the position hadn't been killed in action, then perhaps she might have been a little older when she got the post. And as for Marlow—well, he was shot in the chest during the retreat from the Kepla sector. A very brave young man—I should imagine that a medal or two were handed out there. And it certainly explains the desk job."

It would also explain why both of them seemed just that bit older than their years, Sisko thought.

"Still," Garak went on, "an intelligence officer finding himself in the wrong place at the wrong time and getting shot for his pains—it's good to know some things are no different whether you're human or Cardassian. But both of them were so"—Garak seemed to be struggling to find an appropriately condemnatory word—"so *pleasant!* I was expecting a thinly veiled threat or two, at least. Just for the sake of appearances, if nothing else."

Sisko shook his head. "So, basically, you're disappointed that they didn't try to break your fingers or anything like that?"

"One should always be prepared."

"Torture isn't exactly standard Starfleet practice, Garak."

"A pity. I have a whole host of talents to put at Starfleet's disposal that your colleagues seem unwilling to use."

Sisko refrained from answering. As far as he was concerned, Starfleet had made more than enough use of the full range of Garak's talents already.

"If nothing else, at least it would be *quicker.*" Garak hissed in a breath of air. "It was exactly the same on Starbase 375. All we did was *talk*," he said again. "It almost drove me insane!"

"So you'd prefer it if they were torturing you?"

"At least it would give me a little more confidence in your intelligence service. I mean, *look* at us!" Garak gestured at their surroundings.

"What's your problem, Garak? We're just standing outside."

"And that's *exactly* my point. I'm Cardassian. On Earth. It's *preposterous* I'm able to move around this freely!"

"The Federation isn't in the business of restricting civil liberties, Garak," Sisko murmured. Not since the last time he had been home, at any rate. Not since Leyton. And God only knew, they had been close enough that time round.

"Well, perhaps they should be! Who knows what I could be up to?"

"Right now," Sisko pointed out, "you're just standing outside."

"I can see," Garak muttered, "that I am unlikely to make myself understood on this point." He turned back to contemplating the swans as they progressed unhurriedly toward the other side of the lake. Suddenly, with a great splash, their wings beat the water, and they took flight. Garak leaned forward a little over the railings to see better. They wheeled around overhead, massive and beautiful, before heading off across the wet sky. Garak twisted round to watch them go. *"Extraordinary . . ."* he murmured. As he turned, Sisko saw his expression change as he registered the number of people that had arrived. "This is a lot busier than I imagined it would be," he said. "Was this what you were expecting, Captain?"

"Not really," Sisko admitted. Again, he considered the

distance between Earth and the front line. Was this really what the war meant, back here? The plaza was so full now that people were filling up the space near them, even as far back as Sisko had brought them, and they were attracting more and more curious looks. He gave a curt, polite nod to a young couple standing beside them who had brought their little boy with them. The husband smiled back; the wife did too, a little more cautiously.

"Look," Garak said, gesturing behind them at the water. Sisko twisted his head to see. Another swan was gliding past. It was black. "They come in two colors," Garak said. He seemed charmed by the idea.

"Black swans aren't very common," Sisko told him.

"No?"

"No," he said. Then the sound system blared, and a voice filled the whole of the plaza, welcoming people to the meeting. The crowd began to applaud. The first speaker was coming on.

The bar was busy this evening, but Odo had no trouble picking out his targets in the crowd. Brixhta and Quark were huddled together in conversation. Odo watched them for a little while from the door, and then went inside. He saw Quark register his imminent arrival almost straight away and alert Brixhta.

"Odo," Quark called out to him, "I have something I want to ask you."

Odo reached the bar. "How eager I am to hear this," he said.

"Don't be too quick to dismiss it," Quark said, "because I want to lodge a complaint."

"A *complaint?*" Odo snorted. "Have you nothing better to do this evening, Quark? Is it proving a bad night for profit?"

"A complaint," Quark ignored the interruption entirely, "about the *high-handed* way in which the hard-working business community of this station was informed that part of the Promenade was going to be sealed off. Do you have *any* idea," Quark, Odo saw, was beginning to work himself up into a close facsimile of outrage, "just how *disruptive* that is for commerce? How much of an effect it could have on the proprietors of all those shops? How it shows, once again"—here he remonstrated Odo with the wave of a finger—"how little value you and the major place on the contribution we ordinary people make to everyday life on this station; not to mention the *disgraceful* disregard you're showing for our freedom to move around wherever we choose—"

"I can only assume," Odo cut in, having allowed Quark plenty of rope, "from this laudable display of civic-mindedness that you have not yet worked out that practically the only eating establishment on the Promenade that will *not* be affected by the closure is this bar?"

Quark stopped dead. He ran his thumb thoughtfully along the edge of his ear. "The Replimat will be closed?"

Odo nodded.

"For twenty-six hours?"

"According to our current estimates. It might even," Odo added helpfully, "turn out to be longer."

"Now that I come to think about it . . ." Quark said.

"Yes?" Odo prompted.

"Most of those spaces are to do with administration, aren't they?" Quark waved a vague hand. "Never really sure what goes on round that bit of the Promenade, but nothing essential to the running of the station . . ."

"Yes . . . ?"

"There's Garak's shop, but he isn't here anyway . . ."

"*Yes?*"

"In which case," Quark concluded, "in the spirit of . . ." He thought for a moment. ". . . *civic-mindedness,* perhaps the Merchants' Association *could* see its way to assisting you and the major during what I can only guess must be a particularly busy time for you."

"Quark," Odo said, turning away, "you are deplorable. *Brixhta,*" he said, to his new object of attention, "may I say how very considerate it is of you to spend so much time in this bar—it certainly makes it easier for me to keep an eye on you both. Did you have a successful afternoon?"

Brixhta drained a little from his glass of water. "How kind of you to take an interest, Odo. Indeed I did."

"You were certainly sending out a lot of communications earlier."

"Business, Odo, all business. A number of very rare and interesting pieces are coming onto the market." He sparkled beneath the hat. "Perhaps there will be something I could procure for you? You seemed enchanted by the Bajoran dolls I showed you earlier."

"Bajoran *dolls?*" Quark bared his teeth in a smile. "Odo, I would never have guessed."

Odo growled. He began to look around the bar not, he told himself, for a means of escape, but for someone more pleasant to talk to. As he watched, his eye fell on the conspicuous figure of Worf, rising from a table opposite, bidding goodnight to Bashir. Perhaps this would be as good a time as any, Odo thought, to keep his word to Dax. He left Quark and Brixhta without a further word, and went to join Bashir at his table.

"Doctor," Odo said. "Good evening."

Bashir looked up. "Oh, hello Odo," he said, giving him what looked to Odo's eyes to be a tired smile. "What brings you in here this evening? Keeping an eye on Quark?"

"I'm *always* keeping an eye on Quark, Doctor. And I certainly don't need to be in here to do it." Odo glanced back over at the bar. Quark and Brixhta had hunched together again.

"No, I suppose you don't," Bashir murmured. His attention had strayed back to his drink.

"In fact," Odo continued, "I have another, quite particular reason to be here this evening." He nodded at the chair that Worf had just vacated. "Would you mind if I joined you, Doctor?"

"Yes, of course." Bashir picked up Worf's empty glass and put it to one side. "Be my guest."

Odo placed himself carefully in the seat. "Thank you," he said.

"I was waiting for Miles," Bashir said, "but he's running late. This ship that's due to arrive has had him scrambling around reorganizing the duty rosters."

"The arrival of the *Ariadne* has been keeping us all busy. And, in fact," Odo took his cue from Quark and Brixhta, and leaned toward Bashir, conspiratorially, "that was what I wanted to talk to you about."

Bashir instinctively moved in toward him. "Oh?"

"That's correct, Doctor." Odo lowered his voice, so that it was just audible against the din in the bar and, with exaggerated caution, he looked back over each shoulder, then he leaned his elbows on the table, and shifted further forward. Bashir, he was pleased to see, was starting to look a little intrigued—and the doctor's expression turned into frank amazement at what Odo said next.

"I would like to enlist your help."

"My *help?*"

"Yes. I want you to help me commit a crime."

• • •

Garak had listened to the first two speakers with intense interest and what Sisko was fairly sure was increasing disbelief. Sisko had a certain amount of sympathy. The gap between soldier and civilian had never seemed so wide to him before.

The news had broken about Sybaron; and the mood of the crowd had altered subtly. It was grimmer, more febrile. Some people at the front had begun to chant. The speaker was responding to them; her voice buoyed up by their resentment.

"They said that with new allies," she was shouting, *"this whole war would turn. But what do we have now? Even more dead—"*

Garak could not restrain himself any longer. He covered over his mouth, and leaned in to speak to Sisko. "Is this just a skewed sample," he asked, "or is everyone on Earth this naïve?"

Sisko shrugged. He agreed, but he had his eye on the people standing around. "It's difficult . . ." he murmured.

"But the Seventh Fleet has *held* at Sybaron! I'll admit there were severe losses, yes, but . . . really!"

"You have to remember that not that many civilians on Earth have seen action."

"A case for conscription if ever there was. Perhaps in the meantime they should listen to people with experience—"

The woman standing nearby picked up her little boy. The young man with her turned to Garak. "And I suppose you think you're one of those people with the requisite experience?" His tone, Sisko was glad to hear, was challenging but by no means unfriendly.

"More than I would wish upon anyone," Garak replied, with a courteous tilt of the head.

"So we should listen to you?"

"I would of course naturally suggest that," Garak said, beginning to smile.

"But you're Cardassian," someone else called out. A young woman, Sisko saw, no more than Jake's age, maybe a year or so older. Probably a student at the university. "You're the reason we're at war in the first place."

"My dear young lady," Garak said politely, "looks can be deceptive. I can assure you that the Dominion occupation of Cardassia is neither my fault nor to my benefit."

"No, no!" She shook her head, urgency making her angry. "I'm talking about your whole culture. It's militaristic, expansionist—I mean, just *look* at your history!" She was gathering momentum. Garak was staring at her as if she were an example of some previously undiscovered species. "And I'm not just talking about the invasion of Bajor," she went on, "although that's the *worst* example! It was only a matter of time before the Cardassian Union turned on the rest of the quadrant. The only thing that held you back was that you didn't have the resources! Up until *now,* that is. *That's* all the Dominion have done—given Cardassian imperialism the resources it's always lacked. This is all just . . ." She took a breath before delivering the coup de grâce. ". . . just a logical progression of the tendencies inherent in your society!"

Several of her friends were agreeing warmly, and one or two people standing by gave her a spontaneous round of applause. Garak looked like he had just been hit with a copy of the Federation Constitution. A hardback copy. Sisko began to laugh. Free speech in action, and the humanities had just drawn first blood. "You know," Sisko murmured, leaning toward Garak, "she does have a point there." Garak glared back at him.

"Don't *you* be so smug," the young woman said, turning on Sisko and jabbing a finger at him angrily. "Because *we're* going the same way. It's all about weapons and war now, isn't it? What happened to diplomacy? What happened to peaceful exploration? *Your* generation are making a mess that *we*," she gestured round to her friends, "are going to have to live with." There was another burst of applause, more serious this time. She nodded; satisfied with her words; still angry, but satisfied.

"You know, Captain," Garak said, "she *does* have a point there." He turned back to their challenger. "My dear—" he began.

"Don't *my dear* me!"

"I beg your pardon," he said graciously. "You make a good case, and very persuasively. But the reality is that if Starfleet—if the Allies—struck a deal with the Dominion now, I would give it—" He glanced at Sisko, who shrugged. "—two years, at the outside. In which period of time, they would have rearmed, and they would be even more ready for us. This is a *trade-off*," Garak said, as if surprised to have to make such an obvious point, "between a current conflict and a future, lasting peace."

"But it's not getting us anywhere closer to peace, is it?" someone called from a little way back. "What's just happened at Sybaron?"

"A bloodbath," someone else called out.

"Give people a little knowledge and they'll abuse it," Garak muttered to Sisko. "Now do you see my point about censorship?" He called back, "*That* was holding the line. Do you want to know what a bloodbath would be?" He pointed up past the screens to the roof of the HQ building. Many of the people gathered around them turned to look. "Fifty Jem'Hadar stationed up there, firing on us down here. *That* would be a bloodbath—and it's the Seventh Fleet holding the line at Sybaron that means that *you* can bring your children here and say ill-informed things about war in complete safety!"

Some people around them began to boo. Up on the stage, someone was saying, *"Could we have a little quiet down at the back, please!"*

"Try to tone it down, Garak," Sisko murmured. He looked up at the screens. "Roeder's about to come on. I want to hear what he has to say."

"He's had experience of the war," someone shouted at them, "and he's seen through it all. He wants peace."

"Well, all of us are for *peace!"* Garak called back. "Just not at the price of being . . ." He hunted for the right word. ". . . *enslaved!"* He turned to Sisko impatiently. "Major Kira would know what I'm talking about!"

"I'm sure you're right," Sisko said, trying to calm him down. "Let's just listen to Roeder, shall we?"

"But the captain of the ship is *insistent* that these biometric scans are invulnerable!"

Julian scratched his ear, suppressed a yawn, and tried to listen to Odo's lengthy explanation. He had been planning on having a quick, quiet drink with Miles, and then heading off early to bed. The chief was late, Worf had hijacked him for the first half of the evening, and now Odo—arms folded before him, his frown in full display upon his face—looked like he had settled in for the second half. Julian glanced over at Broik, who lurked glumly behind the bar, and waved his fingers unobtrusively. When he caught the Ferengi's attention, he picked up his empty glass and tilted it. He might as well get started on another drink if he was going to be stuck here all evening. Perhaps he might start thinking about something a little stronger than synthale. . . .

"She is certain that her clients are not the kind of peo-

ple to take risks with this much latinum. She is also very insistent that under no circumstances would she install second-rate systems, and she gave me to understand that these particular clients would not look too kindly upon her if she did." Odo snorted. "I, on the other hand, have *never* come across a security system that cannot be bypassed—should someone happen to be dedicated enough."

Broik slinked up to the table, bearing the fresh glass of synthale, and gawping fearfully at Odo. Odo glared back at the interruption. Julian mumbled his thanks to the waiter, thumbed Broik's padd to ensure payment for the drink, and watched as the Ferengi scurried off gratefully back to the relative safety of the bar. He took a sip of his drink, allowing Odo to pick up his tale once more.

"And *that* amount of latinum would make anyone dedicated, I would think. Which is where you come in, Doctor."

Julian looked up from his drink to see Odo staring at him intently. He rubbed the back of his neck. "Oh yes?"

"Yes. Because if anyone can work his way around these biometric scans—it has to be you."

Julian set his glass down on the table, and shifted about uncomfortably in his chair. "Oh, I don't know, Odo," he shook his head, "it's not something I really have the time for at the moment—"

"But just think about it! Not only are you so intellectually gifted, but this is even in your own field. . . ."

"Really, biometric scans and security systems . . . it all sounds more like the chief that you should be talking to . . ." Julian trailed off when he realized that Odo wasn't listening to him. Instead he was looking down eagerly at a padd he had brought with him.

"Take a look at this, Doctor, " he urged. "I'm sure that

once you start reading, you'll be intrigued." He pushed the padd across the table. With a sigh, Julian began to give the data a cursory scan. Something caught his eye, and he started to look a little more closely. . . .

Don't do it, he told himself firmly. *Don't let yourself get dragged into this.*

He looked up at Odo's expectant face, and tried to think of a good question. "What I don't understand, Constable," he said, "is why you're so sure someone's going to try to steal the latinum."

Odo frowned at him. This clearly was not the answer he had been hoping for.

"I mean, I quite agree," Julian said hurriedly, "that it is an awful lot of latinum, but we've had shipments like this pass through the station before, with no problems at all—at least, none that you've ever mentioned. . . ."

He tailed off as Odo looked over each shoulder, then around the bar, and then leaned toward him. Half-unconsciously, and certainly against his better judgment, Julian leaned in himself, so that he could hear what Odo was about to say.

"Brixhta," Odo growled.

Julian stared at him blankly. "I'm sorry?"

"Here," Odo said, "on the station. Right now."

Julian sat up in his chair. "Odo, I haven't the faintest idea what you're talking about," he said.

"He *says* that he's here to deal in antiques. Antiques?" Odo snorted. "Most of it is just junk. And he's here. Now. With all that latinum on the station." Odo shook his head. "I don't believe a word of this antiques nonsense."

Before Julian could answer, another chair was pulled up next to him. O'Brien sat down.

"Thank god you're here, Miles," Julian said. "Odo is trying to tempt me into a life of crime."

"Sounds like I arrived in the nick of time." O'Brien waved at the bar and pointed at Bashir's glass, then looked back. His expression became suspicious. "What are you two hunched up together like this for? What's going on?"

"You can explain it, Odo," Julian said, just as Odo said again, *"Brixhta . . ."*

"Who or what is Brixhta?" O'Brien said.

"If you can find that out, Miles, you're doing better than I am."

"The name sounds Hamexi," O'Brien said.

"It is. Brixhta and I crossed paths once before. . . ." Odo's face took on a distant expression.

"Well, don't keep us in suspense *too* long, Odo," O'Brien said.

"During the Occupation, Brixhta once attempted to acquire a large amount of Numerian blacksilver. I was obliged to go to Bajor to stop him. And, as a result of my intervention in his plans, he has just finished serving quite a respectable prison sentence." Odo paused. "Don't look, but he's at the bar right now, talking to Quark."

As one man, Bashir and O'Brien turned to look. Quark noticed them at once, and said something to Brixhta. Brixhta turned and tipped his hat at them.

"Stop *staring!*" Odo growled.

As they watched, Brixhta slid out from his chair and progressed in a stately fashion toward the Promenade.

"I see," Julian murmured. He raised his glass to hide his smile, and glanced over at Miles, who grinned back. "So . . . it's almost as if he's your archenemy? You'd best keep quiet about this, Odo. Quark's feelings might get hurt."

Odo favored him with a rather cool stare. "So, Doctor," he said, "when you wonder why I am sure that an attempt will be made to steal this shipment of latinum—my answer is that both it and Mexh Brixhta are here at the same time."

Julian looked at Odo thoughtfully. "You know, I almost hesitate to ask this, but do you have any actual evidence to support that?"

"What do you mean?"

"Well . . ." Julian waved his hand. "It *could* just be a coincidence."

Odo snorted.

"Apart from what he did in the past," Julian said, "for which, I think it should be pointed out, he's paid the price—has Brixhta given you any real reason to think that he's intending to steal this latinum? That he's still a criminal."

"He is an antiques dealer, Doctor. Of course he's still a criminal."

Julian looked at Odo over the rim of his glass. Then he turned to O'Brien. "You know, Miles," he said, "you and your books have a lot to answer for."

"Oh, don't go blaming me for this!"

"Odo," Julian said, "I think you need to start reading something else other than pulp fiction. I can make you some recommendations if you like. Cardassian, if you want to start with something familiar. I'm sure Garak would be more than willing to help. . . ." Seeing that Odo's face was getting—if it were at all possible—even stonier, Julian stopped himself and hid away again behind the safety of his glass. "So, this Brixhta," he said. "Why does he say he's here?"

"He *says* he's here to hold an auction of goods." Odo pushed a piece of card toward Julian, who grimaced slightly at the colors before reading the ornate script upon it. *Brixhta,* it said. *Antiques.*

Julian pushed the card back. "When?"

"Tomorrow morning, here in the bar," Odo said. "As if Brixhta weren't trouble enough without going into business with Quark!"

"Well, leaving that complication aside for the moment," Julian said, "has he brought anything to sell with him?"

"Yes. I went and had a look at them earlier, in fact."

"And did you see anything suspicious about them? Anything at all?"

"Not a thing," Odo said unhappily.

"Well then," Julian took another swig of ale. "Is it not just possible, then, that this Brixhta has no intention of stealing a shipment of latinum under the watchful eye of the very person who once put him in prison?"

Odo frowned and folded his arms, deep in thought. Julian returned to his drink. He glanced across at Miles and raised an eyebrow. *Problem solved, I think!*

O'Brien grinned back, and reached for the padd. He began reading through it. "Are these the security systems from the *Ariadne?*" he said.

Odo nodded.

"I thought they were pretty impressive," O'Brien said, and put the padd back down again in front of the doctor. He looked back at the bar. "Is Quark ever going to bring me that drink?" he muttered, and then looked down at the padd again, thoughtfully. "Hey, that's someone we should talk to," he said. "If anyone would know how to steal this latinum, it would be Quark. Takes a thief to catch a thief, doesn't it?" He swung back on his chair and twisted round to look at the bar. "Quark!" he yelled, over the noise. "Come over here for a minute. And bring my drink with you when you come."

• • •

Roeder was turning out to have quite the gift for public speaking, one that Sisko would never have guessed from serving with him. How many years ago now? People could change in that length of time. Sisko studied the once familiar face, overlarge on the screen. Roeder was a little older than the people who had spoken so far, and he had a harder edge, particularly when he talked about his time in Starfleet. Judith was right. It gave him credibility. Sisko watched him speak, and wondered what the hell had brought about this change of heart; what the hell had brought him here. The people around were responding to his words. Someone jostled Sisko's arm. He looked around for the couple with their son to make sure that they were safe, but he couldn't see them. He supposed it was starting to get late.

Roeder said a little about his grief on hearing the news from Sybaron, and then he paused. When he spoke again, Sisko could hear a new steel in his voice.

"We're here this evening outside Starfleet Headquarters for a particular reason. Inside, there are people making decisions about this war. And we're here this evening because we want to make sure that our voices are heard, and we want to make sure that the right *decisions are made."*

"Let's hope that if your voice *is* heard, it's summarily dismissed," Garak muttered. Some of the people around began expressing their displeasure again. Sisko murmured to Garak to keep quiet. Up on the stage, Roeder seemed to be aware that there was discontent toward the back of the crowd.

"You know, I can see a lot of people here this evening in uniform. I salute them. I know all about their courage and the choices they have to make. But I ask them to think

again about what is being done in their names; what they are allowing to be done."

Sisko looked again at Roeder's face up on the screen. *You don't know the half of it.* He stared around the crowd. They hated the everyday business of war because it was bloody, he knew, and dirty—but what they failed to realize was that it was clean in comparison to what else it permitted. For a second, Sisko regretted his uniform again; and then he caught himself angrily. He was damned if he was going to let Roeder manipulate him like that. He was damned if he was going to be made to feel ashamed of this uniform. People here didn't know the first thing about the front line; hell, *Jake* had a better idea. Someone shoved him, and then Garak was jostled too. Garak held his hands up briefly, palms outward; a gesture of appeasement.

"I don't know how you can wear that uniform," someone new shouted from close by. "You're a commander, right?"

"Captain, in fact," Sisko said. He looked around until he could see Chaplin. There were about ten or fifteen people between them, but he was fairly certain she was reaching toward the phaser she carried openly at her waist. Sisko shook his head, ever so slightly. The last thing that was needed right now was someone in uniform to fire a weapon.

"So you must be ordering young men and women in to battle, all the time," another new voice shouted. "And getting them killed." The mood was becoming angrier. "I bet you're safe on the bridge of your ship all the time— you should be *ashamed* of yourself!"

"Now I really must protest!" Garak interrupted. "I doubt that anything could make the captain ashamed of his uniform."

Sisko shot him an irritated look.

"And why should he be?" Garak continued, cheerfully, having not missed Sisko's expression. "He has conducted himself judiciously throughout this entire war, and with consummate skill, both strategic and tactical. I can honestly say that it has been an *honor* to serve alongside him. Captain," Garak said, breaking off his eulogy to turn and address Sisko directly, "have you noticed that the callow young students and families with whom we were enjoying such a lively exchange of opinions appear to have moved on and been replaced with a crowd considerably less friendly?"

"I know that on Cardassia you don't have much experience of gatherings like this," Sisko said, turning to face him and keeping one eye on the people pressing up close, "but one thing you *should* know about them is that sometimes a certain element may be looking for a focus for less than peaceful action."

"I see," Garak's eyes widened. "Captain, I almost hesitate to ask—but do *we*, by any chance, happen to be providing such a focus?"

"I think we're just about to find out," Sisko replied, moving forward to block the fist that was heading in Garak's direction.

This was by no means, Odo thought, the direction in which he had intended this conversation to go. He had come over for a quiet chat with the doctor, and the entire station was being drawn into the affair. All that was needed now was for Dax to turn up and start offering more of her questionable advice. He berated himself for starting this conversation with the doctor in such a public place. He should have gone to see him in the privacy of the infirmary.

"Chief," he said, watching Quark come over to them, "I must urge caution on you—"

"Don't worry, I just want to sound him out." O'Brien grinned. "Maybe we can find out whether he knows anything—and how much."

"You're assuming that I don't already have that matter well under control—" Odo stopped speaking as Quark arrived. He was bearing a tray, and he set O'Brien's drink down in front of him.

"You're a little less patient than usual this evening, Chief," Quark said.

"Got a lot on my mind," O'Brien said, and glanced round the table. "As have we all."

With a smooth and rapid movement, Quark tucked the tray under his arm, leaned his elbow on the table, and looked round at the three of them. "So . . . are you talking about the *Ariadne,* by any chance?" he said.

"How do *you* know about that?" Odo retorted.

Quark shrugged. "Word gets around."

"Again," Odo said, "I have to ask the question—*how?*"

"It's a small station, Odo," Quark answered. "Anyone watching could have seen you and the chief here running around the past couple of days."

That did not, Odo noted, explain how Quark knew the name of the ship that was due to arrive. It seemed that despite his continuing efforts, it was once again time for him to check upon the extent of Quark's monitoring of station communications.

"You think someone's got their eye on all that latinum," Quark said.

"Stop licking your lips, Quark," O'Brien said. "What do you think could happen?"

"Well, I don't really know," Quark said. "It's not as

if I know anything about the security systems on the *Ariadne*—"

Odo watched him carefully. Was it his imagination, or had Quark's eyes strayed toward the padd on the table?

"And it's not something I have a great deal of experience in," Quark said. "Having said that, friends of mine—"

"Yes, of course," Odo said. "*Friends* of yours."

"Some of us *have* friends, Odo," Quark said, "And friends of mine who *do* have this kind of experience tell me that no system is entirely without faults. And that people can be endlessly creative in finding out what they are . . . if the profit is worth it." He shrugged. "It's just a question of patience and skill, Chief," he said. "You should know that. Anyone can work their way around a technology."

"So people are the flaws in the system, huh?" O'Brien said.

"So I hear," Quark replied.

O'Brien laughed. "Think I could have told you that myself, Quark!"

"But there's your answer, Odo," Bashir said. "You need the kind of person who deals a lot with technologies." He pushed the padd toward O'Brien.

"Funny," O'Brien replied. "The way *I* heard what Quark just said"—he pushed the padd back at the doctor—"Odo needs the kind of person who deals a lot with people."

Odo did not answer. He reached out to stop the padd moving around the table under Quark's greedy eye. Then he looked up at the Ferengi.

"Of course," Quark said, looking straight back at him, "Odo knows of one very simple way to solve the whole problem. Don't you, Odo?"

"Well," Odo said, drawing the padd closer to him, and spreading out across it a millimeter or two, "this will certainly be worth hearing. What is your expert advice then, Quark?"

Quark gave him a predatory smile. "Simple. Arrest Brixhta and keep him locked in a holding cell all the time the latinum is here."

Bashir coughed up some of his synthale. O'Brien whistled. "Quark! I thought you and Brixhta had gone into business together. With friends like you, who needs enemies?"

Odo stared at Quark, who was watching him back with more than a little interest. Then he looked back down at the padd and slowly, cautiously, began to give it a false cover.

"It was just a thought." Quark shrugged. "Well, Odo," he challenged, "what do you think of it?"

"He can't just do that, Quark!" Bashir was outraged.

Odo turned to Bashir and looked at him blankly. "Why not?"

Quark laughed.

"Odo!" Bashir shot back. "Because Brixhta hasn't *done* anything, that's why!"

"Yet," Odo said, pointedly.

There was a slight pause, then Bashir collected himself. "You can't just go around locking people up on the off chance that they're going to commit a crime!" he said. "Where would it end?"

"In this particular case, it could very well end with this shipment of latinum leaving the station safely in the possession of its owners," Odo pointed out.

"But you've no grounds for arresting him! Nothing apart from some suspicions based on what he did in the past." Bashir put down his glass. "You know, I can't be-lieve we're even discussing this."

"Why are you not surprised, Doctor?" Quark said. "It's a very tidy answer to the problem, after all. I can definitely see the appeal of it. For Odo."

Odo did not respond, but stared down at the table, and expanded his cover a little more.

"Well," Quark said, "if we're all done here, I still have a bar to run."

The silence lengthened after Quark left.

"No need to take drastic measures, Odo," O'Brien said soothingly, into the quiet. "We've done this kind of thing before plenty of times with no problem."

Odo did not answer. He began to draw himself in from covering the padd. He glanced over at the bar where Quark was busy with a new customer. What, Odo thought, were he and Brixhta playing at?

"I really am sure, Odo," Bashir said, in a quieter tone of voice, "that if you just do what you usually do, every-thing will work out fine."

Odo arranged his features into a frown. Bashir sighed, then picked up his glass and drained it. "Well," he said, and stood up, "it's been a long day. I should get to bed."

"Doctor."

Bashir sighed. "Yes, Constable?"

Odo pointed down on the table in front of him. "Don't forget the padd."

They ran as if they had a squadron of Jem'Hadar on their heels. Sisko decided to think of it as a strategic withdrawal. *"Take a left!"* he hissed, veering off, and Garak followed. They went, still running, into and along a narrow alley. Sisko led, with Garak just behind. They came out into a wide road that ran past the harbor. It was busy, full of people out in the early evening at the cafés and restaurants on the front. They lost themselves as best a Starfleet captain and a Cardassian could in the crowd, and then Sisko signaled Garak toward a set of stone steps leading down off the harborfront onto the sand.

When they got to the bottom, they stopped. They listened for a moment or two, but nobody was following. Garak leaned back against the wall, gulping in the sea air. He caught Sisko looking at him, and he began to laugh. "I haven't done anything like that for years," he said.

"Well, I hope you enjoyed yourself," Sisko said, trying to catch his breath. "Do you think that you've got Rhemet out of your system now?"

Garak grinned back at him. "I think so," he replied. His eyes glittered. "And have you taken my point about censorship now?" His eyes glittered and he reached up carefully to touch his cheek. He winced slightly. "Thank you for stopping that young man for me, Captain. He was beginning to do some serious damage."

"Any time," Sisko muttered. He heard footsteps hurrying down the steps toward them. Both of them peered up anxiously.

It was Chaplin. She stopped when she saw them, halfway down the steps, and glared at Garak. Then she hit her combadge and said, "I've got him, Marlow."

"Oh dear," Garak murmured to Sisko. "The lieutenant does not look pleased."

When Odo returned to his office, he settled behind his desk, and retrieved from his files a recent communication he had received. It was a Starfleet Special Order, and it was concerned with a series of new security measures that had been introduced since the Dominion had invaded Betazed.

Odo examined the text of the order carefully. There it was, in plain language: Odo was now empowered to "neutralize security threats to the station by whatever means necessary." No specific examples were given, but Odo was capable of supplying those for himself. For example, there was no specific need to charge an individual with a crime. Just hold them, until the threat was over. Or neutralized, as the order preferred.

Odo regarded the file thoughtfully. Now he came to think about it, the language was not that plain at all. In fact, it left quite a lot of room for interpretation. Was it, for example, stretching the meaning of the order to include a possible theft of a shipment of latinum as a "security threat to the station"? It was certainly a threat to the latinum. And it was certainly taking up too much time and causing far too many distractions from the point of view of the station's chief of security. Did that make it a threat to station security? One that should therefore be "neutralized"? Odo had a very strong suspicion that he might know what Bashir would have to say in answer to that question. He himself was not entirely sure how he would answer the question. But he was absolutely certain that implementing the order would put some stability back into what had hitherto been a most disrupted day.

4

SISKO SLEPT BADLY. The adrenaline from the fight kept him awake until the early hours. Then the dream that took him to the bridge of the Jem'Hadar ship woke him two hours before his call, and he did not get back to sleep.

The day itself was filled with wrangling and circumlocution. The consequences of the counteroffensive at Sybaron had, as predicted, led to some strife among the tenuous alliance, and, as the day wore on, Sisko was increasingly aware that he was being watched. Ross, beside him, was the worst culprit, but he could feel Garak's eyes upon his back too, although Garak had, at least, been mercifully quiet throughout the day's sessions. And every time Sisko looked across the table, there was Veral, smiling back at him. When the last session of the day wound up, Sisko was out of his chair immediately.

"Ben—" Ross said.

"I have to go," Sisko murmured, turning away from him. "Off to see an old friend."

He went quickly through the conference room. Out of

the corner of his eye, he saw Chaplin and Marlow with Garak. They were almost glued to him. Sisko turned away and went out into the corridor at a great pace. He took the turbolift down to the reception area, where he arranged for a transporter to take him to his destination, and sent out a communication to announce his imminent arrival. It was no more than fifteen minutes after he had left the conference that he was standing in the white New Zealand sunlight outside a bland gray building, with a security officer waiting to escort him inside.

Back in his quarters, Garak stood by the window and looked out. The afternoon sun was shining, but it seemed to him that the world outside was made of water. It had been raining on and off throughout the day, and the sky had been washed a pale, clean blue. Beyond the verdant ranks of the trees, just on the horizon, there was the grand sweep of the bridge. But what really fascinated him was the bay. The extent of it; the sheer expanse . . . Garak rested his hand against the wall and stared at the water. He thought of Lake Masad, the largest lake on Cardassia Prime, lying high and narrow between barren, yellow mountains. Its surface was like black glass, and it lay still and unchanging in the harsh sun and sullen heat of home. What lay before him now was entirely different and wholly alien to him; bright blues shimmering and varying in the bright sunlight, water rippling in the breeze. He found it mesmerizing. He raised his other hand, absently, to shield his eyes.

Much as Garak admired the water, he felt that he was not likely to get any closer to it in the foreseeable future. He tutted to himself in frustration, tapped his fingers against the window frame, and then pressed the control panel set on the wall. The glass darkened, taking some of the glare away from the room. Garak turned from the already half-hidden view, put his back to the window, and looked thoughtfully around him.

Despite Garak's insistence that the events of the previous evening had been a complete misunderstanding, Lieutenant Chaplin had not been amused by her charge's account. She had asked that, outside of conference sessions and their meetings, Garak henceforth remain inside; and not just within the confines of HQ, but within the quarters that had been set aside for the duration of his visit. Marlow, by way of contrast, *had* seemed to be a little amused—but had firmly seconded his colleague's request. Garak had more than enough experience to recognize that very special subset of request with which one was well advised to comply; and, anyway, if Starfleet Intelligence now wanted to keep a closer eye on him— well, really, he only had himself to blame.

It was entirely consonant with everything else going on at the conference, Garak thought. Everyone was watching everyone else. Chaplin and Marlow, as he knew, were aware of his every move. Rhemet, too, Garak had been pleased to notice, had not now been able to ignore him entirely; indeed, every time Rhemet had opened his mouth to speak, he had glanced at Garak first. In the row behind Cretak and Veral, a veritable phalanx of Romulans was lined up, subjecting the other delegations to near-permanent surveillance. And Garak himself had spent a large part of the day watching Sisko. The events of the previous evening had not served, as Garak had hoped they might, to lift even a little of the captain's mood. Sisko had been, if it were possible, even more preoccupied. All throughout the day, Garak had found himself wondering again exactly what had gone on in the captain's impromptu meeting with his superiors. Garak's worry had only increased with Sisko's abrupt departure; when the afternoon's sessions had closed, Sisko had absented himself as soon as he decently could. The prompt arrival of Chaplin and Marlow, ever efficiently at his disposal, had prevented Garak from following Sisko even a little way beyond the conference room, and had certainly done nothing to alleviate Garak's own concerns.

Garak sighed, and looked around his quarters. As prisons went, he had to admit that it was by no means the worst he had ever encountered. It was, for example, considerably better appointed than anything the Dominion had offered him. It was rather more spacious than the holding cells on DS9, with which he had, on one occasion, become quite unfortunately, but intimately acquainted. Still, even if the lock was metaphorical (and Garak *had* tried the door—it opened too, but Marlow had been sitting at the far end of the corridor, looking rather implacably impassable), a cell was still a cell, no matter how charming the view. And he would have liked very much to be able to open the window.

Garak drew in a breath and told himself, not for the first time, that he had nothing to worry about. If Sisko had informed his superiors of the details of Vreenak's death, then surely Garak would know by now? Surely someone would have come to arrest him? Surely someone would have come to *speak* to him, at least? It looked, Garak thought, as if he was just going to have to believe Sisko when he had said that nothing had happened. Although it went against his better nature, Garak was starting to think that he would have to assume that Sisko had told him the truth.

For Sisko, after all, is an honorable man. . . .

Garak heaved another sigh. "Well," he said, to the walls, "whatever shall we do now?"

• • •

It was only midmorning, and Quark's was already more than half-full. *I imagine he'll be pleased about that,* Odo thought, watching with ill temper as Broik and a couple of the other barkeeps struggled to keep up with the orders. There was a certain something in the air too, Odo thought—an atmosphere of lively anticipation. Odo snorted. People often came to Quark's filled with hope, and more often than not they left disappointed. Buying something from Brixhta was unlikely to make much of a difference to that.

Odo scanned the room. There was a podium set up in front of the dabo table, and chairs had been set out in lines before it. They were already filling up. The clientele was a mix of visitors and locals, with a couple of unexpected faces; it looked like Kaga wanted to acquire some bits and pieces of history after all. Quark and Brixhta themselves were nowhere to be seen. However, just on the other side of the entrance, leaning back against the wall, Bashir was propped up, looking around with interest. Dax was standing next to him—a more than usually amused smile lighting her eyes. Odo went cautiously across to join them, walking slowly so as to create an opportunity to make an assessment of the doctor's disposition. Bashir didn't look quite so unapproachable this morning, he thought; perhaps giving him that padd last night had provided him with some distraction after all. Not that the doctor had been an enthusiastic audience, of course, despite all of Odo's quite considerable effort. . . . Dax had better appreciate this example of his good nature.

"Good morning, Doctor; good morning, Commander," Odo said, nodding to them in turn when he got closer. "I had no idea that either of you were interested in buying antiques."

Bashir grinned back. "I'm more interested in the seller, actually, Constable," he said. "Until last night, I'd never seen an Hamexi in the . . ." He stopped, as if to consider his choice of word. "Well, in the flesh before, although I did read a little about them while I was at the academy. A very interesting species, from a biological point of view—"

Dax groaned. "Don't talk shop, Julian, it's far too early in the morning."

"It's well past eleven hundred hours," Bashir pointed out, but Dax was no longer listening.

"When is the famous Brixhta due to arrive, Odo?" she said. "I assume that's why you're here? To keep an eye on him?"

So Bashir had told Dax about Brixhta? Odo glanced over at Bashir, who gave an eloquently apologetic shrug. *She made me tell her everything,* it said. Of course.

Odo nodded at Dax. "Indeed. I suspect he'll be busy somewhere with Quark."

"Partners in crime?" Jadzia's eyes were laughing.

"So it seems," Odo said, settling his face into a frown. "I suppose, at least, that if they're together, they're not free to cause as much trouble."

"Or else they're causing double." Bashir's grin got a little broader.

Yes, the doctor was *definitely* in a better mood this morning. "Tell me, Doctor," Odo said, "have you had a chance to look over the information I gave you?"

Bashir's smile faded, and he looked at Odo guiltily. "Oh . . . I'm sorry, Odo, I didn't really get a chance last night. I was pretty tired—I just went straight off to bed."

Odo nodded, surprised to discover that he felt a little disappointed. It seemed he had been starting to enjoy his new appointment as provider of distractions for Bashir.

"It doesn't matter," he said, more carelessly than he felt, "I'm sure you'll take the trouble as soon as you have the time."

"Um, later on, I hope . . ." Bashir said.

"Julian—look over there," Dax said with sudden excitement, grabbing the doctor's arm, "could *that* be Brixhta, by any chance?"

Odo looked out across the bar. "Oh yes," he said, with a sigh, "that's Brixhta."

"Is he everything you were expecting, Jadzia?" Bashir said.

"Quite a bit more. Quite a *lot* more, actually. How does he hold himself up?" Dax said.

"He really is something else, isn't he? The surface tension alone must be remarkable," said Bashir. Both of them stood and stared at the Hamexi for a little while, and then Bashir shook himself from his reverie. "So— have you decided what you're going to do about him?"

Odo made a noncommittal sound.

"That's still proving a tricky one, is it?" Bashir grinned again. "Well, I can't stay here and gawp around the bar all morning," he said. "I should be in the infirmary. I really *will* try and take a look at that padd, Odo. Drop by the infirmary later on—it's not exactly frantic there today."

"That hardly seems like something to complain about, Doctor."

"No . . . but I've got out of the habit of being quiet," he said. "Never mind, I've got plenty of reading to catch up on."

"Read the padd," Odo said pointedly. "That will keep you busy."

"Persistent, aren't you?" Bashir laughed. "I'll do my best. See you both later!"

Odo nodded a goodbye, and he and Dax watched as Bashir made his way out onto the Promenade. Then Dax turned to him.

"Well?" she prompted.

"Yes?" he replied.

"He was in a much better mood this morning," Dax said. "Have you been working on him? Did you think of a case for him?"

Odo folded his arms. "That, Commander," he said loftily, "is a matter of station security." Dax gave him a good-humored scowl. Odo turned his attention back to the proceedings unfolding in front of them. All the seats were full now, and Brixhta was making his way around his potential customers. He seemed to be giving something to people as he went past. Eventually, he reached Odo.

"Constable Odo," he said, "what a delight to see you here. May I offer you this?" A padd was held out. "You may find it of interest."

Odo did not unfold his arms. "No, thank you."

Brixhta waved it to and fro, just a little. "Are you sure? It might come in useful at a later date."

Odo reached out and took the padd, quite abruptly. "What is it?" he snapped.

"It is the catalogue for the sale, Odo," Brixhta said, his voice filled with a patient pity. "Press that button *there*—"

Odo did as he was told, with marked reluctance. The padd sprang into life, and a little animation began to play, with a tinny, mechanical tune, resolving into the legend: *Q & B Enterprises*. It filled Odo with a sense of foreboding. Beside him, Dax appeared to be stifling a cough.

"And then that one *there*—"

To Odo's everlasting gratitude, the music stopped and the logo disappeared.

"And you will see all the lots for today's sale."

As Brixhta had promised, the screen on the padd was now showing a list of merchandise, with a brief description, details of reserve prices, and a summary of provenance. It all looked quite in order—which only served to increase Odo's suspicions further.

"I'm beginning to think, Brixhta," he said, ruminatively, "that I should probably just arrest you now."

A slight wheezing sound came out from beneath the hat. Brixhta, Odo realized, was chuckling. "I suppose you could," Brixhta replied, "but think how terribly disappointed all these poor people would be."

Odo looked out across the bar. At the far end, Quark had appeared, and he was taking up his place, behind the podium. He seemed, to Odo's eye, to be even more gaudily dressed than usual, if that was possible; his jacket was an explosion of bright green and gold. He was extremely pleased with himself. He looked around until he saw Brixhta, and gave him a quick nod.

"That will be my summons, Constable. Which means that you must excuse me—unless you really do intend to apprehend me before the sale begins?"

"Get up there," Odo growled. "I can wait a little bit longer."

By the time the door chimed, Garak had once again been reduced to Shakespeare. He put down the padd and frowned, at a loss to think who it could be. Sisko had not been gone very long, and Garak doubted, somehow, that it was Rhemet, coming to reminisce about the people and places they had once both known.

"Computer," he said, rising from his chair, "open the door."

It slid open, and two men entered, both wearing

Starfleet uniforms. Red-trimmed. Garak checked the rank pips of each. Commanders. He narrowed his eyes in suspicion as they came further into the room.

One of the men was thickset, carrying a little too much weight, but he moved across the room toward Garak with a heavy grace. The other man, a shade taller, was younger, and lean, and lugubrious. He was carrying a couple of padds, and was looking at Garak through bored eyes. He spoke first.

"Mister Garak," he said, giving him a brief nod. His voice was flat and soft and too precise; Garak was reminded of Bashir. "My name is Enderby. Starfleet Intelligence. And this," he nodded to his colleague, "is Jedburgh. Also of Starfleet Intelligence."

The big man smiled at Garak, leisurely, and genially. "Ten years we've worked together," he said lazily, favoring Enderby with a look that almost achieved exasperation. "And he's never once managed to get my name right." He stuck out a large hand. "Jedburgh." He pronounced the *g*.

Garak took the proffered hand. Jedburgh clamped hard, shook vigorously, and then dropped it abruptly. Again, he gave the languid smile. "Welcome to Earth. Your first visit here, yeah?"

"That's correct." Garak folded his arms in front of him, and began smoothing at his sleeve with the edge of his thumb.

Jedburgh broadened his smile, generously. "Well, you be sure you see some of this beautiful city," he drawled. "After we're through."

All of a sudden, Garak felt himself relax. He allowed a slight smile to play across his mouth. Chaplin and Marlow really had been too good to be true. Their discussions had been almost pedestrian, by-the-book. Low-level.

This was the contact he had been waiting for. These were the kind of people he had dealt with before. These were the kind of people he understood best. He knew exactly how they worked.

"Rest assured," he said back to Jedburgh, "that I am *very* anxious for the opportunity to arise. Unfortunately . . ." He gave a meaningful look around the confines of his quarters. ". . . at the present moment, I am unable to go any further than this room."

"Well," Jedburgh said, shaking his head, "I think that's a damn shame. A damn shame. But, you know, I think maybe Enderby and I can do something about that. In fact, I'm pretty damn sure of it. What do you say, Enderby?"

Throughout this exchange, Enderby's lips had been thinning even further, and he had begun to tap the padds he was carrying against his palm. "If you are sure you have quite finished, Jedburgh . . .?" he murmured. He had not, Garak noted, corrected his pronunciation.

Jedburgh grinned back at him, ear to ear. "Oh, I'd say so, Enderby. Why don't you just go right on ahead?"

Enderby gave something of a weary sigh and addressed Garak directly. "We're aware of the incident yesterday and the subsequent restrictions that have been placed upon your movements. Nevertheless, we have a sufficiently high security rating to accompany you outside . . ." He paused, and ran the corner of one of the padds against his cheek. It left a mark against his pale skin. "And we'd prefer to hold this conversation outside."

Garak shrugged. "If that's what would make you happy," he said.

For a brief moment, Enderby looked puzzled, as if he had not considered the matter in terms of his own contentment. Then he collected himself, and gestured toward the door. "Follow me, please," he said. Garak fell in just behind him. Jedburgh ambled along at the rear. They went out into an empty corridor. Marlow was nowhere to be seen. They walked on toward the turbolift. Garak looked around.

"Now, I do find myself wondering," he murmured, "where the admirable young lieutenant who has been stationed here has gone? He didn't exactly look the type to just wander off."

"He needed a break," Jedburgh said simply, in a manner that suggested he would not be elaborating.

The auction was well under way, and the bar was full, of customers and expectation. The bidding had just closed on the Ferengi automata; two collectors, coaxed on by Quark, had driven the price high. Odo watched the proceedings in wonder, shaking his head. Why anyone would buy any of this rubbish was beyond him. He watched as Quark took from Brixhta a little parcel.

"Well," said Dax, from beside him, "what about this next one?"

"Commander," Odo said firmly, "I am not buying *anything*. Perhaps you might consider refraining from asking me whether I will for every single lot?"

Dax was not listening; she was peering over the crowd toward the podium, trying to see what Brixhta had just handed Quark. "I wonder what that is?" she muttered.

"Now," Quark said, "we come to something small, but *very* special. If you take a look in your catalogues, ladies and gentlemen, this is lot number twenty-eight."

Dutifully, Odo thumbed at the padd, keying in *twenty-eight*. Dax leaned over his shoulder to look. A picture popped up; Odo saw that it was the little set of figures that he had noticed when conducting his search

of Brixhta's crates. There was an animation onscreen,
demonstrating how the dolls unfolded and then were
tucked back one inside another. Odo admired it once
again; the colors, the symbols, the design, the way that it
all interlocked so tidily.

"It really is such a pretty thing," Dax murmured. "You
know, I'm *sure* that Nerys would love it."

Odo ignored her, and began instead to listen to the bidding. It was slow at first—or so Quark seemed to think,
as he cajoled and wheedled the crowd, trying to tempt
them little by little to go higher. But there were only two
bidders, and one of those dropped out, shaking his head,
after only a few calls. Then, just as Quark was about to
close the sale, Odo slowly raised his hand.

If it was something of a surprise to Odo himself,
Quark was staring over at him in amazement. Odo enjoyed that for a moment—chances to wrong-foot Quark
so thoroughly didn't present themselves every day—and
then he saw Quark's voracious smile. Odo scowled back
at him, across the backs of the assembled company.

"Well, what do we have here?" Quark said gleefully,
curling his lip in delight. "A new bidder—and, I have to
say, a most unexpected one. Well, Constable, the bidding
is with you—at four slips of latinum."

The other bidder, an elderly vedek, responded but,
with Dax urging him on, Odo came back, almost
fiercely. His rival tugged at her earring and pulled a
face. She had, according to Odo's careful monitoring of
events, already picked up a number of small religious
artifacts—a series of icons of the Presati pantheon,
some Lissepian prayer beads. It seemed, from the way
that she was shaking her head, that this was one item too
many. Quark offered the bidding one more time, there
were no responses, and so he raised his little hammer

and then—*bang*. The figures were Odo's. Six slips of latinum. Odo felt a momentary thrill, and then his spirits sank at the enormity of what he had just done. He thought of trying to present these toys to Nerys; of how he would go about explaining to her this unusually impulsive piece of behavior. . . .

"Well *done*, Odo!" Dax was almost in raptures beside him. She patted his arm in delight. Odo grunted. He put aside his growing sense of regret at the purchase, and tried to bring his attention back to the real business of the day. Brixhta.

There was only one lot left now, the old food machine. Brixhta wheeled it out on a trolley, to widespread and appreciative murmuring from its potential owners. Odo began to shift toward the front, only half-listening to the bidding, which seemed to be going very high. It was of no particular interest to him; he just wanted to be in place, ready and waiting, close to Brixhta when finally the sale came to a close.

Quark hit the hammer down one last time. The antiquated food machine had been sold for what Odo thought was an extortionate two bars of latinum. To *Kaga*, of all people . . . Odo blinked. Now that he thought about it, he supposed it did make some kind of sense. . . .

"Ladies, gentlemen, buyers all," Quark said, "if you could make your way to the front, you can collect your purchases."

A queue hastily formed in front of Quark. Odo joined it, with Dax close behind. When they finally got to the front, Quark gave him one of his toothier smiles and held out a padd. Odo thumbed at it to pay. "A pleasure doing business with you, Odo," Quark said, handing over the box of dolls. He turned to Dax. "I suppose it's you I should be thanking?"

Dax shook her head. "Much as I'd love to have done you a favor, Quark, I can't take any credit for this," she replied. "Odo acted entirely on his own initiative."

"No." Quark stared back at Odo. "You know, for some reason," he said to Dax, "that makes me feel even better." He looked at Odo once again, shook his head, laughed, and turned to his next customer.

Odo set his sights firmly on Brixhta. He offered the box to Dax. "Would you make sure this gets to my office, please, Commander?" he said. "I still have some business to attend to here."

"Odo," Dax said, taking the box, her voice more serious, "are you really going to arrest him?"

So Bashir had mentioned that to her too? Information, Odo thought, did pass around the station at a quite alarming rate. "Watch," he replied bluntly.

The Talavian in front wanted to pay in her own currency, and it was a laborious process complicated by her haggling over the exchange rate with Brixhta. Odo folded his arms and waited patiently. Eventually, they came to an agreement. Quark, with a sly wink at Brixhta, took the chance at this point to step in and offer the woman his services to help her exchange her currency— but whatever arrangement Quark and Brixhta had come up with between them for *that* was not Odo's concern . . . for the moment, anyway. Odo moved politely aside to let the woman past, and then he stepped forward and put his hand on Brixhta.

"I wonder," Odo said, "if you would mind coming along with me?"

Brixhta seemed not in the least put out. If anything, he was almost preening. "Odo," he said, "with you—anywhere."

• • •

Sisko was escorted into a small room; it was very bare, and very functional. There was a table, a couple of chairs, and a single window. A flat lamp encased in the ceiling shed a grayish light that was successfully enfeebling the daylight. Sisko looked around with neither much hope nor eventual success for a way to turn it off. He took the seat facing the door, and waited.

A few minutes passed, and then the door slid open with quiet efficiency. Sisko stood up, but kept his fingertips in contact with the table in front of him, as if to anchor himself. A man walked in, and a security officer followed right behind him, taking up his position inside the room and near the door.

"It's all right," Sisko told him. "You can leave us alone."

The security officer nodded. "Will an hour be enough, sir?"

"I think so."

The officer left them alone. The other man sat down slowly across the table, keeping his eyes on Sisko as he took his seat. Seeing him again, Sisko realized he had expected to see something different about him. But the man opposite had not changed. Close-cropped hair; beard with white in it, still kept short and trim. No, he had not changed at all.

Sisko took his seat again, and each man warily appraised the other.

"Hello, Ben," Leyton said finally, breaking the silence. "You look older."

5

GARAK WATCHED with wry amusement as his companions took up their places. He let them escort him in this fashion out of the building. They passed through the security checks on the doors without any delay. Then they cut across the plaza and into the park, taking a direct route that avoided the pathways. The area was not busy, but there were some people moving around on business. Jedburgh, now leading the way, steered his party clear of them. Garak looked up appreciatively at the pale blue sky printed with white clouds. There was a taste of water in the air. It really was another beautiful day. Heavenly.

Down toward the bay it was even quieter. They hit a path that curved with the water, and began to walk along it. Garak saw no reason not to let the other two men continue flanking him. For the moment, he was content enough simply to enjoy the sight of the sky, and the feel of the air against his face. He was outdoors too rarely these days.

After they had been walking for a few minutes, the

pathway became shady; a long line of trees had been set there, and had grown enough so that their uppermost branches overhung the path. There was a little breeze, and the leaves were idly jostling one another. It all felt very fresh and clean, and the trees gave a comforting impression of privacy.

They came to a pleasant spot where a bench had been set beneath one of the trees, apparently for the benefit of anyone who wished to sit and look out across the water. As they approached, Jedburgh slowed down, and finally he came to a halt, standing and staring out across the lake. Garak came to stand beside him, resting his hands on the railings in front of them. The sunlight shifted through the branches of the trees overhead, dappling the water with light and shadow. The sea stretched out before them, rippling in the slight wind. Garak found himself marveling once again at the profligacy of the water.

After a moment or two, Jedburgh turned, and gestured toward the bench. "Why don't you take a seat, Mister Garak," he said.

Garak obligingly sat down, and Jedburgh joined him, sitting on his left-hand side. Enderby moved into the shadow of one of the trees, with his back to the water. From where he was standing, he had a good view of the path as it bent away from them in both directions.

"So, we hear you had something of an adventure last night," Jedburgh said.

"Something like that," Garak replied. He watched with fascination as Enderby arranged himself precisely against the tree. Enderby kept on glancing up to check that he had the best view of the path, and then he would make some minor adjustment to his position.

"Were the speeches interesting?"

"The whole evening was an education," Garak replied.

As he watched, Enderby shifted himself almost imperceptibly, and then gave a slight nod, apparently satisfied now with how he was placed. He was still holding the padds, clasped together in front of him.

Garak turned back to Jedburgh. "I thought that the keynote speaker in particular had many . . . intriguing things to say."

"Tomas Roeder is a man in whom we take a great deal of interest," Jedburgh said.

A little of his geniality had leached away. Garak took a moment to construct a careful response. "Well," he replied, eventually, "a war is hard enough to fight without high-profile people unhelpfully pointing out its ambiguities."

"There is no ambiguity about this war," Enderby stated, from beneath his tree.

Garak didn't reply. He himself had come to the opinion over the years that every situation had its ambiguities. War was certainly no exception; in fact, it was probably the paradigm case. Still, Garak could recognize devotion to duty when he saw it, and experience of *that* made him certain it would be pointless to argue with Enderby. But not everyone, Garak reminded himself, was busy selling out their homeland. Not everyone was fighting a war quite as ambivalent as his own. "Roeder," he tried again, "did intrigue me."

"Probably not as much as he intrigues us," Jedburgh said, "but it's good to know that we're starting from some common ground."

The breeze picked up. A prickle of apprehension went down Garak's spine. He watched as Enderby looked up and then down the path.

"Before we progress any further," Enderby said, "there is something that you must understand. Tomas

Roeder was Starfleet Intelligence's agent within the anti-war campaign."

Garak considered again the passion with which that speech had been delivered. "Then you should be glad he's on your side," he said, "because he's doing a *very* good job of being undercover—"

"You'll notice," Jedburgh drawled, "that Enderby said he *was* our agent."

Which presumably, Garak thought, staring across the water, meant that he was still an agent. But not Starfleet's. . . . "So you think Roeder has made a new cause of his own?" he said. It made sense. Converts usually made the best zealots.

Jedburgh waggled a finger. "Now, Enderby and I, we wondered about that for a while," he said. "But, you know, some people just aren't very enterprising." He shrugged lazily. "I don't know what happens to them. Maybe they get a bit institutionalized. They've gotten used to hierarchy. And it just doesn't feel right to them if they're not serving some kind of master." He nodded across at the figure standing in the shadow of the tree. "Take Enderby there. You know, I don't think he'd be happy if he had no one to report to. Not happy at all."

Garak took a moment to assess the full meaning of what Jedburgh had just said. And then he laughed into Jedburgh's face. "Forgive me my discourtesy," he said, incredulously, "but I'm afraid I find it very hard to believe that a Starfleet officer would sell out the Federation to the Dominion!"

Jedburgh leaned back against the arm of the bench. He looked at Garak, and began to shake his head. "Now, that's strange," he mused. He seemed genuinely perplexed. "Very strange indeed. Because I'd have thought that you of all people would understand that there might be circumstances where betraying your home could be necessary."

Garak's sense of foreboding became a little stronger. That barb was just a little too well aimed. It really must be a very good file that they had on him. He was starting to worry what else might be in it. "That's . . . a fair point," he conceded. "But are you saying that Roeder's apparent . . . conversion is necessary to the advancement of your interests?"

"There is no ambiguity," Enderby said again, "about this war."

"And, at this stage, Roeder's continued participation in events," Jedburgh said, "really would complicate things. Now," Jedburgh said, with a slow smile, "Enderby and I—we like a quiet life. We don't much like complications. And we both believe our lives would be a lot less complicated if Tomas Roeder were no longer on the scene. His little walk-on is over."

The privacy beneath the trees had begun to feel a little stifling. *Less complicated for who, exactly?* Garak inclined his head. "I have no doubt that that is the case, gentlemen," he said. "And although I am naturally troubled to see either of you inconvenienced in any fashion, this really is none of my concern—"

"Well, I'm going to have to contradict you there," Jedburgh said. "Because—from what we've heard—we think you're just the man to help us out."

"I'm gratified," Garak said, through gritted teeth, "to think that my reputation precedes me, but you really shouldn't believe everything you hear about me. The rumors are usually disgracefully vague and wholly inaccurate."

"We have something quite specific in mind," Enderby said.

Yes, I thought you might.

Garak rubbed his thumb against his palm. If he was being honest with himself, it hardly came as a surprise. Sisko, after all, was an honorable man; certainly far too honorable to keep his part in a double murder from his superiors. And while Garak would have gladly welcomed a small demonstration of personal loyalty from the captain, he had to admit that he had not really been expecting it.

"It only came up on our radar yesterday, but it did pique our interest," Jedburgh said. "So Enderby went off and did a little poking around. He's good at that kind of thing. You see, we were both intrigued to find out what the hell could possibly connect a senator to a forger. Apart from them both being on DS9 at the same time. Oh, and both of them turning up dead shortly afterward, of course." He leaned past Garak and addressed Enderby directly, counting off on his fingers. "A senator . . . a forger . . . was there anybody else?"

"According to my information," Enderby said, from the shade, "the senator was traveling with four bodyguards."

Jedburgh beamed. "I just don't know what I'd do without him," he confided in Garak.

"Oh, I'm sure you'd cope," Garak said acidly.

"Maybe, maybe." Jedburgh grinned. He counted off four more, holding up all the fingers on one hand, and his thumb on the other. "So, each one of those comes with . . ." He looked over at the tree again. "How long is it now, Enderby?"

"Twenty-five years each," Enderby said. "Served concurrently, however."

Jedburgh whistled. "Well, I'd say myself the senator is the one that really counts. Particularly with all the visitors we have around these parts at the moment. Still—

twenty-five years for a forger . . ." He trailed off, shaking his head and looking around. Garak glanced at him surreptitiously, and tried to guess not so much what was coming next, but how it exactly would be phrased.

Enderby took a couple of steps away from the tree, and joined them on the bench, sitting down on Garak's right. Garak felt a perverse admiration for the precision of the maneuver, which pinned him once again between them both. He stared ahead, at the railings and the emptiness beyond. There was, he thought, a distinct lack of exit routes. He gave Enderby a cautious, sideways look. Enderby had placed the padds in front of him, on his knees. He was holding them in place. They were perfectly symmetrical. On Garak's other side, Jedburgh had folded his arms and was now leaning back comfortably against the bench.

"But, you know," Jedburgh was saying, "there are far worse places than a Federation prison. Tell me, Garak," he continued, conversationally, "just how long *is* it since you were last on Cardassia Prime?"

People kept on asking him that question, Garak thought. Very solicitous of them—although he had to say that when Sisko had asked it, it hadn't made him go cold. Garak sucked in a breath of air. He looked at his hands, and then clasped them together.

"Seven years," he said, leaning forward, and staring down at the gravel on the path beneath his feet. The next bit of the conversation played out almost exactly as he expected it would.

"You also made a very short trip back two years ago," Enderby corrected, from just behind him. He was pressing the edge of one of the padds into his palm again. Garak watched with morbid fascination. He pictured the red mark it must be making against the white flesh.

"It's still a long time," Jedburgh said. "And seven years is a lot longer. To be away from home. So I'd imagine." He stopped. Garak resisted the temptation to glance up at him. "You anxious to go back there, Garak?" he said.

Garak stared down at the stones on the ground. He swallowed. "Not under the current administration," he said. "As I'm sure you are *quite* aware."

"Yeah. In fact, we were kind of counting on that." Jedburgh leaned forward. Garak turned to look at him. They were face to face, and Jedburgh wasn't smiling at all. "You ready to do business now?"

Sisko and Leyton talked for a little while, about inconsequentialities. The hour wore on. Sisko began to wonder whether this had been a good idea. Leyton had been shifting restlessly in his chair. He was clearly having the same thought. After the conversation ground to a halt for the third or fourth time, Leyton leaned back in his chair and regarded Sisko thoughtfully.

"Ben," he said, "why have you come here?"

"What makes you think I had a particular reason?"

"Well, we've talked about my health, your health, and the weather. We've even talked a bit about how the war is progressing in your part of the quadrant. But you must only be here on Earth for a few days, and you must have a very busy schedule while you're home." Leyton gave him an unfriendly smile. "I can't believe you took a whole heap of time out of your diary, just to spend an hour with your old commanding officer."

He had thought that Leyton was unchanged, but now there was a doubt—a thought that there was something different about him after all. Sisko suddenly wanted to look away from the other man in front of him. He began to search restlessly around the impersonal room, but there was nothing to take his attention. "I did want to see how you were doing," he said. "But you're right," he confessed, glancing at Leyton again, "that isn't the only reason I came today."

Leyton gave a short nod; his suspicions were confirmed. "So . . . are you going to tell me why you're here?"

Sisko stared down at the table. Anywhere other than at Leyton. Now that it came down to it, he found himself unsure of how or where to begin. So he picked the place that let him make the most sense of it all; the place that, at the time, had seemed to justify every decision that came afterwards. Sisko started with the casualty lists. And he went on from there. He found that it got easier as he went on; got easier to tell Leyton everything. To tell him all about biomimetic gel and optolythic datarods. All about a senator, and a forger. All about making a deal with the devil.

He got to the point where the Romulans declared war on the Dominion, and then stopped. He thought of going on to tell Leyton about his conversation the previous day with Ross and Batanides, but his voice died away. It was, Sisko realized, because he wanted to give Leyton the chance to say something. The chance to speak his piece. Leyton had bent the law—had broken it—to suit his ends. He had ordered officers to open fire on other officers; had been prepared to murder for his ends. Was it right, Sisko thought, that Leyton was locked up while he remained free?

Leyton had been listening to his account in silence, and with no reaction. Partway through, he had leaned his elbows on the table, and rested his chin in his hands. When Sisko finished, he stayed in that position, just looking at him. Sisko looked back. Then Leyton relaxed, and put his hands down on the table in front of him. He interleaved his fingers, and contemplated them for a moment or two, before looking up again at Sisko, and giving him a wry smile.

"You know," he said, "as you get older, you come to realize you've cast yourself, or you've ended up being cast, in a lot of different roles. I've been an officer, an admiral, a prisoner—" He glanced around him. "—a traitor . . ." Something about Leyton's expression suggested to Sisko that perhaps he thought that the last of those had been miscast. "But never, in my wildest dreams," Leyton finished, "did I imagine myself playing the part of *your* confessor." He gave Sisko a sharp, calculating look. "Have you told this story to anyone else?"

"Yes," Sisko answered, and left Leyton to work out the rest.

A look of comprehension spread across Leyton's face. "I see," he said, and gave a slight smile. "And there hasn't even been a slap on the wrist, has there?"

"No."

Leyton gave a short laugh. "Well, what the hell were you expecting, Ben?" He waved a hand around. "To join me here?"

"I was expecting *something!*" It exploded from him. "Surely *someone* has to be held accountable for what was done? For what was *allowed* to be done?" With an abrupt and angry movement, Sisko got up from his chair. He began prowling around the little room, as if he were the one that was caged.

"So that's what you want from me, is it?" Leyton was watching him as he paced up and down. "You want me to tell you that you did the wrong thing? Then you're going to have to wait a long time, Ben. Because from everything you've told me, I don't think you did. In fact, I think you did the right thing—"

"But he *murdered* them!"

"No, Ben," Leyton said, shaking his head emphatically. "It was war."

"There are *rules* to war—!"

"Ben, wake up!" Leyton's anger lanced through his words. "Listen to yourself! You don't still really believe that, do you?"

Sisko came to a halt, by the window. He tapped the frame, and stared out onto a blank space of rough grass with a high wall rising beyond it. It seemed to him to be a bleak outlook. Leyton was still speaking from behind him.

"Look around you, Ben," he was saying. "Look at the situations you've faced. Look at the choices you've made. Do you *really* still think there's a rule book you should be following? This isn't the Academy any more. This is the way the world works."

Sisko stared out of the window. "Is that what you told yourself?" he asked, very quietly. "Is that how you justified it to yourself?" He looked back over his shoulder.

Leyton just smiled at him. "What makes you think I felt a need for justifications? Or feel a need even now?" he said. "The Federation was threatened, Ben. And I tried to defend it. It was my duty. That's the only justification I need."

Sisko turned round to face him. "You went too far," he said.

"And you didn't?"

Sisko said nothing. A shaft of bright sunlight came in from behind him, hitting the gray table just in front of Leyton. Sisko could see little bits of dust swirling in the dry air. It suddenly struck him what it was that was different about Leyton. He had hardly ever seen him out of uniform before. Sisko leaned his head back against the wall, and stared up at the bare ceiling. Tried to keep it all under control.

"Aren't you angry?" Sisko said, at last. His voice sounded composed. Like the voice of a completely different man.

"Angry?" Leyton was puzzled. "Why would I be angry?"

Sisko continued examining the ceiling. It was turning out not to be so bare after all. There was a crack over in one corner. "You're here," he said. "And I'm not."

"But that doesn't make me angry, Ben. If anything, I feel . . . validated."

"Validated . . . ?"

"Well, from everything you've told me," Leyton sighed, "it seems my real mistake was to make my move too soon. Another year, eighteen months . . . Maybe what I did would have seemed more comprehensible to others. I think perhaps *you* understand my actions a little better now." He gave a quiet laugh. "Now that you've seen a little more of how the universe *really* works."

"It should have worked differently." Sisko remembered how Garak had come back to him, again and again, asking for just a little bit more each time. "There was chance after chance to call a halt, but every time, it just went a step further. Every time. It *should* have worked differently."

Leyton did not answer. Sisko listened to the silence for a while, and then gave up and looked at him. Leyton pointed at the empty chair in front of him. "Sit down, Ben," he said. There was still something of the commander about him. Sisko pushed himself away from the wall, and took his seat again. Leyton wove his fingers together again, and sat for a moment quietly, deep in thought.

"When I put troops on every street corner," he said, at last, "I know that many people saw them as a threat. To our way of life. Our liberties. I know you saw them that way," he glanced at Sisko. "Saw them as dangerous."

Sisko nodded. "I did. They were."

"But what I saw," Leyton carried on, "was something much more threatening. I could see the alternative— Jem'Hadar on every street corner. Jem'Hadar, here, on Earth." He shook his head. "I wonder if you saw a little of what I could see. Can still see."

"What happened . . . they were crimes. Acts of violence. An abuse of power—"

"And you thought governments didn't do that kind of thing?" Leyton raised his eyebrows. "No, they just have a more highly developed apparatus for dealing out violence. More bureaucracy, certainly. Sometimes we even call it law—"

The door slid open, and Leyton stopped speaking. The guard came back in. Sisko looked over at him, and nodded.

"Right on time," Leyton noted. "They're good like that." He glanced at Sisko. "I'm sorry, Ben," he said, frankly. "I know you came looking for a reprimand. But you're not going to get it from me. Still, I'm glad you came," he said, as he stood up. "I'm glad the war is in your hands. And as for the rest of it . . ." He looked around the little room, and then gave Sisko a rueful smile. "Well, we all make mistakes. And then we have to pay the price. Whatever that turns out to be."

Leyton offered his hand across the table. As Sisko stood up and shook it, Leyton added, "Don't torture yourself over this. You did the right thing. And you had the sense to do it at the right moment." He smiled. "I wish I'd had some of your judgment," he said. "Or, at least," he added, "more of your sense of timing."

He left, and Sisko went back out into a bright and indifferent world.

Garak predicted they would only need to talk for a short while longer. He was right, but still it was long enough for the wind to lift and send clouds scudding quickly over the sky. The sunlight sharpened in intensity, and the shadows grew longer beneath the trees. By the time they had finished their conversation, there was a definite threat of rain.

"We all done?" Jedburgh said. "Enderby? You got anything you want to add?"

Enderby slipped the padds into his inside pocket, and stood up. He looked at the heavy sky, pursed his lips in disdain, and fastened a button on his jacket. "I believe that's everything, Jedburgh," he said. He was still blurring that last sound, Garak noticed.

Jedburgh heaved himself up. Garak made himself relax against the bench. He stretched out his legs and crossed them in front of him. "By the way," he said, addressing Enderby. "It's three years."

Enderby looked down at him. "I beg your pardon?"

"It's been three years, since I last set foot on Cardassia Prime. Not two."

Enderby blinked at him, and it occurred to Garak that it might be in distress. Enderby reached up to touch his face, and tapped a fingertip against his cheekbone a couple of times. "Are you sure?" The finger stopped tapping, but it stayed in place, Garak saw.

"Mister Enderby," he replied, "my ability to visit Cardassia Prime has been severely curtailed over the last few years. You can rest assured that I know *exactly* when I was last there." He arranged himself a little more comfortably on the bench. "You might want to consider updating your files."

There was a noise like a lightly wounded rhino. Garak had never heard, nor even heard of a rhino, but it still took him a few moments to realize that Jedburgh was laughing.

Jedburgh had still not quite controlled himself when he stuck out his hand, offering it to his guest. Garak looked at it, and then pointedly folded his arms. Jedburgh did not take the slightest offense. He just raised his hand and gave Garak a mock salute. "You know," he drawled, "it's been a real pleasure meeting you."

"Oh yes," Garak replied, "it's certainly been a lot of fun."

Jedburgh grinned at him. "You won't need our help to get back inside HQ," he said. "And I'm guessing you might stay out here for a while and get a breath of fresh air. Collect your thoughts. But I'd be obliged to you if you could remember that I told that young lieutenant we'd only keep you for an hour at the outside. I guess he might start worrying if you don't turn up. And you're not really going to want to draw more attention to yourself right now than is strictly necessary." He nodded in farewell. "Good luck, Garak," he said. "Be seeing you."

I certainly hope not.

They walked off back along the path. Garak stayed on the bench and watched them for a little while, until the curve of the path put them out of sight. Then he leaned forward again and stared at the ground. After a moment or two, he reached down and picked up a handful of gravel. He went to stand in front of the railings, where Enderby had just been, under the shadow of the tree. He picked out one of the pebbles, tested its weight and its shape, and then flipped it into the water. It landed with a gentle splash, and the ripples spread outward. Garak gave them serious thought.

So Sisko had indeed decided to come clean, as he had suspected he would; and now Garak found himself attracting the full attention of Starfleet Intelligence—and not in any way he had been hoping for when he had agreed to come along on this little jaunt to Earth. Assassination certainly lay within his field of expertise—as Vreenak's case well demonstrated—but Garak took a certain pride in his work. Bespoke, rather than off-the-rack. He did not simply murder on demand.

Why come to me? he wondered. *Why not just use one of their own men?* If Roeder really had gone over to the Dominion—and Garak had no intention of taking on face value everything those two misfits had just told him—then there must have been some kind of plan to remove him before Garak's trip to Earth had been arranged. But all Garak knew for certain was that now two officers from Starfleet Intelligence had decided that Garak was the man for the job. He had no idea what else had been planned. He had no real idea why; there were many reasons that Starfleet Intelligence might decide that Roeder was now surplus to requirements. Gone over to the Dominion? Garak snorted. It was just as likely that Roeder was exactly what he seemed—yet another disillusioned idealist, but one vocal enough and influential enough to be an unwelcome complication in the midst of a difficult and expensive war. Garak simply had no idea. And that, really, was the problem: There were far too many unknowns for his taste. Far too many. He took aim, and threw another pebble into the water. It landed dead in the center of a clump of rocks. Assassination was a precision instrument. You didn't just wander in off the street and shoot someone. . . . Well, you *could*, but there tended to be ramifications to murder, and Garak did have a somewhat fastidious attitude toward preparation. Particularly when he was this easily identifiable. The holoreconstruction of the assailant the witness saw fleeing from the scene—it would not need to be all that accurate, would it?

He rolled another stone around in his hand. Supposing he did kill Roeder, he thought, and further supposing that it all went to plan and nobody saw a Cardassian anywhere near the scene of the crime? Garak was by no means naïve enough to assume that would be the end of it. Starfleet Intelligence would have yet another hold over him and—as Vreenak's case well demonstrated once again—they would not be averse to using it. Garak took that personally. He took it seriously, too. He had experienced extortion at the hands of a Starfleet officer in the past, and he hadn't enjoyed it much that time either. This stone hit the water with greater force than the ones that had gone before.

Of course, he always had the option *not* to kill Roeder. Now, *there* was a bold move, he thought, laughing to himself as he picked out another stone, and it was probably not one that his new associates would expect. There were risks to it, of course—a hastily arranged and not remotely welcome return to Cardassia Prime being one of them. . . . He clutched hard at the stone and took a deep breath. It was not a risk he could take without having allies—but who could he get on his side? These men were part of Starfleet Intelligence, and they were obviously a significant part. Chaplin and Marlow would be of no use: Jedburgh and Enderby certainly outranked them. And here, Garak thought, was another problem of the unknown; he had no idea just how far their influence ran.

Were there limits to it? Was there *anyone* he could approach safely? It was a distinct possibility that even a whole glittering constellation of admirals would be unable to help. He clenched and unclenched his fist, staring down at the pebble lying on his palm.

There was always Sisko . . . Sisko, whose tussle with his conscience was what had put Garak into this predicament. Sisko, who thought he didn't owe Garak a thing. Who had once blackmailed him to go back to Cardassia Prime . . . Garak found himself fondly imagining the conversation he could have with Sisko. *I have a favor to ask you, Captain. Just a very small matter. Could you possibly introduce me to the man your intelligence service has asked me to assassinate for them? You know which man I mean—the peace campaigner. It seems that your government wants him dead.* If the captain had been experiencing a crisis of conscience before, it really would be nothing to the effect *that* piece of information would have on him. Unfortunately, Garak was fairly certain that, not long after, the conversation would take its usual downward plunge into recrimination—and Sisko did hit *very* hard. . . . Even worse, if you took into account the captain's current flirtation with sanctimony, Sisko would probably tell Garak do the right thing and accept the prison sentence as his due. And Garak had a number of very cogent objections to raise against those who wanted to put him into a confined space.

Ahead, the water was rippling now without any intervention on Garak's part. The wind had been picking up steadily, and the sky emptying of its color, turning from blue to gray. Garak pressed his hands together, rubbing the remaining pebbles around within his palms. There was another option he had yet to consider. *What if I did it,* he thought, *but I got caught?* He felt himself go cold,

colder than the wind was making him. There were not
that many Cardassians on Earth, and fewer still with a
known predilection toward political killings. If he was
seen at all . . . murdering a man of peace . . . if there was
the *slightest* thing to connect him to Roeder's death . . .
Would it break up the conference? Would it break up the
alliance . . .? Garak carefully selected another stone.
That would be something of a shame, given the lengths to
which he had gone in order to stitch the whole thing together in the first place. . . . Or was *that* why Jedburgh
and Enderby had come to him? He rolled the stone between his thumb and forefinger. It would all be so much
easier to blame Roeder's death on a Cardassian, after all.
Much easier to keep the alliance together after the event.
Treachery, disloyalty, murder . . . what else could anyone
expect from a Cardassian? Would it turn out that Garak
too had been "working for the Dominion" all along?
Garak flung the stone into the water. That, he thought,
would be one irony too many.

Although it did bring him to one more option. One so
obvious it was almost ridiculous. One he was certain his
new acquaintances would not have considered or—if
they had—would have dismissed as incredible. He could
talk to Roeder himself.

Once Brixhta was safely ensconced in a holding cell,
with a pair of security officers stationed at the door, Odo
checked the time. Dealing with the Hamexi had taken up
almost all of his morning and, consequently, he was very
late making his second round of the Promenade. Nevertheless, Odo had to admit, as he walked along a little
more briskly than usual, it was a weight off his mind. He
could now concentrate all his energies on the arrival of
the *Ariadne* . . . almost all his energies, that was. He still

was not entirely satisfied yet that he had got to the bottom of the business arrangement that had been put in place between Quark and Brixhta. . . .

When he reached the entrance to the infirmary, Odo hesitated. He was still behind schedule. He glanced inside. It looked quiet. He decided he might as well keep Bashir informed about what was happening with Brixhta.

Nurse Jabara nodded him through to the back of the infirmary. Bashir was in there; so was O'Brien, who was sitting on the edge of a biobed. Bashir was standing next to him, running a medical tricorder over O'Brien's left hand. Odo observed with fascination, recognizing someone else who followed their own very precise rituals.

As he watched, the cut on O'Brien's hand began to heal. "Is that serious?" he asked the doctor.

"It will be as good as ever in just a moment . . ." Bashir murmured.

"Good," said Odo. "We can hardly afford to have the chief out of action at the present time."

"All will be well. . . ." Bashir glanced up at Odo from his work. "Well, Constable," he said. "I hear you've been very busy this morning."

Odo frowned. Had Bashir heard about Brixhta already?

"Have I?" he said.

Bashir grinned up at him again. "Jadzia tells me you bought something for Kira at the auction."

"Oh, really?" O'Brien said, looking up at Odo with great interest.

"Does *anything* remain private on this station?" Odo said.

"I shouldn't think so for a moment," Bashir laughed.

"We have to have something to talk about," O'Brien added. "So—what did you get her?"

Odo scowled at him.

"Dolls, Jadzia said," Bashir offered, with just the faintest glimmer of a smile.

"Dolls?" O'Brien frowned. "Doesn't sound much like Kira's sort of thing."

"I believe that they have religious significance," Odo said quickly.

"Now, *that* sounds much more like her. . . . Hey, careful with that, Julian!" O'Brien glowered up at him. "That hurt!"

Julian shot him a warning look. "Behave yourself, Miles," he murmured. "And do try to sit still."

Odo watched for a moment or two, then said, as casually as he could manage, "I thought you might be interested in hearing how matters are progressing with Brixhta."

"Of course you did," Bashir murmured. "Well?" he said, with a slight sigh, looking down at the tricorder.

"I arrested him."

It was very interesting, Odo thought, watching Bashir freeze, how the human response to surprise fell into two main categories.

"You *arrested* him?" Bashir repeated.

Sometimes they reacted on instinct and fought back.

"Yes," Odo confirmed.

And sometimes they seemed to take a long time to process news. Even when their brains were genetically enhanced. Bashir seemed to be weighing the tricorder.

"You know, Odo," O'Brien said, "When Quark said that, he was only trying to get a reaction from you."

"I know," Odo said. "And he got a reaction. I did exactly what he suggested. Brixhta is in a holding cell right now."

"Are you actually allowed to do that, Odo?" O'Brien

said. "I mean, I would have thought there were laws about that kind of thing?"

"I'm well within my rights," Odo said firmly.

Bashir put down the tricorder with an unusual amount of force. "I find that very hard to believe," he said, folding his arms and looking directly at Odo.

Odo gestured to a padd that was lying nearby. "May I?" he said.

"Be my guest," Bashir replied, enunciating each word very carefully.

Odo punched up the details of the Starfleet Special Order. Then, without another word, he handed the padd back to Bashir. The doctor started to read.

O'Brien leaned over to see. " '. . . *neutralize security threats to the station by whatever means necessary,*' " he read out. He whistled softly. "That's a bit vague. Do you not think you might be stretching it a bit, Odo? Is it meant to include theft, do you think?"

Bashir, meanwhile, had gone very still. Odo noted this immobility with fascination. He was sure that what Bashir was exhibiting was fury. At last, the doctor opened his mouth to say something, but Odo spoke first. "I know what you are going to say, Doctor," he said. "But I *do* consider Brixhta to pose a serious threat to the security of this station—"

"To your pride, you mean!" Bashir shot back.

Odo retreated, a little hurt. "I think that's unfair."

Bashir looked at back him. "I'm sorry, that was uncalled-for." He stared down at the padd again, embarrassed, Odo thought, by his outburst. After a moment or two, he put the padd down and turned his attention back to treating O'Brien's hand.

"Well," O'Brien said at last, into the silence, "I suppose if it sets your mind at ease . . ." He frowned. "I don't know though. I don't think I like the idea of locking someone up like that. It all seems a bit like Cardassian justice to me."

"It's not," Odo said, curtly. "It's not like Cardassian justice at all." He picked up the padd, and made sure the text of the special order was no longer visible. Then he put it back down. "Thank you for your time, Doctor," he said. "Chief, I hope the hand gets better soon." Then he retreated from the infirmary, back to the routines of the Promenade.

Garak had always flattered himself that he could spot a liar within seconds of a man opening his mouth. He had seen only a very little of Roeder—and he accepted he only had himself to blame for that—but from what he *had* seen, Garak was ready to believe that Roeder was the real thing. It was the passion. There was something about it you just couldn't fake. If Roeder was working for the Dominion, then they all were.

Garak contemplated the ground.

Why do they really *want him dead? And what would Roeder himself say if I asked him?* That would certainly make for another fascinating conversation—and Cardassians did excel at conversation. . . . Of course, Garak thought, with a certain gruesome cheer, he could well have got the whole thing completely wrong. It was not beyond the realms of possibility that Roeder was exactly as corrupted as everyone else. In which case, he would deserve everything he got—and it might as well be Garak as anyone else to deliver the coup de grâce. But in this woeful web in which he was now thoroughly woven, there was one thing Garak was sure about. If Roeder died at his hands, it would be on his own terms. Not Starfleet's.

Garak felt a spot of water against his face. It had finally started raining. He peered up again at the sky. It was all gray now, and some of the clouds had begun to look threatening. The evening was drawing on. He dropped the last few pebbles on the ground, got back onto the path, and hurried to get inside before the downpour.

Transporters?

"There are, in total, twenty-five personnel and cargo transporters throughout the station. Personnel transporters are located all around the station; cargo transporters operate within the docking ring. The system itself is of Cardassian design."

Very good. Turbolifts?

"The turbolift system runs on two distinct networks—for personnel and for cargo—and operates across all habitable and operational sections of the station. Shall I describe the composition of the turbo cabs? It is something of a mouthful."

You need only remember it, not repeat it. Now: What procedures are conducted following a breach in security?

When Odo got back to his office, the dolls were waiting for him. All five of them were lined up in a row on his desk, facing the door, as if to greet him on his return. Dax had left a note there for him too, propped up in front of the little yellow kai. *She is going to love them,* she had written.

Odo growled, and reached for the kai, twisting the figure in half with a grim and purposeful ferocity. As if the arrival of the *Ariadne* the following morning and Bashir's outburst were not quite sufficient. Trust Dax to introduce even more chaos into an already unsatisfactorily turbulent day.

6

AUGER STEPPED OFF THE TURBOLIFT and had his first encounter with the color and the commotion of the Promenade.

The lighting didn't go with the architecture, was his immediate thought. The place was meant to be a whole lot darker. And the effect it had was weird—all the metal detail on the walls stood out more harshly than it should. Auger had to blink a few times before things settled a bit and began to make sense. Just before they'd docked, Steyn had managed to fit in a two-minute course in Bajoran history. The Bajorans owned the station, Auger knew, but it had been built by Cardassians, and now it was run by Starfleet. No wonder everything looked just a little bit out of place. But understanding why still didn't stop him losing his bearings, and it didn't help that the walls were bending away from him. He realized he was swaying a little. There was a strange scent too, pungent and spicy. It reminded him a bit of the chapels back at home. Steyn had definitely said something about the Bajorans being religious. . . . Auger decided that what he could smell was incense. And then there was the noise, and the people making the noise, with strange clothes and stranger faces. . . . It was all a lot bigger and busier than he had ever imagined a place could be.

Steyn came up beside him, and put her arm around his shoulders. "So—what do you think, Auger?"

"Different," he said, at last. His voice came out small; it sounded lost in all the noise.

Steyn began to laugh. "You should have seen it when it was full of Cardassians. Terok Nor, they called it then."

"Did the lights work properly back then?" Auger asked.

Steyn gave him a curious look. "How did you know that?" she said. "Oh, never mind." She shook her head. "I don't think I'll ever work you out. Well, you're right—it did used to be a lot darker here. Cardassians don't like bright light so much."

From behind them, Mechter said, "It was a lot easier to do business here back then."

Auger sensed a beat of silence and then Steyn replied, "Yeah, well, life is full of all kinds of disappointment. Look," she said, "Here's our welcome committee, I think."

Auger looked over to where she was pointing. Some people were approaching. People in uniforms. Two men in front; one was in a black and gold uniform, the other was tan. The eight men behind them were carrying weapons. Auger felt things begin to sway again. He was glad when Steyn gripped his shoulder a little more.

The man in tan spoke to them first. Most other new people that Auger met had something about them that helped him read them. The man in black and gold was about as open as you could get. But the man wearing tan was different. His face was flat and empty. After a moment or two staring at it, Auger had to look away.

"Captain Steyn," the man in tan was saying, "I'm the station's chief of security, Odo. We have spoken several times already." He gestured to the man beside him. "Mr. O'Brien, our chief of operations. He'll be leading the team that will be carrying out the repairs on your ship. I imagine he'll want to meet your own engineer. . . ."

The man in black and gold stepped forward and shook hands with Steyn. "We'll get straight to work, Captain," he said. "Won't keep you here longer than we need to."

"I left my engineer on board," Steyn was saying. "Trasser. If he's horizontal, kick him. That usually works."

The man called O'Brien laughed. Yes, Auger thought, there was nothing hidden there. He risked another look at the empty man.

"These gentlemen," Odo pointed behind him, "are, of course, here to look after your cargo as we bring it onto the station."

"I'm very glad to see them," said Steyn. "And I bet Mr. Mechter here is too. . . . As I told you, he represents the consortium that employed me to carry their cargo. I'm sure he'd like to accompany us while we bring it onto the station."

Mechter nodded silently. The man with the empty face considered him for a moment, then turned to look pointedly at Auger.

"Oh," said Steyn, offhandedly, "that's just Auger. He's part of my crew. Hasn't traveled much, so I thought he'd like a look at the station." She frowned at Odo. "That is all right, isn't it?"

The man called Odo continued his inspection of Auger. Auger stared back. He had made a mistake, he quickly realized, in thinking of this man as being empty. If anything, it was the opposite; in fact, Auger thought there was more wound up within him than in anyone he had ever met before. Still, looking at that flat, expression-less face, Auger was fairly certain he wouldn't like to play him at poker. After a moment or two, the not-empty man nodded and, seeming to be satisfied, he looked away and back at the captain, much to Auger's relief.

"He's your responsibility, Captain Steyn," he said.

"Of course," she said. "Well, shall we think about getting the cargo on the station then?"

The third morning session ended with only provisional agreement between the delegates about the access they were willing to provide each other to front line starbases. Sisko watched Veral. She had stood up but as yet made no move to leave the room, and was slowly picking up the padds that had been laid out in front of her.

Ross leaned in toward Sisko, shielding his mouth. "Wanted a word with you after yesterday's session, Ben," he murmured. "You went off in a bit of a rush."

Veral was now piling up the padds, one of top of another.

"I'm sorry," Sisko replied. Keeping his voice quiet. "Was it urgent?"

"Not particularly, I just wanted your opinion on a point of detail on Romulan access to our starbases. The commander of Starbase 375 had more than a few security concerns, but I managed to come up with a couple of bright ideas that should keep him happy."

"Sorry you couldn't find me."

Ross contemplated him. "I thought you might have gone to see your father, but when I contacted your sister she said you hadn't been in touch for a day or so."

"I wasn't at the restaurant," Sisko said. "I went to see James Leyton."

A silence opened up between them. Veral had turned

her attention from the padds to the cup from which she had been drinking all morning. She twisted the handle until it was at ninety degrees from her.

"Oh," Ross said. He pressed the back of his hand against his mouth. It muffled his voice even further, and Sisko had to lean in closer to hear him.

"How was he?"

"Unrepentant."

Ross said nothing.

"Even more so," Sisko said, "by the time I left."

Veral laid the spoon straight beneath the handle of her cup. This ritual complete, she tucked the padds beneath her arm, and addressed the two men opposite. "A productive morning, wouldn't you agree?" she said.

Sisko nodded. Ross made a noise that could count as agreement.

"I am very glad," she continued, "that we came to a resolution on the staff we are able to make available to your starbases. Let us hope the afternoon progresses toward putting some of them there."

"I'm sure we'll have every success," Ross said, with an official smile that Veral met with one so correct Sisko was sure it could cut.

"Until this afternoon," she said, then nodded a farewell, and made for the door. Sisko glanced over his shoulder to watch her leave. The whole room was emptying, he saw, quite slowly, since some of the other delegates were hanging back to continue conversations. Sisko turned his attention back to the table in front of him. He reached across for the spoon Veral had so carefully positioned, picked it up, and began to twist it between his forefinger and his thumb.

"Leyton said," Sisko continued, "that he was glad the war was in my hands."

Ross seemed to consider that for a moment, then he stood up, and pushed the chair under the table. He leaned against it, bringing himself close to Sisko once again. "Well, so am I," he said. He straightened himself up again. "Would you mind if I gave you a bit of advice, Ben?"

"Be my guest."

"Try to get away from here, even if you can only manage a few hours. Try and put it all aside. And no more good works." Ross gave him a dry look. "Including prison visits. Go and see your folks."

"I'd love to," he said, "but I can't tonight." He looked up at Ross and admonished him with the spoon. "Don't tell me you've forgotten? We have to go and drink champagne and make small talk."

Ross's face fell. "Hell, that's all I need right now." He stifled a yawn. "Oh well," he said, with a sigh, "at least Councillor Huang knows how to put on a good show. I suppose we may as well enjoy ourselves." He patted the back of Sisko's chair. "I'll see you later, Ben."

Sisko stayed in his seat and stared out of the window ahead. Outside, he guessed, the midday sun would be high in the sky. Daylight should have been pouring in, bright and revealing, but instead its glare was curbed by the tinted glass. He played with the spoon, catching a little of the light with it and reflecting it onto the tabletop opposite. Perhaps Ross was right, he thought, he should try to put it aside. It was done, and there was nothing to be said about it. And he still had a war to win. . . .

"Captain?"

Sisko turned and looked round. Garak was standing beside him, one hand resting on the back of the next chair along, just where Ross had been, moments before.

"You seem reflective," Garak said. "Am I disturbing you?"

"No," Sisko replied. "No, it's all right."

"Do you mind if I sit down?" Garak tapped his fingers against the chair.

Sisko gestured with the spoon. "Be my guest."

Garak sat down and settled himself, and then turned to look at Sisko, an odd gleam in his eye. Sisko twisted at the handle of the spoon.

"What did you want, Garak?"

"Oh," Garak said, and smiled, "nothing particularly important. It was just that . . . I had a small favor that I wanted to ask you."

Steyn was proving more competent than her tardiness at keeping appointments had suggested to Odo. She was thoroughly briefed on the arrangements that had been made to unload the latinum from the *Ariadne*. Odo had been tempted to put it down to the severe Lissepian who seemed never to be farther than a few inches from her shoulder, but he had grudgingly come to the decision that Steyn was capable enough in her own right. For example, now that he had taken a closer look, Odo had to admit that Steyn had not been overstating the case about her security systems. The biometric scanning systems she had in place were extremely impressive.

The systems were permanently scanning for life-forms within three meters of the crates, and any signature that passed within that space which did not match those contained in its database would automatically trigger two forcefields. One around the crate, to keep them out, and another a few feet away, to keep them in. Since the system could not be altered remotely, adding Odo's signature to the ones that the scanners would accept meant that

Steyn had to go on ahead to enable Odo to come on board the *Ariadne*. He and Mechter stood in uneasy silence until Steyn gave them the go ahead to join her.

The hold of the *Ariadne* was cramped with the three of them inside. Odo surreptitiously made himself a few millimeters thinner. Steyn opened the crate, and Odo looked inside. A rack of vials, nestled within, each one filled with liquid latinum. No children's toys this time, Odo thought. These were the kind of thing for which people might even kill. He glanced at Steyn, and she nodded. He picked up one of the vials. Mechter moved in a little more. Odo contracted another millimeter, and then gestured to some tiny marks engraved on the flat bottom of the vial.

"What are these?" he asked.

"Identification number," Steyn explained. "Each one is unique to a specific vial. When the latinum gets to the other end, the recipient has to match their own numbers up to the codes they have before the latinum is credited to them."

"But they have to get past the biometric scanners before they can begin to read off the codes," Odo said.

Steyn smiled at him. "That's right," she said.

"I'm gratified that I've been permitted to get so close," Odo said.

"Couldn't do it without you, I'm sure," Steyn said cheerfully. She glanced over her shoulder, and her expression became a little dryer. "We'll need to be where you are, Mr. Mechter," she said, "if we're going to get these bloody things off the ship."

Now we come to the weak spot. Where will you come out on the Promenade?

"A turbolift on the main floor."

Look to your left. Describe what is there.

"Close by, there are shops and restaurants. They will all be closed."

Remember that. Look to your right and describe what is there.

"There is a staircase leading up to a platform which overlooks the thoroughfare. On the main floor, beyond the staircase, there is a clothing shop. Next door to the clothing shop is the assay office."

And which way do you go?

"Right, of course."

Odo removed the crate of latinum from the *Ariadne* himself. Once it was off the ship, he and Steyn, with Mechter close behind, brought it through the cargo bay. Four of Odo's officers kept the cargo bay secure while the crate and its convoy transferred to the turbolift. Steyn had been unwilling to risk the biometric scanners in the transporter and, besides, Odo wanted to have the latinum in sight for the entire length of time it took to bring it from the *Ariadne* to the assay office.

Eventually, they reached the Promenade. Eight more well-armed security officers were waiting for them and took up their positions, four in front and four behind, keeping clear of the range of the scanners. Other security teams were dotted about, around the other lifts, and at regular intervals along the Promenade. The procession moved slowly toward the assay office. When they got there, Odo and Steyn took the crate inside, under Mechter's watchful eye, and Odo secured the door after them. A pair of security officers peeled off from the rest and positioned themselves outside. Mechter studied them critically for a moment or two. From the slow nod he eventually gave, Odo assumed he was satisfied with what he saw.

"If you come this way, Mister Mechter," Odo said, gesturing to him to follow, "then we can close off this area."

The Lissepian gave another nod, and Odo led him and Steyn back round the way they had just come. Half of the security team followed Odo, and the rest went down the Promenade in the other direction. When Odo got almost as far as his office, he stopped and waited until his officers were clear, and then signaled their readiness up to ops. Within a few moments, the forcefield was up, and a few seconds after that the other team confirmed that the second forcefield had also been raised.

A third of the Promenade on either side of the assay office had now been sealed off, and the latinum with it. Odo gave a grunt of approval, and tapped his combadge. "Mister O'Brien," he said, "the *Ariadne* is clear. You can take your crew on board."

"Got you, Odo. Thanks."

Odo turned to Steyn. "The work will be starting on your ship very soon, Captain," he said. "I imagine Mister O'Brien will be able to give a better estimate of when the repairs will be complete."

"Thank you," Steyn said and let out a sigh. "I tell you," she said, giving Odo a smile, "it's a relief to have your people working on the ship at last. And to know the latinum is safe and sound, of course. . . ."

"As safe as it is possible for us to make it, Captain," Odo replied.

"More than good enough for me," Steyn said. "Now that I've seen you in action."

They exchanged satisfied smiles.

"May I ask," Odo said, "what your immediate plans are? I believe some quarters have been set aside for you and your crew. Will I be able to find you there if I need you?"

Steyn looked around her, taking in her surroundings. Odo noticed her young crewman hanging about nearby, clearly waiting to join her when she was ready for him. When Steyn caught sight of him, she grinned and stuck her thumbs up at him. Odo watched the young man smile back, shyly.

"That was a bar I saw on the Promenade, wasn't it, Mister Odo?" Steyn asked.

"Yes," Odo confirmed. "Quark's bar."

Steyn's interest was piqued. "The name sounds Ferengi," she remarked. "Or Klingon."

"Quark is Ferengi," Odo answered. "Among other things."

"I see." Steyn chewed at her bottom lip. Odo saw that she was looking at her young crewman again. Then she nodded, as if having made a decision. "Maybe I'll take Auger there before I go and catch up on my sleep. Something else new for him to see."

"If your young colleague is as little traveled as you say he is, I think it is almost a shame to give him such a poor view on the quadrant at large as he will find in Quark's."

Steyn laughed. "I guess from that you won't be joining us then?"

"Thank you, Captain, but I believe I have plenty to occupy my time at the moment." Odo glanced across at the dark and looming figure of Mechter, looking around the Promenade. He had one hand pressed against his chest. "To begin with . . ." Odo murmured. He went over to Mechter.

"The weapon, please," he said.

Mechter stared back at him and did not move a muscle.

"No weapons on the Promenade," Odo said. Behind him, he heard Steyn start laughing.

"I'd do what he says if I were you, Mechter," she said. "Unless you want to take that bunch on as well." She nodded back toward the security team, who were watching the exchange with a certain amount of professional interest. Mechter contemplated them for a moment, as if gauging his chances and then, with ill grace, he reached into his jacket, pulled out the weapon, and surrendered it to Odo.

"Thank you," said Odo. "You can get it back when you leave the station." He went back over to Steyn. "Is *he* likely to accompany you to Quark's?" he murmured, examining the little pistol and noting its weight and impeccable pedigree.

Steyn pulled a face. "I can almost guarantee it. Can't seem to shake him off."

"I can imagine his employers might take that amount of latinum very seriously."

"Probably almost as seriously as I do. I've had enough trouble with this job, and I want it finished up. . . ." She frowned at Mechter's back.

"At least you must be making a good fee from it—"

"I should be so lucky," she replied, glumly. "I'm not making a damned thing out of any of this. Not to mention the cost of repairs."

"I beg your pardon?" Odo gave her a puzzled look. "I'm not sure that I understand—"

"Well, not to get into the extremely complicated details—"

"However complicated, I am always very interested in listening to details, Captain Steyn," Odo said, "as you have no doubt already ascertained."

"Well," Steyn said, giving him a shrewd look, "I'm afraid I'm not particularly eager to relate them."

Odo inclined his head. That was, of course, Steyn's privilege. Should the truncated story she told prove of interest, Odo had his own methods of filling in detail.

"So," Steyn carried on, "let's just say that I made something of a miscalculation a little while back. And as a result I owe Mechter's employers . . ." She frowned. "Well, let's just say that I owe them. And this trip is part of the payment. Just my kind of luck to get stuck with this job." She turned back to Odo and gave him a bright smile. "Anyway, this bar you were telling me about. Any games there?"

"What kind of games were you thinking of playing, Captain Steyn?"

"Oh, I wasn't thinking of playing anything!" she laughed. "I told you—I've got no luck." She nodded over at her silent crewman. "But Auger likes a game of chance."

Quark watched with fascination as the cavalcade surrounding the latinum progressed past the bar in a very stately fashion, and slowly on along the Promenade. He turned to Dax, standing with him at the sealed door of the bar. "Where do you think shapeshifters go when they die?" he said to her. "To the Great Link in the Sky?"

"What makes you think they go anywhere?" Dax said. "They're gods already, don't forget."

"That," Quark replied, "is something that is *definitely* a matter of perspective—"

Dax quirked an eyebrow at him. "What, I wonder, could be making you so metaphysical this morning?"

"*Look* at all that!" Quark pointed at the last of the security guards—stern-faced and heavily armed—as they went past the area just outside of the bar. "I haven't seen so much security on the Promenade since the Cardassians were running the place. If there *is* a changeling heaven, Odo must be in it right now."

"How about the sight of all that latinum?" Dax said slyly. "That must be like seeing the Divine Treasury set up next door."

"Take it from me," Quark said, "I can imagine a *lot* more latinum than that."

"But I can imagine it must pose a temptation . . ." Dax said. "So close, and yet so far. . . ."

Quark looked back at her with a shocked expression. "Commander," he said, "are you saying what I think you're saying?"

"I'm just saying it must be tempting—"

"And I'm saying that it's not."

She gave him a disbelieving look.

"Have I *ever* lied to you?" he said, in an injured tone.

"Let me see," she laughed. "How about every time we play *tongo?*"

"That's different—"

"So you're telling me, Quark," she said, "that you have absolutely no designs on all that latinum?"

"I have *absolutely* no designs on all that latinum."

Dax moved a little closer to him. He found himself staring at her thick dark hair.

"And what about your friends?" she said.

"My friends?" He looked at the patterns made by the marks that so delicately lined her neck.

"People who come in and out of the bar," she said, reaching out and straightening his collar for him. "Who want to talk and tell somebody their business. I know you're always willing to lend an ear to people like that, Quark."

Quark looked into the depths of her dazzling eyes and sighed. *Females,* he thought. *They always* were *my down-*

fall. "So," he murmured to her, "you want to know all of my secrets?"

Jadzia gave him her most beautiful smile.

Quark returned it with a smile considerably less beautiful, but easily as cunning.

"Then you shouldn't have married the Klingon," he said.

Dax burst out laughing. She pressed a fingertip against her lips and then tapped it against Quark's nose. "It's going to be a stressful few days," she said. "Try to leave Odo alone."

"He'd hate it if I did," he replied.

Dax checked the door. The locks had been released. "Goodbye, Quark," she said, still laughing as she left.

Quark went back to the bar, still with a smile on his face. It broadened when he saw two new people come in. They looked like they were bringing a whole array of opportunities with them.

First came a woman, human, more than a little frayed around the seams, and Quark did not miss how her eye fell straight on the dabo table. He knew the type, welcomed them with open arms. They were the kind that never failed to turn opportunity into profit . . . for Quark, that was. Walking just a little behind was a young man—still a boy, really—who was staring around the bar as if it was the most remarkable sight he had ever seen. Quark knew his type too: fresh-faced, trusting . . . the pockets were usually light, but that did not, in Quark's opinion, make them any less worth emptying.

"So," Quark murmured, looking fondly from one to the other as they came toward the bar, "*what* do we have here?"

• • •

A very small matter, but nonetheless Garak seemed to be taking his time to ask about it, Sisko thought. He examined the bowl of the spoon with more interest than it merited, looking at his own face, upside down. Garak had not referred to Vreenak even in passing since their conversation, but surely all these Romulans must have been keeping the matter at the forefront of his mind too . . . and Sisko knew Garak had been watching him very closely all day.

"Am I correct in thinking," Garak said, at last, "that there is some sort of reception being held this evening?"

Sisko looked at him in surprise. He had been assuming this would be another series of leading questions about Ross and Batanides. "That's right," he said cautiously. "Councillor Huang is holding it at her embassy." He glanced at Garak. "She has been one of the councillors most supportive of continuing the war. When the peace initiative was underway before the Romulans joined the alliance, Huang was one of its main critics."

"You may assume, Captain," Garak said, "that I have taken the trouble to find out exactly who she is." Then he lightened his tone again. "Now, as I understand it, the idea behind this event is to foster dialogue between all the conference attendees. A very fine goal and I, for one, am all for fostering dialogue. I've said it before, and I'll say it again—Cardassians excel at conversation."

Sisko frowned. "Are you going where I think you are with this, Garak?"

Garak smiled back. "Well, I would like to come along this evening, if that's what you mean."

Sisko snorted. "After that fiasco the other night? Why the hell would I let you anywhere near this reception?"

"Oh come, Captain." Garak frowned back at him. "You and I both know that was just an unfortunate series of misunderstandings. Opinions expressed in the wrong place and at the wrong time. Which brings me to my point—"

Sisko threw the spoon into his own cup with rough impatience. It landed there with a clatter. "At last," he said.

"I hear that the leaders of the antiwar campaign have also been invited to this little soirée. Which means that . . . Tomas Roeder will be there this evening."

"I should think he would be, yes," Sisko said. "He's the most high-profile member of the campaign after all."

"Indeed he is. And *I*," Garak tapped his chest, "am one of the few Cardassians on Earth. So—in the professed interests of fostering dialogue—I would very much like to meet him."

Sisko leaned an elbow on the table and looked across at him. Garak's expression was bland, polite, and thoroughly inscrutable.

"Why all this sudden interest in Roeder?" Sisko said suspiciously.

"I'd hardly say it was sudden," Garak pointed out. "I did want to hear him express his views at the meeting the other night, remember. It's just that . . . the way things turned out I didn't exactly get to hear much of them."

"You really only have yourself to blame for that."

"Forgive me for being so unfamiliar with your customs, Captain," Garak replied, with an attempt at penitence that was blatant in its falsity. "I am after all a *very* long way from home."

Sisko began to laugh. What had Ross said? *Might as well enjoy ourselves.* Making polite conversation to conference delegates who were only talking to him in the hope he might inadvertently let something slip rated very low on Sisko's list of entertainments. Watching a conversation between Garak and Roeder had at least something to recommend it. So long as Garak wasn't up to something . . .

Sisko looked thoughtfully at the tailor, still smiling blandly. Garak had managed to cause quite a scene at the rally the other night, but Sisko suspected that had more to do with his frustration with Rhemet than with any hidden agenda. Perhaps he'd gotten that out of his system now. Perhaps this was a genuinely innocent request . . . if Garak was constitutionally capable of making a genuinely innocent request.

"I was under the impression," Sisko said, rubbing a finger along the side of his nose, "that the security team assigned to you had requested that you not go any further than the HQ building."

"In its immeasurable wisdom, Starfleet Intelligence has seen fit to change its mind about that for this evening."

"Oh yes? And how exactly did you manage to persuade the two lieutenants that that was a good idea?"

Garak gave an unrevealing shrug.

"Don't tell me," Sisko murmured. "I already know you excel at conversation."

"Something like that. But," Garak raised a finger, "they were insistent that I would only be permitted to attend if somebody they trusted accompanied me. Someone such as you, Captain. And I am loath to make life harder for your intelligence services than I already have." Sisko watched him suppress a smile. "Call it collegiality."

Sisko really could believe that Garak had just kept on talking until Chaplin and Marlow had given him what he wanted. "All right," he said, softly, "say I do agree to take you along this evening to meet Tomas. Just what exactly do you plan to say to him?"

"Rest assured, Captain, I have nothing to say that will make you feel uncomfortable at having made the introduction. Very simply put, I am intrigued to know why a Starfleet officer decides to resign his commission and speak out against the evils of war. Particularly *this* war, which," Garak smiled, "is surely a just one, if ever there was."

A fair enough question. Sisko had, after all, been wondering the same thing too. "And that's the only reason you want to come this evening?"

"Well . . ." Garak hesitated. "I suppose there is another reason too."

"Oh?"

Garak gave a sigh. "I've been stuck in this building with nothing better to listen to than the blustering of the Klingons, the insinuations of the Romulans, and—forgive me—the homilies of Starfleet. I'm *bored*, Captain. I want to hear something new. And what Roeder has to say . . ." He shrugged. ". . . intrigues me."

Intrigue. That word again. Still it was, Sisko suspected, probably the closest thing to the truth that Garak was going to tell him. "I suppose," he said, "that's as good a reason as any." He straightened himself up in the chair and made his decision. "All right, Garak, I'll introduce you to Tomas. Just—stay close and don't wander off anywhere. And don't cause any trouble."

Garak beamed at him. "Captain," he promised, "you have my most solemn word."

Back in his office, Odo was listening to O'Brien's assessment of the state of affairs on the *Ariadne*.

"*I've had a good look around now,*" O'Brien was saying. "*It was definitely sabotage, Odo. Someone's made a real mess of pretty much all the systems here. The engi-*

neer here has done a good job of patching things together till they could get here, but we've got plenty of work to be getting on with. Anyway, I thought you should know in case it made a difference to security at your end."

"Thank you, Chief. I believe I have everything under control. Are you willing to make an estimate yet of how long the repairs will take?"

"I think we can get everything done here within thirty hours. The sooner we can send the Ariadne back on her way the better, I think."

"I certainly won't disagree with that, Chief. And any time you can take off that thirty hours will be most appreciated. So I'll leave you to your work. Thank you for all your assistance."

"You're welcome, Constable."

Odo cut the com, and came out from behind his desk. Thirty hours. It was still plenty of time for something to go wrong. He stood for a while in the doorway of his office, looking along the Promenade. It was very quiet. He nodded in satisfaction.

He went out into the unusual silence. As he walked past Quark's he peered inside, and caught a glimpse of the captain of the *Ariadne* down by the dabo table. When he reached the forcefield, barring his way, he tapped on his combadge, and, after a moment or two, one of the officers detailed to the doors of the assay office came up to the field to speak to him.

"Is everything in order, Lieutenant?" he asked.

"Everything's stayed quiet, sir," he answered, "in the twenty minutes since you were last here." He gave a smile. Odo arranged his features into a frown.

"Although," the lieutenant said, "as you predicted, someone wanted to get in here to retrieve something from the assay office."

"Really?" Odo pursed his lips. All residents and visitors to the station had been given ample warning that access to the assay office would be restricted, and when those restrictions would apply. Whoever it was should have accessed their property the previous day. "I assume that you didn't let them in?"

"Of course not, sir!"

"Do you know who it was?"

"A visitor to the station, I think. I've seen him around the station the past day or two. I would have known if he was a resident. He looked . . . well, odd. I think he's Hamexi."

All of a sudden, things no longer seemed to Odo to be quite so well under control.

"Hamexi?"

7

THE BAR WAS FULL; full of more noise and more color.
Auger was feeling the station as an assault on his senses.
He was relieved when Steyn took him gently by the
elbow and began to navigate him over to the bar. But
there was something there. It was orange, and it had ears.
Auger stared at them. It was an epiphany. He realized
now that all the ears he had ever seen before had just been
fooling with him. Pretending that they deserved to be
called ears. Because *these* were ears—

"Auger," Steyn was saying, "would you like something to drink?"

Auger felt Mechter step into place just behind him and
the captain. "Water," he gasped at Steyn. "Water."

"We don't serve water," said a voice, coming from between the ears.

"Isn't there a *law* about that kind of thing?" Steyn
was complaining. One of life's sureties. Auger took a
deep breath, and looked properly at the alien behind the
bar.

"There should be a law against people coming into a

bar just to ask for a drink of water," it said. He. It was definitely a he. Auger thought.

"All right," Steyn said, "some kind of tonic water. And I'll have a Samarian sunset. Auger," she said, turning to him, "I *have* to get you drinking. The markup on nonalcoholic stuff is criminal."

The alien put down a glass in front of Auger. "I have to draw the line at criminal," he said.

"How about—opportunistic?"

The alien smiled. Which meant that he was showing teeth. "Now that," he said, handing Steyn her drink, "I'm prepared to take as a compliment." The alien looked at Mechter. "And can I get anything for you, sir?"

Mechter stared at the alien until he took a step back. "Synthale," he said.

Steyn put her glass down on the bar. "Watch this, Auger," she said. "You'll like this." The drink was clear, like water, and then Steyn tapped the edge of the glass, and the liquid exploded into a blaze of color before settling to bright orange.

"A Samarian sunset," Steyn declared. "Pretty, isn't it?"

"Yes," Auger murmured. "It is." He admired the color a bit longer, and then smiled up at the captain. She looked back at him fondly.

"You feeling better now?" she said.

"A *lot* better," he said.

"Ready for a game?"

Auger took a fortifying sip of his tonic water and then looked at Steyn's face. He liked the creases at the corners of her eyes, and he liked the way that her hair did not stay tied back. She had pulled him from a backwater, and shown him strange stars, and planets with moons, and now a Samarian sunset. She was funny, and sometimes a bit sad; he had a strong suspicion she was addicted to risk, and he knew without doubt she was shameless in using his talents toward this end. He liked her for all of these things.

"Am I ready for a game?" he said. "You bet."

Steyn started to laugh. "So, have you ever played dabo before, Auger?"

"What do you think, Captain?"

Steyn stood up. "I don't think it will make much difference either way." She nodded toward the back of the bar. "Shall we go and find out?"

Auger grabbed his glass, spilling only a little of the contents, and followed her over to the table at the back of the bar. Mechter was close behind them, but Auger was getting close to familiar territory. He and Steyn eased past some of the punters to get closer to the table. There was a wheel on it.

"This is dabo," Steyn said. "Have a look, see what you think."

Auger watched the wheel. It began to spin. And with it—like with the twist of a kaleidoscope—the whole universe fell into a beautiful shape.

Brixhta was still there, situated at one end of the bench, his hat serving as camouflage. Hearing Odo's approach, he eased himself up into a sitting position, and raised his hat ever so slightly. "Odo," he said, cheerfully.

"You're there," Odo said, unnecessarily.

"Now, where ever else would I be?"

Odo did not reply. He checked the setting on the lock. The last time it had been activated was when he himself had sealed Brixhta in.

"Although when one has experienced incarceration, one's perspective on it does change."

"Does it indeed?" Odo said.

"Why yes. A man's body may be caged, but . . ." Brixhta raised his hand and moved it in a slow, meaningful arc.

Odo checked a few of the less obvious settings on the door. There was nothing suspicious. No sign of tampering.

"Is there something troubling you, Odo?"

"Not in the slightest," Odo replied, with more confidence than he felt. He checked all the door settings once again, but they brought him to the same conclusion. There was no way that Brixhta had been anywhere other than where he was now.

The Centaurian Embassy took up the whole of a row of what had once been four tall, terraced town houses. Sisko and Garak materialized in a small flower garden at the front of one of the houses, at the foot of a set of wide stone steps that led up into the buildings.

It was late evening in early autumn. The air was damp and smelled of leaves. Twilight. Looking out from where they stood, with the embassy behind, there was a quiet street running parallel to the row of terraces. Over the road, running left to right, was a line of trees and then a row of lamps that went along the length of the embankment. Beyond the thread of lights, Sisko could see the dark line of the river.

"Where are we now?" Garak said, staring up at the gray wash of the sky, and then taking in the outline of grayer buildings that spread out along the far bank of the river.

"London," Sisko said.

"I think I may have heard the doctor mention it."

"Well, this is certainly more his part of the world."

"It's . . . a little darker than I expected," Garak said.

"Not that I'm complaining. Are we very far from San Francisco?"

Sisko was sure he felt a spot of rain. "About as far as you can be," he muttered to himself. "We're on a completely different continent," he said, for Garak's benefit.

"And an even wetter one, apparently," Garak said. "Although it seems to me as if this entire planet is wet. Even more so than Bajor."

"What are you basing that on?" Sisko said curiously. "I thought you'd only been to Bajor a few times?"

Garak turned away to stare across the river. "In my situation, it's difficult not to hear a lot about it."

They went up the steps and through two ornate doors into the embassy, passing through a security field as they went in. Two men in tuxedos on either side of the doorway watched them enter, and one spoke discreetly into a communication device fixed to the back of his hand. Inside, the foyer was white and high-ceilinged; the walls were hung with landscapes and pastoral scenes. A wide staircase opened out to the right, but they were guided politely but firmly toward open doors straight ahead.

They went into a large reception room, with high ceilings, bright chandeliers, and more paintings. Seascapes, this time, Sisko noticed; scenes of flagships of a long gone empire. Little groups of people had gathered together here and there, making light and insubstantial conversation, rising and falling in harmony, counterpointed with the sound of strings. The wall opposite was almost entirely given over to windows—two bays on either side of French windows, which were standing open. They led out onto a terrace; some of the guests had decided to brave the evening chill and take their drinks outside. Looking into the garden, Sisko could see spots of candlelight flickering against the graying sky, and dark lines of trees in the garden beyond.

A waiter passed by, carrying a tray of drinks. Sisko grabbed a couple of glasses and handed one over to Garak. "Champagne," he said. "That's . . . a kind of fizzy wine," he added, by way of explanation, when Garak gave him a questioning look.

Garak peered down at the contents, and then took a taste of it, cautiously. "Odd," he said. "Not unpleasant, but odd." He took another sip.

Sisko looked around the room. The reception seemed to be in full swing. The room was full and busy but not yet crowded. Sisko spotted the source of the music: a string quartet was sitting in the space opened up by the bay windows, playing something that he recognized but could not place. It was all so very civilized. A shame, really, that the Romulans all seemed to be at one end of the room, and the Klingons at the other. Or maybe it was the safest option for the décor.

Their host, at least, was not letting this segregation trouble her, Sisko thought, although she was clearly conscious of it. He watched Councillor Huang, dazzling in electric blue, as she threaded her way between the little groups, stopping to speak to people now and again. After she had passed, one or two people would peel off from their set, and make the effort to speak to others beyond their obvious circle. Huang was very skilled at this, so Sisko had heard. Who knew—by the time the evening was over, a lot more of the work might have been done to make the whole conference a success.

Huang moved away, laughing, from what looked like it had been a spirited conversation with a Klingon attaché. Her eye fell on Sisko, and on Garak. She made a direct line for them. Closer to, her dress seemed to shimmer a little; the blue silk was shot through with silver thread.

"Captain," she said, brisk and businesslike, and smiling as they shook hands. "It's a pleasure. Your fame precedes you."

"So does yours, Councillor," he said, and nodded around the room. "The evening looks set to be a great success."

She leaned in toward them, as if drawing them into her confidence, the silk of her dress rustling as she came close. "Between you and me," she said, lowering her voice, "I would have liked to see a little more integration between my various guests from the outset. Never mind! I have an hour or two yet in which to achieve it." From the assurance of her smile, Sisko found that he did not doubt her ability to make it happen.

Huang turned her attention sharply toward Garak. "Welcome to Earth, Mr. Garak," she said. "I had hoped that some members of your government-in-exile would be able to attend this evening, but they declined the invitation. I believe they preferred to remain within the safety of Starfleet Headquarters. A pity."

Garak inclined his head. "They are not my government," he said politely, "but I believe it to be possible that a period of exile can induce a rather suspicious cast of mind. May I apologize for any offense they might have inadvertently given?"

"No offense has been taken. I can sympathize with their security concerns. Although, as you can see," she glanced over at the door, "I am not taking any chances this evening." She smiled at them. "Well, good evening, gentlemen; duty calls. Try some of the caviar, Mr. Garak," she ordered him, as she turned away. "I suppose you shouldn't leave Earth without that particular experience. Personally, I think it's foul stuff, but people seem to expect it."

They watched her head back into the fray.

"What an exquisite dress," Garak remarked.

"Yes," Sisko said. "Very nice."

Garak smiled down at his champagne. "Look," he said softly, raising one finger from his glass to gesture across the room. "There's Roeder."

Bashir was, Odo guessed, as embarrassed about his outburst the previous day as Odo was embarrassed to have been the cause of it.

"Odo," the doctor said, "I didn't expect to see you back here so soon." He gave a rueful smile. "I'm sorry if I was short-tempered yesterday. Locking up the Hamexi—I guess it just didn't seem right . . ." He stopped himself. "But under the circumstances . . . Well, let's not get into all that again. Are you satisfied now that the latinum is safe?"

Odo began to look around the infirmary. It seemed he would have to be embarrassed once more. "Not *exactly* . . ." he said.

"No?" Bashir said sharply.

"I have just," Odo said, staring at a flashing light on the console with an intense and thoroughly unnecessary degree of interest, "concluded my latest check on the security around the latinum shipment. . . ." He risked a glance at the doctor.

"And?" Bashir had folded his arms and was now leaning back against the console. Odo looked back quickly at the flashing lights.

"And one of my officers told me that an Hamexi had asked to be allowed into the assay office. However, when I checked on Brixhta, he was still in his cell and the door had not been activated since I put him in there." He glanced up again.

Bashir was grinning at him. "That must be very puzzling for you, Constable," he said.

Odo made a low, noncommittal sound.

"Well," Bashir said, straightening himself up, "it doesn't really surprise me."

"Would you care to enlighten me as to why?"

"I'm not entirely sure that you deserve this information after being so quick off the mark to lock the man up, but Hamexi are a very interesting species from a medical point of view." He reached for the padd, and punched a few controls. "There you go," he said, offering it to Odo. "It's all there."

Odo took the padd, and glanced down at a meaningless stream of numbers. "I think that I will have to ask you to interpret this data for me, Doctor."

Bashir grinned again. At least he wasn't angry anymore, Odo thought. Although he could try to be a bit less self-satisfied about it.

"Hamexi share an unusually high level of genetic information," Bashir explained, obviously enjoying himself. "They're often particularly indistinguishable to members of other species. So you see, Odo—it's very simple." He smiled. "Your security officer saw an entirely different person. A traveling companion of Brixhta's, I imagine."

Odo stared down at the padd, and then pointed to the console. "Do you mind if I check something?"

Bashir stepped courteously out of his way. "Be my guest."

It took a minute or two, but Odo soon had the information he needed. "I'm afraid you'll need to come up with another hypothesis, Doctor. There's no record of any other Hamexi arriving on DS9. And a scan insists that there is no other Hamexi on the station. Apart from Brixhta himself, that is."

Bashir blinked. "Oh," he said. He looked rather crestfallen. "Well. Yes, that does put a rather different complexion on things. . . ."

Sisko looked across the reception room. Roeder had positioned himself in front of one of the windows. It put him on the edge of the party, and he was standing silently, watching, and seeming to monitor the little groups that had gathered, sipping his champagne, and filing away who was talking to whom. *You can take the officer out of Starfleet security . . .*

Sisko downed another mouthful of champagne. "All right," he said, unwillingly, "shall we get this over with?"

"Try not to sound so enthusiastic, Captain."

"And *you* try not to—" Sisko stopped himself and wondered how best to put it. "Just . . . try not to provoke him."

Garak was affronted. "Captain, I am *genuinely* interested in hearing what he has to say! Quite frankly, I am *insulted* by the assumption that I might—"

"All right, all right," Sisko cut off the tirade. "But he hits even harder than me. So don't say I didn't warn you."

They went across the room. As they got a little closer, Sisko noted that there were flecks of gray against Roeder's dark hair. They had all gotten older, it seemed. And who could say which of them it was that had gotten wiser?

"Tomas."

Roeder turned at the sound of his voice, and looked straight at him. His eyes widened; for just a second, Sisko thought he looked shocked, but then it seemed to be no more than surprise.

"Ben," he said quietly, in greeting, and came toward him. He offered his hand, and Sisko took it. Roeder's grip was strong and certain. "I didn't expect to see you here. I wouldn't have thought anything could bring you away from DS9 right now."

"Well, it's an important conference, Tomas. I have a lot to say—and I mean to be heard."

A faint smile crossed Roeder's face. He nodded, as if something had become clearer to him. "You haven't changed a bit, Ben," he said. "It's good to see you again. How's Judith?"

Sisko smiled back. "She's very well. Just got back from a tour."

"I never seem to get the chance to hear her play. Always offworld, or speaking somewhere . . ."

"She was asking after you."

Roeder's smile became distant. "Remember me to her, please."

"Of course I will. I should be catching up with her later in the week."

"And your father—how is he? And the restaurant?"

"Both still going strong."

Roeder nodded. "It's good to know some things remain the same." He took some of his champagne, and seemed to fall into thought. For a moment, Sisko thought, it was almost as if Roeder had absented himself from the room, although the fingers around the glass were still following the arpeggios in the background. At last he spoke. "I heard the news about the Seventh Fleet," he said. "There were a lot of familiar names on the list."

"There are always a lot of familiar names these days."

"I'm very sorry." Roeder looked away, out across the room.

"So you don't think we're just getting what we deserve?" Sisko's voice had softened, but the words did not lose their edge. Beside him, he heard Garak draw in a sharp breath.

Roeder turned his head, and looked at Sisko with something like compassion. "It's the cost of it all, isn't it?" Roeder said, with pity. "The realization that comes—early one morning, or late one night, or whenever it is that the dreams wake you up—that it just isn't worth that cost. That whatever credit is on offer right now, one day there will have to be a reckoning. One day, we'll be held to account."

Sisko drew his finger round the perfect crystal circle of the rim of his glass. The comfortable distance of Earth permitted many persuasive fictions. But the truth, Sisko knew, lay back on the front line. He tapped his nail against the thin glass. It rang, a hollow sound. "I don't doubt I'll pay a lot more yet for victory," he said.

Roeder did not answer, and the sound of strings intervened.

"I heard your speech the other night," Sisko said, as a peace offering. "Well, as much of it as you were able to give."

Roeder's mouth tightened at the corners. "It was not," he said, "exactly how I would hope a peace rally to end." He gestured impatiently with his glass. "Sometimes I'm sure there are agents provocateurs in our ranks—"

"I don't believe that for a moment, Tomas—"

"Yes, well—then I think I'm probably being paranoid." He gave a short laugh. "Still," he said, looking around the room, "these are strange days. Sometimes it's hard to pick out our enemies from among our friends." His gaze, perhaps inevitably, came to rest on Garak, who had been standing by, patiently. "Forgive me," Roeder said, "I don't think we've met before. . . ." He glanced quickly at Sisko and quirked a dark eyebrow up at him.

Sisko roused himself. "I'm sorry," he said. "I should have introduced you straight away. Tomas, this is Elim Garak. He . . ." Sisko struggled for a moment to think of an adequate way to explain away Garak. "He's come this evening very eager to hear about your reasons for joining the antiwar campaign." *That* was pretty heavily edited, Sisko thought, as Garak and Roeder shook hands, but it was enough as a start. If Roeder really wanted to know anything, he could try getting it out of Garak himself. It would be interesting to watch.

"So, Mister Garak," Roeder said, addressing him directly, "explain to me—how does a Cardassian find himself here on Earth in the middle of a war between us?"

"That's not difficult to explain at all," Garak replied, easily. "By being at odds with the current regime."

"Something that can happen to the best of us," Roeder pointed out. "So—does that make you a peacemaker too?"

"A peacemaker?" Garak smiled down into his glass. "I am a Cardassian, Mister Roeder, first and foremost." His smile thinned. "And a very long way from home." He stopped speaking, and the sound of a solitary cello began to filter through again.

"I was once fortunate enough," Roeder said, into the gap, "to hear one of your finest musicians. Ilani Tarn."

"You heard Ilani Tarn *play?*" Garak switched his attention back to him, eagerly.

"She gave a performance here on Earth, eighteen months ago. A cultural exchange, arranged just before your civilian government fell, I think."

"It was not my government," Garak corrected him, with a polite nod of the head, and with what Sisko was beginning to think was an unusual degree of attention to the truth by Garak on this particular point, "but it must have been a unique occasion."

"It was," Roeder agreed. "Mostly Cardassian compositions, but she did some Beethoven sonatas too, if I remember right. Arranged for the *trikolat*, of course."

Garak was enchanted. "Her performances were so few and far between. I only heard her once, right back at the start of her career. She was astonishing even then. I imagine she's improved substantially since."

"She was magnificent," Roeder said, nodding. "The dynamics, the quality of the sounds she could produce . . ." He drew his glass across the space before him, briefly becoming absorbed in the memory.

Garak turned to Sisko, his eyes bright and alive, shining with enthusiasm. "Ilani Tarn is Cardassia's greatest living musician, captain. Her instrument—the *trikolat*—is a string instrument, but percussive too. . . ." He waved his hand impatiently. "It's difficult to explain," he admitted. "Really, you would need to listen to her."

"I'd like that," Sisko said softly, thinking he should have brought Judith along.

"I understand the Cardassian Institute of Arts finally granted Tarn a full license last year," Roeder remarked.

"Yes . . ." Garak too seemed to become lost in thought for a moment. Then he collected himself. "Yes, they did."

"A full license?" Sisko said. "What does that mean?"

"Musical and theatrical performances on Cardassia are regulated by the Institute of Arts, Captain," Garak explained, "and artists are required to apply for permission from the Institute for each performance. But full licenses can be awarded to particularly prestigious artists, who then have more freedom—"

"But they're still regulated to some degree?" Sisko asked.

"Naturally," Garak replied, and took a sip of his champagne.

Naturally. . . . "So what was the delay in giving her the license?" Sisko said. "If she's Cardassia's greatest musician?"

"Her willingness to embrace alien composers most likely did not win her many friends," Roeder suggested.

"Perhaps," Garak said. "But I suspect that it was more than just a political statement on the part of the Institute. Tarn is a very subtle artist, Captain," Garak said, turning back to him, "but she refuses to be obscure." He glanced across at Roeder. "I have heard it said now and again that perhaps there is a little too much truth in her style for Cardassian taste. A little too much honesty."

Roeder drank from his glass. "And would you agree with that assessment, Mr. Garak? *Is* she too honest for Cardassian taste?"

"Now that," Garak said, with a smile, "would be telling."

Roeder laughed. Sisko frowned. He had forgotten Roeder's liking for cryptic conversation. He had equally forgotten just how much it grated on him. He took a mouthful of champagne that he did not want and stared beyond Roeder, out of the window, at the faded sky and the candlelight lining the terrace. Three officials from the Romulan delegation had gathered just outside. They were leaning together, looking inside, watching, and saying nothing to each other. Veral stood among them. *The cost of it all . . . ?* Sisko doubted that Roeder could guess the full extent of it. He doubted that even Leyton could.

Someone passed beside him, accidentally jogging his elbow, murmuring a polite apology when Sisko turned to see. The room had gotten very crowded now, he noticed. As he looked around, he felt a sudden need for some fresh air. He turned back to Roeder and Garak, now talking about one of the paintings that was hanging on the wall nearby. Roeder seemed to be giving Garak an abridged history of naval warfare. Garak seemed enthralled.

"If you'll excuse me," Sisko said to them both, "I think I'll just step outside and get some fresh air."

In Quark's, Odo saw the captain of the *Ariadne* and her odd young crewman sitting at the dabo table. Auger was staring at the wheel with a fixed intensity. He seemed, Odo thought, to have accumulated a great deal in the way of winnings. Steyn was watching the table closely, but her attention was split between Auger and the brooding figure of Mechter, who was standing very close to her left shoulder. Odo filed away the picture for later consideration and went over to the bar.

He and Quark took each other's measure.

"Well, Odo," Quark said, breaking the silence first, "this has turned out to be a great day, hasn't it?"

"You're not in prison, Quark. Which prevents it from being a great day from my perspective."

"Well, I'll never forget today, Odo. The day that *you* had to admit you'd made a mistake." Quark dusted one of the bottles lightly. "You should never have arrested him in the first place, you know. That way you wouldn't have lost face when you had to release him."

"*What* are you talking about?"

"Brixhta, of course," Quark replied. "You made a mistake there, Odo. But he's out now, and you were wrong, and that makes the day a great one for me."

"Someone has been telling you lies, Quark. I hate to have to disappoint you, but Brixhta is still safely sitting in his holding cell."

Quark blinked at him. He put down the bottle he was holding, leaned on the bar, and pushed himself up to get a good look at the Promenade. "Strange," he muttered, and shook his head.

"What do you mean?" Odo said.

"Oh, nothing. It's just that . . ."

"Yes?"

"Well, I was sure that I saw Brixhta walking along the Promenade earlier."

"That's impossible," Odo denied bluntly. "Brixhta is down in the holding cells. I saw him there myself not even half an hour ago."

For a moment, Quark looked to Odo to be genuinely puzzled. He peered out onto the Promenade again. "Huh," he said, and then turned his attention back to the bottles.

Odo leaned across the bar. "Quark," he growled, "whatever scheme you and Mexh Brixhta have got together, I *will* find out what it is. In the meantime, I am not in the least amused by this pathetic attempt to distract me."

Quark shrugged. "Have it your own way," he said. "I'm just telling you what I saw. I suppose it would explain why he didn't come to talk to me. And you're so stubborn I guess I didn't really see you releasing him, even when you must know you've made a mistake. Not to mention overstepped your authority—"

"As a matter of fact," Odo said frostily, "I am well within my authority to hold Brixhta, for as long as he presents what I believe is a threat to station security. You might want to bear that in mind, Quark, before you decide to meddle again." He glanced over at the dabo table. "It seems to me that you have enough to worry about. How *are* profits looking today?"

Quark laughed, showing most of his teeth. "That's my business, Odo. Perhaps *you* should be worrying about whether that holding cell really is as secure as you think it is."

"Of course it is," Odo said, with considerably more certainty than he felt.

"Of course it is," mimicked Quark. "Or maybe, just maybe—Mexh Brixhta really is smarter than you after all."

If it wasn't one thing, Julian thought, then it was another. One minute the Dominion were kidnapping you and sticking you in a prison camp, the next it was a covert ops outfit operating within your own government that was spiriting you away. Either way, Julian had found that the net result was that you ended up with an awful lot of conference papers to catch up on. At least the infirmary was quiet at the moment. O'Brien would be kept busy on the *Ariadne* for the next day or so; he was expecting no distractions from that quarter. And while Julian could hardly agree with Odo's methods, it seemed that arresting Brixhta had finally put the constable's mind sufficiently at rest to leave him in peace for a while.

He scanned through the list of papers from the conference he had missed on Casperia Prime, looking at the titles. Lined up alongside each other, they made for grim reading, Julian reflected; they were all devoted to mitigating the effects of war. Only one or two articles on changeling physiology came close to what Julian would call pure scholarship, and even then their applications were primarily defensive. It was one of Julian's greatest regrets in recent years that even though so much research was being done, all of it was aimed at better waging of the war.

He began methodically, almost ritualistically, opening the first file on the list, a paper concerned with the treatments of plasma burns. Familiar as he was with the trauma, he knew that he would see a lot more of these appalling wounds. He scrolled onward to see how long the paper was, and then started to give it his full attention. He was partway through a particularly grueling section, when he heard someone give a cough that managed to be ineffably polite and yet still was judged perfectly to interrupt.

Julian looked up. Sure enough, there was Odo, hovering in the doorway. "Am I disturbing you, Doctor?" he asked.

Julian looked back down at the padd. He had lost the thread of the paper. He would have to come back to it later. He had heard Quark complain many times about Odo's doggedness, and had always felt it was largely deserved. Now he was starting to feel some sympathy toward Quark's point of view. And Julian had not, as far as he knew, even committed a crime.

"No, Constable," he said, automatically marking his place, and setting the padd to one side. He twisted round on his seat, and gave Odo his full concentration. "What can I do for you?"

Odo stepped toward him, eagerly. He was anxious too, Julian thought. "There's been another sighting of Brixhta," Odo said.

"Odo," Julian sighed, "you've got him locked up. I thought you'd decided your security officer had just made a mistake—"

"Quark saw him this time."

"Oh, well, if it was *Quark* . . ." Julian stopped as a thought struck him. "Brixhta still *is* locked up, isn't he?"

"Yes, I went and checked. He's spread out in the cell. Asleep, I think."

"Then Quark can't have seen him."

Odo began pacing around the room. "That was what I thought. That Quark had invented the story to take my attention away from whatever it is that Brixhta is up to. But both Quark and one of my security officers telling the same story?" Odo shook his head. "That seems too much."

"Maybe the security officer was telling the story in the bar and Quark overheard?"

"The officer," Odo said, "is behind a forcefield, and will be for several hours yet."

"All right . . ." Julian started running through options. "Perhaps Quark has managed to bribe your security officer to take part in whatever escapade he and Brixhta are carrying out, and he's the one letting Brixhta out—" He started shaking his head. "Odo, this conversation is becoming preposterous! You have Brixhta in one of your holding cells. Neither Quark nor your security officer can have seen him. And we know that there isn't another Hamexi on board—"

"But still," Odo urged, "I am not able to explain why two people have seen an Hamexi wandering around the station. They are hardly easy to mistake!"

"But that's what it has to be—they both made a mistake—"

"Which is what I fear I might be saying if I don't treat these sightings seriously."

"All right," Julian sighed. "Let's go through what we know. We're assuming that Brixhta can't get out, is that right?"

"Yes," Odo said dryly, "I think we can safely assume both the competence and the incorruptibility of my security team."

"Fair point. Sorry, Odo." Julian gave an apologetic smile. "Well, that would mean it *is* another Hamexi."

"But the only life signs we picked up were Brixhta's," Odo pointed out.

"If it were a clone . . ." Julian mused. "That would show the same life signs. . . . No, that wouldn't work. It would show another reading—we'd have picked him up before."

"A twin?" Odo suggested.

"Same thing with the readings. And, anyway, Hamexi don't reproduce multiply; it's part of their genetic profiles."

Odo gave a wan smile. "I knew you were the right person to come to, Doctor. Chief O'Brien would never have known that."

"Well, it's certainly good to be appreciated," Julian murmured. He looked back down at the padd he had been reading when Odo arrived. One of the titles leaped out at him now. "Odo," he said, more urgently, "there is one thing we should have considered."

"Yes?"

"What kind of alien can assume the form of another?"

"One of my people?" Odo looked alarmed. "Why? What purpose would it serve?"

"I don't know!" Julian said, but the thought of another changeling on the station spurred him to invention. "Maybe there are . . . political or strategic reasons for the theft. It's a lot of latinum, isn't it?"

"It is a great deal of latinum, Doctor, but by no means enough to bring down an economy, for example. Moreover, I run twice daily scans for the presence of any of my people on this station." Odo shook his head decisively. "There are no changelings on Deep Space 9. Other than myself."

Julian nodded in relief. "Then we just have to go with the most likely explanation. Quark and the security officer both made a mistake."

Odo looked very unsatisfied with that answer.

Julian sighed. "You really are convinced that someone is going to try to steal this latinum, aren't you?"

"I'm absolutely certain of it," Odo said fervently.

"Well . . . why does it have to Brixhta? Aren't most crimes done by people who are on the inside?" He shrugged. "Think about it—who doesn't own the latinum, but has been very close to it all this time? Who knows about all the security you have around it? And is here on the station, right now?"

Odo stared at him for a moment, and then turned on his heel and headed out of the infirmary. "Thank you, Doctor!" he called back over his shoulder. Julian watched him go, laughed a little, and returned to the doubtful pleasure of reading.

Outside, Sisko saw, the evening was drawing on. The clouds were clearing, and the sky was deepening to a clear blue-black. The stars were coming out, and a thin wedge of moonlight had already sliced its way through the branches of the trees and into the grounds that lay behind the embassy. Sisko walked past the cabal of Romulans gathered on the steps, and felt their eyes upon him as he passed. He decided that he would not acknowledge them.

At the edge of the terrace ran a low wall, with steps leading down onto the lawn. Sisko stopped at the wall, setting his champagne glass down, and staring out into the shadows of the garden. A breeze was picking up, shifting the leaves on the dark trees. He shivered a little at the chill, and rubbed his hands together, warming them.

Then he glanced back over his shoulder. One of the Romulans had gone back inside. Veral was still there, now talking intently to her colleague. Their voices were low, the words indistinct. Beyond the pair of them, Sisko had a clear view back into the reception room, lit up brightly. Just by the window, Garak and Roeder were still deep in conversation. Roeder was pointing up at one of the paintings, his hand moving purposefully as he explained some intricacy of ship construction, no doubt; or maybe the aesthetic charm of the piece. Garak looked completely fascinated. Councillor Huang might not have any more triumphs tonight, but Roeder and Garak at least looked set to be a success.

Sisko picked up his glass and drained it. Then he went down the steps into the garden, holding the glass upside down by its thin stem, swinging it back and forth ever so slightly.

He walked out across the lawn. The four buildings that had once been the row of houses—and that now made up the embassy—had each had its own garden, and the gardens were now combined into a single open space right in the heart of the town. The chatter and clatter from the reception receded; he could hear more clearly the distant thrum of the city traffic. He walked on, into the darkness, breathing in the damp of the evening air, until he came at last to a wooden bench situated beneath what he guessed was an apple tree. He put the glass down on the arm of the bench, and sat down, stretching out his legs before him. He looked back at the bright hall. He looked up through the branches of the tree at the night sky. Then he put his hands behind his head and closed his eyes. The noise of the reception receded further; so did Roeder, so did Garak. And Ross, and Batanides; even Leyton. All that was left was the bottom line; the whisper of his conscience, muffled and clumsily silenced.

"Captain Sisko?"

With a start, Sisko opened his eyes and straightened himself. He looked up. Veral was standing in front of him, her perpetual expression of slight amusement still on her face. She was clasping a champagne glass before her.

"Have I disturbed you?" she said. "Please, allow me to apologize."

"No," Sisko said. "No, you're not disturbing me. I was just . . ." He gestured back toward the reception. ". . . just taking a break."

"Would it be an unwelcome imposition, Captain, if I joined you? It would be only for a moment or two."

Sisko shifted over to one side of the bench. "Be my guest," he said softly. Veral, he thought, had seemed to have something to say since they had first set eyes upon each other. Perhaps now he was going to find out what the hell it was.

Veral sat down beside him, and put her glass down upon the ground. "I'm sorry to say that this drink is not very pleasant," she remarked. "The bubbles . . . I did not particularly want to mention it to the councillor—she has been most welcoming this evening, and the drink seems to have some special cultural significance. But should any further gatherings of this sort take place . . ." She gestured suggestively with her fingers.

"Well, that's certainly something we should bear in mind," Sisko said.

"Thank you, Captain."

He watched her fold her hands before her, and waited for her to speak. But she just sat, staring out across the lawn.

• • •

Odo had, as a matter of course, done background checks on the crew of the *Ariadne*. He ran background checks on everyone who came aboard Deep Space 9. Nothing had shown in either Steyn's or Trasser's file. He had, however, been able to find out very little about Auger, except in relation to the *Ariadne*. He had so far put this down to Auger's youth, and Steyn's comments that he was not much traveled. Inexperience, after all, was not a crime. Nevertheless, Odo thought, perhaps it was time he went to have a word with that young man. And Steyn too. Who seemed to spend a lot of time gambling. And talked about being in debt to unmistakably shady characters.

As Odo was assembling his files on the *Ariadne*'s crew, the door to his office slid open and Bashir came in. He seemed most excited.

"Doctor," Odo said, rising from his chair. "How can I help you?"

"I've cracked it," Bashir said. He was grinning from ear to ear.

"I beg your pardon?"

"The *latinum!*" Bashir said. "Odo, I think I know what's going on."

"I was just about to go and speak to Captain Steyn again, and her young crewman—"

"No, you were right all along." Bashir's eyes were shining. "It's Brixhta, I'm absolutely sure of it."

Odo eyed him with interest. "That is something of a change of heart, Doctor—"

"Odo, we've been working from *completely* the wrong premises."

"Have we?" Odo glanced past Bashir out onto the Promenade. Now that he had a new avenue of investigation, he was keen to get started. Of course, he thought glumly, this would be *exactly* the moment that Bashir would decide to become interested in the case. "In what way?" he said.

"Well, think about it. What have almost all your questions to me been about?"

"About Brixhta—"

"No, more than that—about Hamexi, and about Hamexi physiology. Odo, we've been assuming that what we needed to track on the station was a biological entity. But what if it isn't biological. What if it's *mechanical?*"

Odo took a good look at the doctor's eager face. It was touching, in a way, to see Bashir become so enthusiastic about the whole business. Nevertheless, an investigation was not advanced by ignoring the facts and details of the case in favor of someone's flight of fancy.

"A mechanical *Hamexi?* Don't be ridiculous," Odo said, flatly.

Something wasn't working. Auger could feel it. The wheel was spinning just as it should, and it was telling him things, just like it should—but it just wasn't quite right. . . . The picture, he thought, was splintering.

He reached for his glass of water and began to play with it. After a moment or two, it was shifted away from him, and then he felt a touch upon his arm. He jumped, his already fractured concentration thoroughly interrupted, but when he looked it turned out to be Steyn.

"Auger," she said softly, "are you okay? Is something the matter?"

Auger looked fretfully around the colors of the bar. Something dark impinged on his vision.

"It's him," he muttered, jerking his head at Mechter. "He's getting in the way."

• • •

"No, Odo, I mean it! Think about it!"

Bashir was sufficiently thick-skinned, Odo noted, that being told his ideas were nonsense did not lessen his zeal in any way. He thought impatiently of the interview he wanted to conduct with Auger, and then looked at Bashir's keen face. This was not a man who was going to be passed over without a hearing. He leaned back against his desk.

"Present a little more of your thinking to me, Doctor," he sighed.

Bashir's excitement visibly rose. "Brixhta calls himself an antiques dealer," he said. "Now, I don't know about you, but when *I* hear the word 'antiques,' I think of things like furniture, or paintings. But most of the merchandise Brixhta brought with him to the station was toys. And some of them were mechanical. *Machines,* Odo. I *told* you it was the chief you should have been talking to!"

"A mechanical Hamexi?" Odo snorted again. "Doctor, you've seen what they look like!"

"If he's selling this stuff, he must know something about how to restore them, or . . . or how to build them." Bashir leaned across the desk eagerly. "Miles would know better than me, but my guess is that it could have come in quite easily in any of the crates which Brixhta brought with him to the station. Nothing would have been detected on any of the scans you and I did looking for lifesigns. And even with Brixhta safely locked up in one of your holding cells, this machine—or whatever it is—can be going around doing . . . well, whatever it needs to do in order to steal the latinum. And if someone saw it, they would just assume it was the Hamexi that they had seen before. Odo," he stopped for breath, "they *all look the same!*"

Odo looked down at the padd he was holding. It was still showing the security reviews of Steyn and her crew.

"Odo, don't you think it's possible?"

"It's *possible*," Odo admitted, "but whether or not it is very *likely*—"

"Possible enough that it's worth checking out?"

"I still want to speak to Steyn and that young man as soon as I can—"

"You don't have to do it yourself, you know. Just get someone to check."

Odo looked at Bashir's face. Having gone to so much trouble to intrigue the doctor in the case, it seemed a shame, he thought, not to follow up on his suggestions. However unlikely they seemed.

"Oh, very well," he growled.

Bashir looked back at him in delight. "Good man!"

"Although my team is very stretched at the moment, Doctor . . ." Odo grumbled as he went back around his desk and started to punch at the comm.

"And I appreciate you taking the time even to think about it."

Odo frowned, and tried a few more buttons.

"Is something the matter, Odo?" Bashir's voice had faltered a little.

"Yes," Odo replied. "This is odd. I can't seem to open a channel on the com."

Bashir leaned over. "Are you sure?"

Odo kept on trying for a moment or two more. "There's nothing," he said, and moved around from behind the desk. "I wonder if this is stationwide, or just in here." He walked over to the door of his office. And then stayed standing in front of it, because it had not opened.

• • •

Sisko stirred impatiently in his seat. Garak, Roeder, now Veral . . . He was getting tired of all this opacity in the conversations round here. "Subcommander Veral," he said, "was there something you wanted to talk to me about?"

She turned and looked at him, seeming startled, as if he had unexpectedly cursed. "Nothing of particular importance, Captain," she said. "I do wonder, however, what you make of occasions such as this." She nodded back toward the building.

Sisko shrugged. "It's just part of the way things work, I guess," he said. "What do *you* make of them?"

"I find them frivolous," she said, coolly. "A waste of time. Perhaps that is something else to bear in mind."

"You don't see any use in bringing the delegates together informally?" Sisko said, a little sharply, on Huang's account, if nothing else. "You don't think it might help us all—not just now but in the future—to find some areas of common ground other than the fact that we all want the Dominion driven from the Alpha Quadrant?"

"That sounds to me very like many lectures I have heard given by Starfleet officers on how others should behave, but I am willing to admit it might be useful," she conceded. "And yet . . ." She gave him another of her half-smiles. ". . . in practice, the delegates from the Klingon Empire stand at one end of the room, and my own colleagues stand at the opposite end, and between us flutter your own delegates, as pliant and ineffective as ever."

Ineffective? Sisko felt a flash of fury. *Who the hell was it brought you into the war?* he thought. *That was pretty damn effective!* He had a sudden urge to find out just how self-satisfied Veral would look once he had told her exactly what had happened to the late Senator Vreenak. He suppressed that desire quickly. Admitting his responsibility to his superiors was one thing. Being provoked into breaching security was another. He looked again at her smile, and felt the sharp stab of anger that had become common but not comfortable over the past weeks. *Although perhaps they're both a kind of confession. . . .*

"Adaptability isn't a bad thing, Subcommander," he said, with an effort. He kept looking resolutely out at the garden, rather than risk meeting her eye. "Particularly in wartime."

"I notice you have ignored my charge of incompetence, Captain, but otherwise it seems we are in accord with each other. Everything changes—particularly in wartime," she agreed, nodding her head. "The old enemies no longer seem so inimical. The old certainties become fluid, perhaps; the line between good and bad is no longer so clear-cut. And I find myself wondering," she said, with a studied carelessness, "how fascinating it would be to discover quite how adaptable the Federation and Starfleet are. How pliable their principles might be. Given enough pressure."

Again, that half-smile. Sisko found himself almost shuddering, and he had to look away. He stared upward, up through the dark leaves of the apple tree, up at the sky beyond. The branches shivered in the breeze, and a sliver of moonlight slipped through. As he watched it touch the leaves of the tree, it filtered through Sisko's mind that maybe this was not an academic discussion. That maybe Veral was talking about something very particular. Talking about Vreenak.

"I can find myself imagining," Veral was saying, so softly, "a situation in which a Starfleet officer might face a difficult choice. A choice between his principles, and a choice to adapt those principles in a new and hostile environment. I can easily imagine him adapting; and adapting to the new circumstances very well. And I would not blame him, Captain. Rather, I would applaud him. Everything changes, everything adapts. But only the strongest can survive. The strongest, and their allies."

Sisko listened to her voice almost as if he was dreaming. He watched the clouds slipping past the moon. There was no one to condemn what had been done. Not Ross, not Batanides—certainly not Leyton. And not even, it seemed, the Romulans themselves.

"I welcome that," Veral said, "in an ally." She picked up her glass, and held it again by the stem, between both hands. "To our alliance, Captain Sisko. May it continue as it began." Then, with a quick, decided movement, Veral stood up. She straightened the tunic of her uniform. "Perhaps you will excuse me now. I would like to explore a little more of this garden before the evening ends." Sisko sat and stared at her. She gave her enigmatic smile, and then her expression changed, and became more sober.

"There is one other thing I feel I ought to mention, Captain," she said, hesitating. "I have noticed that you find yourself in some interesting company. I have no doubt that Mr. Garak has his uses. But you might wish to keep a closer eye on him."

Sisko looked back over his shoulder at the reception room. His eyes had become accustomed to the outside, and he found himself squinting against the lights. It was difficult to be certain, but he was fairly sure he could no longer see either Garak or Roeder standing by the window. . . .

"Goodnight, Captain," Veral said, quietly.

It was like a splash of cold water on his face. Sisko got up and almost ran back indoors. There was nobody in front of the painting of the *H.M.S. Victory*. He glanced around the room, until he saw Huang, still darting through the company like a hummingbird. He made his way over to her, gently touched her elbow until she smiled up at him, and then drew her aside.

"Councillor," he said, quietly, "you don't know where Tomas Roeder is, do you?"

Huang caught the urgency in his voice. She looked at him with concern. "Mr. Roeder? Didn't he come and find you, Captain? He left with your friend. It seems that Mr. Garak was keen to see a little more of the city, and Roeder knows it very well, of course. They went . . ." She checked the time on a delicate silver wristwatch. ". . . I'm not sure exactly, five or ten minutes perhaps? It can't be much longer. If you hurry, you might catch them. I should imagine they'll head up the river."

"Thank you, Councillor," Sisko murmured, turning to leave. He felt his fury rising again. *I specifically told him not to wander off anywhere!*

He contained himself enough to avoid actually running out of the embassy, but he took the steps down onto the road two at a time. The street was dark and empty. Then he ran across the road, hopped over the wall, and stood for a moment looking up and down the embankment. A couple walked past, looking at him curiously in his dress uniform. There was no one else around that he could see. The lamplight winked down at him. The moon was bright. And the river flowed on by, broad and brown and slow.

8

ROEDER NAVIGATED A PATH slowly but purposefully through the reception crowd. Garak kept him just to his right side, and slightly ahead. The press of people thinned out as they reached the foyer, and the security guards at the door nodded at them as they went on outside. There were a couple of people out there, dotted about on the steps, making conversation, enjoying a drink and the evening. Roeder went down the steps. Garak sucked in a breath and followed his lead, still keeping the other man just a little in front.

The night air was cool, but it seemed to Garak that the threat of rain had passed. The clouds had cleared and the moon had come out. Roeder led Garak across the street, and they went down toward the embankment. A line of railings ran along the line of the water, several yards from the river's edge. Roeder stopped at them. Garak came to stand beside him. The sky was dark, and the moon was broken on the ripples of the river.

"The Thames," Roeder said.

Garak glanced at him. "I'm sorry?"

"That's the name of the river."

"I see."

"This isn't the best view," Roeder said, turning his back to the water. "We should go south of the river, and look back this way."

"Whatever you suggest."

"There's a bridge a short walk away. We can cross the water there."

Roeder started off, and Garak fell in step on his right, putting Roeder between him and the river.

"I was interested," Roeder said, after a moment or two, "that you came to the reception this evening with Ben Sisko. You know that we served together?"

"Yes, he told me."

"I knew him pretty well at one point. Sisko is Starfleet to the core. You'll forgive me, Mister Garak—but you're not what I would have picked out as being an obvious choice of friend for him."

"The same could stand in reverse," Garak pointed out. "My home is being occupied by our mutual enemies, Mister Roeder. I have very few allies. But Starfleet is willing to fight the same war that I am fighting."

"Of course," Roeder said, smiling down at the ground. "I should have guessed. What's that expression? 'My enemy's enemy is my friend.' "

I really rather like this man, Garak thought. *I don't particularly want to kill him.*

"Which I've always found to be a very pragmatic philosophy. Whereas you . . ." Garak glanced at Roeder's still face. ". . . you would say that you have no enemies?"

Roeder remained impassive. "Oh, no," he said. "I wouldn't say that at all."

Garak risked a glance at the other man's pale, thoughtful face. He frowned. Roeder was proving harder to crack than a *canka* nut. *Talk to me,* Garak urged him silently. *Give me a reason to keep you alive.*

"Then . . . you choose not to fight them?" Garak hazarded. "Is that a little closer?"

Roeder gave a thin smile. "A little," he allowed. Then he added, in a low but still conversational tone, "By the way, I don't know if you've noticed, but we're being followed. Have been since we left the embassy."

"I had been wondering if you were aware of that."

"Shall we go and find out which of us it is that's attracting all this attention?"

"To be perfectly honest, Mister Roeder, I would rather we were left in peace."

"Peace?" Roeder gave a quiet laugh. "All right, Mister Garak. Let's go and find some peace."

Dax looked up from her station. "Nerys, something isn't right here."

Kira picked up the mug from the replicator. "What sort of something?"

"I was just running the level-three diagnostic on the environmental systems, and everything has seized up on me."

"Seized up?" Kira abandoned her *raktajino* and went to join Dax at her station.

"And now none of the systems are responding," Dax said, shaking her head.

"Communications?" Kira said.

"Nothing. . . ."

Kira hit her combadge. "Kira to Odo." There was a silence. "Kira to Worf." No reply.

Dax tried the same routine, but with no success. "Combadges too," she said.

"I don't like having no idea what's happening anywhere else on the station," Kira said. "Try the doors," she ordered.

Dax nodded and tapped at a few controls.

Nothing happened.

"The turbolift?"

Again, there was nothing.

"Transporter?"

Nothing.

"Could this be something left over from when the Dominion were on the station?" Kira said. "The Cardassians had access to all of the systems then. Could they have left something behind, something that would start running at a predetermined time?"

"It could be that," Dax acknowledged, leaning over her station. "Although the chief and I were very thorough in our housecleaning afterward. . . ." She started working at the controls. "I'm going to try bypassing the primary command pathways. That should let me get past whatever program is running. . . ."

"Try to be quick about it," Kira said. "Because if this *is* the prelude to an attack on the station, I'd like to know *before* things start exploding around me."

Dax worked for a little while, and then began to frown.

"What's the matter?" Kira said.

"Well, every procedure that I try is being blocked; it's as if the program can counter everything I throw at it." She jabbed, irritated, at the console. "And then it goes on to block that route in entirely. I've tried with a whole array of security protocols, but so far it's no use. . . ." Dax carried on working for a while, and then shook her head. "Whoever's doing this had a very good idea of what we would try to do to get past it."

"I really don't like the sound of that," Kira said. "All right—what do we do next?"

"When all else fails me," Dax said, giving her a wry look, "what I usually try next is to ask the chief to hit things very hard. That always does the job."

"This is *ridiculous . . .*" Kira ground out. She put her hands on her hips and glared around ops. Then, with one swift, decisive movement, she pulled out her phaser.

"Nerys, *no!*" Dax yelped, putting her hands over her face and closing her eyes, wincing in anticipation of the explosion she was sure would inevitably follow.

There was a short silence. Dax risked looking out. Kira was standing with one hand still resting on her hip and the other pointing her phaser at the control panel of the entrance into ops. She had a thoughtful expression on her face. Dax heaved a sigh of relief and relaxed again, leaning on the console in front of her.

"You know," Kira said, pensively, putting her phaser away, "I'm sure that the last time I tried that, it ended with the station almost exploding." She glanced over at Dax and raised an eyebrow. "Maybe you should try a few more things before I start blowing the doors off."

"I think that's a *very* good idea," Dax replied earnestly.

Kira lifted a finger in warning. "Just don't take too long about it, Jadzia."

Odo studied the inside of the locking mechanism to the door of his office, all too conscious of the irritating presence of Bashir hovering anxiously at his shoulder.

"Any luck?" Bashir said, for about the fifth time.

"If I were having any luck, Doctor," Odo replied, "then you would not still be staring at a locked door." He pushed the panel closed.

"Odo," Bashir said urgently, "I know you think I've been talking nonsense, but I really am worried that something is about to happen to the latinum—"

Odo nodded slowly. "It seems reasonable to conjecture that if anyone is making an attempt to steal the latinum, they would do so not long after putting the station's chief of security out of circulation."

"Exactly," Bashir said.

Odo went over to his desk, and tried the com. "Odo to ops." There was nothing. "Odo to security." Still nothing. "Odo to anyone who can hear me."

"Combadges?" Bashir said. They both tried, with no success. "So we're stuck in here," Bashir said, folding his arms in frustration, "with no way of raising anyone and letting them know about the latinum."

"No," Odo said, shaking his head decidedly. "I can get out of this office, even when the door is barred." He gave Bashir a knowing look. "You may recall that I found myself trapped in here once before, Doctor," he explained. "When Gul Dukat's defense program was mistakenly activated."

"I remember," Bashir said, nodding. The whole station had locked down around them, and it was in part because of Dukat's assistance that the station itself had not been destroyed. Bashir could only hope that they were not facing a similar situation now. They were hardly in a position to apply to Dukat for his help this time round.

"As you may remember, I was not able to escape from my office because there were forcefields running down the decks and along the bulkheads."

"I guess you decided not to make the same mistake a second time?" Bashir said, starting to grin.

Odo tilted his head. "Being trapped here with Quark provided a sufficiently strong incentive to insure it would never happen again," he said. "If there is a breach of station security, then the forcefield still covers the door, protecting this office from intruders. But I had the chief install stasis interrupters in the field, which means I am not prevented from shapeshifting out of my office." He came from behind the desk. "I can get out beneath the door. Whatever situation is currently unfolding on the station, I'll soon have it resolved."

"Well, that's some good news," Bashir said. "At last." He took a step back, to give Odo space to change into whatever shape he needed.

There was a slight pause, in which nothing happened.

"Do you want me to look the other way, Constable?" Bashir said, suddenly uncertain of etiquette.

Odo did not answer. He was staring down at his hand. Then he said, "Something isn't right."

"What's the matter?"

"I can't . . ." Odo jerked his hand downward, as if he were trying to shake something loose.

"Odo?"

"It appears, Doctor, that I cannot alter my form," he said. There was a rising note of alarm in his voice.

Bashir reached for his tricorder. "Give me your hand," he said. Odo pulled away from him. Bashir drew back, raised a palm in apology. "I'm sorry, Odo—I just want to make sure you're all right."

"There's no need, Doctor." Odo clasped his arms across him, sealing himself away further. "I know what this is," he said, bitterly, adding Garak to the list of people with whom he intended to have a long conversation once this situation was resolved. "I've experienced something like it before."

They walked onward slowly, Garak waiting for Roeder to give him the signal. They reached the place where the river was crossed by a wide bridge, and the road they were following sloped down to enter an underpass.

Roeder began to steer them away from the river. Just before they went into the underpass, Roeder pointed right. They peeled off into a dark side street alongside them.

"There's a gate up ahead," Roeder muttered. "It opens into some gardens. Go in there. Move quickly. Keep quiet."

Sure enough, they soon came upon the gate. It eased open on its hinges, barely making a sound. They hurried in. Garak quickly took in his surroundings. The garden was small and secluded, and surrounded on three sides by what he guessed would be office buildings. There were still one or two lights on in some of them. Anyone looking down from there and out into the garden would almost certainly see them. Garak frowned.

"Keep walking along this path," Roeder whispered. "It will fork. We'll go left."

Again, it was just as Roeder described. They went quickly down the new path; Garak had time only to feel rather than see the dark shapes of trees as they hurried on. The new path ended at another gate. Roeder raised his hand to signal to Garak that they should stop, then he stepped off the path onto the grass, to one side of the gate. He gestured to Garak to take the other side. Garak took up his position, and watched for Roeder's next move. Roeder put his finger to his lips; then, *"Listen,"* he mouthed to Garak.

Garak leaned back against the wall. He did not take his eyes off Roeder. They both stood, completely still, staring at each other, listening for footsteps, listening for anyone following. There was nothing. Just the soft, distant sounds of the night. It was not, Garak reflected, the usual means of going about seeing the sights of a city.

A minute or two passed. A light went off in one of the buildings across from where they were standing. Roeder blinked and looked away, up to where the light had been. Then he turned back to Garak.

"Whoever it was," he said, calmly, "I think we've lost them."

"I didn't doubt we could," Garak replied, with a smile. "Where now?"

Roeder jerked his head at the gate. "We'll take a back way." He reached for the latch on the gate, and paused. "Will people be looking for you now?"

"Would you let a Cardassian wander around Earth unattended?"

"Probably not." Roeder pushed open the gate. "But then, you're not unattended, are you?"

Dax was running her latest test when a comm channel crackled with static, and a voice unexpectedly came through. It kept breaking up, but it was still instantly recognizable.

"This is O'Brien to Deep Space 9. Is there anybody there who can hear me?"

Kira and Dax exchanged relieved looks.

"The voice of the machine," Dax murmured.

"Chief, this is Major Kira—are you able to hear to me?"

"Just about. . . ."

"You're breaking up quite badly," Kira informed him, "but we're still glad to hear from you. Where are you right now?"

"I'm still over on the Ariadne. What have you been doing to the station?"

"More what it's been doing to us," Kira replied. "We seem to have some kind of systems lockdown, Chief. None of the doors are opening, none of the systems are responding to us—we can't raise any communications . . ." She stopped and frowned. "How is it you can talk to us?"

There was a brief burst of static loud enough to make both women wince, and then the channel went dead.

"Chief?" Kira said urgently. "Are you still there? Chief? *Dammit!*"

The channel spluttered back into life. *"Sorry, Major, lost you for a moment—what did you say?"*

"We can't raise *any* communications here, Chief," she replied, speaking more clearly. "How are you able to speak to us?"

"Nothing over here on the Ariadne *has been affected—except for the airlocks back onto DS9. As soon as I realized something was going on, we used the systems here to patch into the station's com—but this ship's nowhere near fully operational yet. We're going to get breakdowns on the channel . . ."*

"Is there any way you can get back over here?" Kira said. "So far as we can tell communications, doors, turbolifts—none of them are working. Certainly nothing here in ops. We could really do with you right now."

"The Ariadne *doesn't have a transporter. And from what you've just said, I'm guessing ours aren't working right now."*

"Good guess," Kira said, in exasperation.

"Then, no—I can't get back. But perhaps I can do something from here."

"Wait a minute," Dax murmured. "What's this?"

Kira came over to see and, as they watched, one of the viewscreens flickered and then came back on.

"Chief," Dax said, "we seem to be getting some monitoring devices back. Have you managed to get some other systems up and running at your end?"

"Much as I'd like to take the credit, that's all your own work."

"It's certainly nothing we've done," Kira said. "We can't *do* anything!"

"Well, whoever's behind all this seems to be showing a great deal of attention to detail. My guess is somebody wants you to see something."

Kira leaned over Dax's shoulder to take a look at the image on the screen. It was showing a closed door.

"Habitat ring," Dax murmured. Kira nodded. Then, as they watched, the door slid open, to reveal the distinctive shape of an Hamexi, coming through.

"That can't be," Dax said.

"What's going on, Dax?"

"What we can see right now," Dax said, "is an Hamexi making its way along the habitat ring—" She was stopped by a startled interruption from O'Brien.

"An Hamexi?"

Kira frowned. "What do you two know about this?"

"Well, just that Odo has been worried about an Hamexi visiting the station right now. Thought he had his eyes or whatever it is on the latinum. But last I heard Odo had put him in the holding cells."

"Yes, he arrested him yesterday, after the auction," Dax said.

"Well, he's out now," Kira replied. "And he seems to be able to pass through all the doors . . ." She shook her head in disbelief. "They're just opening as he comes up to them and closing as he comes through!"

"He also seems to be right on route for the Promenade," Dax pointed out. "Will there be anyone there to stop him?"

"We cleared most of that area when the latinum came on board," Kira said. "But the route he's taking leads up to the airlock just along from the assay office. He's going to hit the forcefields soon enough."

"This is fascinating stuff," O'Brien said, *"but I don't know how long this channel will stay open. Tell me what you've been trying so far to get things working."*

In between bursts of static and sudden breakdowns in the channel, Dax managed to give him a rundown of her attempts to bypass the command pathways.

"From what you're saying, it sounds like this program is faking security protocols," O'Brien said. *"There are some high-level ones that give you the authority to lock down an area and stop any access to it."*

"Is there any way we can work around that, Chief?" Kira said. "Any way we can use those protocols to our advantage?"

"That's my advice—there's not a lot else to try. I want to get through to Odo. He'll know the higher level security codes; maybe we can use those to find some way to override this program."

"Whatever you both say about this Hamexi," Kira put in, "I'm still not ruling out the possibility that this is something left over from when the Dominion were here."

"Sounds reasonable."

"I don't want us to find ourselves sitting targets for a fleet!" Kira said. "Will you try to find out what's going on from up there?"

"Not everything's working here properly yet, Major, but I'll get onto it."

"Thanks, Chief," Kira said. An idea struck her. "Back when the Cardassians' counterinsurgency program locked the station down, Garak had some access codes that let him move around. Odo will know about them, I'm sure. At least if we have those then we could get out of ops."

"That's exactly the kind of thing Odo will know about.

I'll get onto it straightaway. Oh, and try not to hit the consoles so hard, will you? You really need to know where to do it."

Kira and Dax looked at each other guiltily.

"Typical of Cardassians when you think about it. Only they would build systems that respond to violence—"

"You're getting off the point, Chief," Kira said, with a slight twist of her lips.

"Sorry, Major."

"All right, we'll wait until you get through to Odo. One other thing," she said, "if you can get any information on what's going on elsewhere. We've got no idea how much of the station is affected, whether anybody has been hurt—*anything* you can find out."

"All right, I'll do my best."

"Thanks, Chief."

The channel went dead.

"Well," Kira said, looking over at Dax, "at least we're not quite back to blowing off the doors. Not yet," she added darkly.

"I'm sure between them the chief and Odo will be able to work something out—"

"But we don't know how long that's going to take," Kira said in frustration. She looked down again at the viewscreen. The Hamexi was advancing toward the Promenade. "And I have a feeling a forcefield isn't going to hold this one. We need to get onto the Promenade before it does—"

"Major," O'Brien's voice came through again. Even taking into account the static he sounded unusually acerbic. *"Give me a couple of minutes before you start going out with all guns blazing. I doubt you'd beat the Hamexi anyway, and I'm not thrilled at the thought of having to fix every single door between the Promenade and ops."*

• • •

Sisko swore at the night sky and tried to make up his mind what to do next. He was not familiar with the city, and he could not guess where Roeder would take someone who had claimed an interest in learning about it. He stared in both directions down the embankment. East, downriver, he had a pretty clear view, and despite the dark it seemed the less promising way. Westward, the river ran beneath a bridge, and then bent away to the south. And *up the river,* the councillor had said. It could just have been a figure of speech, but it helped him make his decision. He set off west walking at a rapid pace, with the river to his left. Veral's mocking smile as she had given her warning about Garak came back to him. He found himself with an overwhelming urge to kill Garak when he saw him again.

Sisko kicked a stone out of his way. Again, he thought, he should have predicted that Garak would try something like this. He drew closer to the bridge, and scanned the length of it. There was nobody there. He walked on. The river began to curve, and the street bent with it. Looking ahead, he could see that it was darker in the underpass, away from the streetlamps. Then he heard footsteps— someone running toward him. He slowed down, thinking he would rather see who it was in the relative light of the street.

The dark figure came out from the under the bridge. It was Lieutenant Chaplin. She no longer had her air of brisk efficiency, Sisko noted. In fact, she looked frantic.

"Good evening, Lieutenant," Sisko called out to her, calmly. She stopped running, and he made his way over to her. "Are we looking for the same man, by any chance?"

• • •

Roeder led Garak down a narrow street. They took a sharp right, into another street. Trying to keep his bearings, Garak guessed that they were now going in front of the buildings that overlooked the garden. More of these tall terraces, like the embassy. He peered at some of the brass plaques on the walls as they went past. Art societies. Historical institutes. They took another right. This street seemed at first to Garak to be ending in darkness; then he realized that it was the river straight ahead.

Roeder, watching him, said, "Do you know where you are now?"

"Yes," Garak said, glancing around. "We've come right back on our tracks."

"With any luck, our follower will have carried on along the river. Which means, in effect, that we're now following him. Or her."

They came out onto the embankment and turned right. The dark mouth of the underpass opened up ahead, but Roeder did not take Garak in. He bore left, closer to the river, leading Garak down some narrow steps.

It suddenly went very dark. For a moment, Garak lost all sense of direction. He made himself concentrate on remembering the map of the area he had studied before leaving Starfleet HQ and, as his eyes became accustomed to the darkness, he recalled a narrow towpath running under the bridge. He glanced around, taking in the whole of his surroundings. They were walking along a wooden pier that ran along the side of the underpass. There were some railings to the left, and then the river; and some dim lights lining the wall of the underpass to the right. Garak could not see anything across the river; could not see another building, could not see if there was anyone out there to witness.

Roeder walked on a little way, and then came to a halt,

just beyond one of the lights. His face was obscured.
Garak stopped walking too, leaving a couple of feet between them, keeping to the shadows himself.

"Well," said Roeder. "Shall we get down to business?"
His voice was flat; it sounded emptied out.

"I'd like that," Garak replied, his gaze flickering between the figure standing opposite and the dark all around
him, trying to pick out some information from both.

"You're still with Starfleet Intelligence, aren't you,
Roeder?" he said, stalling for time; trying to invent ahead
of himself how this conversation might go. He was beginning to get very impatient with the other man. He had
been as unthreatening as he knew how, given Roeder several opportunities to open up—but he had remained im-
penetrable. Garak was starting to think that Roeder might
need to be presented with a more immediate threat to get
him talking. People so often did.

"Your association with the antiwar campaign," Garak
said, "it's a front, isn't it? You're the man inside." He
reached up and slid his hand toward his inside jacket
pocket.

"I wonder," Roeder murmured, "who could have told
you a thing like that?" He eyes followed the route of
Garak's hand, and he shifted his weight slightly to one
side. It brought him no closer, although it did seem to put
him farther into the darkness.

"Well, I have my sources," Garak replied blithely,
mirroring his movement. He had a much better sense of
the river now. There were some lights, dotted here and
there along the water. But he couldn't quite make out
where they were coming from. Buildings on the other
bank? Boats? He could not tell if there was anyone
close, and before he made a decision about what to do
next, he had to know if he could be seen.

"And I also have to wonder," Roeder said, "if that were indeed the case, why that information would be interesting to you."

"Well . . . perhaps it would put us on the same side," Garak suggested. He moved his hand further across his chest. From what he could make out of Roeder's shape, black against black, he seemed to lean in a little in response.

"Would it? Is there something you want to tell me about yourself, Mister Garak?"

Garak pressed his hand against his chest and suppressed a sigh. Roeder seemed to meet every question with a question of his own. It seemed he would have to give Roeder a little more information, if he was going to get him to talk. If he wanted to stop this before it all got completely out of hand . . .

"Imagine if you will," Garak replied, "a former agent of the Obsidian Order, cast out from Cardassian space, who deplores the new regime, and wishes to see it destroyed. Who wants to keep Starfleet in the fight. And who would like to know a little more about how he might assist Starfleet Intelligence toward this end." Something splashed into the river. Somewhere, a light went out. Garak slid his hand more into his jacket, trying to make it look real, trying to make sure it was not too unreal.

"That's a fascinating story," Roeder said. "And not even remotely plausible."

Roeder could move at warp speed, Garak realized, as he crossed the distance between them and grabbed Garak's wrist with his left hand, stopping him from reaching further into his jacket and the knife concealed within.

Roeder began to reach for his own pocket. With a swift movement, Garak slammed the heel of his hand into Roeder's face. He heard the crack of bone, felt blood trickle warm down his wrist, caught Roeder's curse cold in the night air. That was perhaps a little too real, he thought, guiltily. They both fell backward awkwardly, away from each other. Quick as a flash, Garak had the knife out and held in front of him. He stepped in; not to kill, to take control—

And found himself looking down at the snub nose of a phaser.

Garak fell back a step. He looked up at Roeder, and jerked his head back in the direction of the embassy. "How did you get that in there?" he said.

"It pays," Roeder coughed out, voice thick and breathless, "to make friends with the men on the door." He kept the phaser trained on Garak and, with his other hand, reached down into his pocket. There was a flash of metal. Garak jerked back again, expecting a knife—and then saw what it was.

A hypospray.

Roeder gestured with it toward the knife in Garak's hand. "Drop it," he said. Garak looked at the phaser, considered his options—and then did what he was told. Roeder took a step forward, and kicked the knife away beyond the railings. It made a quiet *splash* as it hit the water.

This, Garak thought, *might well turn out to be one of my riskier strategies.*

"Now," Roeder said, his voice still muffled, but his breathing settling a little, becoming steadier, "The choice is yours, Mister Garak. We can do this the quick way," he lifted the phaser, "or the easy way," he lifted the hypospray.

"Easy for who?" Garak asked, eyes flicking between his two immediate options.

"Well—which one of us is armed?"

"That's a very good point," Garak murmured. "And since you put it that way," he looked up and could not help but smile at the sight of Roeder's nose, "I think I'll take it easy."

Standing at the bar, Quark could hear music, conversation, people eating and drinking . . . but underneath it all there was the grim and steady grind of the dabo wheel. Yet another spin, and Quark heard his profits take yet another plunge. He wiped a glass disconsolately, and put it clattering on the shelf behind him.

Over at the wheel, the captain of the freighter patted her young crewman on the back, then she bent down and whispered something in his ear. He nodded absently, his attention entirely on the wheel in front of him. The captain stood up, and ambled over to the bar, settling herself on the stool right in front of Quark. She pointed up at one of the bottles behind his ear, so Quark poured her a drink from it and slammed the glass down in front of her. But it could not quite drown out the sound of the wheel spinning away more of his latinum.

It was heartbreaking, Quark thought. From what he could make out, the entire station was locked down. Nobody could get in and—more importantly—nobody could get out. He had customers trapped in here. *Trapped.* And yet still somehow all this profit was slipping through his fingers. . . .

Steyn drank deeply and then smiled at him across the bar. "So . . ." she said.

Quark glowered back at her. "So?"

"I was hoping that you and I could have a chat."

"Do you think you really have something I want to hear?"

"Maybe," she said. She started tapping her fingernail against the inside of the glass. Quark ground his teeth. As if she wasn't irritating enough. "I thought," the captain said, "that you might like to hear a little about my friend Auger over there."

"I can hear the damage he's doing to my dabo table."

Steyn looked over toward Auger with a maternal pride. "That boy," she said, "was a find. I tell you, it was like digging up treasure."

"Not from where I'm standing."

"You'd never think it on a day-to-day basis. He drops things, he breaks things . . . practically trips over his own feet. And yet I have never seen him lose a game. Of anything." She stared down into her glass, tapping her nail against it again, and shook her head in admiration. Then she looked back up at Quark. "You ever heard a dog whistle?" she asked.

A *dog* . . . That was some kind of Earth animal, wasn't it? Quark thought he could remember something about fur. And fangs. He was certain there had been fangs. He looked back at Steyn in complete bewilderment. "*Can* they whistle?" he said.

Steyn put her hand to her eyes for a moment. "No," she explained patiently, "I meant, have you heard it. A whistle. For dogs."

"I'm not entirely sure what a dog looks like, Captain Steyn. Do you think I'm likely to have heard a whistle for one?"

Steyn held up her hands. "Fair enough," she said. "All right—the thing you need to know about a dog whistle is, it's pitched at a high frequency."

In Quark's opinion it sounded close to cruelty. He shuddered, and drew back a little further from Steyn. Was this meant to be some kind of threat? *Hew-mons* too often turned out to have an aggressive side. "What has this all got to do with my dabo table?" he said.

"The high frequency," Steyn said, tapping more vigorously at her glass, "means that people can't hear the whistle but that dogs can. And sometimes," Steyn nodded at Auger, "I think that boy's a bit like that when it comes to gambling. Like he's working on some higher frequency."

"Which just happens," Quark said resignedly, "to be the same frequency my dabo wheel works on."

A guilty smile spread over Steyn's face. "Yeah," she said. "Sorry about that."

"Oh, I'm sure that makes you sorry." Quark looked mournfully at the table. "What you're telling me is that he's going to clean me out."

Steyn shrugged. "Who knows? The game's only just started, hasn't it? But going on past experience, Auger *will* clean you out, and the rest of those poor mug punters—unless you're running a much smarter program than anyone else we've come across yet. What are the odds on that?"

So this boy's gameplaying was up against Rom's programming. It was like a battle of wills between the two village idiots . . . but while Quark was well aware of just how far his brother's talents stretched, what he was less sure about was the extent of Auger's talents. When it came to odds, Quark was a pragmatist. That was why he preferred stacking them. And watching the way the wheel had been turning for Auger, Quark thought that right now the odds were not stacked in his favor.

"I think," he said, unhappily, "that your young friend might well be on his way to cleaning me out."

"And *that*," Steyn said, "is why we should have a little chat. Because I have a proposition for you."

• • •

Chaplin's relief at seeing Sisko was palpable.

"I've lost him, sir," she said, the apology clear in her voice. "He was with Tomas Roeder. And I just don't know where they got to. . . ." She took a few deep breaths, steadied herself, and fell into step beside Sisko. "One minute they were walking a few yards ahead of me—and then the next thing . . ." She shook her head. "If they used a transporter, they could be anywhere. I can't believe I *lost* him!" She kicked a stone out of her way. "I'm sorry, sir," she said.

"Roeder has about twenty years of Starfleet security experience," Sisko replied, gently. "And Garak . . . well, I'm not sure of the full range of his talents." He glanced across at her dejected face. "If they combined their expertise and really put their mind to losing you, I don't think you stood much of a chance against them." He smiled. "They didn't exactly have much trouble shaking me off either," he pointed out.

That seemed to console her. Not much, but at least it helped her focus and give him a proper report. "Thank you, sir," she said, and nodded. "I'm in contact with Marlow back at HQ—he's doing a planetwide sweep for Cardassian life signs."

"Good." He had been right about her competence. She had not panicked, no matter how fraught she looked right now. They passed out into the street again, into the moonlight. The river was still bending south, and there was another bridge coming up.

"It'll take a bit of time," Chaplin said, "but at least we're looking for something specific and not exactly very common on Earth."

"Well, I certainly hope not," Sisko murmured. "Don't worry too much, Lieutenant," he said, at her rueful smile. "Councillor Huang said they were going to take a look at the city. I think it's best if we just keep on searching while Marlow finishes up his sweep." He pointed to the dark length of the bridge, spanning the river ahead. "I figure we'll find them up there, swapping epigrams."

It made her laugh, as he had intended. "So you've noticed that about Mr. Garak too, sir?"

"I'd say it was one of his distinguishing features."

In the security office, Julian sat leaning against the desk, his arms folded, his head slightly down. But he watched covertly as Odo trod a narrow line back and forth in front of the locked door.

"Odo—" he said.

"No, Doctor," Odo replied firmly. "I do *not* require your attention."

"I just wanted to ask," Julian said mildly, "if you were due to regenerate soon."

He watched Odo's pace quicken.

"Yes," Odo replied.

Julian nodded slowly. "Do you keep a medkit in this office?" he said.

"As I have already said, Doctor—"

"You may not require my attention now," Julian said, "but you might later. My medkit is safely locked away in the infirmary. Do you keep one here?"

Odo gestured over to the desk and, as he did so, Julian saw a flake come away from the constable's hand. He went calmly over to the desk and looked around. He opened one box and, looking inside, he saw a small figurine of a Bajoran. It was painted to look like the kai. He fastened the lid again quickly, and kept looking around the desk. Eventually, he found the medkit.

"Odo," he said, carefully, making sure he was looking away from his patient and examining his medical supplies, "you said that you had experienced something like this before—"

"I'm afraid that that is a security matter, Doctor."

"I understand," Julian said quickly. "I don't want to know how or where—I just want to know what the likely effects are going to be on you. I have to know a little about what's happening to you, Odo."

"Is that *really* necessary, Doctor?"

Julian knew how closely guarded Odo was, but he was not prepared to sit back and watch the constable suffer just to honor his stubborn streak. Before he could answer, there was a burst of static from the comm on Odo's desk, and then O'Brien's voice came through; very distant and breaking up. *"Anyone there? Odo?"*

"Thank god," Julian muttered to himself. "Miles," he said urgently, "am I glad to hear your voice. What the hell is going on?" He looked up. Odo had ceased his pacing to come and stand beside him at the desk. Julian took the opportunity to survey his patient. It was as if Odo was drying, he thought, watching the coarsening and flaking.

"Hallo Julian," O'Brien said. *"Seems we're having a few problems with the station. Well, one problem, actually—it's not under our control right now."*

"That's what I would call a fairly large problem," Julian agreed.

"And you're the smart one. You got Odo there with you?"

"Yes, he's here. . . ."

Odo did not miss his hesitation. "I am quite well, thank you, Doctor—"

"I do think that I should be the judge of that—"

"I am *certainly* well enough to speak to the chief!"

Julian got out of his way.

"How may I help you, Chief?" Odo said.

Dax is trying to bypass this program from ops, but none of the standard protocols are working. Can you give us some higher-level ones, Odo?

To an accompaniment of static, Odo supplied the protocols. "Is it possible to put me through directly to ops?" he asked.

It's all I can do to keep this one channel open—we're going to be pretty low tech for a while yet. Odo, do you remember when that counterinsurgency program of Dukat's locked down the station?

"I remember the occasion extremely well."

Didn't Garak have some security codes that let him access systems? I was thinking that if we could at least have a look round—

"After the event," Odo said, "I came to the conclusion that leaving Garak with an array of access codes was not in the interests of station security. As a result—and, regrettably, given the circumstances—they do not work any more."

Huh. Well, can't say I blame you, Odo.

"Miles," Bashir said, urgently. "Odo and I think that someone is in the process of stealing the latinum."

There was a pause.

"Miles? Are you still there? Miles?"

You might want to see if you can switch on the viewscreen in there.

Odo went across the office and turned on the viewscreen, and Julian came to join him. They stood and watched, aghast, as they saw the Hamexi moving effortlessly around the station. Without cloak or hat, and the doors opening and closing behind him, it was an eerie sight.

"Well," Julian breathed after they had watched for a while. "That's . . . uncanny."

"I'm by no means convinced as yet by your theory that this is a machine," Odo said. "We have no way of knowing what's been happening in the holding cells."

This new turn in events had the benefit of taking Odo's mind off being trapped, Julian thought. "You think Brixhta might have got free?"

"Part of this program might have been to enable Brixhta to get out of his cell," Odo said. "I am assuming that anyone who has this level of control over the station will be able to deal with the forcefields sealing off that section of the Promenade. But Brixhta would still have to get past the security team outside the assay office. And then there are the biometric scanners on the crates—"

As if on cue, the monitor switched to a view just outside the assay office. There was a slight haze to the air, as if the area was filled with some sort of mist. Peering through, Julian saw the two security guards, slumped against the bulkheads.

"I admit it's difficult to make a proper diagnosis from this range," Julian said, "but I'm going to make a guess and say that they've been drugged." They carried on watching for a little while, and then a shape began to emerge from the mist.

"And I notice," Julian added, "that it's not holding up that Hamexi for a second." He glanced over at Odo. "Have you changed your mind about it being mechanical now?"

"You see that gentleman back there?" Steyn jerked her head toward the dabo table. "Standing right behind Auger?"

Quark looked over. "You mean the one with the hidden weapon and the cravat?"

"That's the one. His name is Mechter. He represents my current employers."

"I have a strange feeling that the weapon might be part of the uniform they issued him," Quark murmured. Steyn narrowed her eyes in confirmation. "But what about the cravat?"

Steyn smiled up at him. "I don't think we need to worry about that too much. What really worries me—"

"Apart from the hidden weapon?"

"*Apart* from that, what worries me about Mechter is that he makes Auger even more jumpy than usual. Saw it again and again back on the ship. When Mechter's around it makes Auger drop more cups, break more machinery, all kinds of disasters. Now, I don't *think* it's the cravat that's doing it, though you can never be quite sure with Auger . . ." She frowned. "Anyway, I'm starting to get worried about whether that could eat into our winnings."

"I hope you don't think that makes me feel sorry for you, Captain Steyn."

"Not at all—but what it *does* mean is that I'm looking for someone to keep Mechter busy for me. Which would leave Auger free from distractions, and we'd end up doing so nicely at that wheel of yours that I'd be grateful enough to pay the person looking after Mechter very well. Very well indeed."

Between Steyn's fingernail tapping against the glass and the crashing sound from the dabo table, Quark almost—*almost*—couldn't believe his ears.

"Run that past me again," he said. "I don't think I misheard, but I'm sure you just asked me to help you clean out my own dabo table."

Steyn looked aggrieved. "Well, for a *very* good fee!" she pointed out, hotly.

"You're insane!"

"Well, *maybe*—but that's got absolutely nothing to do with it! You've been watching us and listening to that wheel spinning ever since we came in, and I know that *you* know," here she jabbed a finger at him, "that even with Mechter breathing down his neck, that boy over there is still going to make a fortune at your table." She came up for air. "We seem to be locked in, and while I'm not Auger, I'm still willing to bet that you don't know how long we're going to be stuck here. Auger could be playing right through the night. And the gaming laws are really *quite* strict about letting a player play, aren't they?"

Quark shivered at the sound of that.

"So, why don't we come up with something mutually beneficial. For us. If not the other players. Wouldn't you like the chance to make some of that latinum back?" She flicked her fingernail against her glass again.

Quark listened to the wheel, and then looked at Mechter. He set his own finger on Steyn's glass, stopping it from resonating. He reached behind him for the bottle.

"Ah . . . the gentleman with the cravat," he said, filling up Steyn's glass. "What can you tell me about him?"

Steyn grinned at him. "I thought you might hear what I was saying," she said.

"I need to hear more. What does he like?"

"This is part of my problem," Steyn said. "Because Mechter doesn't seem to drink. Nor does he partake of any other illicit substances, as far as I know. I'm starting to think he's incorruptible."

Quark bared his fangs. "Now you're making it sound like a challenge."

Steyn winked back at him. "I knew you were the man for the job."

"And, anyway," Quark philosophized ruefully as Auger claimed another pile of chips, "if ever there was an application of the one-hundred-and-eighty-third Rule of Acquisition this would have to be it. When life hands you ungaberries—"

"You have to make ungaberry juice?" Steyn guessed.

Quark pulled back from her. Sometimes *hew-mons* were revolting. "No," he said, in disgust. "Detergent."

Garak woke to a dry mouth and a splitting headache. A bright light was shining. He winced and squeezed his eyes tight shut again. Whatever Roeder had used on him, it seemed not to sit too well with Cardassian physiology. He thought about putting a hand up to his head, but suspected this was not an option open to him. He tested the hypothesis and, with a certain dreary predictability, it turned out to be true. His arms and legs were tied to the chair he was sitting on. You could travel light years, and some things did not change. Not even on Earth.

He opened his eyes again, slowly. It had gone dark. He shook his head. It stayed dark. He licked his lips and blinked, several times. Shaking his head had been a mistake. He had to hope it was the only one he had made so far this evening.

"Roeder," he called out, trying to sound bored and not entirely sure that he was managing it, "I'm awake now. Let's get this over with, shall we?"

There was no answer.

Garak sighed. "Preferably with the minimum amount of fuss," he said.

The light appeared again, dimmer this time. That constituted progress of a sort. Garak heard footsteps, slow against what sounded like a concrete floor, coming nearer.

"Come, Roeder," he said, straining forward ineffectually. "Let us skip the formalities."

Something scraped along the floor. It felt like knives in Garak's head. His stomach twisted and lurched. He began to cough, and struggled to stop. He urged himself to concentration, willed himself to self-control. Games like this did not win themselves.

"It's all right." Roeder's voice, muted in the darkness. "I'm just pulling up a chair."

Garak peered out. The light became bright again, almost dazzling. In silhouette ahead, like in a shadow play, he watched the dark figure of Roeder stretching out in his seat. As Garak's eyes adjusted, he was able to pick out details: the short distance between them, Roeder's legs crossed at the ankles as if he were at ease, the accuracy with which he was pointing the phaser at Garak. The light lessened and, in the shadows to which he was adapted, Garak saw the lie behind Roeder's easy posture: saw the tension in the muscles of his shoulders and his arm, saw the unsteadiness with which he drew each breath. He was a man expecting a threat and readying himself to deal with it. Where, Garak wondered, did Roeder think that the danger lay? It was hardly as if Garak himself posed much of a threat right now.

Garak glanced around. They were sitting in a dark, small room. It was damp; filled with the scent of the river. Looking for options, he picked out the doorway, over to his left. He felt as if there was a weight of buildings above them. He would have guessed that they were in a cellar, except that there were windows straight ahead. He realized now what the source of the light was. It was the moon. It shone on his face and put Roeder in darkness.

"I don't remember threatening you, Garak," Roeder said. "So what was the knife for?" His voice was still coming out thick, Garak noted contritely. He really had not meant to hit him that hard.

"You took me away from the crowd, and my security, and then led me under a bridge," Garak pointed out. "Would you not have felt a little threatened? Would you not have become a little suspicious yourself?"

"I was already suspicious," Roeder answered. "When Ben Sisko turns up out of the blue with a Cardassian in tow? *That's* when I become suspicious." Roeder ran his free hand along the phaser. "Why did he bring you along this evening? Why did you want to meet me?"

"There's nothing suspicious about that." Garak spoke confidently. Here he could be truthful; or, at least, the small part of the story that he told would not be lies. "I asked the captain to introduce us because you interested me—"

"*Interested* you?" Roeder's fingers strayed around the phaser.

A misstep, Garak thought, a little frantically. "I wanted to know," he said quickly, "what could make a Starfleet officer resign his commission. What could turn him against the war."

There was a silence. The light went out. The moon must have gone behind a cloud. Then there was the sound of the chair scraping, and then slow steps.

"Don't you know already?" Roeder was now close by.

Garak felt a certain amount of sharp impatience at that question. If he knew already, he thought, he would not be subjecting himself to this charade. He turned his head slowly, and took a good, clinical look at Roeder. He saw that he had read the man correctly. The blood around Roeder's nose was almost black against the pallor of his face. The hand that came up to wipe at it was shaking; the one around the phaser was too tight. His breath was coming out in rasps, and Garak could almost smell it on the other man's breath. Desperation.

Garak did not know how—could not guess how—but it was clear to him that Roeder had known from the outset that Garak had come to kill him. And Roeder was afraid, Garak could see; afraid that this was all part of an ambush, afraid that he had gone too far already, afraid that they had been missed at the embassy, afraid that any moment now someone would arrive to finish the job that Garak had started. This was a man who needed to make Garak talk, but it was not a man who felt he was in control of the conversation. Which was where Garak's opening lay. Because Cardassians, after all, excelled at conversation.

Garak began to speak. Every few words, he would shift his eyes, ever so slightly, to glance past Roeder's shoulder, looking for a rescue that he did not in fact believe was coming. But each time he looked, it made Roeder twitch a little closer to the edge.

"Cardassians," Garak said, "are trained from birth in duty, and in loyalty. We are *patriots,* Mister Roeder; love of our country is the rock upon which our empire is built. It lies at the very heart of us." He glanced over Roeder's shoulder. "When we see these qualities in others, we understand them. We admire them. But, in the time I have spent away from my own people, it has been my observation that duty and loyalty are not always sufficient for others. Other races are more pliable. They *give.*" Another glance. "And the reasons can be so very different. Love. Power. Greed. So many frailties! And I am *fascinated* by them." He smiled up at the blood on Roeder's face. "I came to meet you this evening, Mister Roeder," Garak taunted, "because I wanted to find out which one of those it was that turned you into a traitor."

It had exactly the desired effect. Roeder stared down at him for a shocked, empty moment. Then he drew back his arm and smashed the phaser hard across Garak's face.

9

QUARK CONTEMPLATED Mechter. Wine. Females. Holosuites. One of them would be his downfall.

Still, that glass of synthale looked almost untouched. . . .

"Brother?"

And he seemed to prefer watching the dabo wheel to admiring M'Pella . . .

"Brother . . ."

Holosuites. That had to be it. Their charms were infinite; imagination was the only limit. . . .

"Brother!"

"Rom, *will* you be quiet! I'm thinking!"

"But, brother, this is *important*—"

Reluctantly, Quark dragged himself away from his plans for Mechter.

"I think," Rom's voice was low and urgent, "that I've found a way out."

He got Quark's full attention, right then.

"What?" he whispered. *"Where?"*

"Follow me. . . ."

Quark came out from behind the bar, and scurried after his brother. Rom led him to one of the storerooms. On one side of the room stood a fair-sized crate that Quark had agreed to store for Brixhta. For a fair-sized fee. The lid of this crate, Quark noticed, was slightly askew. He went over to it, reached out a hand and then, quickly, lifted the lid and peered inside.

It was empty.

Quark lowered the lid, and fastened it shut.

"Not *there*," Rom was saying, "over *here*. . . ." Quark glared at him to quiet him down. He stood for a while in contemplation, listening to the shouts drifting in from the dabo wheel. He heard Steyn give a yell of triumph. . . .

Quark put his hand on his brother's shoulder. "Rom," he said, "we don't want to put anyone in danger."

"But we can get *out* of here—"

"Rom!" Quark stopped him. He licked his lips. "Who knows," he extemporized, "*what* could be happening across the station right now? There could be . . ." He waved his free hand. . . . "a whole Dominion fleet arriving, squadrons of Jem'Hadar battling through to ops *right* now—"

Rom shuddered beneath his hand. "Oh," he said. "I hadn't thought of that, brother."

"Well, don't you worry, Rom," Quark said. "We'll *all* be safe, here in the bar. And we'll hear from Major Kira or from Odo when it's okay to come out. Don't worry about that . . . it's probably for the best." He ushered Rom away from the crate and out of the storeroom. "We'll forget we ever saw it."

Sisko and Chaplin drew closer to the next bridge. There were several dark figures walking along it; and Sisko could see a pair standing toward the center, looking back

the way he and Chaplin had just come. He took in a
breath of night air, and prayed that his sense of relief was
not premature.

"Do you think that will be them, Captain?"

He shrugged. "Can't say from down here, Lieutenant.
But I certainly think we should take a look and find out."
They started to walk toward the steps leading up onto the
bridge. Then Chaplin's combadge chimed.

She tapped it. "Lieutenant Chaplin," she said.

"It's Marlow."

"We're just about to check out a couple of people we
think could be them."

There was a brief pause, and then Marlow spoke
again. *"Who's 'we'?"*

"I have Captain Sisko here with me."

There was a silence. Sisko could practically hear Marlow's dismay that such a senior officer was now aware
that they had lost their charge. He covered his smile but
Chaplin saw it, and bit at her lower lip.

"Have you got anything else for us to go on?" she said,
turning away. They started to go up the steps.

"I have some coordinates from the sweep," Marlow
said. Sisko noted that he was keeping his voice smooth.
*"It picked up the delegation here in San Francisco.
And—you're not going to believe this, Wendy—there was
a Cardassian signature in Beijing—"*

"Perhaps somebody should check that out," Sisko suggested.

"Are we planning to do anything about that, Guy?"

*"Someone at this end is on it. Now. And the only other
Cardassian life sign was there in London all right—I'm
patching the coordinates through to you."*

Chaplin took out her tricorder. Sisko looked over her
shoulder at the data streaming across the screen.

"Those are our coordinates, sir," she said, tapping a set of numbers with her forefinger. "And these are what Marlow has just sent . . . which puts Mr. Garak very close."

Sisko peered along the bridge. The two figures were embracing now.

"But it's not along there, Captain," Chaplin said. She was still looking down to read the data.

"I think I could have told you that myself."

She glanced up, saw the couple, and gave a wry smile. "Well, these coordinates put him back on the north side of the river, just a little way over there." She turned to face the way they had just come, and pointed to the left.

"Any idea what's over there?" Sisko asked. If Chaplin had scoped out the area properly before coming out on this evening's assignment, she would have a good sense of the immediate geography.

She didn't let him down. "Well, further on are the real city sights, the historical buildings that are left," she said, promptly. "But these coordinates aren't as far as that." She screwed up her face. "The reading puts him practically beneath the bridge. Which seems a strange place to be if you want to see the city."

Sisko frowned. "Yes, it does. . . ."

Her combadge chimed again and she tapped it. "Chaplin."

"Marlow. There's something else."

"I'm listening."

"I did a trace on the signature near you. I wanted to see if I could track his route from the embassy. It's odd— I followed it as far as the underpass, and then there was a break in the reading. When I picked it up again, it was showing where he is now. He's stationary right now, by the way."

"What do you think would cause a break like that?" Chaplin asked.

"The process I was using can be a bit haphazard, so it could just be something went wrong at this end. Or . . . well, the other immediate explanation that comes to mind is that he used a transporter."

"But, Guy, that doesn't make any sense. It's hardly any distance," Chaplin said, looking around and frowning.

Sisko gestured at her tricorder and held out his hand. Chaplin passed it over, and he started thumbing at it.

"I can't help you with that," Marlow was saying. *"But it seemed worth telling you."*

Sisko read the data. "A transporter *has* been used here recently," he said, after a moment or two. "There's no way we can know for sure that it has anything to do with Garak, of course, but it *would* explain the anomaly Marlow picked up reading the signature."

"But it wouldn't explain why someone would transport themselves—" Chaplin glanced back toward the embassy, measuring the distance. "—a hundred yards down the road? That's odd." She gave Sisko an embarrassed smile. "I'd certainly *like* to think I lost them because they transported out, but if I'm being honest, it doesn't make sense."

"No, not really," Sisko agreed. A distance that short, you would just walk it. Unless you were moving something heavy. Or someone. Someone who was unable to walk . . .

Sisko looked out across the dark north bank again. He reached instinctively to his side, and then remembered where the evening had started. "Lieutenant," he said, "we're going to go and take a good look down there. But I might just have to ask you for the loan of your phaser."

• • •

Garak gasped. His headache had just become considerably worse. Tasting blood, he ran his tongue against the inside of his mouth. One of his upper teeth felt a little loose. Possibly two. He grinned up at Roeder. "For a peace campaigner," he said, in between gulps of air, "your choice of tactics is very interesting. I'm just glad our paths didn't cross when you were still a soldier."

This time, the blow was to his ribs. When the shock of it began to pass, Garak was able to feel a certain nostalgia for the wire. *No pain, no gain,* he thought, rather more hysterically than he would have liked. When Roeder pressed the nose of the phaser up against his throat his panic rose further, but he swallowed it back. It really would be the most dreadful waste of effort to lose control now. Now that Roeder was so close to the edge.

"Tell me," Roeder rasped out, "why Sisko brought you with him tonight. What do you know? Who else knows?"

Garak had no idea what Roeder was talking about. Not yet. He knew there was something, and he meant for Roeder to tell him. Until then, what Garak *did* know—and knew a great deal about—was the application of violence. He knew as well as any other how it worked. And he also knew well, too well, how much it took to use it as a tool. Roeder's nose had begun to bleed again; the phaser up against him was shaking. And, Garak thought, what better way to break a man of peace?

"What do you think the cost of this will be, Roeder?" Garak whispered. Roeder's own words, to Sisko. "Is it worth it? Will you be held to account?"

Roeder hit him in the chest again but now, Garak saw, he was weeping.

• • •

"These new codes are just not working," Dax said in frustration. "Whatever I do, it seems to know *exactly* what I'm going to try."

"I have some news for you two, if you'd like to hear it."

"Make it good news, Chief," Kira said, "because that Hamexi is just about to lay its hands—or whatever they are—on those crates of latinum."

"Pretty good news. I finally got through to Worf."

"He picked just the right time to be off-duty," Dax noted.

"He's not in a great mood, though."

"Who is?" Kira muttered.

The channel went dead. Dax and Kira waited patiently.

"You both still there?"

"You can count on that," Kira said.

"And we also managed to coax some life into some of the systems here: enough to run some scans of the station. There's no problems with life support. So unless people are busy injuring themselves, there doesn't seem to be any immediate threat to anyone on the station."

"Just to the latinum," Kira said, looking back at the screen.

"Just to the latinum," O'Brien agreed.

Built into the structure of the second bridge, there was a narrow alleyway. Chaplin led them in, reading from the coordinates on her tricorder. A line of lamps on the wall to the left cast orange light and uncertain shadows. Along the wall to the right, up the length of the alley, Sisko could see a row of four or five doors. Judging from the curve of the bridge, he guessed that there was a series of small, cellar-like rooms set behind the doors.

Sisko glanced over at Chaplin. She gestured with the tricorder further down the alley. When they came to the final door on the right, she stopped.

"In here, sir," she whispered.

Sisko nodded. He pointed beyond the bridge. They went on, out of the alleyway, and scouted out the far side of the bridge. There were some high windows set into the wall on the outside; too high for them to climb to take a look inside. Sisko went back beneath the bridge. He tested the handle on the door, very carefully. It gave a little; soundlessly, he noted with relief. He released it and looked at Chaplin.

"What do you think, sir?" Chaplin whispered. "Shall we go in?"

"Not we," Sisko murmured back. He held out his hand, gesturing to her phaser. She passed it over. "Me. You're going to get us some backup, and then stay here by the door. You got that?" She nodded. "Nobody gets past you," he said. "Nobody."

"It seems," Odo said, "we have just discovered the flaw in Captain Steyn's flawless security systems." He watched as the Hamexi went up to the crates of latinum, and began deactivating the security programs. Then he turned away from the viewscreen and went to sit, heavily, in his chair.

"I suppose," Bashir said thoughtfully, still staring at the screen, "that given the thing's a machine, the scanners might not even be recognizing it as an intervention. . . ." He shrugged and looked at Odo. "I suppose you're more than satisfied now that this is all Brixhta's work?"

"I was already more than satisfied."

"It's all so elaborate," Bashir mused. "Although that does make sense. In terms of motivation, I mean." He stopped himself and glanced over at Odo, wishing there was something he could do. Odo caught his look.

"If you want to help, Doctor," Odo replied sharply, "you can stop fussing, and start telling me more about what you mean by 'motivation.' "

"Well," Bashir sighed, "I was thinking about Hamexi psychology. Like I said, physiologically, they're all very alike. And this puts some very specific cultural and psychological stresses on them. There's a great emphasis on social cohesion but, at the same time, individual Hamexi feel under a great deal of pressure to differentiate themselves from the rest." He glanced at Odo and bit his lip.

"Go on," Odo said. He shuddered. Another few flakes fell away from him. He saw the doctor look away, down at the tricorder in his hand. "I *am* listening."

"Well, think about Brixhta," Bashir said. "The way he talks, and that hat . . . it's all about standing out from the crowd."

"I do find myself wondering," Odo said, "how you know so much about Hamexi. Aren't they known to be a reclusive species? Did you study them at the Academy?"

"Hardly at all, in fact," Bashir said. "Hamexi physiology was mentioned in passing, in a single lecture." He gave a quiet laugh. "No, all my conjectures about the psychology of the species are in the finest traditions of evidence-based medicine. They rely on a single anecdote."

"Although I find your deductions fascinating, Doctor," Odo said, "I do wonder if I am in quite the right frame of mind to listen to one of your stories of over-achievement at Starfleet Academy." He felt another tremor pass through him.

Bashir came over to the desk and leaned against it. He gestured with the tricorder. Odo sat in isolation for a moment, and then reached out his hand.

"Then you can rest easy, Constable," Bashir said, as he got to work. "Because this isn't one of my stories. It's one of Garak's."

Mechter, Quark decided, was devoid of appetite. He had brushed aside all of M'Pella's expert advances, turned down several offers of cheap, cheaper, and eventually free use of one of the holosuites, and the same glass of synthale stood beside him. He had even managed to block Morn's conversational gambits. And now it looked like Rom was bothering him.

"*Rom* . . ." Quark muttered. Mechter was going to squash him like a tube grub. And Quark could see that Steyn was beginning to get annoyed. She slid out of her chair, wandered about the bar for a little while, and then came to a halt a few feet behind Mechter. She glared over at Quark. *What the hell is going on?* she mouthed.

"Rom!" Quark yelled. "Here! *Right* now!"

Rom jumped, and then hurried over to the bar. Mechter frowned at him as he departed. *Just in time,* Quark thought.

"What is it, brother?" Rom said.

"If you're going to be stuck in here with the rest of us, you can make yourself useful instead of wasting time talking. Start putting things away."

Dutifully, Rom came behind the bar and started picking up glasses. Quark could see him shooting concerned looks at him.

"You seem worried about something, brother," Rom ventured after a moment or two.

"Well," said Quark, glancing across the bar at Mechter, who had gone back to watching the dabo wheel, "it must be because I'm looking ruin in the face."

"I'm sure it'll all turn out fine, brother." Rom soothed,

and looked to see where Quark was staring. "Have you been talking to Mister Mechter too?" he asked. "He's a nice man."

"A *nice* man?"

"We got on just fine."

"You have been talking to him?"

"Yes, brother. We have a lot in common."

"Rom, that 'nice man' over there is a hired killer. You have more in common with the replicators. For a start, they're not sentient."

"I'm sure you're right, brother," Rom said humbly. "But he did get engaged to a Nausicaan woman at the start of the year. And her family don't like the idea of an interspecies marriage, so they're making it difficult for the final ceremonies to take place." Rom piled up a few more glasses. "Just before you called me over here, I was telling him about me and Leeta, and how we got things to work out between us . . ." Rom looked at Mechter sorrowfully. "It's so sad," he said. "I think he's losing hope. He just needs someone to talk to."

Females, thought Quark, with some vindication. "Well, then," he said, retrieving a glass from his brother's hand, twisting him round bodily, and pushing him back in Mechter's direction, "what are you doing still standing here? Get over there right now and talk to him some more!"

He watched Rom head across the bar. When Mechter saw him, his mouth twitched into what Quark assumed was a smile. Quark took a look at Steyn. She raised her eyebrows at him. He tapped one of his lobes and winked. She grinned, gave him the thumbs-up and then went back to her chair to carry on watching Auger's success at the wheel.

Rom, you're an idiot. But I don't know what I'd do without you.

The moon had come out again. Garak turned his head to the side. Roeder was sitting on the floor now, his knees drawn up, his back against the wall. His hands were balanced on his knees, and the phaser was hanging limply from one of them.

"One of the dark places," he murmured to himself. He leaned his head against the wall, and then turned it so that he was looking at Garak. "You've been in places like this before, haven't you?"

Garak looked straight ahead again; back at the moonlight. "Yes," he said.

"And not always in the chair."

"Not always, no."

Roeder nodded. "I thought so," he said, turning away. "You can always recognize them, can't you? Recognize the people like us." Garak watched as Roeder ran his thumb mechanically up and down the edge of the phaser, and said nothing. Roeder was right. You did come to recognize them: the men who lost themselves in violence, who let themselves be hollowed, who cut out their souls and filled the space with something they called duty. You learned to grasp their loves, and the limits of their loves. You learned to see what would bring them to those limits. Roeder was close now, Garak could tell. Garak had brought him there.

"Did you ever reach a point," Roeder asked, "where you had to say, *Enough?* Was there ever a line you couldn't cross? Something you just couldn't bring yourself do?"

Garak closed his eyes. He let his head fall forward. His gamble, it seemed, was about to pay off. Had it, he asked himself, even been that much of a gamble? They always confessed in the end. They always told him everything.

He gave a little thought to Roeder's question; found himself remembering being on the *Defiant* above the Founders' homeworld and, before that, on the bridge of Tain's flagship. He had been quite ready, both times, to wipe out an entire race. *No,* Garak answered Roeder, with complete sincerity, and with a little pity too. *Never.* He opened his eyes again, and glanced across at Roeder, sitting in silence, drawn in upon himself again. The moonlight was landing on his face. He looked wrung-out.

Tell me, Garak willed him. *Tell me what's happening.*

"Roeder," he breathed.

Roeder's hand twitched; the one holding the weapon. Garak licked his lips, and tasted metal in his mouth. He swallowed, and drew in some air.

"Talk to me," Garak urged him, almost tenderly. "Tell me—"

And then there was a noise, from near the door.

Roeder was up on his feet again in a second. He moved to stand next to Garak. He put one hand on the back of the chair, and raised the phaser, pointing it across Garak, toward the entrance. Garak turned his head to peer into the shadows, slowly, trying not to startle the other man. There was a shape moving near the doorway. Garak raised his eyes to the darkness above and prayed to gods he did not believe in that this was not going to turn out to be some well-meaning but remarkably ill-timed rescue attempt.

"Tomas," the figure said quietly, from the darkness. "It's Ben. Ben Sisko."

From just inside his field of vision, Garak watched as Roeder shut his eyes, for the merest moment, and opened them again. Slowly, gently, he felt the blunt nose of Roeder's phaser press against his temple. "Well," Roeder muttered. "You're here."

Sisko. At this moment, Garak came close—closest—to seeing the whole story; unraveling the threads that bound him to this place, these people. But the pain, and the darkness deluded him, and all he understood was Roeder. The charm, the brutality, the whole terrible episode had simply been contrived to find out why *Sisko* had come back to Earth. Not Garak. Not the conference. Not even the protest. Just *Sisko.* After that, Garak could penetrate Roeder's mind no further. Whatever it was that Roeder wanted to know, whatever it was about the commander of Deep Space 9 that had driven Roeder to take these desperate measures—all of this Garak could not begin to guess. He had hoped that Roeder would tell him; had been certain that Roeder was about to tell him. Now he had to doubt whether Roeder was going to get the chance.

"I'm armed, Tomas." Sisko's voice was as smooth as silk. Trying to keep everything calm. Particularly the man waving the gun around. "I have a phaser pointed at you. Why don't you put your weapon down, and we can talk?"

Garak swallowed and looked at Sisko, silhouetted in the doorway, taking slow steps forward. Sisko spoke again. "Tomas," he said, "please—don't do anything you're going to regret. I know we can talk this through."

Something felt like ice, Garak thought. It was not just the headache, he realized. It was the phaser, cold against his temple.

Captain, he thought, *please—don't do anything stupid.*

• • •

The Hamexi figure had now reached runabout pad B. Kira and Dax watched as it boarded, and began the launch procedures. The runabout was ready to leave.

"Chief," Kira said, resignedly, "I'm guessing there's no way you can take the *Ariadne* after the runabout?"

"Can't release the docking clamps, Major."

Kira sighed. "I thought you might say something like that."

Together, she and Dax stood and watched as the runabout was launched. "So," Kira said, "there she goes." She glanced at Dax. "And I'm really not looking forward to explaining *that* to the captain."

From the shadow of the doorway, Sisko took in the tableau before him. Over to the left, moonlight was filtering in through three high windows. It fell upon the scene straight ahead: Roeder, looking right at him, his arm stretched out, holding a phaser up to the forehead of the figure in the chair; Garak, sitting there, facing the windows, unable to move.

Sisko took a few cautious steps forward. They echoed out loud against the concrete.

"Stop," Roeder ordered.

Sisko obeyed, and cast a quick look at Garak. Garak's eyes were intent upon Roeder, but Sisko could almost hear him, warning him. Not to do anything he would regret.

"What's going on, Tomas?" Sisko tried to keep his voice calm. Unthreatening. "When I left the reception, you two were hitting it off just fine. What happened?"

"What happened? Your friend here pulled a knife on me, that's what happened." He sounded breathless.

Sisko glanced at Garak again and frowned. "Is that true?"

"In my defense," Garak said, "I would like to point out that he was attacking me at the time."

Roeder's hand twitched and tightened its grip on the phaser.

"Shut up, Garak," Sisko advised.

"He'd come to kill me, Ben," Roeder said.

Sisko stared at him in disbelief. *"What?"*

"He'd been sent to kill me."

"Tomas, that's *crazy—!*"

"Is that why you're here too? To kill me?"

"I don't want to kill you!" The words came out too loud in the space. Sisko made himself suck in a breath. This conversation had gotten way out of control. He smoothed his voice. "Tomas, I don't know what's happened to make you think that—"

"You. Here. Now. You bring this Cardassian to meet me—an *assassin!*" Roeder pushed the phaser harder against Garak's face. Garak's eyes closed automatically; Sisko watched him swallow, and then look up at Roeder's face. "Ben," Roeder shouted, "I swear, you're not going to stop me. I can't let you stop me. I *will* shoot!"

"Don't do it, Tomas," Sisko said. He raised his own phaser and took aim; targeting right at Roeder's heart. He looked into the other man's face. The moonlight was streaming down upon it; Sisko could see the blood drying around Roeder's nose. People really had been fighting a private little war here.

Sisko glanced down at Garak. Garak was watching him now; watching with bright and glittering intensity. Then, just as on the *Rubicon,* Garak's eyes widened, ever so slightly; it seemed that something had become very clear to him. His lips curved slowly into a cold smile.

Sisko could not say later why that had made the difference. But, at that moment, it seemed to him that everything came together at once: Vreenak's murder, his failed confession, Ross's sanction, Leyton's approval, Veral's consent. All of the lines drew together at this point. Shooting Roeder would not be a crime, but that did not make it right. And Sisko knew he could not do it. He could not cross this line.

Sisko lowered his arm. Slowly, he bent down on one knee, and then he set his phaser deliberately upon the ground. He put his hand on the ground alongside it, spread out the fingers, and contemplated them for a moment. Then he stood up straight and looked at the other man. "I mean it, Tomas," he said, with all his newfound conviction. "I don't want to kill you."

Roeder stared at him. His own hand gripped more tightly at his phaser. He looked back at Garak, sitting motionless in the chair. He turned back to Sisko. His face twisted. "God, Ben, what is this . . . ?" he whispered. "What *is* this?"

"I don't understand what you mean—"

"You're *playing* with me!" His face had bleached white.

"Tomas," Sisko said, "I just want to talk." He took a step toward him. Roeder jerked the phaser away from Garak's head and pointed it straight at him. Sisko raised his hands. "I just want to talk," he said again. He risked another step forward, and then stopped when he saw Roeder begin to shake. His eyes were very blue, Sisko thought. He had never really noticed that about him before. Right now they were staring back at him as if looking right into the face of the enemy.

"What about, Ben? What do you want to talk about?" The shaking was becoming worse. "Do you think I don't know? Do you think I can't guess why you're here, right now? You, of all people?"

"Tomas, I don't know what you're talking about—"

"Stop *lying* to me—!"

"I'm not lying to you! Why the *hell* would I lie to you?"

"Shut up!" It was wrenched out of Roeder, from the very core; and friable, as if there was barely anything left in him to give. Sisko stood still, waited until the other man regained some control.

"Surely we can settle this peacefully?" Sisko kept his voice cool. *"You're* the one that's been campaigning for peace!"

It was the wrong thing to say; he realized his mistake at once. Roeder's newfound control transformed into anger; directed, and with purpose. "You have the nerve to talk to me about peace? You know what we're doing." he said. "Go to *hell,* Sisko!"

Roeder took aim. Sisko looked at the phaser. *Damn,* he thought, wildly, *this wasn't in the script—*

And then:

"Roeder."

Roeder swung round. Sisko stared at Garak, forgotten in the chair. Garak was slumped back. But his arm was free now, and it was raised. He was holding an astonishingly compact, but very functional, phaser.

He fired.

White light screamed out, ripping across the room, scorching Sisko's eyes. He could just make out a dark shape straight ahead; it fell to its knees as if its strings had just been cut. There was a second shot. The figure slid backward, onto the ground. Sisko jerked forward, unwillingly, like a marionette. And then everything settled, and went still.

"I don't much like being hit." Garak's voice, chill in the empty space. "But I didn't think he deserved to be shot in the back."

Sisko stepped forward, and kneeled down. Roeder had fallen awkwardly; he was lying bent back upon himself. Sisko fumbled his fingers beneath Roeder's collar and tried to find a pulse. There was nothing. Roeder was dead.

His eyes were still open, bright blue and sightless. Sisko reached down and closed them for him, and rested his hand for a moment on Roeder's hair. Then he looked up at Garak. "*Why* did you do that?" he said, bitterly angry. "You didn't have to *do* that!"

Garak looked back at him. Cold. Like ice. "You're wrong, Captain. He was going to kill you."

"You don't *know* that!" Sisko shouted back at him. "How could you *know* that?" He was ready to hit Garak himself.

Garak leaned back in the chair, and put his hand up to his head. He was still holding the phaser. "I wonder, Captain," he murmured, "if you could possibly lower your voice? I seem to have the most excruciating headache."

Sisko did not answer. He could still hear the shots. The air tasted acrid; it tasted of failure and disappointment.

"Captain."

Someone right behind him, speaking very softly. Sisko turned. Chaplin was standing there. She had reached out her hand, and was almost touching his shoulder. She was looking at him with a kind of wary pity.

"He's right, sir," she said. "I'm really sorry, sir. Where I was standing, back there—I had a good view of his face. He really was going to shoot you."

He knew she was speaking the truth. He just couldn't get it to make sense.

"All right," he murmured. "All right, Lieutenant." He moved past her and stood staring around. "Try to get some people here, will you?"

Chaplin tapped at her combadge. "Guy," she said, "we could *really* do with that backup now."

Sisko holstered the phaser, and then went over to Garak and began untying him. Neither of them said a word. When he was finally free, Garak slumped forward and put his head in his hands. Sisko waited. Eventually, Garak straightened himself up; slowly, and wincing.

"Think you're going to live?" Sisko said, quietly.

"Possibly. . . ." Garak looked down at himself and frowned at the bloodstains. "Although I may have ruined this jacket."

"You'll get over it."

"No doubt."

Sisko gestured down at the phaser. "Where did that come from?" he said.

"I brought it with me this evening."

"How the hell did you get past security at the embassy?"

Garak gave him a withering look. *"Not* the most difficult task I've ever set myself, Captain."

Sisko decided to let it pass. For the moment. "If we can go out onto the street," he said, "we can get a paramedic to you. Can you stand?"

"Let's find out, shall we?"

Sisko put out a hand to help. It took a moment or two but, eventually, Garak was on his feet, propped up against him. Sisko watched as Garak studied him closely. He seemed to be contemplating Sisko's dress uniform. Garak glanced down again at his own jacket. And then he looked back over at Roeder's body.

"The things we do for Starfleet," he murmured.

Sisko stared at him. He was sure he had misheard. "What did you say?"

Garak shook his head. "Nothing," he said. "It doesn't

matter. Not now." He considered Sisko's uniform again.
"An interesting moment to choose to have a crisis of conscience, Captain."

They went outside. The moon lay bright against the
darkness, carving out a space in the clouds. "It wasn't a
crisis," Sisko said, more to the sky than to Garak. "I think
it might have been clarity."

"So *Garak* decided that the best course of action was to
let the Hamexi go," Bashir explained eagerly, as he read
through the data on the tricorder. "Which *I* think is an interesting aspect of the tale in and of itself . . . but the point
he was trying to make, was just how remarkable it was to
find an Hamexi there in the first place. Given just how
reclusive the species is, that is. So *my* interpretation," the
doctor stopped for a moment to catch his breath, "is that
some—maybe only just a few—Hamexi struggle against
the institutionalization which their wider culture enforces
upon them. And that when they *do* break out of their so-
cietal structures, it's in the most ostentatious ways. Like
Brixhta!" He stopped, and looked up at Odo tri-
umphantly.

"I see," said Odo. There was a pause as a slight ripple
shivered through his body. He brought it under control,
before speaking again. "And that was the story that Garak
told you?"

"Not repeated word for word," Bashir allowed, "but
close enough."

Odo slowly leaned back in his chair, and contemplated
the other man. One eye was closed, and his speech was
blurred now, words struggling from the side of his
mouth.

"So, Doctor," he said, "what you are telling me, in effect, is that Garak admitted to you that he played a key

part in the plot to overthrow the two-hundred-and-nineteenth Autarch of Tzenketh?"

Bashir frowned and ran through the whole story again in his mind. "I hadn't thought of it that way." He chewed his lower lip. "On balance, I suppose that doesn't seem very likely, does it? I could believe the bit about the plot. But not that Garak would actually tell me about it."

"No. It's not very likely," Odo said, closing his eyes completely. "And it might be best," he rasped, "if we elect not to believe a single word of it."

Garak stood outside with his back up against the wall, tasting the sharp night air. Each breath he took turned into mist. He looked up at the velvet of the sky, and tried to pick out patterns in its strange embroidery; tried to force familiar constellations onto the alien sky. The moon was shining bright upon his face, and the stars seemed to be pricking at him. Slowly, he raised his hand and, with his thumb, blotted out the moon. Then he closed his eyes and let his hand fall back down to his side. *Mission accomplished,* he thought. All things considered, he would rather Roeder had lived. But not everything was possible in this life.

He listened to the sound of the river running by. There were voices, low but urgent. Then, even nearer, there were footsteps, approaching. He did not open his eyes. Someone spoke, saying his name. It was Sisko.

Garak cracked his eyes open and moved his head a little to look at him. The captain was standing a couple of feet away, staring down at the ground that lay between them. Still wearing his dress uniform. It looked, Garak thought, rather incongruous. It also looked a mess.

Garak swallowed in some air. He would have preferred to have waited a while before having this conversation. But perhaps now was as good a time as any for them to have this out once and for all.

"Captain," he said quickly, before Sisko could speak again. Some part of him had been fabricating the speech from the moment that Sisko had appeared in the shadows of the doorway; telling and retelling in a mind fogged with pain. He knew the words would come as a flood, or not at all. "I really am very sorry about your friend. I don't think he had to die tonight. But it was perfectly clear that *one* of us was not getting out of there alive. You'll forgive me if I say that I certainly didn't want it to be me. And I couldn't think of a particular reason why it should be you."

There was a silence. Then Sisko said, "I was just coming to let you know that the medic's arrived. He's ready to see you."

Garak opened his eyes a little wider. "Oh," he murmured.

"Also," and now Sisko did look straight at him, "I wanted to thank you. For saving my life."

The sky above was in disarray, and the moonlight had become too bright. Garak shut his eyes. *I even get to be the hero,* he thought. "You really are most welcome, Captain," he said.

"That's it; I've had enough; no more. You can all just stay there."

Kira and Dax roused themselves and looked at each other in surprise.

"Chief," said Dax, "are you *still* at it?"

"Still at it?" The comm fairly crackled with fury. *"What do you think?"*

"Why don't you give yourself a bit of a break, Chief?" Kira said.

"*A break? Do you actually* want *me to just leave you all there—?*"

"I'd rather," Kira replied, "that you worked profitably rather than pointlessly."

There was a pause and a brief burst of static.

"*Might be a good idea, I suppose. I'm going round in circles with this damn program—*"

"You'll come up with something eventually," Dax comforted him.

A deep sigh was transmitted down the com channel.

"*Well,*" O'Brien said, "*this is a piece of good news, at last.*"

"What?" Kira leaned hopefully in toward his voice.

"*Someone here's just dug out a pack of cards.*"

The whole operation to remove the latinum from Deep Space 9 had taken less than an hour, but it was exactly ten hours after the station had locked down before all systems reverted to the crew's control. O'Brien immediately transported back from the *Ariadne* to ops, and started a full systems check. Dax began to run what they all suspected would be a wholly unsuccessful trace on the runabout. Kira and Worf began reestablishing standard security measures. Throughout the station, the doors began to open and the turbolifts began to move.

Bashir, sitting with his chin in his hands on the floor in Odo's office, watched with relief and fascination as Odo at last began to lose his shape. The whole station began its slow, collective exhalation, but Julian knew that he and his fellows could not even begin to conceive of Odo's sense of release at the end of this long and torturous day.

PART THREE

LAST MEETING PLACE

Only disconnect.
—David Lodge

DAWN LIGHT BEGAN TO TRICKLE into the meeting room. Sisko looked up from the viewscreen and out of the window. A chill and watery day was beginning. He glanced across the table at the two lieutenants; saw Marlow yawn and then lean over to say something to Chaplin; saw Chaplin rub at the muscles at the back of her neck and try to listen.

He sighed and turned back to the viewscreen. The news of Roeder's death had now broken. The reporter finished her short biography of him, and then a piece of footage ran of Roeder making a speech at a pro-peace rally. He did speak extremely well, Sisko thought. Passionately. It was clear he believed every word he said.

"We hear a great deal these days," he said, *"about war. We hear a great deal about our enemies. And we hear a great deal about how we should fight."*

The picture cut to the audience, showing their faces as they listened intently to Roeder. Many of them were nodding.

"Oh god," Chaplin said wearily, putting her head in her hands. "This is all my fault. . . ."

"Don't say that," Marlow consoled her. He looked at her anxiously, and reached out across the table, stopping just a little short of touching her. "There wasn't anything you could have done."

"I'd *read* Garak's file," she said. "I should have known he'd try to lose me. I should have got backup the *second* I realized he'd gone—"

"There was something else happening, Wendy," her partner said. "Something with Roeder. You can't hold yourself responsible for that."

"It's five in the morning, Lieutenant Chaplin," Sisko put in quietly, "you've just seen a man shot dead, and I know for a fact you've not had any sleep. Now's not the time to be thinking about blame." Sisko turned back to the screen.

"But we seem to hear a lot less about peace."

Maybe it was just the lack of sleep, but Roeder's death, Sisko thought, seemed unreal, like a swift and hideous dream. He had been playing it over and over in his head in the hours since it had happened; had been trying to work out what had gone wrong, how they had come so quickly and so viciously to the point of no return. There was so much he could not understand: why Roeder had been so angry and so mistrustful, what he had said that had made Roeder raise that phaser to kill him . . .

"And I would ask you—what will you do, when all of our enemies are destroyed? Will you look around and find new wars to fight? Will you make new enemies out of people we once called friends?" He looked out from the viewscreen, straight at Sisko. *"And where you have made a wasteland,"* he asked, *"will you call it peace?"*

Sisko looked across at the lieutenant sitting opposite. "Marlow," he said.

"Sir?"

"What did you think of Roeder?" he said. "His views on the war?"

Marlow gave him a guarded look. "I don't think it's my position to say, sir. . . ."

"No?"

"No, sir. I don't."

"Not your position to say?"

"No," he said again. "Sir."

"Then I'll say it, Guy," Chaplin cut in, "if you're not willing to." She looked Sisko straight in the eye. "May I speak freely, sir?"

"By all means."

"I know he was a friend of yours, sir," she said, "and, believe me, the last thing I wanted was to see him killed—but he was wrong about the war." She was still shaking, Sisko could see; was still angry with herself and how the night had ended. Time for her to get some of this out of her system.

"And a lot of junior officers," she said, "felt betrayed by the things he had been saying in recent months. We've been put on the front line again and again by officers like Roeder, and hearing some of the things he said was like a kick in the face. Like we'd put all our confidence in people who had no confidence in us or what we were trying to do." She stopped, very suddenly.

Marlow had been staring down at the table. When Chaplin finally came to a halt, he looked at Sisko again. "When you've put yourself on the line, sir," he said, quietly, and Sisko remembered what Garak had told him about Marlow, "it's hard to hear the people who asked you to do it start saying it was wrong."

"I'm glad, sir," Chaplin said, "that this war is in the hands of officers like you."

My God, Sisko thought, *we'd better be worthy of it.*

"Thank you," he said, looking back at the screen. "Thank you both."

It had been a very long shift, and it still was not over. Kira gathered the rest of the senior staff in the ward room. "So," she said, looking round, "do *any* of you have some good news for me?"

After a moment or two, Bashir raised a cautious hand.

"Go ahead, Doctor," Kira said, leaning back in her chair.

"Well," Bashir said, "from my perspective at least we really were very lucky. . . ." He glanced around at the others and quirked up his eyebrows, as if to acknowledge that he was perhaps alone in this respect. "There were no serious accidents during the time the station was affected. A few minor cuts and bruises," he thumbed through his report, "just ordinary domestic accidents. Somebody got some minor burns when a door panel that he was trying to force blew up, but that's about it." He looked at each of his colleagues in turn, and at Odo last. "Nobody else was affected."

Kira pushed a hand through her hair. "I guess that's a start," she said, and turned to address Odo. "Constable, how's your investigation coming along? How's it going with your prime suspect?"

"I have very precise information on his whereabouts for the duration of the lockdown," Odo replied. "Unfortunately, that is in the holding cell in which I myself had placed him the previous day."

"And you're absolutely sure of that?" Kira said. "That he didn't get out."

"I have the evidence of the two security guards who were on duty at the time, and who passed the hours mostly in conversation with him," Odo said. "Any proof that Brixhta was involved in the robbery will have to come," he nodded toward Dax and O'Brien, "from what we can determine of the whereabouts of the missing runabout, or from investigations of the programs that were used to seize control of the station."

Dax shook her head. "Nothing on the runabout. It's gone."

"And I've not got much in the way of good news either," O'Brien said. "It's proving impossible to trace how the programs penetrated our systems. It's like they burst their way through our systems, and then burnt themselves out. But it's not how it was done that worries me so much as how *well* it was done. Somebody knew an awful lot about the procedures we would try to get past their blocks."

"I thought that at the time too," Dax agreed. "As if the program was anticipating everything I tried, or everything the chief suggested."

"It is imperative," Worf said, "that we set up new protocols immediately."

"Getting on top of that now," O'Brien said. "It'll set back repairs on the *Ariadne* for a bit though—"

"Which is no longer as urgent," Worf pointed out.

"True enough." O'Brien nodded. "I'll keep a decent-sized team on there; better to get them off as soon as we can. Unless you need to keep the crew here for your investigation, Odo?"

"No need," Odo replied. "Captain Steyn and her crewman Auger were in Quark's almost from when they arrived on the station, and certainly for the duration of the lockdown." He nodded at O'Brien. "And her engineer was with you on the *Ariadne* throughout."

"Never left me for a moment. And obviously knew nothing about the sabotage. He was quite upset about his engines. Retuned them himself—not a bad job. We'll get them fixed and away as soon as we can then."

"Thanks, Chief," Kira said. "Anything else?"

"There is one strange thing," O'Brien said slowly. "Did anyone else notice that Quark's is the only place on the Promenade where you can get something to eat at the moment? The replicators are jammed everywhere else. Have been since the lockdown. I thought you might find that interesting, Constable," O'Brien said. "Given how friendly your prime suspect and Quark have been."

"And yet—much as I would welcome the opportunity to be able to say otherwise—Quark was sealed away just as we all were," Odo pointed out. "As far as I have been able to determine, the business arrangement between Quark and Brixhta is entirely legitimate, and entirely connected with the buying and selling of antiques."

"So," Kira said. "The theft. Where are we with that? Could it really be the case that somehow another Hamexi was on this station and none of us even *knew* about it? I mean, just how difficult *are* they to spot—?"

Odo and Bashir exchanged a glance.

"What is it?" Kira said. "Constable? Doctor?"

"Has the doctor not yet mentioned his theory?" Odo said.

Bashir frowned back at him. "I thought it was *our* theory now?"

"Which is?" Kira prompted.

"Well," Bashir replied, "that it was an android."

"The doctor," Odo put in, "has demonstrated, to my satisfaction at least, that there could not have been another Hamexi on board the station."

Kira had not yet caught up that far. "An android?" she said, looking between the doctor and the constable.

"Yes, Major," Odo replied.

"An Hamexi android?"

Odo and Bashir both nodded.

Kira stared at them both for a moment and then raised her hands in defeat. "After my day," she said, "I'm ready to believe anything."

"Do not be ridiculous. This is *not* a matter for humor," Worf said, impatiently. "At the end of a day's investigations, all we in fact know is that some latinum has been stolen—"

"A great deal of latinum has been stolen," Odo corrected.

Worf gave him a curt nod, acknowledging the correction. "That a runabout has also been taken," he continued, "and that we have a prime suspect who cannot be guilty."

Kira pressed her fingers against her temples. "I really am not looking forward to explaining all of this to the captain."

"Could be worse," O'Brien said.

"Could it?" Kira said.

O'Brien nodded. "We could have lost the station while we were at it."

Steyn and Quark were splitting their winnings. Auger was perched on a seat nearby, still, Quark noticed, gazing in wonder around the bar. He appeared to have no interest in the transaction taking place just beside him. Quark watched the slips of latinum pile up on his side of the bar. Profit from loss. He supposed it had a certain charm, but it wasn't something he'd want to try too often. Still, he thought, listening to the commotion out on the Promenade, he was having a lot more success today than Odo.

Just as Quark had finished doling out the final few slips, a hand slammed itself down upon Steyn's cut. *Nice cuffs,* Quark thought, reaching out to stop Auger's glass before it flew off the bar.

"Hello, Mister Mechter," Steyn said. A note of resignation had crept into her voice.

"Foolproof, Steyn?" Mechter said.

Steyn looked down sorrowfully at her share of the latinum. She reached out and touched it with a sole fingertip, as if to say hello and then goodbye. "Go on then," she said. "Take it. But that's quits."

Mechter claimed his payoff, and was out of the bar before anyone unwise had a chance to ask him whether his employers were likely to see any of this compensation. Quark settled his hand protectively upon his own pile of latinum, and turned to Steyn, leaning glumly on the bar. Profit to loss in less than a minute. The Great River had some truly treacherous turns.

"You have got to be," Quark said, "one of the unluckiest people I have ever met."

Steyn looked up at him and shrugged. "Made it through another day," she said. "More than I expected."

Odo had been putting Bashir off all day, but after the meeting in the ward room, Bashir came with him back to his office and insisted on another checkup.

"I wanted to thank you, Doctor," Odo said, as Bashir worked, "for keeping . . . my situation yesterday to yourself."

"Doctor-patient confidentiality," Bashir murmured, concentrating on the tricorder's display. "Nobody's business, unless you think there's a security risk. . . ." He looked up quickly. "And I suppose that's your business too." He snapped the tricorder shut. "You're fine," he said. "No ill effects that I can see."

Odo nodded slowly.

"What are you going to do about Brixhta?" Bashir said.

"I'm going to the holding cells now," Odo said.

"To question him some more?"

"To release him," Odo said. "Of course."

Bashir looked back him in amazement. "You *can't* be giving up on the investigation?"

"And what evidence do I have, Doctor?"

"We all saw the figure that went round the station. It was Hamexi—isn't that evidence enough?"

"Is it? Of what?"

"That Brixhta allowed himself to be locked up," Bashir replied. "So that he couldn't be held responsible for the crime, of course—"

"Did he?" Odo allowed himself a small smile. "Perhaps somebody used an Hamexi figure in order to point the blame at Brixhta. A most distinctive figure; and someone whom I was likely to suspect from the outset. Did anyone actually *see* the Hamexi in person? All *I* saw—and all I know that *you* saw, Doctor—were images on a viewscreen. And we were *meant* to see those images—again, was that because somebody wanted to put the blame on Brixhta?"

"Oh, come off it, Odo!" Bashir said in disbelief. "You don't believe any of that for a second!"

"It could be anyone on the station. Which seems increasingly likely—the chief told us that whoever prepared the program that sabotaged the station knew a great deal about our security protocols. How would Brixhta get access to information like that? Anyway, I

myself am still not satisfied that I know all there is to
know about Steyn and her crew, for example—"

"And you *certainly* don't believe that," Bashir said.

"In fact, Doctor," Odo admitted, "I am as certain as I
can be that Brixhta is responsible for this theft. But in the
absence of any evidence, it's only conjecture." He gave a
very wry smile. "Now, should Brixhta elect to *tell* me
what happened, *then* I would have evidence—but I think
that you and I both know that that is hardly likely to happen, is it?"

Bashir put the tricorder he was holding down on the
desk, and sighed deeply. Odo watched him carefully.

"Odo," he said, at last, "you showed me that Special
Order—you know you can keep Brixhta in custody for as
long as it takes for you to get him to confess—"

"Doctor," Odo replied, gently, "I am not in the business of forcing confessions from my prisoners. Not even
those that I believe are guilty." He thought a little more
about what he had just said. "*Particularly* not those that I
believe are guilty."

"That device he used," Bashir said, "to stop you
shapeshifting out of your office. It was *terrible. . . .*"

Odo himself had a number of questions about that, but
neither Bashir nor Brixhta were the people to whom he
intended to pose them. "It was, Doctor," he agreed, quietly. "But to keep him imprisoned out of revenge? That
would also be a terrible thing to do."

"It just seems so wrong," Bashir said, staring down
at the tricorder on the desk in front of him, "that nobody will be punished for what happened. I don't mean
the latinum," he said, shaking his head, "I couldn't
care less about that. I mean, for what happened to
you."

"Leaving that aside, Doctor, I will not continue to

keep a man in custody after the crime has been committed, and without proof that he was involved. To hold someone against their will without evidence? That would be unjust. And I am sure, if you thought about that, you would realize that yesterday you would have agreed with me, in the strongest possible terms."

Bashir looked up at him. He looked, Odo thought, quite troubled.

"Yes," Bashir said, quietly. "Yes, I do agree." He picked up the tricorder again. "That was a stupid thing to say," he said. "I'm sorry, Odo; I didn't meant to push. I was out of line."

"It's been my observation," Odo replied, "that even the most scrupulous can find themselves willing to bend or even break the law. In fact, I've begun to suspect that they are the ones most easily tempted to do so."

"Really?" said Bashir. "Why?"

"Because they value morality and justice above the letter of the law. Or," he smiled at Bashir, "so I would like to flatter myself."

Odo watched with interest as Bashir processed all of this; he saw the doctor's expression shift from its angry tension to something more relaxed, if a little resigned. Solids, Odo thought, were very malleable, in their own way.

"So," Odo concluded, briskly, "I shall uphold the principles of the law by operating within its constraints. Therefore," he put his hands down decisively upon the desk in front of him, "Brixhta will be released, and without charge. Besides, as you say—it's only latinum. I'm not Quark to value it so highly that I would sacrifice *all* my principles."

Bashir began to laugh. He made to go, and first reached out to touch the little wooden box standing at the side of Odo's desk. "You should give them to her, you know," he said.

Odo gave him a frosty look. "Your interference in my health I'm willing to permit, Doctor. Your opinions on upholding the law I'll listen to, if under duress." His expression warmed, just a little. "Everything else is none of your business."

Bashir smiled back at him, unreservedly. "I'll bear that in mind for the future," he said. He tapped his fingers on the box and made for the door. "See you later, Odo. And—thank you."

The conference closed with a formal ceremony and on a cautious note of success; with agreement reached on much of the key business. After the documents had been signed, all of the delegates assembled for another reception. Fleet Admiral Shanthi, at the center, was looking very pleased. She deserved to, Sisko thought. The news from Sybaron and the death of Roeder could have derailed the entire summit, but Shanthi had kept things on track.

As Sisko wandered around the reception, he saw Veral, and made a point of passing by. "Another frivolous occasion, I'm afraid," he said.

She smiled at him and bowed her head. "I am sure I can adapt."

Sisko walked on, looking around the gathering until he saw Garak, on the perimeter, talking to . . . Rhemet of all people. Sisko went over, and listened in to some of the conversation.

"Should you ever care," Garak was saying, "to learn something about how the fates of empires are decided—you might wish to speak to me."

Garak was not, however, who Sisko was looking for. "Marlow," he murmured, "A word."

The lieutenant nodded, signaled to Chaplin, and came to join him.

"Did anyone ever get to the bottom of that other Cardassian lifesign you picked up?" Sisko said.

"Yes, sir, they did. It turned out to be something of a strange story—she looks completely human. And yet she seems to have no idea at all that she's actually Cardassian. Have you come across anything like that before, sir?"

"Yes," Sisko said. "The late and entirely unlamented Obsidian Order had a program of placing agents in deep cover; they altered their features and made them undergo memory reprogramming so that they believed their new identities completely." He glanced over at Garak, recalling the whole series of events. "They could remain in the part for years," Sisko went on. "In the case I came across the agent had been on Bajor for a decade—and may still be, for all we know. Still living blissfully unaware as a Bajoran."

Marlow seemed to be fascinated. "What an interesting idea . . ." he murmured. "Even if she found out, you'd have to wonder where her loyalties would be now."

"You think?" Sisko frowned.

"After so long sitting on the other side? Could make anyone go native," Marlow answered.

Sisko nodded, and moved on. He went over to Bill Ross, and they found a quiet place where they could speak.

"You've been busy," Ross commented.

"Not what I'd expected from the week," Sisko said. "How about you?"

Ross handed him a padd. "Had an interview with Michel Le Brun, Roeder's secretary," Ross said. "He'd been with him since Roeder resigned his commission, knew him as well as anyone." He let Sisko scan through the transcript for a while. "Did you know," Ross said, "that Roeder refused to use communications systems, if he could help it?"

Sisko frowned. "No, I didn't know that," he murmured. "That's odd."

"Always wrote by hand, apparently. Turns out there were quite a few idiosyncrasies lurking behind that polished veneer. Le Brun was also of the opinion that Roeder had been getting more and more withdrawn recently."

"He was pretty quiet anyway," Sisko pointed out.

"Well, his secretary seems to think it was more than that—"

"But didn't think to do anything about it?" Sisko glanced up.

"Benefit of hindsight, I think. The man's devastated—he's absolutely dedicated to the work they were doing together. Blames himself for not realizing how close to the edge Roeder was."

Sisko looked up from the padd. "You think that was it? You think Roeder snapped?"

Ross gave him a sharp look. "Why? What's your reading, Ben?"

Sisko rubbed at the muscles in the back of his neck. "It all moved too fast for me to read anything," he said. "He did seem to focus his anger against me particularly—"

"You're the face of the war, Ben."

"I guess so. . . ." He kneaded at the muscles a little more.

"We're only just starting to open up parts of Roeder's file," Ross was saying. "And quite a lot of it makes for bleak reading. Undercover with the Maquis; even spent some time on Bajor before the Occupation ended . . ." Ross shook his head. "People can find themselves in some bad places, Ben; end up seeing some bad things.

Maybe it wasn't something particular that tipped him over. Maybe it was all of it, piling up."

Sisko thought again of what he had seen as the moonlight fell on Roeder's face. Was that *really* what it was? A man whose duty had taken him to extremes, and then who had driven himself further? Had he done things that he regretted, in the name of duty? Had he been unable to tolerate a guilty conscience? Perhaps Roeder's death did make sense, Sisko thought. It still did not make it any less of a tragedy.

Sisko looked out across the room. "How did the members of the other delegations take the news?"

Ross gave a dry laugh. "From what Shanthi told me, that was an interesting series of meetings," he said. "The Romulans have been making a great deal of noise about the fact that an assassin was loose at the reception last night." He gave Sisko a bland look. "I think most of them were talking about Roeder, although Subcommander Veral asked specifically about Mister Garak."

Sisko thought of his conversation with Veral—hell, had that only been last night? "She's shown a certain amount of interest in Garak all week," he said.

"And quite the guardian angel he turned out to be," Ross replied. "I gather you'd be dead now, if it wasn't for him."

Sisko tilted his head in acknowledgment. "He has his uses," he murmured. "I guess." He looked around the room, moving the subject onward. "Did the Romulans manage to use it all to their advantage?"

"It gave them a fair amount of leverage in the discussions," Ross admitted. "Cretak is already talking about need for access to Deep Space 9—"

Sisko gave a slight smile, and looked to where Cretak

and Veral were in what looked to be quite formal conversation with one of the Klingon delegates. "She's
going to have to take that up with the first minister," he
said.

"I'm not worried too much about her, to be honest,"
Ross said. "From all I've seen this week, the senator
seems to be firmly behind the alliance. She's shrewd, and
she's doesn't miss a trick, but . . ." He nodded. "I think
we can do business with her."

"I guess that's all we need," Sisko said. He raised his
hand to his mouth, stifling a yawn. He looked around
the room, at the people talking to each other. Too easy,
he thought, in all of the chaos to forget what the real
business of the week had been: the conference, the attempt to bind the alliance together more tightly. The
business of winning the war. As they stood there, a
silence opened up between the two men; the memory
of their charged conversation seemed to be about to
cast a shadow. They both roused themselves into
motion simultaneously; they both began to speak at
once.

"You first," Sisko murmured.

"I just wanted to ask," Ross said quietly, "will you go
and see your folks, Ben?"

"Yes," Sisko replied, "I think I can do that now."

When Brixhta slid into a seat at the bar, Quark did not
go over to him at first. He watched for a little while as
the Hamexi worked at a little piece of machinery. Another of his toys? Quark had no idea.

At last, Quark made his approach. He poured a glass
of tonic water, and set it in front of the Hamexi. "Thank
you," Brixhta said, and drew it toward him.

"So," Quark said, watching for any clue to emerge from beneath the brim of the hat, "do you want your crate back?"

"No," Brixhta said, busying himself with the water. "Keep it. Sell it. Whichever suits you best."

"All right . . ." Quark tried another way in. "You do know that it made Odo very suspicious that mine was the only place on the Promenade where people could get food for hours—"

"Odo is of an uncommonly suspicious cast of mind." Brixhta drained the water. "I am sure I hardly need to tell *you* of that."

"Not really, no. . . ." Quark watched as Brixhta pushed the glass back toward him. Looked like he was going to have to be more direct. "The auction is over, you don't want your crate back, and . . ." Quark stopped to select his words. "There are—now—plenty of other places on the Promenade where you could eat. Is there something in particular that has brought you into the bar today, Mister Brixhta?"

Brixhta beamed at him. "I've come to settle my bar bill. What else?"

Quark came in closer. He waggled a finger at Brixhta to get him to lean in. The Hamexi obliged. What Quark was about to say he did not want anyone to hear. Not ever. He did not much want to hear himself say it.

"It's on the house," he whispered.

There was a silence. After a moment or two, Quark started to get worried. He ducked his head and peered beneath the hat. When he looked in there, he could see that Brixhta was genuinely moved by his words.

After a moment or two, Brixhta gathered himself together, reached inside his jacket and retrieved a little piece of pink plastic. He pushed it toward Quark. "A pleasure doing business with you, Mister Quark. Truly— a great pleasure."

Brixhta drew himself up from his seat, and touched the brim of his hat. "Farewell," he said, and left.

Quark watched him depart. He picked up the empty glass and stared down into it. He checked under it. Then he shook his head at the door.

"Well," he said, in most aggrieved tones, "he might have a left a *tip*."

At home, the kitchen was warm; its scent and its heat were all-embracing. At the worktop, Ben Sisko, Starfleet captain, commanding officer of Deep Space 9, loving parent of a teenage son, and Emissary to the Prophets of Bajor, was chopping up onions under his father's vigilant eye.

His sister was perched up on the counter nearby, one leg tucked beneath her, watching her brother and her father as they worked. Ever since Judith was a kid, ever since she'd first shown all that promise on the cello, she had been excused from cooking duties. Just in case she did something to her hands; just in case something hot spilled or a knife slipped. Thirty years on, and her brother had still not forgiven her for what was, he reckoned, a blatant and—even more unforgivably—successful strategy to get out of her share of the chores.

"*Finely,*" his father said, leaning over to look. "What are they supposed to be? Piano keys?"

"That's my department," Judith said, and smirked.

Her brother glared up at her. "Can't you make yourself useful *somehow?*" he said. "Dry something, or put something away?"

"I'm keeping you company," she said. "Isn't that useful enough?"

"Not from where I'm standing. . . ." He stopped chopping and put down the knife. His eyes had started watering. He screwed them up and tried to resist rubbing them. Judith picked up a dishcloth and threw it at him.

"Thanks." As he wiped his eyes, he said, "You ever heard of a Cardassian composer called Ilani Tarn?"

Judith looked back at him in surprise. "Well," she said, with a quirk of the lips, "aren't you getting cosmopolitan in your old age?"

He frowned at her and tapped the handle of the knife—once, twice.

"She's Cardassia's greatest living musician," she said. "Why do you ask?"

"Is she any good?"

Judith laughed. "Yeah, Ben, I'd say she was pretty good!"

"The . . ." What was it they'd called it? ". . . the *trikolat*. That's right, isn't it?"

"I don't expect you to study, you know, for when we meet." She looked at him more closely. "What's this all about, Ben?"

He started work on another onion, and had to check to make sure that his father's back was turned when the knife didn't cut too straight. "You saw the news, I guess," he said, "about Tomas Roeder?"

"Yes, I saw it." She shook her head. "Hell, that was sad. You have any idea what happened with him?"

Her brother reached for the cloth and wiped his eyes again. "I think he was pretty sick by the end, Jude. Some kind of breakdown, I think." He went back to work. "He mentioned Ilani Tarn the other night—he was at some concert she gave, a year or two back." He glanced back up at her. "I met him at the embassy. The night he died. He asked about you," he added. "Asked to be remembered to you."

She gave a gentle smile. "That's nice," she murmured. "You know, I was at that concert too. I wish I'd known he was there; it would've been good to catch up." She looked at her brother sharply. "You do know that there was nothing there, don't you? He was just kind once to a friend's little sister when she was a young student all alone in a big city."

"I know." He went back to the chopping. After a moment or two, his sister spoke again.

"Something troubling you about it, Ben?"

"Maybe . . ."

"Care to take a guess what?"

"Oh, I don't know, Jude," he said. "It's not been an easy trip back. And then for that to happen . . ." He sighed. "Somehow," he said, "I just can't help thinking it didn't have to end like that. It didn't have to end with him dying."

Their father came back at this point with the peppers. He looked at his two children disapprovingly. "What's all this talk about people dying?" he scolded. "Not in this kitchen. Not tonight."

So they finished up the cooking and sat and ate together; and talked instead of Judith's last tour, of Joseph's impressions of the station, of how Jake's writing was coming along. When they were done, they sat happily for a while replete amid the comfortable wreckage of the meal. Then Judith got up from the table and went over to the piano. Her brother and her father watched her in the candlelight, and she started playing a few slow chords. She always complained the piano was way out of tune, had done for years, and yet she always managed to get a decent sound from it, at least as far as her brother could tell. After a few bars, the tempo picked up a little, and she began to sing along, softly.

"Heaven," she sang, *"I'm in heaven . . ."*

"So, Ben," Joseph turned to his son, "when are you going to tell me what it is that's on your mind?"

Sisko picked up a piece of bread and began to wipe up the last of the sauce on his plate. "I can't, Dad."

"Oh, I think you can," his father replied. "You can just leave out the details. Doubt I'd understand much about them anyway."

"It's complicated—"

"Well, given the way you've been, I didn't think it was going to be something easy."

Sisko sat up his chair and looked in surprise at his father, who looked straight back. *"How* have I been?"

"Oh, your usual. Big black cloud hanging around your head. Feeling it all just a bit too much and not saying anything about it."

"I see." Sisko bit into the bread and thought for a while. "I went to see James Leyton the other day," he said at last.

"Was he the one who wanted to take my blood without my say-so?"

"Yes," Sisko said. "That's the one."

Joseph's pursed lips said more than enough about what he thought of Leyton. He gave his son a canny look. "Now what could have sent you there, I wonder?"

Sisko shrugged, and pushed the bread around the plate a little more. "I don't know," he said, "maybe, because I put him there, I owed him a visit at least. . . ."

"And now tell me the truth, Ben."

Judith was still singing; the sound of her voice and the

melody filtered through the room, giving each of them space but still binding them together. Her brother listened to her sing for a little while.

"A few weeks back . . ." Sisko began, and then stopped. He looked up at his father, sitting and waiting patiently. "I made some choices, Dad, and did some things," he told him, "and I'm not proud of them."

Joseph nodded slowly. "Did it get you into trouble?" he said.

"No," Sisko said. "No. And that's part of the problem."

"*Should* it have got you into trouble?"

Shrewd old man. "Yes," his son murmured, "yes, it should." He ate the last of the piece of bread.

"And which is worse, Ben?" Joseph asked him. "Thinking you went too far, or knowing you weren't punished for it?"

"I *thought* it was the second—"

"Well, I wouldn't worry yourself too much about that," his father said, "since from what I can see you've been doing a fair enough job of punishing yourself. So we're back to the first. *Did* you go too far?"

Sisko raised his hands. "I don't know, Dad! That's just the problem, I don't know!" He sighed. "It *was* too far; by any measure—but what's come out of it . . ." He thought of how the conference had ended. "I think that may have made it worthwhile."

His father did not answer right away. He piled a couple of dishes together, stacking the knives and forks on top. "This morning," Joseph said at last, "I went out to get the vegetables for our dinner tonight. And I dithered and dithered, over what to get, and how much. Trying to guess how much the two of you would eat tonight. And I ended getting *far* too much. Some of it'll go to waste, I guess," he said ruefully, looking back toward the kitchen, "and you *know* how much I hate that . . ." He gave his son a sharp look. "What I'm saying, Ben—if it's not plain enough to you already—is that the kind of decisions an old chef like me has to make are little ones. How many vegetables should I get in for the day. And still I can't make them easily. But I guess they're nothing," he said, "to the kind of decisions you must have to make."

"But still we have to make the *right* decisions. We have to be willing to do the right thing—"

"Well, you know, Ben," Joseph sighed, "I'm not so sure you can really get the measure of a man by knowing what he's willing to do. It's what he's *not* willing to do that's the real measure."

Sisko picked up another chunk of bread and began to smear sauce around his plate again. His father waited.

"The other night," Sisko said, "I had a choice to do something, something that would have . . . would have been better for me." Because Roeder really had meant it, Sisko understood that completely now. Chaplin had seen it, Garak had seen it—Roeder would have shot Sisko, if he hadn't been shot first.

"And?"

"Couldn't do it." Sisko bit into the bread.

His father sat in silence for a moment, and then he said, "Don't tell me all the details, Benjamin—there are some things an old man with a bad heart doesn't want to hear his son say—but what happened?"

Sisko ran the story through his mind until he had something he could tell his father. "Someone else did it," he said.

"Well," Joseph replied, "so that's on *his* conscience then, isn't it?"

It was true, Sisko realized, relief rushing into him, filling him. His hand had not fired the weapon that killed

Roeder; his hand had not planted the bomb that killed Vreenak.

"And that's why," his father was saying, "I'd rather it was you making those decisions than men like that Leyton fellow. I should think he *still* doesn't know what it was he did wrong."

"And yet sometimes I have to wonder," Sisko murmured, "whether I *should* be the one making those decisions; if there isn't someone else who'd do a better job of it—"

"It's thinking that way that makes you fit for it. And I know you'll make the best decisions that you can," his father said softly. "And that will be enough, *more* than enough. Because no matter what it is you do, you're still a good man, Ben Sisko. You'll do the best you can. So," he finished, "I think you're in just the right place." Joseph picked up a piece of bread and bit into it. "Which is all for the best, since you don't have what it takes to make a really *good* chef."

"*Dad—*"

"You'd think," Joseph complained, "that a man who knows how to build a ship that can sail across space would understand cayenne a little better."

Sisko started to laugh, very softly. He looked out at the candlelight, glowing warmly. The sound of the piano, he realized, had stopped. Judith was coming back over to the table. She took her seat again and eyed her brother and her father fondly. "You two set the world to rights now?"

Joseph Sisko looked lovingly at his son. "As right as it'll ever be," he said.

2

IT WAS A BARREN PLACE, on the border. Nothing happened there. On Federation star charts it was called Santa Helena. The Maquis, with a sense of dark humor borne of their own marginal way of life, had nicknamed it Destiny. The Cardassians had used it as a marker for a place where they passed in and out of their space, but they had not named it, only given it a number. Not even the disaster at Sybaron had been enough to draw it into the fray. One day, perhaps, it might achieve significance, but not yet.

Santa Helena's third moon, however, was a slightly different story. It seemed to attract a certain amount of traffic. The Maquis, for example, had often made use of it; but they, of course, were all gone now. Still, even these days, its location—out on the border—made Santa Helena's third moon a very useful place. The handful of people who knew about it came from all over the quadrant, and connected with each other; they did their business, made their exchanges, and then they went on their way.

When Brixhta made landfall there, the runabout had already arrived. The android was sitting patiently at the helm, waiting for its next set of instructions. He patted it fondly, and switched it off. Everything else was just as it should be. The runabout had not been traced. And in the back, the vials of latinum were stacked up, awaiting collection.

There was only one thing preying upon Brixhta's mind. His employer had been maintaining a stony silence. The last time Brixhta had heard from him had been just before he reached Deep Space 9. He had sent out a transmission to Earth, confirming his imminent arrival on the station. And he had received a reply back, acknowledging his message, and sending him the security files he needed. When at last Odo had released him from the holding cell, and he'd been free to leave DS9, Brixhta had sent out another communication, then another—but there had been nothing in reply. Caution, no doubt. Brixhta had often heard it said that it paid to be cautious.

He settled himself around the controls and, once again, tried the secure frequency. His message was very short, almost cautious:

In my possession.

This time, he received a reply. It had all the right signals.

Coming to collect.

Garak was sewing; had been ever since they'd got back on board the *Rubicon*. Some kind of embroidery, Sisko thought . . . in fact, Sisko didn't know what the hell it was, except it was holding all of Garak's attention. Balanced on the console next to the tailor there was a cup, and Sisko caught the aroma of redleaf tea. Looked like

Garak had given up on Earl Grey after all. Perhaps he had decided it had too much of a nasty aftertaste.

Sisko watched the tailor work for a while; watched the needle go in and out of the cloth. The pattern or whatever it was looked pretty complex. "That's keeping you busy," he said.

"It has to be ready," Garak murmured, "for an *ih'tanu* ceremony taking place only a few days after we get back . . . and I was *far* too distracted to work on it while we were on Earth. . . ."

Sisko watched a little longer, then stood up and stretched. After a moment or two, Garak broke the silence between them.

"You told your superiors all about Vreenak, didn't you?"

Sisko locked his hands behind his head and looked down at the lights on the console. "Yes," he said. "I did."

Garak nodded. "I thought you would," he said. He continued sewing. Sisko studied him as he worked. After a minute or two, it became clear that Garak had nothing else to say on the matter. Sisko turned and went into the back of the runabout, to the replicator. As he sipped his *raktajino,* he thought about what Garak had just said. Perhaps that really was an end to it. All in the past. All that Sisko had to do now was just get on and win the war. . . .

He took his mug back into the front of the runabout and sat down again.

"That really was a quite *fascinating* report which the major delivered earlier," Garak remarked, conversationally.

"Yes it was. . . ." Sisko rubbed the back of his neck. A cargo of latinum and a runabout stolen in his absence. "And I am looking forward to hearing the full version of events."

Garak smiled. "A curious species, the Hamexi," he said. "I knew one once, although I never knew his name. And this despite the fact that he saved my life."

Sisko nodded over at his work. "Comes with the territory, does it?"

Garak bit at a piece of thread. "Tailoring has a whole assortment of occupational hazards, Captain," he murmured. "You really can't imagine. Now," he went on, "in the unusual and rather fraught situation in which we found ourselves, this Hamexi regrettably turned out to be something of a liability. And then, perhaps inevitably, I was presented with an opportunity to rid myself of this . . . encumbrance."

Garak stopped speaking in order to concentrate on threading his needle. Sisko watched him stonily. Garak was, presumably, about to explain how he had killed the Hamexi. Why, Sisko wondered, was he telling him this? Was it meant to be some kind of threat, now that he knew that Sisko had told his superiors about Vreenak's murder? As if Sisko was somehow unaware of the fact that Garak was prepared to kill in cold blood . . .

"But then," Garak continued blithely, "I thought . . . no, not *every* good deed has to be punished." He looked up for a second, giving Sisko a sly look. "So I let him live. It's always interesting," Garak concluded, "to discover what you can't quite bring yourself to do."

And what the hell was *that* supposed to mean? Sisko stared at the tailor and tried to unravel his words. Where did you start? With the deaths, Sisko guessed, and there were two standing between them: Vreenak's and Roeder's. Sisko was sure, as sure as it was possible to be with Garak, that the whole matter of Vreenak had just been closed between them. So this had to be about

Roeder. *I let him live.* . . . Sisko pressed his fingers against his temple. Was Garak drawing a comparison with that and the choice that Sisko had faced as to whether or not he should shoot Roeder? Was Garak saying that he had been there himself; that he understood why Sisko would choose not to shoot? But that choice could well have cost Garak his life. Sisko had known that when he put his phaser down; had been ready to take that risk with Garak's life to keep his own conscience clear, to take back his self-respect . . . and that was one hell of a risk to take with someone else's life. . . .

"Just let me get this straight, Garak," Sisko said, his fingers still pressed hard against his head. "Are you offering me your forgiveness?"

An expression of mild consternation passed over Garak's face. He stopped his work and looked directly at Sisko. "Do you require it?" he said.

Sisko had a flash of memory: of Roeder's hand holding the phaser against Garak's head; of his own hand, spread out flat upon the concrete of the ground.

"Maybe. . . ."

"Then maybe," Garak answered, as he turned away, "I am offering it."

A quiet descended over the runabout. Sisko sat listening to the soft hum of the instrumentation. "I don't think I realized until now," he said, after a little while. "It's not just a game to you after all, is it?"

Garak's hand halted, the needle suspended in midair. He sat staring at his work. "After all this time," he murmured, "and still you fail to understand me." He was, Sisko realized, completely serious. He started sewing again. "Of course it's a game, Captain. The great game."

• • •

The sky had turned vermillion by the time the second ship arrived. The other moons had set, and Santa Helena filled the horizon, solitary and barren. Brixhta watched the squat shape of the ship as it descended; a dark smudge against the vivid purity of the sky. The ship landed. There was a short breath where nothing moved. Then a hatch on the side opened. Somebody disembarked, and came toward his position.

Brixhta revealed himself, and took a good look at the other. Quite a small man, sandy-haired. Not, he had to say, quite what he had been expecting. He stretched to claim ownership of the crate of latinum. This was when he became aware that the other man was holding a phaser.

"You're not Roeder," Brixhta said, in resignation.

"I'm not," confirmed Luther Sloan.

In the wardroom, Sisko eyed his senior staff one by one. Odo was uncomfortable. O'Brien was wincing. Bashir looked disarmingly shamefaced; Kira looked frankly embarrassed. Dax had an unrepentant gleam in her eye, while Worf had the expression of someone vindicated in a deeply felt belief that it was best to do everything yourself.

"You know," Sisko said, keeping his voice low and controlled, "when I left the station, I'm *sure* we had another runabout." He looked at each one of them again. "Who wants to start?"

Kira squared her shoulders, took a deep breath, and opened her mouth. Before she could say a word, Odo began to speak.

"The whole affair, Captain," he said, assuming a stern expression, "is—I believe—the fault of a single man. Brixhta."

"'Brixhta."

"'The Hamexi, Captain."

"'Ah yes. The Hamexi."

"'Yes, Captain. He deals in antiques."

Sisko's eyes went very narrow. *"Antiques?"* he said.

"Open the crate," Sloan instructed.

The Hamexi obeyed, slowly. "You're Federation," he said. "What could you want with latinum?"

Sloan observed him without passion or pity. "It's not the latinum," he said. "Of course it's not the latinum." Keeping the phaser trained on the Hamexi, he reached with his other hand inside his jacket and drew out a padd. "Catch," he said, and threw it over.

The Hamexi did as instructed.

"I'm going to read out some numbers," Sloan said. "Key them into that padd. You'll understand soon enough."

Sloan picked out one of the vials, and read out the number engraved on it. Then he opened up the vial, and poured the latinum onto the ground. It pooled on the surface for a moment, before the thin soil accepted it and it slid into the earth forever. The Hamexi made a slight sound, as if he were in pain.

"I didn't see you key in the number," Sloan remarked. "Do you need me to read it out to you again?"

"No, no. I heard it." The Hamexi busied himself with the padd.

"Good." Sloan dropped the empty vial on the ground. He reached for another and read the number out. The Hamexi entered it obediently into the padd. Sloan opened the vial, and poured the latinum away. They followed this ritual for all of the vials. The sun grew heavy in the sky, the list of numbers on the padd grew longer, and the ground took the latinum.

When it was done, the numbers began to give up their secrets. Sloan himself had no need to look. He could picture the files that were appearing well enough. He already knew the details intimately: of changeling morphology, of the damage being done to it, of the designers and the perpetrators. Sloan knew all about the kind of knowledge that could make a man turn on the institutions that had nurtured him—or make a man believe those institutions had turned on him. Sloan knew about the wrongful weapons of a rightful war.

While the Hamexi examined the files, Sloan stared up at the fabulous sky. "I suppose Tomas intended to cross the border here," he said, looking at Cardassian space.

"You do seem oddly familiar with the affairs of Tomas Roeder," the Hamexi said.

"At one time," Sloan confessed, "I thought that he might be one of us."

"And who, exactly, are you?"

Sloan felt a little pained by that question. "Don't you know?"

"I believe I may have met your kind before." The Hamexi held up the padd. "Why have you shown me this?"

"Perhaps I'm sentimental," Sloan said. It was not intended to convince. "Perhaps I think a man should know what it is he's going to die for."

The Hamexi laughed; a full, melodic sound. "But now you've enlightened me about all your schemes. So surely," he said, extending to touch the brim of his hat, "this is the point where I make an unlikely but dramatic escape?"

Sloan did not answer. Brixhta realized that he was not even looking at him, but absently gazing past into the unknowable space behind. The sun was setting. Santa Helena flared, and then was plunged into darkness. Its moment in history would have to wait a while yet.

Sloan nodded a command.

"No," replied Enderby, right into Brixhta's ear. "It isn't."

Odo stood for a moment outside the tailor's shop, and then he went inside. The lights were dim, and he walked on to the back where, he assumed, Garak would be. Sure enough, the tailor was there, busy at his table. He looked up as Odo approached, and put down his work.

Odo tilted his head almost imperceptibly. "Welcome back," he said, quickly.

Garak gave him a slow but courteous smile. "Thank you."

Odo began to wander round the shop. He was conscious of Garak's eyes upon him, following his every move. He waited for the tailor to speak first.

"I heard about the theft," Garak said.

Odo nodded. "It's been a frustrating few days," he said. He came to a halt in front of one of the mannequins, and considered it.

"Was there something you thought I could do to help?" Garak prompted.

"As a matter of fact there was," Odo said. He put out a finger to touch the mannequin. It was solid. "Do you recall the device that you used in our conversation on Tain's flagship?"

Odo turned round. Garak was frozen to the spot, as

motionless as one of his own mannequins. After a moment or two, Garak swallowed and seemed to collect himself. "I am hardly likely to forget it," Garak said quietly. "And you'll forgive my impertinence, but I was under the distinct impression that we were of the same mind when it came to remembering that whole *regrettable* incident—"

"We most certainly are," Odo said firmly. "However, what appears to be a similar technology came to my attention while you were away from the station." Odo knew that he was a master of understatement, but he also knew that Garak excelled at reading between the lines.

"I am very sorry to hear that, Odo," Garak replied, and Odo suspected him of a rare piece of honesty when he said it.

"It kept me detained during the robbery," Odo explained. "And I wondered whether you might have any thoughts on the matter. For example, how such a technology might have become more widely available?"

"Constable," Garak said, in alarm, "I must assure you that I would *not* have—"

Odo gestured with his hand to stop him speaking. "I most certainly hope you wouldn't," he said dryly. "What I am asking is whether you would care to conjecture how *else* it might have become available?"

Garak wiped his mouth with the back of his hand. "There are any number of ways," he said, after a moment or two. "Not through the Obsidian Order." He glanced at Odo again and held up his empty hands. "Of course."

"The Tal Shiar?"

"Perhaps . . . Although it could as easily be Starfleet Intelligence," Garak pointed out. "We shared all our nformation with them on our return, if you recall."

"Did either of us have enough information to allow the level opment of such a device?"

"Probably not," Garak conceded. "But we had enough o start them *thinking* about developing such a device."

"Hmm." Odo turned his attention briefly back to the mannequin. "Does that not concern you, Garak?" he said at last. "That it might have been acquired from Starfleet?"

"Information gets loose all the time, Odo," Garak replied. "Any intelligence officer could tell you that; it is their greatest success and their deepest sorrow. Or are you thinking it was intentionally leaked?" Garak frowned, and Odo watched the tailor's face as he ran through several options. "You're not saying that *Starfleet* was behind this robbery?" Garak said.

Odo grunted. "No, I was thinking less in specifics and more in the general case. That Starfleet might choose to develop a technology of that kind."

"I see," Garak said. "Then, in answer to your question as to whether it concerns me, I would say that I believe that there are occasions when one has to use every weapon at hand."

Odo tapped the dummy lightly. "That was what I thought you might say."

"I'm horrified to discover myself so predictable," Garak replied, "but I hope it helps. Not, I imagine, that it's an answer you particularly care for."

Another piece of honesty? Two in one evening? Odo felt honored. "Not particularly," he said, paying Garak in the same coin. "But it helps to hear it articulated." He nodded, and turned to leave. "Thank you, Garak. Good night."

• • •

When Odo left, and the door closed after him, Garak took up his sewing again, worked for a while—then tutted, and began undoing the stitches. The constable's questions had shaken him and not least, Garak knew, because if the chance ever came his way, he would do the same again. He would torture with impunity; he would rain fire down on the Great Link itself; he would do whatever it took, if it meant that the Dominion was destroyed and Cardassia saved. He suspected Odo knew it too. Carefully, patiently, Garak unpicked his work. When at last he had returned it to its earlier state, he put it back down onto the desktop, stood up, and looked around the shop.

It was hardly, Garak thought with a sigh, as if such chances presented themselves with great regularity. He thought of the patient and methodical questions posed to him by Chaplin and Marlow; thought of the slow but systematic way in which he had turned over the minutiae of his old life: security protocols, encryption codes . . . Such trifling betrayals. Garak chafed at these limits on his field of action but at least, he consoled himself, he was back at work.

Garak walked slowly over to the nearest mannequin and began to straighten the scarf it wore. It stood there, mute and patient, as he twisted the fabric slowly and thoughtfully through his fingers. There were other forces at work in Starfleet too, he thought. Forces unwilling to allow opposition to this war to become too powerful. Forces willing to blackmail men into murder. Forces that were indeed ready to use the weapons at hand. What else, Garak wondered, were they prepared to do? And who *were* these people? They were not the competent if circumspect Chaplins and Marlows of this universe; nor were they the stolid officers before whom le had sat on Starbase 375. They were not even the Benjamin Siskos of the universe: passionate about their principles, but just corruptible enough . . . Garak knew he had never really credited Starfleet Intelligence with, well, *intelligence,* but such ruthlessness from them was something else entirely. Something new.

For a moment, the idea amused him. Garak felt his lips curve into a slow smile. He tugged at both ends of the scarf. Perhaps, he thought, Starfleet even had its own Obsidian Order. . . . Had it always been there? Or had it come about as a consequence of war? Was it Starfleet's dark heart, he wondered—or was it on the fringes, a law entirely unto itself? Whatever it was, it did seem that at last *some* people—whether in Starfleet or without—were becoming serious about winning this war. And that, surely, had to be all to the good?

Garak went over to his worktable, grabbed the jacket folded over the back of the chair and, absently, began to smooth the creases out of it. All to the good? Whose good? The Federation's, perhaps. But surely these serious and ruthless people would be seeking to have influence beyond that sphere; and, besides, the Federation was not—and never had been—Garak's chief concern. He shrugged his jacket on and looked uncertainly at the shadows crowding around the shop.

"So," he said to the mannequin. "That's that."

Garak decided to head over to Quark's. Because he couldn't stay here, and stare at the walls, and think about Cardassia, falling into hands less constant than his own.

"Can I come in, Benjamin, or will you bite my head off?"

Sisko looked up to see Dax standing at the door of

his office; still unrepentant, he noticed. "That depends, old man," he murmured. "Are you coming to tell me someone's stolen the wormhole from under your nose?"

Her smile widened. "Not that I've noticed."

He waved her in. She took the seat opposite, watched him for a while with that smile still quirking at her lips, and then she became more somber. "I heard about Tomas Roeder."

Sisko reached for the baseball. "A damn mess. Admiral Ross thinks he cracked under the pressure."

"Is that what you think?"

"It's the only thing that makes sense. . . ." He shook his head. "A real tragedy. He was a clever man."

"Curzon didn't like him much," Dax mused. "He thought he was cold."

"That's not fair," Sisko murmured. "There *was* passion there. . . ." He shifted the baseball from hand to hand. "What do you think went wrong, Dax?"

"With Roeder?"

"No, not just *him*. With all of us!" he said. "Our generation. James Leyton, Cal Hudson—hell, even Michael Eddington! What was it that drove them all away?" He clutched the ball within one hand.

"You're still here," Dax pointed out.

"Yes, I am."

But it had been damn close.

"I know we use it as a shorthand," Dax said, "but it's the war, Benjamin. It changes everything."

"Leyton told me he saw it coming, that he thought his mistake was moving too soon. But Cal? Michael Eddington?"

"Were fighting a war too."

"I guess . . ." Sisko murmured. "So Roeder was yet another casualty." Sisko put the baseball down and smiled. "And some of us go on to fight another day?"

Jadzia Dax smiled back. "Well, some of us," she said, "are just indestructible."

Odo eased himself into the seat next to Garak. "I forgot to ask," he said, "how was Earth?" At the far end of the bar, Quark put the stopper in the bottle of Saurian brandy he had been watering and came over eagerly to listen.

Garak put down his glass, opened his mouth to speak, stopped, thought for a while, considered replying, and then thought for a little while longer.

"I was punched repeatedly by pacifists," he said at last.

"So," said Quark, picking up a cloth and wiping the bar. "Much as you expected, then?"

Frankly, Felix had written, *I think your obsession with Earth in the 1960s is verging on the obsessive, but who am I to come between a man and what's obviously a rich fantasy life? So here's a little magic—Vegas-style.*

Obsessive. Julian snorted. This from a man who stayed up till the early hours of the morning tweaking hologram programs. The cheek of it.

PS, Felix had added, *Vic is something special. Treat him right and he'll see you right.* And, Julian had to admit, Felix had told the truth on that score, no matter how poor his psychiatric evaluations. He checked the time. It was fifteen minutes since Ensign Walker had come off duty, and she would be here soon. Julian tugged at his bow tie, and then started fiddling nervously with his cuff links. Up on the stage, Vic had just come to the end of his set. Julian joined in the applause, and waited for Vic to join him at the bar.

"So," Vic said as he sat down beside him, "where's this girl of yours? The one you can't stop talking about?"

"She should be here soon, Vic—she's very excited. Can't wait to meet you."

"Everyone wants a look at the light bulb, huh?"

"Actually, I think she wants to thank you for getting me to ask her out one more time." Julian looked at him anxiously. "You know, after you've met her, if you've got any more advice you'd care to give . . ."

Vic laughed and shook his head. "Hey, pally—I just helped you on your way. What you do with her now is your own business."

Julian laughed too, and leaned back against the bar. Up on the stage, the band had started up again.

"You know," Vic said, "the first time you came in here, your face was so long it left a mark on the carpet."

Julian shrugged. "I think I was going through a bit of a rough patch."

Vic looked at him thoughtfully. "Those spy fantasies," he said. "Running around outside the law. They're fun for a while, and then the charm really wears off, huh?"

"You said it, Vic." It came out a little more fervently than Julian had intended. He saw Vic watching him closely, and he laughed it off. "Believe me, that's one game I do *not* intend to play again any time soon."

"You saw sense?"

"More like a friend talked sense."

"Well, that's what friends are for," Vic said. They stood and watched the band for a while, Vic tapping his fingers against the bar.

Odo *had* talked some good sense, Julian thought, and he was grateful for it. He listened to the music, and found himself thinking about that little wooden box. He had no doubt it was still languishing on Odo's desk.

"Vic," Julian said, suddenly.

"What is it, pally?"

"This friend of mine."

"What about him?"

"I think you might just be able to help him out. . . ."

That was how it happened. Some men went on a journey.
Some strangers came to town.

ABOUT THE AUTHOR

Una McCormack discovered *Deep Space Nine* very late in its run, but loved it immediately for its politics, its wit, its ambiguity, and its tailor. She enjoys classic British television and going to the cinema, and she collects capital cities. She lives with her partner Matthew in Cambridge, England, where she reads, writes and teaches. She is the author of the short story "Face Value," which appeared in the *DS9* tenth anniversary anthology *Prophecy and Change,* and the novel *The Lotus Flower,* which appeared in *Worlds of Star Trek: Deep Space Nine, Volume One.*

It all began in the *New York Times* bestselling book *Ashes of Eden*.

James T. Kirk gave up his life and his wife for Starfleet, now he faces a threat that could bring down the entire Federation... his son.

STAR TREK
CAPTAIN'S GLORY

William Shatner

with

Judith & Garfield Reeves-Stevens

This Summer from Pocket Books

STAR TREK VOYAGER®

Distant Shores

an all-new anthology of tales by

Christopher L. Bennett, Kirsten
Beyer, Ilsa J. Bick, Keith R.A.
DeCandido, Bob Greenberger,
Heather Jarman, Robert T.
Jeschonek, Terri Osborne, Kim
Sheard, James Swallow, Geoffrey
Thorne, Susan Wright

VDS

STAR TREK VOYAGER®

A tenth-anniversary odyssey

STRING THEORY

A new trilogy beginning in July 2005 with

COHESION

by
Jeffrey Lang

From Pocket Books
Available wherever books are sold
Also available as an eBook

STC